Positively Morbid

by

Cara Johns

Positively Morbid

Cover Art by *Jennifer Greeff*

The Wild Rose Press, Inc.
PO Box 708
Adams Basin, NY 14410-0708
Visit us at www.thewildrosepress.com

Publishing History
First Edition, 2023
Trade Paperback ISBN 978-1-5092-4884-1
Digital ISBN 978-1-5092-4885-8

Published in the United States of America

"Race you," she said to Mouse, who accepted the challenge with a joyful burst of speed. The dog wasn't distracted by old, persistent sorrows, and if Parker meant to keep up, she couldn't be either. They sprinted to the steep cliff-side stairs leading up to the boarding house that had been gutted, expanded, and re-branded as the Tyler Bettering Institute.

A bright piece of fabric caught Parker's headlamp beam, and she paused for a closer look, thinking a guest might have lost a hat. Mouse ran to sniff it, then let loose a full-throated volley of barks as she backed away.

Parker shushed her. Mouse quieted, a subsonic growl vibrating in her throat. Parker heard nothing but waves, wind and distant traffic. Could there be an injured cat under there? She fished out her pepper spray. "It's okay," she called, and rounded a pile of driftwood to peer under the stairs, poised to retreat if she met frightened eyes.

It was not a hurt animal. Or rather, it had been a man, and he didn't hurt anymore.

Dedication

To everyone who struggles with the past.

Chapter One

Parker sat cross-legged on the concrete floor of her balcony, eyes closed. A chill seeped into her bones through the yoga mat as she tried to focus on the sensation of salt-tinged air entering and exiting her nostrils. Breathe, and again.

Her phone interrupted with a repeated rhythmic buzzing.

The noise was only another sensation, she told herself. No different from the breeze playing through her short hair, or the skin on her bare biceps contracting into goosebumps.

It didn't help. The buzzing continued, and her stomach tightened in response. Unless it was an emergency, Dad or Krista wouldn't call in the middle of a workday. Surrendering, her eyes flicked open to the pearl-gray sky, and she reached for the offending phone.

The number was unfamiliar, except for an East Coast area code she'd had herself once upon a time. Maybe Dad was calling from a neighbor's house.

"Hello?" she said. Anxiety emerged as brusqueness.

There was an indrawn breath, followed by a hesitation that made her stomach shrivel.

"Hello?" she repeated.

A short cough like clearing a gnat in the throat. Another pause. Then, "Hi. Corey. It's Jess."

That was a gut punch. Jesse Coburn, first love and

onetime soulmate. It had been more than eight years since she'd spoken to him. For a while, Parker had hoped he'd come after her and make everything better—and then she'd moved on to nursing her resentment.

Recently, she'd let that go, too. No one could have made everything better because no one could bring Britt back to life. Parker had started to create an intentional, compassionate adult life. With a few shortcuts here and there, to make up for lost time.

She slipped through the sliding door to collapse on the loveseat next to Mouse, her long-legged rescue mutt, who was stretched across one and a half of the two cushions.

Parker's voice was weirdly calm. "Jess. How did you find me?"

"Your dad gave me your number when he told me you were on the Oregon Coast. I hope you don't mind."

Dad. Of course. Her heart eased a little. Despite the cloud of suspicion that had hung over her and Jess after they found Britt's body, her father, the consummate professor, had argued their innocence to anyone who would listen. Not a popular move, with Britt's own mother spreading lies, but Dad had believed in Parker and Jess both.

Even accounting for her father's collusion, it wasn't okay for Jess to intrude on her life. There could be no good reason after so long a silence and so much hurt. "What do you want?" Parker demanded.

Mouse responded to the tension in her voice with a searching gaze. Parker scratched between her ears, and Mouse sighed and settled her chin on Parker's thigh.

Jess made the gnat-forcing noise again. Parker's anger ratcheted down a notch. He sounded like he'd wanted to make this call even less than she wanted to receive it.

"Corey—"

"I don't even go by that name anymore. It's Parker, okay? Just Parker."

Silence.

Then, "Wasn't that your mom's maiden—?"

"It doesn't matter, Jess! What do you want?" Her stomach was tight with dread.

"Uh, yeah. Okay. Parker. I need to talk to you—"

"Clever of you to call, then."

He soldiered onward, immune to her stress-induced sarcasm. "I'm in San Francisco right now. I have a job lined up in Alaska, so I thought, since you're in Oregon, I could stop by. Talk to you in person."

Parker's hand clenched in the loose fur at Mouse's neck. Mouse shifted and unfolded her legs to climb down in search of a calmer place to lounge.

"Parker?" Jess said.

She bit her lip. It was such a bad idea. It would stir up memories and emotions best left in the past. But she was older, more mature. Maybe it would be easier. Maybe it would bring closure, if such a thing existed. "I'm in Newport at the Tyler Bettering Institute. Text me when you get to Yachats and we'll figure out where to meet."

She ended the call and stared out the window, seeing not the grays of the ocean and sky, but a summer forest from long ago and far away. The bonfire down on the sand, barely visible through the trees. Jess's hand sliding up the back of her shirt as he pulled her close after that electric first meeting of lips. Their friends' voices, distant as a dream, overwhelmed by the sound of eager breath. Then, a piercing shriek of laughter that was definitely Britt. Sudden tension. Jess's whisper warm against Parker's ear. "It's fine. She's moved on."

One small moment, imbued with lust and tenderness and guilt and fear. Her best friend's ex, the attraction between them finally blooming—but what if Britt wanted him back again? She never did, though. She disappeared. And when they found her, she was past wanting anything.

Gentle chimes from Parker's phone, the signal to rise from meditation, interrupted her downward spiral into the dark times. It was a tribute to newly acquired Pavlovian responses that she jerked upright and tried to shake off the miasma of emotion. Sitting up was successful, the shaking off less so, but it was a start. Jess should not have the power to ruin her day, or even her hour. She'd agreed to see him, yes, and it was probably a mistake—She tried to think of a "but," but nothing came. Closure wasn't real. It was better to leave the past in the past. If she'd learned anything, that was it.

Twenty minutes until the next client, for a beginner's guided meditation. Twenty minutes to clear her mind enough to snug the Parker persona around herself, to project calm and wisdom and compassion. Double-check the schedule, get to the assigned room, light some candles, choose a soundtrack. She would fit in a few moments to re-center herself first.

Outside, the clouds had thickened and dark spots of rain appeared on the balcony's floor. On the beach, distant figures hurried toward shelter. The sound of Mouse lapping at her water bowl in the kitchen overlaid the creaks and groans of the drafty old building. Parker paused with her hand on the sliding door handle, letting the normality soak in. Everything was exactly as it had been before Jess's call. *She* was exactly as she had been.

She retrieved the yoga mat from the balcony and resumed her meditation practice inside, in front of the window. A few deep breaths. Her heart rate slowed, and the knot between her shoulders began to unwind. After a moment, her eyes fell shut.

Her inner vision reverted to the trees, the darkness, and Britt. She breathed it away. But instead of the wind against the roof, the forest's hush filled her ears: a breeze through sparse leaves, a distant siren on the other side of the wood.

Parker cringed, but the image was already in her mind. Almost a year after that first kiss, she and Jess discovered Britt's body in a clearing. Britt's clothes were gray with dirt, her suede boots discolored to match mottled skin. Leaves tangled in her long hair, hiding what was left of her face.

Parker's eyes popped open: gray sky, gray-green ocean. Spume leaped into the air from the foaming caps of waves hitting submerged rock. When she sucked in another breath, she smelled sandalwood soap and jasmine tea and just a little eau-de-dog, instead of the thick funk of death. *This* was real. This was the life she had salvaged from the wreckage created by her losses.

One phone call and she was falling apart.

Not true, she insisted to herself. Memories, not reality. Passing emotions, which she could cut off as easily as she'd hung up on Jess.

Chimes from the phone again. Five minutes until her session. She peered into the mirror above the sideboard on her way to the door. Her smile was professionally compassionate. Her eyes were like holes.

Parker debated whether she could fix that with a little mascara, decided probably not, and hurried downstairs. Mr. Ryan Poulos, her 1:30 p.m. client, would be waiting.

****

Parker hurried down four flights of stairs, past the apartments of other on-site co-workers. Judging by the confetti design on the aqua and pink carpeting, the south wing of what was now the Tyler Bettering Institute had last been updated in the nineteen-eighties, but it still showed the bones of its boarding house past: no elevator, low ceilings, and corners warped by decades of damp sea air and layers of paint. Not on-brand for the guests, so until there were funds for renovation, Parker and the other on-site staff got ocean-adjacent housing as part of their employment package.

From the shabby, mildewed hallway at the bottom of the stairs, Parker pushed through the connecting door to the main lobby. Modern abstract paintings in blurred greens and blues graced the walls, and tan leather furniture accented with dark polished wood were gathered in tasteful groupings. Sounds were hushed, ceilings soared, and the air carried a delicate ozone scent reminiscent of the sea, which came straight from bottles plugged discreetly into outlets all over the building.

She tossed a wave in the general direction of the reception desk as she sped toward the stairs. Ellen, the concierge, was one of the few staff who'd been friendly in the six weeks since Parker started. Krista had worked here for over a year before she left, recommending Parker for the position, and she'd warned Parker they were a cliquish bunch. Parker felt like she was back in middle school and everyone knew a secret that she didn't. At least they didn't know her secret, or she wouldn't be here.

She passed the bar area and hooked a sharp turn past the elevators for the stairs to the lower floor, where the kitchen, pool, and gym were located, as well as the smaller "Cove Rooms," which were used for massage or meditation appointments. The one Parker had booked, the Netarts Room, had a lavender door which was currently shut. Biting her lip, she knocked lightly and eased it open with a welcoming smile, which collapsed as soon as she saw the room was empty. She rushed to set up, repeating, "Wise, calm, compassionate," under her breath. No windows down here, but the expensive lighting system could evoke a wide array of effects. She dialed the overhead fixtures to a gentle glow and lit a few soy candles.

For the safety of staff and clients, subtly positioned security cameras watched over each room, but the overall effect was natural luxury, with bamboo furnishings, silk hangings, and plump cushions, which she rearranged. She selected a harp concerto to play on the hidden speakers and dialed the volume one notch above subliminal.

The client still hadn't arrived. Parker listened to the harps and strove for inner harmony, but after a moment she gave in and pulled out her phone to text Krista.

Parker—*Guess who called today?*—

Just as her thumb hovered over the off button, Krista answered.

—*Do I have to?*—

Parker—*Ok, no. it was Jess*—

Krista—*Jess who?*—

Parker rolled her eyes.

—Our Jess! From high school. He's on his way here—

Parker had left the door open and thought she heard the elevator ding at the end of the hall, over the sound of muted voices from the pool area. She hovered in the doorway with one eye on the phone, ready to stuff it in her pocket.

The elevator slid open just as Krista replied.

—Shit!!!—

Yep, Parker had known Krista would understand. Quickly, she muted the phone and set it on a hutch that held massage oils, a few books, and pieces of pewter and pottery that complemented the room. She took a deep, cleansing breath of air scented with eucalyptus and lavender massage oils. All was well, and all would be well. In with the good air. Out with the thoughts of Jess, and Britt, and all the past.

A tentative tap on the door followed by a dark-haired man poking his head into the room. "Hi, am I in the right place? I'm supposed to have a meditation session?"

He was around Parker's age, mid to late twenties, with dark-framed glasses and curly hair falling over his forehead; he was cute in the semi-nerdy "safe guy" way that she tended to like. Parker compensated for the attraction by upping her professional vibe. "I'm Parker James," she said. "Are you…Ryan Poulos? From the Chester-Schoolfield wedding party?" She retrieved her phone from the hutch and swiped through appointments on the scheduling app as if there might be more than one Ryan Poulos.

"Uh, no. I mean, well, probably?"

Parker raised an eyebrow.

He flushed down to the collar of his plaid button-down shirt. "Well, that's a mistake. I mean, yes, I'm Ryan. My buddy is the groom, Doug Chester. He signed me up for this. But that's my girlfriend's last name. Poulos? Larissa Poulos. She was supposed to come with me this weekend, but we broke up. We were signed up for couple's massage, and Doug switched it? I don't know why the name—" He broke off and turned an even darker red.

"Okay, no problem!" Parker said quickly. Someone in the office picked the wrong side of the hyphenation to drop when they rescheduled. What a great start. "So, what is your last name?"

"Bennett." He spelled it, and she entered it and set the phone aside.

"Let's sit down," she said, and settled onto one of the cushioned chairs. He perched on the bamboo couch, stiff and upright, as if afraid it wouldn't hold his weight. Parker smiled with encouragement. "So, have you ever tried meditation before?"

"Not really. I think that Doug was messing with me. Since Larissa dumped—since we broke up, he's been saying I should stop feeling so bad. That I should let go of the past. He thinks I should talk to someone, or, you know, take up meditation or something. So he switched that massage appointment. And I figured, I guess, I would try it?" He shrugged, still pink.

"Has it been long since the breakup?" she asked.

He shrugged again. "Six weeks tomorrow. I mean, not that I'm counting. Sorry, I didn't mean to dump on you. I should probably just go—"

He started to stand, but she reached for his arm. "Wait! You might as well try it, right? Now that you're here?"

He sank down with a grimace. "I don't know…"

"Meditation might not be for you, but you won't know until you try," she said lightly. "Maybe your buddy is right. It could do you good."

He offered a tentative smile. "I don't know why I'm so nervous." He brushed the hair back from his forehead and adjusted his glasses in one move, and Parker realized he wasn't just vaguely her "type." He looked a little like Jess. Jess was fair with straight shaggy hair, but they both wore glasses instead of contacts and had that same way of shifting glasses and bangs at the same time. The Jess of ten years ago, anyway. Parker had changed a lot. Had he?

Ryan stood up again, and she realized she'd failed to respond to his comment. He said, "God, I'm sorry. I don't have the temperament for this. I mean, I'm too jittery. Maybe I should give up coffee. Or alcohol. Probably both."

Well, crud. She sucked at connecting today. "Sit down," she said firmly. "I'm sorry. You reminded me of an old friend for a minute. But you're fine, really. Those of us with jittery minds are the ones who can benefit most from meditation. Trust me. You don't wait until your life is sailing smoothly along to start this—you start when you need it, and it sounds like you need it now. Your friend signed you up for the full package, three sessions through the weekend, and then you can decide if you want to make it part of your routine. If you do, I'll send you home with materials and recommendations. If you don't, no harm done. Okay? It will be painless. I promise."

He lowered himself back down reluctantly, and the

session ticked forward from there. Parker settled into her groove, and if she was more self-conscious than usual, he didn't seem to notice. The little zings of attraction at the length of his fingers and his cedar-scented aftershave or soap barely distracted her at all. He really was cute, except for the anxiety. Which she could fix—maybe after she fixed her own? Would he mind that she was an inch taller and twenty pounds heavier than him? Parker fluffed her short burgundy hair, then mentally smacked herself. Positive and professional, Parker! Be here now!

By the end of the session, Ryan seemed more comfortable. He met her eyes as they shook hands. She wondered briefly if he would ask for her number, but instead he said, "Ten-thirty tomorrow morning, right?"

"Yes. If you're up for it. Could be nice to get centered before the wedding," Parker answered, smiling and stepping back. The ceremony was scheduled for one o'clock on the beach, if the weather allowed, in the chapel if not. To her, it was a free afternoon, as all the guests would be attending.

"The wedding," he repeated. He swallowed, then gave her a quick, tight smile. "Yeah. Great. Thank you."

She closed the door behind him, blew out the candles, and turned off the harps. Her heart rate had jumped with the touch of his hand, but it slowed quickly. Thinking of a client as a potential date would be highly unprofessional. Krista would kill her if Parker lost this job. It was her best opportunity in a while, and she'd lied and cheated to take it—she wasn't going to blow it for some cute guy.

Jess's call had thrown her off, that was all. A silly flirtation would distract her from a blast from the past.

Parker closed her eyes and sighed. If she didn't have

more work to do, she'd go back to bed.

A knock startled her, and the door eased open revealing a buxom girl with grass green hair. Calli, the bosses' teenage daughter, spent half her time reading in out-of-the-way corners and the other half running errands for her parents as an unpaid gofer. Probably the motivation for the out-of-the-way corners.

"Mom says your group is gathering. You should go to Oceanview One." Her voice was surprisingly hoarse for a teenage girl, making her sound like she smoked unfiltered cigarettes between shots of whiskey. According to Krista, she'd had a sinus condition which led to multiple surgeries when she was little.

Glancing at her watch, Parker groaned a little. The group mindfulness session wasn't supposed to start for forty-five minutes. "I was hoping for a break," she said. Her stomach felt hollow, and she'd looked forward to grabbing an energy bar and a few moments with Mouse.

Calli opened the door wider as if she'd been invited in. "You're so not what I expected. You're very different from Krista."

"Oh, yeah?" Krista had described Calli dismissively as a typical spoiled rich kid, and Parker wondered if that had been too harsh. Krista sometimes jumped to conclusions about people who hadn't had to deal with the kind of trauma they both had when they were younger, and Parker knew she could be guilty of that, too.

Calli bit her lip, thinking. "She's a lot...I don't know. Kind of smoother?"

Parker snorted. Yep, Krista was and always would be the smooth one, although Parker knew her well enough that she couldn't write her off as over-privileged. More so than Calli, Krista had grown up with a pampered lifestyle, but only until her brother's accident and her parents' acrimonious divorce laid waste to the family during high school. Suddenly, the girl who'd expected a sports car for her sweet sixteen was lucky to get a birthday cake. These days, Krista had resumed the sleek façade of her childhood, but Parker recognized it as the armor it was. Calli was seventeen, easy to fool with a lift of a threaded brow and a flash of whitened teeth. Skinny, blonde, shiny Krista probably seemed like the epitome of togetherness.

"I'm having a rough day," Parker admitted. "Wish it didn't show, though. I'll be up in a few minutes. You can let your mom know if you want."

Instead, Calli plopped onto the couch where Ryan had recently perched, looking around curiously at the sage-green walls and natural fiber decorations as if she'd never been in one of the Cove Rooms before. With a pang, Parker realized she was probably lonely. Except for the servers and housekeepers, who would get in big trouble for socializing on duty, Parker was one of the youngest women on staff. But why did Calli hang around here instead of with her own friends?

"I'm having a rough day, too," Calli said. "Maybe I should stay in here. It's nice. Do you think anyone would notice?"

"Notice you were missing? Or notice an extra person hiding behind the couch during the next meditation session?"

Calli grinned and shrugged. "Mom said this is a slow week. Maybe you can just work around me."

Parker sat reluctantly on one of the chairs. "Did you have a tough day at school?"

Calli looked away, fiddling with a dangling

sequined earring. "Nah. School's okay. I'm doing it on the computer, so I can pretty much go at my own pace."

"I didn't know that. I wish they had that when I was a kid."

"Mom had to fill out a ton of paperwork," Calli said. "I wouldn't mind going to a regular school, actually."

"Oh." Parker snuck a look at her watch again, as she let go of the idea of a snack. Like it or not, she was still on probation, and if Marta wanted her to start the group session early, she would start it early.

Calli noticed and stood up. "Just procrastinating," she said. "I should go get some things done. But hey, I wanted to tell you, I really like your dog. If you need someone to walk him some time, I could take him to the beach."

Parker smiled. Mouse wasn't the friendliest dog in the world, possibly due to her not-so-stable previous owner, but she did have her fans. Calli must have seen Parker and Mouse out at dawn or dusk, when they made a habit of jogging down the beach or walking to the little pizzeria that sold by the slice. A jar of dog biscuits sat right inside the door, and sometimes Parker and Mouse would eat on the patio and people-watch all the tourists going by.

"Mouse does love the beach," Parker said. "I'm sure she'd appreciate an extra walk sometime. But she's doesn't listen well to people she doesn't know, so we'd need to get her comfortable with you first."

Calli grinned, which lit her face with sudden prettiness. "Great! Can I come up later today?"

Parker's mind jumped to Jess's impending arrival. It shouldn't be for a couple of days, but frankly, she felt crappy and antisocial. And she wasn't responsible for this kid's well-being. "Tomorrow or the next day would be better. Can I text you? Or I bet we'll just see each other."

"Oh, okay." Calli sounded a little hurt, but Parker dictated her number and then saved Calli's into her phone.

"I better head out, I guess," Parker said. "Hope the rest of your day goes better."

"Yeah. Like that's gonna happen."

Chapter Two

Parker slipped through the heavy door into Oceanview A, a mid-sized conference room whose west wall was entirely composed of windows overlooking Nye Beach, now concealed behind vertical blinds. A loose knot of people milled around the circular tables, with Marta slightly to one side, frowning down at her phone. Blonde tendrils had escaped her chignon and her face was pink and wind-chapped, her leather jacket dripping rain onto her snug designer jeans. The diamonds at ear and throat were large and real, but her nose was red-tipped and her mascara had smudged.

Parker hesitated. She'd only known Marta for six weeks, but she could guess being caught in the rain would seriously piss Marta off. Krista had warned her Marta could be tightly wound, but this was only the second time Parker had seen the woman off her game. The first time had been a doozy. When Parker first arrived, pulling up late outside the Institute after a long day of driving, she hadn't expected the owners to welcome her immediately. She had just released Mouse from the passenger seat when Seth and Marta rushed out from the glass-fronted lobby to greet them. Marta exclaimed loudly as she swooped toward Mouse, who jerked away and growled softly, showing her teeth.

Marta yelped and darted behind Seth. He calmed Marta, Parker soothed Mouse, and after a few moments of awkwardness, they tried again. Marta held her closed hand out to Mouse, who deigned to sniff it, and all was well. Marta even apologized. But the next day during Parker's orientation, Marta had expressed skepticism about Parker's claim that Mouse was normally gentle and tolerant. If she heard a single complaint about Mouse's behavior, Marta said, the dog would have to go.

Since then, Parker kept Mouse far from her, and Marta had been nice enough, if exacting. The Tyler Bettering "Code of Conduct" was an eighteen-page manual Marta had developed, detailing how to relate to clients in various situations in order to receive exemplary feedback, which equaled bonuses. Tips were forbidden, so the staff carried surveys to hand out after providing services.

Parker was not a fan. But so far, she'd been getting decent feedback despite not knowing what she was doing, so Marta was happy.

"First the stables had a plumbing issue and canceled at the last minute," Marta whispered. "So we drove to the shops, started walking around, and the sky opened up. We got back on the bus, and a fire truck was blocking the exit. We were trapped there, in our damp clothes, for fifteen minutes. And now there's an issue with the fish delivery, so dinner will be late! Could you stretch your session so I have time to arrange a snack table?"

Parker blinked. She was starting half an hour early already. What could she do with these people for almost two hours? A line appeared between Marta's pale eyebrows and Parker's mouth opened by itself. "I'll extend the introduction and add in some stretching at the end. No problem. Really."

Marta beamed, missing the edge of resentment in

Parker's voice, and hurried out with a long stride, without even introducing her to the group. With a sigh, Parker approached the tables, re-assessing the mood of the room. Fortunately, the many bartending jobs which hadn't made it to her fake resume helped with this. Several guests were still wearing coats and scarves and even riding boots, although others had peeled off damp outer layers and set them on the tables. Still chatting loudly and poking at their phones, they were a picture of restlessness and irritation, more like people stranded at the airport than guests at a wellness-themed wedding. Parker had a powerful impulse to turn and leave. They wouldn't want to listen to her, and what good could she do for them? Parker had her own fear and melancholy to chew on.

Boy, that sounded like the old Corey. Washed-down-the-drain Corey. Parker pushed her away. Krista had said, "Fake it till you make it," and Parker had said, "Wherever you go, there you are." But she'd agreed to this crazy plan anyway, expecting failure but finding that a new place with new habits and new expectations made a difference. Until today.

Parker squeezed her eyes shut. This is what I do now, she reminded herself sternly. No one here, including me, is in a great state of mind. But we can all move forward.

Deep breath from the diaphragm. She opened her eyes, straightened her spine, and moved to the light controls. Wise, calm, and compassionate, she reminded herself. Without saying a word, she dimmed the lights. There were some surprised laughs, and the volume in the room fell, leaving one voice chattering on and a moment later, self-conscious silence.

Another press of a button slid the blinds open to reveal gray sky and gray-green waves, breaking white-caps on the rain-spattered beach below. Parker shed her shoes and sweater, laid them carefully to one side, and heard shuffling as others followed suit. When she switched on a background soundtrack that featured a soft flute blended with wind and ocean sounds, the room hushed into stillness and she knew she had them. Again, she felt the bright swelling in her chest that she recognized as the bud of her new self, her hopeful, kind, optimistic self.

"For those of you who haven't met me yet," she said, "my name is Parker James." A lie, of course. Her name was Corey Jantzen, and the internet would forever remember her as the girl who got away with her best friend's murder. "I've been practicing various forms of meditation and mindfulness for many years now." Vast exaggeration. She was almost done with an eight-week online course, and she prayed every night that she wouldn't run into an actual expert. "I'll be your Meditation and Mindfulness coach for the duration of your visit, and I'm so happy to meet you all and share what has been for me, a source of joy and healing." Sure it was. Parker couldn't help it if she felt a little ambivalent right now.

Oh, Jess.

****

The smile dropped off her face as soon as the last guest disappeared through the double doors to the hallway. Parker's professional front had held up through the session, but there were cracks. Impatience, snarky inner commentary, an inability to stay in the moment for more than, well, a moment. Her delivery had leaned toward rote rather than sincere.

In zombie mode, she grabbed a wrapped sandwich from the staff dining hall and her mail from the front desk, and carried them upstairs. Flyers went in the recycling, dinner went in the fridge, and, trying to stifle her thoughts, she checked the tide and surf online. Mouse was eager and restless, signaling her readiness with bright eyes, sticking right by Parker's side as she changed into her purple running bra and a tech shirt celebrating a race she'd run in California, plus green tights with a phone pocket, ankle socks, and running shoes.

Mouse knew the routine and was certain Parker could speed it up. She nosed Parker's calf.

"Easy, girl. I'm coming. Don't worry," Parker said.

Mouse woofed and trotted to the fire escape door, then gazed reproachfully as Parker hurried into the bedroom one last time to fish for the headlamp and pepper spray. The spray was a tiny canister that fit into the thigh pocket of her tights, along with her phone. She'd never used it, but better to have it than not. The headlamp she wrapped around her wrist. It made her look like a coal miner, so she'd wait until full dark to put it on. Tonight, she wasn't sure how far she'd run, or how long she would run for. Long enough to sweat out the day and any thoughts of Jess, whatever it took.

The rain had softened to a light mist, and the sun glowed beyond a veil of clouds right at the horizon. They had the beach to themselves, and her tension shook out as they jogged north. Parker used to keep Mouse leashed, worried that the expanse of sand stretching for miles would overexcite her, or some other dog would tempt her away. But Mouse stayed close, even when a pair of tiny, unleashed hairballs chased after them as Parker passed their oblivious owners.

Waves licked the beach, but the tide was low, the sand hard and flat. Parker settled into a brisk, comfortable rhythm. Fresh salt air filled her lungs, and she became hyper-aware of the breeze on her skin, the sound of her own breath, and Mouse's even, tireless steps padding along the sand. It was another kind of meditation, and she was grateful as always that Mouse had come into her life and led her to this.

Still, there was an ache in her chest. Grief was a permanent resident, but she had finally learned to broaden her perspective to encompass the beauty she also saw, without discounting or denying the pain. It was a tricky balance, but with practice, it was getting easier. Unless, like today, something threw her off-kilter.

As Parker approached the headland where they'd turn and head south toward home, her phone buzzed. She awkwardly she fished it out of her pocket without pausing. There was one text.

Krista—*Talk soon?*—

Parker considered calling her right back. She and Mouse could walk for a while, a pleasant cool-down in the ocean breeze, as she told Krista about Jess's call and her fragile-feeling day.

But Parker knew what would happen. Krista would sympathize, Parker would cry. Mouse would worry. And instead of feeling comforted, Parker would feel like she'd given in to her old, broken self. Krista was her best friend, and had the best intentions, but Parker needed to regain her balance on her own this time. She texted back.

—*Tomorrow*—

She slipped the phone back into her pocket before

picking up the pace again.

"Race you," she said to Mouse, who accepted the challenge with a joyful burst of speed. The dog was not distracted by old and persistent sorrows, and if Parker wanted to keep up, she couldn't be either. They sped all the way to the steep cliff-side stairs leading up to the boarding house that had been gutted, expanded, and re-branded as the Tyler Bettering Institute, much as Corey Jantzen had become Parker James.

Erosion was a constant issue on the coast. The public access at Nye Beach occurred at a natural low point and took the form of a ramp instead of stairs, but most of the hotels were up on the bluff, thirty or forty feet above sea level, and struggled to maintain private access points which had to be rebuilt or rebolted every few years. The Tyler Bettering stairs zig-zagged three flights up the cliff, and the lowest flight started in the soft sand at the base, with a landing on stilts to allow for the natural movement of sand. It created a sheltered cave partially hidden by beach grass and driftwood from the recent storms.

A bright piece of reflective fabric caught Parker's headlamp beam. She paused to take a closer look, thinking one of the guests might have stashed a jacket or hat there earlier and forgotten to retrieve it. Mouse, sensing her curiosity, ran ahead to sniff at the fabric, but instead of fetching it she barked, again and again, her eyes fixed on the recess under the stairs as she backed away.

Parker shushed her with a hand on her neck. Mouse quieted reluctantly, but a subsonic growl vibrated in her throat. Parker heard nothing but waves and wind and distant traffic—no nearby creatures. Could there be a raccoon under there? An injured cat or dog? She fished out the pepper spray, just in case.

"It's okay," she called, and rounded the pile of driftwood to peer beneath the landing, poised to jump back if she met scared or angry eyes.

It was not a hurt animal. Or rather, it had been a man, but he didn't hurt anymore.

Parker jerked away with an involuntary shriek. If hearing Jess's voice had been a punch in the gut, this was being hit by a truck. All breath left her lungs and her skin prickled with terror. She was filled with broken glass; She was burning and numb and panting and dizzy, all at once.

The white fabric was part of a ball cap, lying two feet from the head of a man whose eyes, nose, and mouth were hidden by a generous application of duct tape. Parker recognized him anyway. The wavy hair and dark-rimmed glasses, now askew on his forehead and offering no help with vision, were devastatingly familiar.

Ryan Bennett didn't move. She froze too, for far too long. Mouse whined. Parker forced herself to breathe and breathe again past the constriction in her chest, and after an agonizing stretch of time, she collapsed to her knees next to him and hunted for a pulse. His throat felt clammy and slightly warm under her chilled fingers, but there was no doubt he was dead. She retched, tears streaming from her eyes, and swallowed down bile.

She longed to yank the tape from his nose and mouth, to remove the glasses from his face and peel the adhesive gently from his eyes, but she forced herself not to, just rose and stumbled away toward the stairs. Hackles still raised, Mouse settled next to Parker on the bottom step. Parker lowered her head to her knees, took a deep breath and tried to calm them both with soft words.

"It's okay, Mouse. It's okay. It's over. It's all over."

A lie. That bleak and empty feeling in her chest had grown as huge and frigid as the ocean. She wrapped her arms around Mouse, but Parker barely felt the dog's warmth. Mouse licked her ear worriedly.

If only she hadn't noticed the hat. But no. He would still be dead, a guy no older than her, who would never get the chance to move on from a bad breakup. Someone else would have found his body, if not tonight, then tomorrow. He would have been disturbed by some other dog-walker, or a convoy of rats and seagulls and crows would have drawn the attention of a passerby in the morning. And the police would trace him to the wedding party at Tyler Bettering, and inevitably from there to Parker James. A woman living under an alias.

She felt so horrible for Ryan, for his stolen life, for the pain and fear of his last moments, but that didn't stop her from focusing on herself, even if that meant she was a twisted narcissist. She would be revealed as Corey Jantzen. Corey Jantzen, murder suspect. Corey Jantzen, finder of bodies, four times now. Corey Jantzen, whose mother had been murdered and wrapped in duct tape, whose babysitter had been stabbed in the chest, whose best friend had been kidnapped, tortured, and killed. Even if it was all coincidence, it must have warped Corey, or so the papers had said, implying she was a teenaged killer.

She dialed 911 anyway.

Chapter Three

Parker shivered. Huddled on the stairs with Ryan's body yards away, she couldn't help thinking of Uncle Danny. Part of her loved him and hurt for him, but he was the monster she pictured when she pictured a killer. Daniel William Evers, the goofy college student who played tea party with her and her stuffed giraffe, was the same guy who strangled her mother more than twenty years ago and he was still locked away. She hadn't seen him in person since she was five, but despite all her efforts to scrub him from her thoughts, he was a constant presence in her life, tied to her by pain and love.

She absently stroked Mouse's neck. Mom's death hadn't made sense, especially with five-year-old Corey in the house. She'd been too young to understand anything about mental illness, and when people tried to tell her Danny was sick, she would say, "No, he wasn't. We ate spaghetti and then we played hide and seek." But even adult Parker still wondered. Why hadn't there been more signs? How could he wash dishes, joke around with friends, babysit Corey, and at the same time hide his paranoid delusions?

At thirteen, she'd concocted an elaborate theory about Danny being a fall guy and a victim of a lazy and misguided medical establishment. She put together a website, presenting the facts as she remembered them; he hadn't been schizophrenic or delusional or psychotic, therefore his doctors must be using a murder he hadn't done to justify locking him away.

When he discovered the website, Dad showed her the stack of letters that Danny mailed monthly from the psychiatric hospital where he was serving his sentence. Long rants about Mom, himself, their parents, his professors, even Corey—and how they all set him up to fail—interspersed with spates of self-castigation and apology. She took the website down. Uncle Danny's voice could be heard in brief flashes, but his illness was undeniable.

Clipping on Mouse's leash in anticipation of the cops' arrival, Parker suppressed tears and pulled the dog close. Finding Mom's body was etched indelibly in her memory. The blue gauzy scarf trailing from under the door of the coat closet like a deliberate clue. Little Corey, uneasy because of the silence but tantalized, expected a giant "Boo!" when she opened the door. Instead she was met by the silver duct tape covering Mom's face, as if she were wearing a mask—probably a mercy, hiding bulging eyes and tongue, but now featured in all of Parker's nightmares. Mom's face, a death mask in silver...so like Ryan's.

Parker restlessly stood. For all she knew, Ryan's death had been a simple robbery, the tape just an overenthusiastic way to shut him up. Duct tape was ubiquitous, it probably showed up in crimes every day. She paced a small circle with Mouse at her side and forced her mind to leave Uncle Danny and her mother. Not relevant, and she was just freaking herself out.

Ryan's handshake jumped into her head—that little inappropriate shock of attraction. She could feel the sensation of his hand in hers, his bony fingers, soft and cool. From there, Jess's phone call came to mind, the sound of his voice, the way Britt's murder had been haunting Parker hours before. Britt's corpse, abandoned and inanimate. And Mrs. Gilford. And Mom, and then Danny and his duct tape again. His duct tape, which one talk show psychiatrist surmised might signify either remorse or a deep need to shut her up and make her stop staring. And finally, five-year-old Corey, falling into a doze on lavender-scented towels under the upstairs bathroom cabinet, while her mother struggled and died downstairs.

Parker swallowed. Today was really too much. Today was the kind of day that proved she had never left her past behind. It would just keep grinding her down. Where had Parker been when Ryan was breathing his last? Loping along the beach, exhilarated by salty air and the joyful bounding of Mouse? Fixated on poor little Parker having to face her ex-boyfriend, boo-hoo? She was spiraling into a neurotic loop of guilt and horror that she knew all too well.

Why did Ryan have to die? And why did Parker have to be the one to find him? She was already broken enough, goddammit.

Finally, sirens drew close, and she turned to see flashing lights in the TBI parking lot at the top of the cliff. Her phone buzzed, and she checked it quickly.

Krista—*Got a question, sure you can't talk?*—

Parker—*Not now. Something bad happened.*—

Krista—*You ok?*—

Parker—*No*—

Krista—*Should I come?*—

Parker half-sobbed and half-chuckled, her pain easing just a little. It was a ridiculously kind and generous offer. Krista's new position was at a swanky resort near Seattle. It would take her half a day just to drive here. Plus, she was still proving herself in a much more corporate, competitive environment.

Parker—*No! I'm fine. Can't talk now, deets later.*—

She shifted the volume from vibrate to silent and slid the phone into her pocket. Watching the lights flash above, where two cop cars were parked with engines running, she realized she should have called Seth and Marta in addition to the cops. They would have appreciated a heads-up before police swarmed all over their wellness wedding. Shit. Too late.

Now there were flashing lights at Nye Beach as well, and a car jounced slowly toward her over the sand.

Behind her someone called out, and Parker turned. A shadowy figure approached from the darkness of the beach to the north, and Parker tightened her hand on Mouse's leash. Fear jolted through her, but then she recognized the form hurrying awkwardly over the soft sand.

"What's going on?" Calli called out. "What's wrong?"

Her face reflected red and blue lights. Her eyes were wide and panicky. The vehicle, an SUV with a light bar, stopped about twenty feet away, and two uniformed figures got out.

"It's okay," Parker called to Calli over the sound of waves and wind. "But wait there."

Calli halted, frowning.

The officers approached. Parker spoke to them, "I'm the one who called. He's back here, by the steps."

Calli's hearing was sharp. "Who? Who's back there?"

28

One of the officers, a man, stepped past Parker and toward Ryan's body. The other, a woman with a curly ponytail blowing across her face, joined Parker just as Calli drew close.

"What's going on? Is it my dad?" Calli demanded.

"No, no, don't worry, Calli. It's nothing to do with you, it's just—an accident."

The pony-tailed cop said, "Can I get your names? I'm Officer Connelly."

"She has nothing to do with this. She just got here," Parker told Connelly. "She's just a kid. Can she go up to the hotel?"

"I'm seventeen!" Calli protested frantically, her eyes darting from Parker's face to Connelly's.

Parker raised her eyebrows, nonplussed. What was Calli so anxious about? She'd approached from the same part of the beach where Parker and Mouse had been running, but Parker hadn't noticed her at any point. Had Calli been on the beach all along? Did she witness whatever happened to Ryan?

"Okay, okay," the officer said soothingly. "Let's get your names, and you can both tell me what's going on."

The male cop came up beside Connelly and eyed Calli. Out of the side of his mouth, he said, "We definitely have a body."

"*Who?*" Calli's voice pitched high. Parker put an arm around her instinctively, and Calli huddled close. The girl's black T-shirt was long-sleeved, but thin and gauzy, and she was shivering more than Parker.

"Stay right here," Connelly told them both, and she followed her partner to peer around the driftwood pile.

Calli pulled away from Parker to look her in the face. "Who is it?"

"It's one of the wedding guests," Parker said. "Ryan Bennett. Did you see something? When did you come down to the beach?" It occurred to her he had been youngish, cute, apparently non-threatening. Too old for Calli, but still. Could the girl have been meeting up with him? Flirting with him?

Calli's shoulders caved. "I didn't know him," she breathed, but there was a hitch in her voice. She folded her arms tightly across her chest and rocked from foot to foot.

Connelly returned and observed the girl dispassionately. "Names?" she asked again.

Parker introduced herself and Calli, then repeated that Calli was just a kid who hadn't been with her when Parker had found the body, and wasn't dressed for the weather, and should be sent up to her parents at the Institute. Connelly nodded and made notes, but hadn't responded to the request by the time another vehicle approached.

More people in uniform were coming via the cliff stairs as well. Mouse pressed against Parker's legs. Parker could feel her alert energy as she shifted watchfully in the sand.

Connelly and her partner spoke quietly, then the partner stepped forward and said, "I'm Officer Martinez. I can take Ms. Tyler up to the hotel."

"Before we let you go, the detective needs to ask you some questions," Connelly added to Parker. "It won't be long. She's heading over right now."

Calli joined Martinez but looked back at Parker and asked, "Do you want me to take Mouse?"

"No, thanks though. She'll be fine with me."

"Okay," Calli said, voice small, and Parker realized

the girl had been hoping for moral support from the dog. Parker felt selfish for a moment, then pictured the look on Marta's face if Calli walked into the middle of whatever chaos was happening up there with Mouse in tow. Not a great idea.

The officer led Calli to the SUV. Parker paced, rubbing her hands and arms to keep warm, until the detective approached. Short and bundled in a bulky hip-length police jacket, the detective diverted briefly to observe Ryan's resting place before angling toward Parker. She wore gloves and a watch cap pulled down on her forehead, and Parker shivered harder in envy. It hadn't been a very intense run, but Parker's tights and tech shirt were damp with sweat and mist, which were still leaching heat from her body.

The detective's eyes flicked over Parker. "Can you get her a blanket or sweater or something?" she asked Connelly.

Connelly pulled a face. "I'll try. Martinez took our vehicle. I'll see what I can find."

The detective stuck out her hand. "I'm Detective Balderas. Sorry, you're freezing. We'll get you inside in just a second. Can you tell me what happened here?"

Parker drew a blank and realized her little freak-out on the stairs and her attempt to pull herself together had done no good. She hadn't gotten around to planning what to say. Was she going to tell them her birth name or let them discover it for themselves? But what if they didn't? What if Ryan had an enemy, a stalker, and Parker outed herself, overcomplicating everything for no reason? It would look like a grab for attention, the exact opposite of what she wanted, and she couldn't bear that.

She said, "My name is Parker James. I work at Tyler

Bettering Institute, right up there on the cliff. Tonight I went for a run with my dog, Mouse, and on the way back, we noticed a hat in the sand."

"We?"

"Me and Mouse."

"The hat?"

Parker pointed to where the white object had been showing, but driftwood and beach grass blocked the view from here. "Ryan—the dead guy's hat had fallen off his head. It was white, kind of reflective in my headlamp, and I thought someone might have forgotten it. One of the guests maybe. So I was going to bring it up…" She stopped when she realized she was babbling.

Balderas nodded as if she were making perfect sense. "So you were running on the beach in the dark?"

"It wasn't really dark when I started, more like twilight. The sun set and even then it takes a while to get completely dark. I usually run twice a day, morning and evening, and I'm used to it."

"Always here?"

Parker shook her head. "No, sometimes I run on the street. The sidewalks. Or south, over the bridge."

"Okay. You knew the victim?"

The detective's voice was sympathetic, but her eyes studied Parker carefully.

"I don't *know him,* know him," Parker said, then realized that sounded shifty. "I met him yesterday. I mean, today, this afternoon. We had an appointment."

Balderas gave the slow nod again. "For?"

"Excuse me." Connelly came up and offered a fleece blanket. The wind blew pieces of her curly ponytail into her mouth, and she made a face as she pulled her hair back. Parker took the blanket and wrapped it gratefully around her shoulders.

"What was your appointment for?" Balderas reminded her.

"Oh." That should be a simple question, but Parker's mind lost traction in the weeds. Did she need to explain how it was couple's massage, and someone put his name in the books wrong? Probably not. "Meditation. He wasn't really interested. His friend had signed him up."

Connelly touched Balderas's shoulder, and the two withdrew to speak together. Parker huddled in the blanket, blowing on her hands. Mouse sighed and lay down at her feet. Above, clouds still streaked the sky, but a patch of starry purple shone over the ocean. Parker fixed her eyes on that and tried not to let her teeth chatter.

Balderas stomped away through the soft sand, a cell phone to her ear. Connelly said, "The detective says she'll get your official statement later. For now, let's get you home. Where do you live?"

"The hotel. The Institute." Parker looked up the steps. Garlands of crime scene tape rippled in the wind at the top and bottom.

"Really? I don't think I'd want to live and work in the same place. You'd never get to go home." Connelly shuddered theatrically.

Parker shrugged. "Saves a lot of commuting time."

They walked along the beach toward the parking lot access in silence. Mouse sniffed happily at the line of seaweed, driftwood, and other detritus left by high tide hours ago. Parker second-guessed herself. Maybe she should ask Connelly about whether her old name or relationship to long ago cases might be important.

Three separate encounters with murder, now four. If there was a prize for how many times someone's name appeared in the news in relation to murder, Parker would probably be number one in the amateur category. Who else could beat that, aside from cops and lawyers? Hitmen. Serial killers. Only the guilty.

That was not a good train of thought. It led to questions like, would the cops be right to care about her past? Was the similarity between her mother's death and Ryan's meaningful?

She already knew the answer though. Danny strangled her mother with the gauzy long scarf she sometimes wore to work. Ryan's neck had been bare above his shirt collar, the stubble on the underside of his chin clearly visible, with no sign of ligature marks.

Parker shivered, wishing she couldn't see his corpse so clearly in her mind's eye. Images like this, popping up almost randomly, already haunted her. Drugs and alcohol had helped a bit when she was younger but had side effects, like making her life a piece of crap. Running helped, too, but one tool was not enough. She was down to meditation or suicide, and suicide, she thought darkly, was too much of a last resort to suit.

So meditation *had* to work. And it seemed to be. Sure, she'd had bad sessions, when the intimate knowledge of violent death would crawl over her until she didn't think she could bear it, no matter how much she tried to focus minutely on air traveling through her nostrils. But she was learning to let that excruciating sensation come and go, just as every breath did.

One more dead body would not take that away from her. She had too much riding on it.

Parker flashed again on their short encounter, which she would no doubt have quickly forgotten if he hadn't died, but now would remember forever. Would they have met again tomorrow morning? Would they have come dangerously close to flirting?

Would he have left after the weekend wedding with her phone number?

Much more likely, the momentary thrill would have faded at their second meeting, professionalism would have smoothed it over, and next week or next month he'd be recovered from the break-up and laughing with his friends about his brief and pointless experiment with woo-woo meditation.

Parker and the officer walked up the ramp to the parking lot at Nye Beach. Two City police vehicles were parked there, lights still flashing. The shops and restaurants that lined the street were closed for the night, but gawkers lined the beachside benches. She envied their separation from the events. For them, it was just one step closer than a TV show, not a matter of grief and devastation.

Parker caught herself before she fell into her own trap. She refused to be devastated by this. She'd worked too hard to turn her life around. Jess wasn't allowed to throw her off, and neither was this.

Stronger at the break, she reminded herself. And wise, calm, and compassionate. For all the wounds in her soul, for however broken she had been, she was healing. She knew where the cracks were, and she'd begun to fill them with peace and a commitment to helping others. Her dad had asked a while back if she would consider seeing a counselor and she'd told him she had seen plenty. In fact, it had been two, despite years of subpar health insurance. The first creeped her out with a seemingly ghoulish interest in each death. No doubt he had an endgame, but she didn't wait to find out what it was. The second wanted Parker to reinterpret her life in ways she wasn't comfortable with or ready for. Maybe she would try again, someday, but for now, belief in her own power to heal had to be good enough.

Officer Connelly asked her to wait and chatted with another cop through the squad car window. Finally, she shrugged, and they resumed their trek up the steep sidewalk toward the hotel entrance two blocks away.

"No more room in the parking lot," Connelly said. "I guess this wedding was going to be pretty big."

"It's a pretty small lot," Parker said, echoing a complaint often expressed by Marta, who hoped to purchase a property across the street as an additional guest parking area, if she could get permission from the city.

The renovated TBI building was dark gray with teal accents and beautiful landscaping. Exotic grasses, impatiens, nasturtiums, and ivy spilled over pottery tubs in rich glazed colors, even in autumn. Connelly led the way to the front lobby door, and Parker and Mouse followed obediently.

Comforting warmth blasted out as soon as the door opened, and Parker let it wash over her in relief as they stepped inside and the doors swung shut behind them. The lobby, with its multiple seating areas and strategically placed screens, could divide an excited crowd into softly murmuring get-togethers. But now it held a collection of people reeling from shock, and the air of devastation would not be tamed. Parker recognized a young woman with a large nose and a thick black braid as the bride-to-be, thanks to the "Welcome to the Chester-Schoolfield Wedding" poster at the front desk. The bride sagged on the groom's shoulder, her face hidden, his head turned down toward hers. Parker took in his puffy eyes, his slack expression. This must be Doug, the friend who'd pointed Ryan in her direction for help in leaving the past behind.

Others stood with uncomprehending faces, drinks still in hand. They'd likely been at the rehearsal dinner when the awful news broke.

Marta and Seth stood in a small curl of armchairs near the entrance, Calli scribbling in a leather-bound notebook on a bench behind them. The splayed pages were dense with ink. Marta and Seth regarded Parker with sharp eyes and closed expressions, and she hesitated. They couldn't blame her for finding the body, could they? Someone else would have if she hadn't. But she knew she should have called them from the beach. It had been a stressful moment, though, and she'd done as well as she could. Defensively, Parker snugged the fleece blanket around her shoulders and approached.

Marta grabbed her by the bicep and pulled her close enough for Parker to see a clump of mascara stuck in Marta's lower lashes. She squeezed Parker's arm hard. "How could you?" she demanded.

Chapter Four

Marta's fingers bit into Parker's arm. Wide-eyed, Parker tried to step back, but Marta wouldn't let go.

"Your poor judgment! I am shocked. Just shocked."

Parker looked from Marta to Seth in confusion.

Calli flipped her notebook closed and said, "Mom!" but Seth interrupted her.

"She's right, Calli. Let your mother speak."

"I don't understand," Parker said.

Officer Connelly edged between them. She was a large woman and used her bulk to good effect. "What's the issue here, ma'am?"

Marta released Parker's arm and stepped back, but was not noticeably calmed. "The issue is that this young woman exposed my daughter to murder!" Marta's voice rose in a hissing whisper that no doubt pierced the hum of every conversation in the room.

"No!" was all Parker could say. "I had nothing to do with it!" She panicked, reviewing the moments when Calli approached her on the beach. What had she done that could be misconstrued as "exposing"? Parker's eyes sought Calli's again, but the girl avoided her gaze.

Connelly looked with interest from Calli's downcast eyes to Parker's confusion to Marta's rage, and said, "Well, why don't we just briefly take your statements and then let you all go about your business? Ma'am— Mrs. Tyler, is it? Why don't you go first? I know you're eager to deal with your guests when we're done."

Marta looked somewhat mollified, although she quickly corrected, "It's Ms. Reinhardt, please. My husband and I don't share a last name." She led Connelly behind the reception desk to the staff area door, which led to a few offices, the staff dining room, and a private staff conference room.

Seth sighed and sank back into the armchair next to Calli, rubbing his tanned face. "I think she's over-reacting a little," he said. "But I do wish you'd been able to shield Calli better."

Parker opened her mouth to protest, then shut it and nodded. She wished that too. She just hadn't had any say in the matter.

Parker was never sure what to think of Seth. His blue eyes and oversized features gave him a theatrical air, even when he seemed sincere. Seth played to an invisible audience, consistently aware of himself as the center of a three-dimensional composition.

He was an author of self-help books, a self-deprecating guru of charisma, who had supplemented his authorial income by offering leadership and success trainings at professional conferences until he made it big. His boyish enthusiasm and aw-shucks confidence had gone over well on morning talk shows, and his last two books were New York Times bestsellers. Running his own wellness resort was his "retirement" project, according to the TBI website, but it was common knowledge among the staff that he was also working on another book, this one about parenting.

Parker wanted him to stop being "on" all the time, and to walk around with a big piece of spinach between his teeth all day. Or maybe he could trip over a dead body. Anything to undermine his overconfidence and make him stop pretending to have all the answers all the time.

"These things are so hard," he said, his head in his hands. "I never know what to do." He looked up and blinked at her as if noticing her for the first time. "Oh my goodness, Parker, you look beat. Sit down. You poor thing."

Internally, Parker rolled her eyes. He was so good he could sense and combat her skepticism. Or he wasn't as bad as she thought? Against her will, she warmed to him, as she always seemed to do in his presence. "I should bring Mouse upstairs," she said.

Seth raised his eyebrows. "Didn't that officer say to wait here?"

"Can you tell her I'll be right back? We were out for a run, and Mouse hasn't even had any water yet."

They both looked at Mouse, whose delicate build, while not as sleek as a purebred greyhound, made strangers think she must be starving all the time.

"I could take her up for you," Calli offered eagerly.

"You're not going anywhere," her father said.

"You'd like that," Calli grumbled, but settled back to scribbling.

Parker surveyed the room, relieved at the thought of getting away for even a few moments. The staff corridor, although it would take her past Marta's office, would be quickest, so she led Mouse through the same door behind reception that Connelly and Marta had disappeared through. They were visible through the window on Marta's door: Marta's tired, strained face on the far side of the desk, Connelly's curly ponytail closer to Parker as she hurried by. The cop was rising from one of the visitors' chairs, so Parker's absence would be noticed in a moment. As she hurried past the staff dining room, she saw other police inside, including Detective Balderas talking to an unfamiliar older man in a suit. The scent of coffee drifted through the open doors.

Parker slipped quietly into the south wing and up the carpeted stairs. In their suite, Mouse went straight to her water bowl, and without flipping the lights on, Parker poured fresh kibble for her before collapsing on the loveseat in the dim living room. On the beach below, red and blue lights still flashed, and she wondered numbly when they would move Ryan's body. The tide would come in soon, although it would not reach the level of the stairs barring a big storm.

She'd wanted to water Mouse, but she'd also been desperate for a moment alone, to regroup and fortify her boundaries. She'd intended to do some deep breathing exercises and light a relaxation candle, but a wave of exhaustion rolled over her and she sat, staring out the window. She should change out of the damp clothes, get back downstairs, but she couldn't seem to make herself move.

When the phone buzzed, she jolted upright out of a dreamlike train of unremembered thought. Mouse rose in protest from the loveseat cushion and stalked to her bed in the corner. Parker checked her phone.

Krista—*I'm dying of curiosity! R u ok?*—

Parker's eyes moved from the text notification to the time up in the corner of the screen. She'd lost twenty minutes. Damn, she should head back downstairs or the cops would probably come looking.

Quickly she responded.

—*Yeah. I'm fine. Busy now, txt later*—

Krista answered immediately.

—*What's happening?!*—

Parker pocketed the phone and pushed to her feet.

In the dark of the room, she headed toward the door, running her fingers through her hair and glancing automatically at the large mirror over the sideboard. She looked as terrible as Seth had said, hollow-eyed and beaten down. She drew in a deep breath and pulled her shoulders back. Stronger at the break, she reminded herself. Wise, calm, and compassionate.

She checked the mirror for confirmation, but those eyes weren't selling it.

"I'll be back," she told Mouse, who sighed and settled her chin between her paws.

Downstairs, the mood had shifted. Less shock and panic, more quiet chatter. Seth and Marta mingled among the guests. Boxes of tissue had sprouted on every side table, and Calli was nowhere to be seen. No one appeared to be searching for Parker, so perhaps they had taken Calli back for an interview, although it seemed strange that her parents weren't with her.

Parker perched on the armchair where she'd left the blanket, leaving it folded on the back despite the chill. As far as she could tell, except for her bosses, and Ellen doing busywork behind the reception desk long past her end-of-shift, the rest of the staff had been left to their own pursuits. Assuming bureaucracy continued at its normal lugubrious pace, Parker could be waiting here until midnight. She gave up on maintaining a façade of alertness and sank back into the chair, pulling the fleece over herself. Why hadn't she taken two minutes to change her clothes?

Much sooner than expected, Officer Connelly

appeared and led her back to Marta's office. On the way, they passed Marta, whose expression was somewhere between a polite smile and a glare. The office was the same as always: a gleaming dark wood desk holding a sleek monitor kitty-corner to the leather chair. There was one picture of Marta with Seth and one with them together with a ten-year-old Calli. A mix of coastal photography and framed quotes from Gandhi, Shakespeare, and Seth hung on the muted turquoise walls.

Connelly and Parker faced each other in the visitors' chairs. "I already told you what happened. It's not going to be different," Parker said.

"Great," Connelly said. "Let's just go over it one more time, and then I can let you go. I'm recording this on the body cam, okay?"

Parker glanced at the little rectangular device on the officer's sternum. "Uh, yeah, that's fine." She folded her chilly fingers together in her lap nervously.

The officer identified them both for the benefit of the video, then said, "You got your dog settled?"

Parker nodded. "She's fine."

"Good. So let's start at the beginning."

"Can I ask a question first? What happened with Marta and Calli? Did you find out why she was so angry?" Parker asked.

Connelly shook her head. "Actually, that's a good place to start. Did you have any conversation with Calli having to do with her coming down to the beach or her being on the beach, this evening or earlier in the day?"

Parker raised her eyebrows. "No, I didn't. I saw her this afternoon and she asked if she could walk Mouse. I told her not tonight."

"And why was that?"

Because Parker needed some alone time after her dead best friend's ex-boyfriend and onetime murder suspect called her out of the blue, but she didn't want to go there. Parker managed, "I was feeling like I'd had no time to myself all day. She's a nice kid, but…"

Connelly nodded sympathetically.

"I can't imagine what Marta thinks I did."

Connelly's face was youthful, with apple cheeks and bright dark eyes, but her expression sagged. "Mothers and daughters," she said.

"I wouldn't know."

"Oh?"

Parker wanted to take it back, but all she could do was downplay. "Uh, yeah. My mother died when I was little. My dad raised me on his own."

"No stepmother?"

"Nope."

"Okay, well, go ahead. Start with why you went out this evening."

"I run pretty much every day, at least once, usually twice. After work today, I changed clothes and headed down to the beach around seven o'clock. It was just starting to get dark. My dog Mouse was with me, and we did about three miles. When we arrived back at the stairs to TBI, I noticed a hat in the sand."

She'd gone over the moment enough times by now that it had lost some of its potency. Her mother's scarf, trailing out of the coat closet door like the tail of some mystical creature, still came to mind, but Parker moved past it without mentally opening the closet and seeing the silver mask of tape. She continued, describing her shock at seeing the body, her sudden fear that the killer might

44

still be present.

When she reached the end, the point where Connelly herself had approached nearly at the same time that Calli did, Parker asked, "Did you tell Marta you saw Calli coming up the beach?"

Connelly shrugged. "For all I know, she was with you before I arrived. Not that I think she was," she added with a smile. "But me vouching for you won't settle that woman. You're going to have to do that yourself." She paused, looking thoughtful. "I guess that covers it. Is there anything else you want to add? You didn't see anyone from the wedding party on the stairs or on the beach when you headed out for your run, for instance?"

Parker shook her head.

"Okay. That wraps it up for tonight. Detective Balderas may follow up with you, or if you think of anything, call us."

"You have my cell phone number," Parker said, and stood.

Connelly stood as well. "You sure there's nothing you want to add?"

Parker tried not to look guilty. Had they already checked her out? Did they know she was hiding something?

"No, I can't think of anything." With luck, they'd figure out who killed Ryan Bennett without having to dig deeper into anyone but the wedding guests. Maybe it would be some newly released felon who'd mugged him on the beach, who had a duct tape fetish.

But Parker had never been lucky.

****

When Parker opened her eyes and gazed at the candles she'd lit for the second time that night, relief

Cara Johns

washed over her. Her heartbeat had slowed. Her thoughts were clearer. Ryan was still dead, but however horrible that was, she was going to get through it.

She cringed to recall her state of mind when she'd walked in the door—the knee-jerk impulse to obliterate her anxiety and sadness by draining dry the fancy bottle of wine from the welcome basket that still lived in the cupboard over the fridge. Old habits would have led her straight through that bottle and into another, only to emerge tomorrow, hungover and miserable and even less ready to face reality.

Not that she was looking forward to it. Ryan's death could unmask her, put her back in the news, and threaten her employment. But she'd rather be clear-headed to face all that, and capable of keeping it in perspective as a relatively minor inconvenience in the shadow of his stolen life.

Letting out a final long breath, she stretched and headed to the kitchen, where she pulled out the sandwich she'd grabbed earlier. Yay for the perks of the job, which discounted food from the TBI kitchens for the staff.

In the living room, she stared out the balcony door as she ate. Silvery clouds trailed over a dark sea patterned with moonlight. Her phone lay on the side table, and she stretched over Mouse to grab it. Krista must be worried sick.

Parker—*You still awake?*—

Krista responded immediately.

—*Yes. you ok now? What's up?*—

Parker—*I'm fine. But someone died here. A client.*—

Krista—*Who?*—

Parker—*No one you would know, a guest*—

Krista—*Did you know them? It was your client?*—

Parker—*Only one session—*

Krista—*Died in session?!—*

Parker—*No! Found on beach—*

Krista—*Terrible! Sorry :(—*

Parker—*Yeah—*

Parker hesitated, but Krista would find out as soon as she looked at the news. It was probably up on a website somewhere already.

Parker—*And it was murder—*

Krista—*Oh shit. Are they sure?—* She included a line of emoticons: horror, sadness, sickness.

Parker—*Really sad and awful. Police are here.—*

Krista understood right away.

—Know who you are?—

Parker—*I didn't tell them.—*

Krista—*They'll find out—*

Parker—*They shouldn't care—*

Krista—*Yeah. but they will if they can't find killer—*

Parker—*They will—*

Krista—*Fast, I mean—*

Parker—*They will—*

Krista—*Ok—*

Parker could sense her dubiousness, even on the small screen.

—Just wanted to let u know I'm ok.—

Krista—*Good—*

Parker—*Need to sleep, tho—*

Krista—*You home?—*

Parker drew her brows together. Where else would she be? Maybe Krista imagined her texting from the police station.

—Yeah, ready for bed—

Krista—*All locked up safe?—*

Parker—*Don't creep me out. All fine, sleepytime*—
Krista—*Goodnight*—

Parker closed the app, smile fading. Krista was teasing in a very Krista fashion, because if she'd discovered a murder victim, she'd drama-queen it up like she was next on the hit-list. That wasn't Parker. She knew most victims were killed by someone they knew, and Ryan had been a stranger to her. Her little apartment was safe. But Krista had zeroed in on her biggest worry, that the police would think Parker had something to do with Ryan's death because of her history. And because of the duct tape. Not "something to do with" like she'd killed him, necessarily, although Mouse wasn't a very good alibi and no one else could have seen her very well out there at dusk.

She was making a good case for being a legitimate suspect, which was a ridiculous idea, proving she was too tired to think straight. Time to call it a night. Everything would be clearer tomorrow.

The candle still flickered on the small table by the window. She stared at it for a moment, suddenly realizing she hadn't thought of Jess's impending visit in hours. That particular horror from the past had been forced into perspective. Thanks, Ryan.

Parker closed her eyes, feeling a few hot tears, and tried to push the self-pity away with a wish for peace for him, wherever and whatever he might be or not be.

After a few minutes she returned her plate to the kitchen, rinsed and left it on the drying rack next to the sink. Then she blew out the candle and looked out to sea. The tide had advanced, and the waves licked at the tire tracks left by police vehicles in the sand, already erasing the end of a young man's life.

Parker turned away. "Let's go to bed," she murmured, and Mouse padded after her to the bedroom door. Tonight, she wanted her coziest pajamas. She wanted to feel safe and warm, and for her soft bed to drown out any sneaky thoughts about Ryan, cold forever.

When she crouched to open the bottom drawer by nightlight, she noticed something out of place on top of the dresser. She didn't need books on how to get rid of stuff, because years of bouncing from place to place were not conducive to accumulation. Plus, clear surfaces relaxed her, so no decorations or knick-knacks or miscellaneous junk lay around gathering dust. The tiny vase of dried flowers on her dresser was an interloper.

Parker's skin pulsed with a brief burst of pain. Even in the dimness, she could see the flowers were dried sprigs of lavender, old and crumbly, so that flower heads already littered the surface around the vase. So old they shouldn't hold any scent, and yet their strong distinctive odor overwhelmed her. Blinking, she flashed to a sensation of thick, soft towels against her cheek and the sense of a small, dark place.

Uncle Danny's voice sing-songed from downstairs…"I lost count, Corey. Hope you found a good hiding place! Was I on fifty-six, or forty-six? No, thirty-six, right? Thirty-six, thirty-seven…" The darkness, the towels, the lavender soaps stored under the sink, were oddly soporific, as if she'd been hypnotized by his voice, now louder, now fading. Falling asleep, unforgivably, as her mother struggled below.

She backed away from the dresser and flipped the light switch. An overhead bulb flooded her cramped bedroom with glaring light, shrinking the vase to a mundane, meaningless decoration. Housekeeping. It had to have been left by housekeeping, because who else would have a key to the suite? Could it be left over from the wedding party's decorations? Something like that. They would have no way to know that for Parker, lavender was not a charming touch, but a reminder of grief and madness. It was just a decoration. That was all. Nothing else made sense.

****

But she was no longer sleepy.

She swept the vase, dried lavender, and crumbly detritus from the top of the dresser straight into the garbage, then tied off the trash-bag and scrubbed her hands with lime-scented dish soap.

Mouse followed her back and forth from kitchen to bedroom to kitchen, perplexed by this departure from routine and sensing Parker's dismay. "No biggie," Parker said. "I just don't like flowers that much."

Then she sat on the edge of the loveseat again. It really wasn't a big deal. Housekeeping had never done anything like that before, but Parker had only worked here for six weeks, which was a very short never. They came in every Friday to vacuum, wash the floor, change the sheets. It was another perk of living in a furnished hotel suite instead of in her own place. Next Friday, Parker would leave a note saying thanks, but that she was allergic to flowers and would they please not leave any in the future. Problem solved.

Mouse, who'd been sitting by the bedroom door to remind her it was time for bed, gave up and climbed onto the love seat next to Parker with a little groan, setting her chin on Parker's thigh. Parker rubbed her velvety ears and stared out the window.

Uncle Danny was safely locked away. He was not

coming for her.

Duct tape and lavender both occurred commonly in the world, and while it was deeply disturbing that Ryan's face had been hidden like her mom's, the lavender bouquet did not make it any more likely to have something to do with Parker.

Nevertheless, her brain wanted to chew at it, as if it were a puzzle she could solve. She knew it was an illusion, that her mind was falling into the old pattern of anxious perseveration, but it felt real.

Parker adjusted her posture and tried some breathing exercises, but she couldn't stick with it. The scent of lavender, real or imagined, was deep in her nose and she kept drawing it in. After a while, she pulled out cleaning supplies from under the sink and scrubbed the top of the dresser and the wall behind it with pine-scented ammonia, then opened the window and let the ocean breeze clear out the room.

In the bathroom, she showered with eucalyptus shampoo and put on her coziest pajamas. Thinking of Krista, she double-checked the locks on the interior and fire-escape doors, and hauled a kitchen chair into the bedroom to shove under the doorknob. Even if all those precautions failed, if anyone tried to enter, they'd disturb Mouse. Even if Parker fell deeply asleep, which there was no way she would, Mouse would alert her.

Parker climbed into bed and lay tensely, listening to the creaking of the old building and the ocean waves until she conked out like someone had hit her over the head.

Chapter Five

The wedding party left the following morning in a grim and shell-shocked state. Parker didn't know what she'd expected—dramatic scenes of "Ryan would have wanted us to go on."—but everything felt funereal, a mood reflected by the steel gray sky. When she checked the TBI scheduling app for her day's sessions, it was empty. More tired than she should be, and heavy-hearted, she jogged south at a slow pace with Mouse by her side and her headphones channeling music loud enough to drown out her thoughts.

She stretched out the run despite her lack of energy, not wanting to deal with what would face her when she got back. More questions from the police, maybe. More anger from Marta. More anxiety about duct tape and lavender and Jess's upcoming visit. She jogged over the bridge that spanned Yaquina Bay and picked up the beach on the other side, which stretched eight miles before hitting another headland. At Ona Beach, she stopped to water Mouse and use the restroom, then kept going.

At some point, the sun burned through the cloud cover and the day became bright and autumnal, the air chill enough to cool the sweat on her skin even as it formed. The ocean sparkled, and Mouse pranced toward a colony of seagulls splashing in a stream with a broad doggie smile on her face.

Returning north, they approached the beach access parking lot that had been filled with police vehicles last night, and a small shape launched itself from the benches that lined the retaining wall and torpedoed toward them. Mouse diverted to intercept her friend Pepper, and they peeled off together toward the surf, the smaller dog galloping double-time to keep up.

Pepper's human slouched on a bench with legs stretched out in front, a baseball cap low over his eyes. Despite the chill in the air, he wore khaki shorts and a stained white T-shirt under an open flannel shirt. He looked to be in his seventies, with snow-white invaders in his scruffy dark beard and thick eyebrows. As Parker slowed to a walk, he called out, "Looks like you're not running your dog enough. Shame on you!"

Parker grinned and rolled her eyes. Mouse and Pepper were wrestling with a two-foot-long twist of driftwood in the surf, and it was impossible to tell who—or what—was winning. Pepper was a third of Mouse's size, if that, but they seemed not to notice as they ganged up on the stick.

"What's up, Adam?"

"Not much. Some fishing later, probably."

"What, again?"

Shortly after she'd arrived in Newport, she'd met Adam and his dog, Pepper, who often hung around Nye Beach when Adam wasn't on his boat in the bay. Mouse and Pepper instantly became great friends, their meeting and greeting rituals extending into play sessions that would go on for as long as Adam and Parker allowed. A retired mechanic who'd spent the last decade fishing and walking the beach, he was unexpectedly easy to talk to, conversing about the dogs, Newport's history, fishing and seafood and cooking and whatever else, all without prying into her personal life. They'd chatted many times as the dogs played, and once, after getting caught in a sudden, icy downpour that shifted from mist to sleet to hail and back within minutes, he'd invited her to warm up in front of the woodstove in his cottage and have some coffee. She'd hesitated, but he'd never given off a dirty-old-man vibe, and after an hour in front of the fire, she knew she'd made a new friend. When it started pouring down again, Parker had accepted the loan of a rain slicker to walk the half-mile home—and then never returned it.

"Oh man," she blurted. "I forgot to get your jacket back to you."

"Nah," he said. "It's an extra. Plus, when's it gonna rain?"

"Aren't we still on the Oregon Coast?"

"Oh, yeah," he said comfortably. "Well, whatever. No rush."

The dogs curved toward the bench where Parker and Adam sat, the driftwood held victoriously in both their jaws. Adam said, "You see all the excitement on the beach last night? Must've been down near you. I saw about, what, five cop cars and an ambulance pull down into the turnaround. You think another drowning?"

He'd warned Parker that every year saw drownings up and down the coastline, mostly tourists who didn't understand the power of the ocean, but sometimes locals, too. She hesitated, then decided he'd learn soon enough. "It was a murder," she said. "I found a dead body. I'm the one who called 911."

The thick eyebrows drew together. "That must've been terrible. Sorry to hear that," he said. "A murder. I wasn't expecting that. You sure?"

She shrugged, not wanting to get into how unlikely someone was to apply duct tape to their own face. "Think so."

"Body found not too long ago in the Walmart parking lot, turned out to be a drug thing."

Parker shrugged again. "Yeah, it could be something like that."

He shot her a concerned look. "Well, I really am sorry to hear that. You hate for something like that to strike so close to home. But you'll be okay," he said. "Just be careful out here. You got your pepper spray?"

She patted the pocket of her tights, where the tiny canister snugged down beneath her cell phone. "Got it."

"Good. Always be prepared." He nodded, agreeing with his own sentiment, and then stood creakily. "Time for me and Pepper to head back if we want to get some fishing in before the wind picks up."

Parker stood too. "Yeah. Seriously, I *will* drop off your jacket."

"No rush."

"How can you be prepared without it?" she said.

****

After getting cleaned up, Parker braced herself to check in with Marta. It was almost nine, and some of the wedding party were gathered for the breakfast buffet, while others waited in groups in the lobby. The bride sat alone, now in sweatpants, with dark circles under her eyes. She looked hung over, with a pasty sweatiness that may have explained why she was skipping breakfast.

Parker wondered where the groom was, but just then she spotted Marta chatting with a foursome of middle-aged folks. Parker caught up with her as she left them.

Marta eyed her coolly, but without anger. "What can I do for you, Parker?"

"I just wanted to check in. I saw the schedule was cleared out. Is everyone leaving?"

Marta nodded and motioned her to follow. "Yes. The wedding is canceled, of course, and we had no other events today. I've notified the wait staff, and put the cleaning staff on a deep clean. We'll give the Sunday people a day off as well…" Her voice was distracted, and she thumbed her phone as she walked. When they reached her office, she swung around her desk and immediately started typing on her computer, mumbling to herself.

Parker lowered herself into one of the visitor chairs and waited, not sure if Marta wanted to talk or had meant to dismiss her. She gazed at one of the abstract paintings on Marta's wall, a geometric extravaganza in blues and purples, decided there were too many stripes and hard edges, and stood to go.

Marta blinked at her, as if just remembering Parker's presence. "Oh, sorry, I just had to get that down. Did you need something?"

"Sorry to bother you. I know you must be busy," Parker said. "I can come back later."

"Oh, no, that's okay. Go ahead." She let her hands fall to her lap. Parker noticed lipstick was smeared on her teeth but decided this wasn't the time to bring it up.

"I wanted to tell you I was sorry about last night. About Calli coming down to the beach," Parker said, and stopped. She was sorry that it had happened, but still didn't feel responsible. Even so, apologizing seemed like the only way forward.

Marta smiled thinly. "Sit down, Parker."

Parker sat.

"You're young. You probably remember what it's like to be a teenage girl."

Yes, but Parker's experience was probably nothing like Marta's. Or Calli's, hopefully. She nodded anyway.

"Well, it turns out that Calli's original version of what happened was not entirely accurate. In other words, she lied. Seth and I should be apologizing to you."

"Oh?" Parker said. Her face warmed, thinking of her own lies. Probably Marta wouldn't be apologizing if she knew Parker's whole resume was fiction.

"She'd been grounded, so her father and I couldn't understand how she was even present on the beach. I guess she hoped that in all the fuss about the murder, a teeny white lie about you asking her to watch Mouse while you talked to the police wouldn't be noticed."

"Oh," Parker said again. "I'm sorry." This time, she had even less of an idea what she was apologizing for. The ways of teenagers?

"No, I'm sorry," Marta said. "I should have realized that didn't quite make sense, but I was so upset about that poor boy, it didn't hit me until one of the officers asked Calli about the differences in your accounts."

"It's okay. I understand," Parker said.

"Anyway, I do apologize," Marta said briskly. "It's not easy parenting a teenager. And when something awful happens, you just want your child to be as far away from it as possible."

"Of course."

"So."

Parker stood again, taking that as a hint to leave. "Did Calli ever say why she went down to the beach?"

Marta's face tightened. "A small misunderstanding

about what grounding means. Anyway, staff meeting, Tuesday, nine a.m. sharp. We'll be gearing up for next week. Thank goodness we have the holistic dentists and then that finance company next weekend. I was worried it would be too much all in a row, but they should offset this fiasco. If they don't cancel."

"Okay," Parker said again. The rest of the weekend stretched ahead, strangely empty. She'd been booked solid except for the three hours of the wedding and reception, all the way through Sunday evening, and then Monday had been a day off. Now, she had Saturday, Sunday, and Monday to fill.

She should be happy. Time to recover. Time to center herself before Jess intruded into her life. But the weekend stretched in front of her like a void, filled with unseen threats. If Jess didn't conveniently become lost or change his mind about stopping by, if the cops examined the background of random people at the hotel, if ambushes from the past were around every corner…

"Marta?" Parker asked.

"What?" She was already looking at her monitor.

"Does housekeeping sometimes leave extra flowers in the staff suites?"

Marta frowned and gave Parker a funny look. "I wouldn't think so. We're not made of money, you know. Christ, I have no idea what this murder is going to do to our bookings…" She trailed off, fingers twitching on her keyboard, a line deepening between her eyes.

"Right. Silly question," Parker said, and waited ten more seconds to see if Marta would say anything else. Belatedly remembering that she was supposed to embody wellness and peace of spirit, to her boss more than anyone, Parker attempted to come up with a piece of wisdom that would cover murder, the loss of thousands of dollars in revenue, and parenting stress.

No calming aphorism came to her lips, so she retreated instead. Thank God for Mouse; without her Parker would be entirely unmoored, but since she still had to feed the dog, water her, take her outside, and keep her company, Parker had at least some structure. Today could be a good time to get away from the beach and try hiking inland. They could drive to Cape Perpetua, hike through the forest.

As she drew closer to her room, her steps slowed and her stomach tightened. Despite what Marta had said, housekeeping must have left the flowers. And she hadn't sounded certain, just disgusted. Maybe housekeeping went rogue sometimes.

Making up her mind, Parker retraced her steps and headed to the basement office that was housekeeping headquarters, trying to remember the name of the guy in charge. She'd met him a couple of times: in the blur of unfamiliar names and faces at the meet and greet when she first arrived, and at a baby shower for one of the nutritionists a couple weeks ago. Both times, he'd been wearing a wireless earbud which flashed a tiny blue light, which made Parker wonder if housekeeping in this place was really so urgent and stressful that he needed minute by minute updates, like air traffic controllers or the Secret Service. At the time, it struck her as pretentious, but for all she knew, he could have been listening to a football game or studying for the bar exam. She still couldn't recall his name, though.

The office was in a warren of rooms in a part of the basement which reminded her of high school, because of the painted cinderblock walls plastered with public service announcements: employee info about minimum wage laws and family leave, and an Employee of the Month display that showed that Rita P., Cleaner III, had demonstrated "Extraordinary Diligence" in September. A woman with graying red hair smiled brightly from the frame, holding up a fifty-dollar gift certificate.

The corridor was empty, but as Parker approached, the door to housekeeping opened and the balding ear-budded manager strode out, brushing past. He was stout and short, only reaching Parker's shoulder, and she could glance down at the top of his head like a giantess. Just in time, she spotted his name on a little plate next to the door. Kim Hesp. Just as she said, "Excuse me, Mr. Hesp?" the name clicked, and she remembered Krista had called him a creep. Unless there was another Kim.

He turned, tapping at his earbud. "Yeah? That's me."

"I'm Parker James. We met a couple of times. I'm the new Meditation Guide."

He nodded slowly. "Sure, sure."

"I have a quick question for you, if that's okay."

He glanced down the corridor. "I was just heading off for a break—"

"Seriously quick. Like, one sentence." She smiled her best charming smile.

"Okay, shoot."

"Do you guys, I mean, does housekeeping put flowers in the staff apartments?"

He raised his eyebrows like she might be making a joke, the punch line yet to come. "You want us to put flowers in your room? What, like weekly?"

She flushed, feeling accused of something. Thinking she was at the Ritz? "No! Not at all. I found flowers in

60

my room, and I was wondering if housekeeping put them there."

He shook his head. "You mean, someone sent you a bouquet, you're not sure who delivered them? What, like, housekeeping found them in your doorway and put them inside? Sure, yeah, maybe. I can see that. That a problem?"

She grimaced. "I wasn't thinking it was a delivery. No note, no card, no plastic wrap. It was in the bedroom, on my dresser. I thought it could be an extra decoration from the wedding…?" She trailed off, as he was already shaking his head.

"Never happen," he said, smiling, his finger poised to tap at his earbud again. "Nah. All that stuff costs money. The clients pay for everything, and the boss lady watches the bottom line like a hawk. No extras. Sorry."

"But—"

"Listen, I really gotta go," he said, already moving down the hall. "Let me know if you have any more questions." He waved a hand perfunctorily, pushed through a swinging door on the left, and disappeared. Parker started to follow but was stopped by the sign on the door: Restroom.

She stood in the corridor, biting her lip, wondering whether to wait and try again. He'd been in a hurry and very dismissive. And he was talking about rules, not reality. She could see Marta being obsessive about ordering and using just exactly what the guests paid for, but surely there were margins of error. Accidental overages that weren't returnable or re-usable, like dried flowers that would fall apart when they got too old.

Parker realized she was answering her own question. The only person who would really know whether the cleaner had put some extra flowers in her room, and why, was the cleaner. Parker should wait and leave a note next Friday, like she'd planned.

Reluctantly, she headed for the stairs.

****

Parker trudged to her rooms and greeted Mouse, who was waiting at the door and seemed her usual self. Even though no one could hide in the suite without disturbing her, Parker checked every space where someone could fit. In the small apartment, it came down to the coat closet—barely large enough for an ironing board—the bedroom closet, or crammed under the kitchen sink, assuming the intruder was a small child. The bed was a platform bed, so on second thought she heaved up the mattress to see if someone could hide inside, but all the pieces were secured tightly together.

"Okay, Mouse, what do you think is going on?" Parker said, settling on the loveseat and giving the dog a serious look. Mouse sighed and rested her head between her paws. She'd observed the entire process with an air of perplexity and now reclined near the balcony, monitoring the seagulls. It was only ten in the morning and Parker wanted to go back to bed. She texted Krista instead.

—Are you busy?—

Krista—*Just heading out to meet friends for coffee. what's up?—*

Parker—*Is it nice there—?*

Krista—*Bright sunshiny day :)—*

Parker—*Here too—*

Krista—*What's up?—*

Parker hesitated.

—Trying to decide whether to tell police

something—

Krista—*About the murder?—*

Parker—*Maybe? Someone left something in my room—*

Krista—*Sounds mysterious. When? What? Why?—*

Parker hesitated again.

Krista—*???—*

Parker—*Did you ever get flowers in your room?—*

Krista—*Sometimes. That guy Tom was big on flowers—*

Parker—*Not a delivery. Just, in your room—*

Krista—*Not unless I put them there. I don't get what you mean—*

Parker—*Someone left a vase on my dresser. No card, no note, no wrapping.—*

Krista—*A decoration? Housekeeping?—*

Parker—*They were crumbly and old. And lavender—*

Krista—*You hate lavender!—*

Parker—*Yeah—*

Krista—*Oh. OH. hang on, I'm gonna call—*

A second later, she did. "What the heck?" she demanded. "Someone literally left this gross lavender in your bedroom? That is so weird!"

"It's worse than weird, considering my history. Am I being paranoid?" Parker told her about the duct tape on Ryan's face.

"Jeez," Krista said slowly. "But I guess duct tape is pretty common for tying people up, right?"

"Common probably isn't the right word. But, I guess?"

"Well. I'm just saying. Just because you found a body that also had duct tape on it doesn't mean that it has anything to do with you. Duct tape is…duct tape. It's good for everything."

Krista was saying the same things Parker had told herself last night. Somehow, Parker still couldn't tell if they were good points or desperate denial.

Parker said, "But now that there's lavender, too…"

"Now you feel like you have to talk to the cops, because it seems even more connected, and it's going to make you look bad," Krista replied. "Oh, dammit, Parker. Don't do that. It's a weird coincidence, but that's all. Stop making everything about you." This last had become a joke between them, considering how often they said it to each other.

"Someone duct-taped that poor guy in almost the same way my mother's face was taped, and the same day, someone put lavender in my room for no reason," Parker insisted.

"But no one knows about your mother. I mean, details. At this point, it's in your head and in police files, that's it. And the lavender part. Who would know about that?"

"My dad…" she responded slowly, but she was stymied. Krista was right. The newspapers hadn't had details about Mom's defacement, only that she'd been strangled and left in a closet for her five-year-old daughter to find. And Parker's fragrant hiding place. Had that been in any articles? She'd gone through a phase in her teens of reading everything she could find about the murder, but she burned out after Dad showed her the letters from Danny. At fifteen, she turned down two 'ten years later' interviews, even when they offered serious money. Had a friend or cousin or neighbor shared personal details of Parker's story for a few bucks, and she never found out because she was avoiding the media rehash like the plague?

Krista waited quietly.

"I don't know what to think," Parker said finally. "I stopped reading news articles at some point. My uncle's locked up and what more is there to say about it? As far as I know, anybody could know anything."

Krista was silent for a couple more moments and then did a typical Krista one-eighty. "Listen, Parker. I know you're upset, and you have a right to be. Hell, you should take some time off, you're probably all traumatized and shit. But listen to me. This is not all about you, okay? Even if you have to tell the friggin' cops your real name, even if you have to explain why duct tape freaks you out, it's all about that poor guy that got dead, right? And if someone's messing with you, leaving you creepy flowers—well, just tell the cops. Get it over with. Then you can stop sweating about it and it's off your plate."

Krista had majored in hospitality services in college and added yoga and massage and meditation certification later, but despite her seeming focus on welcoming and wellness, she was a true cynic. Her career was designed to pull in good money doing easy work while living at vacation resorts, meeting rich marriage prospects, and staying in shape. End goal until Mr. Right came along— a position at a ritzy resort in the tropics, or possibly on an elite cruise ship.

Parker's foul-mouthed but practical friend was often good at cutting through bullshit, and it helped.

"You're right," Parker said. "Thanks. I'll stop by the station later."

"Okay, bud, love you, got to go!" Krista said, and hung up.

Shaking her head, Parker smiled.

Chapter Six

Parker's stomach tied itself in knots and bile roiled around threateningly in her stomach. Maybe she'd contracted some terrible disease, Ebola possibly, and she'd die here wracked with nausea before she had to follow through with her decision to speak with the police. Wouldn't that be a relief? Or maybe the killer playing games with her had her phone tapped, now knew she was going to the cops, and would finish her off before she ruined their fun. Almost as likely as the Ebola scenario.

She groaned and forced herself to stand up before she spiraled further down into dark imaginings. With one hand on the cool glass of the sliding door, she drank in the sight of the ocean under the robin's egg sky, and acknowledged her thoughts were fueled by panic and fear. But the emotions would pass, and the ocean would still be there. She breathed deeply and reminded herself what rock bottom felt like. This was not that, not even close.

"Mouse, car!" she called, and Mouse jumped to her feet and fetched her leash from the basket as if Parker might change her mind if she wasn't quick enough.

"Good girl," Parker said, giving her a scratch as she clipped it to her collar. Talk about remembering to feel grateful. How could she ever forget when she shared her life with Mouse's kind and hopeful soul? "We're going to run an errand, and then we are going on a beautiful hike in the woods. You won't believe your nose."

Parker tossed hiking shoes and a water-resistant jacket into a bag, along with nut bars and dog biscuits and her stainless-steel water bottle. Her little canister of pepper spray got zipped into the jacket's pocket. In the car, there was a backup jug of water, along with a travel bowl for Mouse and a stash of doggy waste bags. They were set. If only Parker could prepare so thoroughly for her errand.

They trotted down the stairs, and though they passed several rooms belonging to staff, everything felt deserted. Word must have spread about having the weekend off. Mouse and Parker exited onto the street to walk to the parking lot, and she spotted a few coworkers through the lobby windows. Plus Calli, who jumped up and waved.

Parker smiled and waved back, not wanting to get derailed by a chat right now, but a moment later, Calli called, "Hey!" from the open lobby door. When Parker paused, Calli jogged up the sidewalk toward her. She wore a crocheted black tunic over black leggings, and her face looked pale and washed out under her sea-green hair.

"Morning," Parker said.

"Hi." Calli tried a smile, but it collapsed back into an anxious look.

"You okay?" Parker didn't want to get sucked into teenage girl drama, but Calli looked pretty upset. "Are you grounded again?"

"My mom told you?" Color infused her face. "Yeah. Sorry I got you in trouble. I didn't think it through."

"No worries. I was sixteen once. I know it's hard to

deal with parents."

Calli stared at her feet, then looked up. "Are you taking Mouse for a run? Can I go with you?"

"I'm going to talk to the police. No big deal, just a quick follow up from last night," Parker added quickly when Calli's face paled further. "But I should head out. You go back inside, okay? You look cold."

Calli hugged herself, goose-fleshed shoulders visible through the lacy fabric. "Um, wait. I know this is weird, but I do really need to talk to you before you go. Because I did something stupid. And it has to do with you."

Parker snorted. "What do you mean, with me? What are you talking about?"

"Can we sit down?"

There was a stone bench in the landscaping next to the sidewalk, and they sat just a few feet from the front doors. Mouse leaned against their knees, graciously allowing Calli to scratch behind her ears.

Calli glanced sideways at Parker, who noticed freckles showing under the layers of powder on Calli's nose and cheeks.

"Go ahead," Parker prodded.

"This is going to sound worse than it is…" Calli started. "I mean, it sounds worse than I thought it was, but I thought it was just, like, a surprise."

"Okay…"

In a rush, the girl said, "I got a note that said to sneak into your apartment and leave you some flowers."

"Ahh."

"I thought, like, maybe someone had a crush on you. I thought it would be mysterious and romantic. And you would guess who it was from, and it would be really sweet, and I would be part of it too."

Parker's heart pounded as her brain reeled, trying to untangle the lavender from what happened when she was a kid and what happened to Ryan. Was it really just a prank, after all? A surprise from a crush? But that should be a nice bright bouquet, not a dried out little vase, her mind argued.

Calli stared down at the green-painted toenails showing through her gladiator sandals.

Parker finally made her mouth work. "But then you figured out it might not be so harmless?"

Calli shot her a look, face flushing, then talked to her shoes. "When I snuck in, I felt like a stalker. Like, I'd never been in your place before and I wasn't invited, and there I was, going into your bedroom. I could have been anyone. I could have been a bad guy."

She sounded so full of shame that it undermined Parker's anger. Calli was gullible and inexperienced. It had probably sounded no worse than sticking a candy bar in someone's locker at school. "Whose idea was it?" Parker said, trying for stern.

"I don't even know," she said with a sob in her voice. "I really don't know. I found the note in my coat pocket last week. God, you must think I'm an idiot!"

"Last week?" Parker's voice rose.

Calli nodded.

"So, you found the note last week, and then you waited until someone was murdered to sneak into my room? Plus, you do whatever anonymous notes tell you to do?!" Parker could hear the anger in her own voice now, but no longer cared.

"No! I just…I assumed it was one of the staff. I know it was stupid. But I thought it was sweet."

"Calli. Jeez. If someone thought it was such a great idea, why wouldn't they do it themselves?"

"I already admitted I'm a freaking moron, okay?" Her shouted words seemed to echo up and down the street.

Parker checked out the lobby over her shoulder. No one on the other side of the thick glass paid them any attention. She took a deep breath. "Okay, you got this note. You thought it was an inside joke or a secret admirer or something harmless. And you were glad to be included. So, again, why did you wait until the night someone was murdered to break into my room?"

Calli pulled her green ponytail around to hide her face. "It had nothing to do with that!" she insisted. "It just took me a while to figure out how to get in. I didn't want to get anyone in trouble, so I had to get a blank keycard that wouldn't leave a trail in the system. I stole one of the cleaner's cards and she thought she misplaced it, so she borrowed a master to use temporarily. Then I snatched the master from her apron after she went home for the day."

"Won't she get in more trouble for losing a master than for losing her own card? If I was the boss, I'd be pretty suspicious."

"I returned it! I hid it under some towels on a cart. Someone probably found it already, and they'll think it was just an innocent mistake."

Except it wasn't. Parker gritted her teeth. "Okay. Go on."

"So, I was all ready to go in yesterday morning, but I had second thoughts. You seemed a little on edge when I talked to you, remember? I thought you might yell at me if you caught me." She stole a look at Parker, whose cheeks heated. Was that how she seemed to people? Edgy? It was true that Jess's call had thrown her for a loop. Maybe Calli was especially observant.

"Go on," Parker said.

"Not like you were going to explode," Calli said hurriedly. "More like you were trying to make everyone happy, and you might, you know…think it was childish and annoying? So I wasn't going to do it at all, and then I got another note in my pocket yesterday."

She reached into the pocket of her tunic and pulled out a triangle of paper, folded in a way Parker remembered from high school.

Parker unfolded it slowly. On the inside, in block letters written in faded pencil, it said: HURRY! DO IT NOW! OR ELSE…

"Or else what?" Parker asked.

"I don't know. I thought, or else the right moment will be lost, or something like that. So what, right? And then that guy died. And I got scared. It can't have anything to do with me, right? He probably pissed someone off. Obviously. But. I grabbed my chance when you were talking to the police." Calli was talking so quickly she tripped over her tongue, trying not to come out and say that she felt threatened by a vague and anonymous note.

"Yeah," Parker exhaled. "I guess I would have been scared too. But Calli, are you sure this isn't some friend of yours messing with you? Who else would have been able to get close enough to put something in your pocket?"

"I don't have any friends here. I mean, not kids. It's got to be a friend of yours, someone on the staff. A tennis coach or one of the cute waiters or something. Satoru."

Satoru was an extremely ripped waiter, whose hotness level even Parker had noticed. "A: Satoru is barely twenty-one years old. He's way too young for me. But too old for you! And B: I don't know anyone very well yet, either."

"But someone might want to get to know you."

Parker considered. Was it possible? "Wait, Calli. The first note—did it say lavender flowers?"

"Yeah. Lavender means serenity, it said. I thought, because you're like, Miss Meditation. I just couldn't find any good ones, so I pulled them out of this wreath my mom has."

Parker looked at her, shivering in the autumn breeze. If Calli were to be believed, Parker was as clueless as before. Lavender flowers for serenity. Funny, she didn't feel serene.

"Okay," Parker said finally. "It all sounds super weird, and I feel really uncomfortable about it, and I want you never, ever to go into my rooms or anyone else's rooms without a specific invitation again. You totally abused your knowledge of the keycard system. I should tell your parents."

Calli jerked back. "You can't!"

"I can. I should."

"I told you, I just…it was just for fun! I just wanted to be, you know…" She covered her face.

Parker resisted the urge to comfort her. "I was about to go tell the police about the intruder, because I was scared it had something to do with the murder."

"It didn't! I swear!"

"You don't actually know that if you don't know who gave you the notes or why," Parker pointed out. It was still lavender. It was still a disturbing coincidence.

Calli shook, her hands covering her face. Great, now there was a sobbing teenager in the middle of everything.

Okay. What if, instead of someone wanting to remind Parker of her mother's death, it really was someone with a crush on her? Someone with an adolescent level of social intelligence, one of the younger waiters or cleaners or fitness coaches, who saw her as an attractive older woman. Or even someone closer to her own age. The part-time trainer who oversaw the weights room seemed really awkward. Was he someone who might look up the meaning of flowers online and think it was clever? By that logic, anyone might pick lavender because meditation and lavender were both associated with calm. Maybe someone would come clean soon and ask her out, and all this anxiety would be for nothing.

Parker blew out her breath. "Calli, you just told me you were scared when the note said, 'or else.' If you felt threatened, it's definitely a police matter."

Calli shook her head again. A tear glimmered in her eyelashes but didn't fall. "I was just being stupid. I don't think it was supposed to scare me. Nobody could have known there would be a murder!"

"Calli, do you know who wrote the notes?"

"No!"

"I'm not sure I can believe you."

"You should!" she said defiantly, and met Parker's eyes. Calli's were hazel, brown and green with a little fleck of gold in the left like a chip of mica.

Parker thought for a moment, then asked, "Did you keep the first note?"

"No. It said to destroy it. Like a spy movie." Calli shrugged, and her earrings, little plastic hula girls,

74

danced.

"Can you remember what it said?"

She considered. "Not exactly, but pretty close. It was something like, 'You are the only one who can help me. Flowers for PJ—lavender for serenity. In her room, as a special surprise. Please help!'"

Then she added, "Down at the bottom, at the end, it said: 'thank you this is important don't mess up!'"

"Did it look like the same handwriting as the one you showed me? Block letters?"

Calli nodded.

Parker narrowed her eyes. Another coincidence had just occurred to her. Getting flowers in her room the same day she heard from Jess. He knew a lot of personal things about her that no one here knew. Could he have arranged for Calli to get the notes? Or could he secretly be here already? But unless Jess had changed a lot, he wouldn't think this kind of thing was amusing.

Parker turned to Calli. "Okay, fine," she said. "I won't report it to the police, at least not yet."

Hope lit up Calli's face. "Really?"

"Yeah, really. I think you're probably right. Someone has a crush and a weird way of showing it." She didn't add, *or someone wants to scare me, and used you to do it*. "But I don't want to get you in trouble, and now that I know it was you that got into my room, I'm less scared."

"I'm really sorry," Calli said softly. She looked like such a kid. A busty, green-haired kid, but still a kid. Isolated in a backwater town, befriending the staff at her parents' resort instead of hanging out with regular kids. Parker wondered if Seth and Marta had done anything to get her to mix with the locals. Sure, homeschooling was great, and Calli was obviously smart and sophisticated and mature in some ways, but she seemed awfully lonely.

"Do you like hiking?" Parker asked abruptly. "Mouse and I were going to drive down to Cape Perpetua and go for a hike in the woods."

Calli's face lit up. "Um, yeah. I would love that, but—"

"Oh, right, you're grounded?"

"No, I mean, they'd probably let me go hiking. It's all healthy and everything. It's just, I'm not dressed for the outdoors."

"That's okay. I can wait a few minutes," Parker said.

"Um, yeah! Thanks! I'll be right back."

Parker texted Krista as she waited.

—Not going to police. you'd never guess, break in was Calli—

Krista—*Kali, destroyer of worlds. Should have guessed—*

Parker—*Ha, great nickname. Are u still in touch?—*

Maybe she could get Krista to reiterate how stupid it was to do things anonymous notes told you to do.

Krista—*Facebook friend I think? Can't remember—*

Parker—*But you don't talk?—*

Krista—*She's, like, 8 years old. Why?—*

Parker—*17. As you know. Nevermind, long story—*

Krista—*You should still go to police—*

Parker—*Idk. Prob not—*

Parker saw Calli through the glass and added a quick *gtg*, hit send, and stood. If she got to know Calli a little better, she could figure out if there was more to this story.

Calli had changed into jeans and switched the black fishnet sweater for a heavy purple poncho that hung almost to her knees, with a green knit hat and a fuzzy black scarf for added warmth. Fingerless gloves accented her green fingernails.

"Ta-da! Better?" she asked.

Her knitted hat had big froggy googly eyes, and ear flaps shaped like frog legs. Parker gave her a thumbs up, then noticed her new-looking hi-tops. "It might be a little muddy. You don't mind if those get dirty?"

Calli looked dubiously at her spotless canvas high-tops. "Um, no…? I don't have anything better."

"They'll work," Parker assured her. "You can always hose them down. Okay, Mouse, finally, car!"

Mouse grinned.

****

Parker drove south with a sense of relief. Fluffy clouds had re-populated the sky, and the air felt moist and cool. Rain was in the forecast, but she thought it would hold off until evening, long after their hike was over.

She looked sideways at Calli. The girl stared out the passenger window as if she'd never seen the ocean before. Maybe she'd never come this far down the highway. Her preparation for the hike must have included reapplication of perfume, and a fug of patchouli mixed with the salty air blowing in. Parker rolled her eyes internally. What made the girl douse herself for a walk in the woods? At seventeen, Parker's mind had been full of morbid preoccupations and the grim reality of Britt's murder, but despite last night's events, Calli was probably the picture of what 'normal' growing pains looked like.

It made Parker nostalgic for the adolescence she never had. Britt and Krista hadn't either, which had drawn them together. Between the three of them, they had more than enough dysfunctional exposure to be teenaged cynics. Britt with her overbearing mother, cold and judgmental to the point of cruelty. Krista with her parents' marriage imploding in torturous slow motion, even before her brother's accident. Parker had been overexposed to death, but compared to either of their families, at least her dad had been dependable and loving. Funny how, at the time, she'd barely noticed.

Mouse bathed her nose in the airstream of the open window behind Calli, eyes bright. Nothing like seaweed and fish molecules from the beach mixed with exhaust fumes and roadside restaurant burgers to make a dog happy. Mouse basked in the present moment, and Parker envied that, but she couldn't keep herself from continuing to shuffle and reshuffle Calli's story.

Theory number one: the strongest theory. Calli was lying about pretty much everything, and had conveniently destroyed the most important piece of proof, the original detailed note, *if* it had ever existed. She was lonely, curious about Parker, and interested in Mouse, so she'd made up a reason to sneak into Parker's apartment and have an excuse to connect. The notes were a lie—Calli wrote the second one herself. The lavender was a coincidence, the easiest flower to get her hands on because her mom had some in their apartment. And she could have looked up the serenity thing. Yes, it was a strange and even stalker-like thing to do, but she was a strange girl, prone to lurking in out of the way corners and scribbling in notebooks or tapping on screens at all hours. A shy and lonely girl, desperate for a dash of drama but mostly needing a friend before she got too caught up in her own obsessions.

Parker thought that sounded pretty solid. It only became a stretch when paired with Ryan's death, and with Calli's odd choice of timing. She could have broken into the apartment anytime, so why choose the night of the murder?

Parker had to consider other options.

Theory number two: Calli was telling the truth and nothing but the truth. The note-writer was real, and had a stalker-like crush on Parker, as Calli had suggested. Or, theory three: Calli was telling the truth, the note-writer was real, but Calli was wrong about their motives. They were trying for unknown reasons to torment Parker with pieces of her past, and Calli was a gullible tool. In both scenarios, Calli either knew who they were and was covering for them, or really didn't know who they were, as she claimed.

A fourth theory occurred to Parker as she stole a glance at the back of Calli's tangled hair and the curve of her pale cheek; this girl had somehow learned Parker's birth name, uncovered details about her past, killed Ryan and defaced him with duct tape, then left Parker the lavender to further undermine her stability, for some motive known only to Calli. Parker was no psychiatrist, and she realized that there were sociopaths out there who were really good at seeming harmless—but still. Too ridiculous. Calli would have to be an award-winning actress to fake the awkward vulnerability which she constantly broadcasted. Plus, how could she have figured out Parker's birth name? Why would she have thought to look? Calli made the most unlikely teenage psycho ever, and it was only the influence of too many horror movies that led Parker to consider it.

She strove to push away the irrational suspicions and hold on to her "shy and lonely girl making an excuse to connect" theory. Would Parker have to resist the feeling of paranoia until the police caught Ryan's killer? Would she have to leave the Tyler Bettering Institute to escape her newly raised ghosts? Her heart ached at the thought. As recently as yesterday at lunch, she'd dared to believe things were working out, that she could pull this off and keep her new, upbeat, contented life.

A brown sign with a pictograph of hikers loomed up abruptly after a blind corner, and Parker swung off the road onto a gravel pull-out. "Look, we're here!" she announced. She'd chosen a less well-known hike just south of Yachats instead of the popular Cape Perpetua, and there was only one other car parked there.

Calli looked around. "Where are we?"

"Just past Yachats. This is a beautiful hike. You'll like it."

Calli's face was dubious. Parker got out of the car and clipped on Mouse's leash, and Calli climbed out to join them. The head of the dirt trail looked narrow and dark amid a tangle of overgrown blackberry vines scattered with roadside trash, and cars continued to whiz by at sixty miles an hour on the highway.

"I promise," Parker said. "When we're twenty yards in, you'll barely hear the cars, and the trees open up. We'll have a bit of a climb, but when we get to the top, there's a great view of the ocean."

"You mean the ocean I see every day from my window?"

Parker narrowed her eyes at her. "You asked to come, remember?"

"Um, yeah, I just got a little carsick, sorry. I'm sure it'll be great." Calli flashed a smile.

Parker stuffed the leash into the girl's hands, and Calli yelped in surprise as Mouse leaped forward, pulling her up the trail. Parker followed, and they hiked at a good pace for a while, their breath coming faster. The air was rich with the scents of damp soil and pine. Calli's shoes slipped a few times on slick earth or tree roots, but she had good balance and Mouse kept her scrambling forward. She exclaimed over mushrooms on the side of the trail and the newts and slugs making their slow way across dirt and fallen spruce needles.

Eventually they came to a bench fashioned from a fallen tree, and Calli plopped down despite Mouse's evident desire to continue. "How much farther?" Calli said breathlessly.

"Another twenty or thirty minutes until we get to the viewpoint. The rest won't be as steep, though!" Parker added when her face fell.

"I'm not really used to hiking," Calli said, rubbing her legs. "I thought I was in pretty good shape, but I guess not."

"You're doing fine. It's okay to take a break whenever you want. We're not in a rush."

They sat for a few minutes, and Parker considered and rejected asking more questions about the lavender incident. She didn't want to put Calli on the defensive again. Instead, Parker casually asked her about what online high school was like.

"It's fine," Calli shrugged. "I'm a year ahead of most kids my age."

"That's amazing. Good for you. Does that mean you'll graduate early?"

Calli looked down at her lap, letting a swoop of loose hair fall across her face. "I guess. Maybe I'll take some college classes for credit or something. Like, before I graduate."

"What about sports teams? Or being part of the band? Do you play an instrument?"

Calli snorted and shot Parker a wry look. "Yeah, right. No, I'm completely non-athletic, as you can see. And non-musical. If I did a thing like that, I'd do theater. Last year I got a part in a community play. It was pretty cool, but kind of intense, and my mom got annoyed because practice would go past ten at night sometimes. She didn't like having to be at the theater that late."

"Wow, that's great. I wish I had seen it," Parker said. "I could never get up on a stage like that."

Calli blushed and grinned. "Yeah. It was kind of a rush. Maybe Mom will let me try again. I'm old enough to go by myself and walk home alone. The theater is just a few blocks away."

"I could even come and walk with you," Parker offered. "Mouse needs a quick walk before bed, anyway."

"Really?" Calli said hopefully.

"Totally. I'd be happy to. I mean, if it's okay with your parents."

"Yeah, I bet they would say yes for sure if you were walking with me! Auditions are coming up in a couple weeks for *Four Weddings and an Elvis*. I could maybe talk them into it in time for that!" Calli was gleeful, sounding all of twelve years old, and Mouse pranced around eagerly, picking up on her mood.

"That sounds good." In a couple of weeks, everything would be back to normal. The murder would be solved and settled. Jess would have come and gone. Parker would be two weeks deeper into her new job. All would be well, and the weird thing Calli had done, breaking into her apartment, could be left safely in the past.

Parker took a deep breath of pine-scented air, feeling grateful and hopeful for the future. The pinch of guilt that she was pushing away Ryan's death so quickly barely registered at all.

Chapter Seven

By the time they arrived back in town, the fluffy clouds had morphed into full cloud cover, and a downpour chased them from the employee parking lot into the lobby. Calli's cheeks were pink, raindrops glistening in her hair, as she waved and disappeared down the back hallway toward the Tyler apartment. Unlike the rest of the staff, the bosses lived in the refurbished main building instead of the older south wing.

Parker headed more soberly up the internal stairway with Mouse. As they'd driven back up the coast, the sense of wellness brought on by the hike dissipated quickly. She liked Calli, but still didn't know what to think about her story. Jess was on his way, and Ryan was still dead. When Parker glanced at the mirror over the dresser as she changed out of damp hiking clothes, her face looked pale and haunted.

To counteract that, she'd decided to ground herself by using the rest of the afternoon to do laundry and buy groceries. TBI provided room and board, but she kept a stock of healthy lunches and snacks in her little kitchen. When she sat down at her laptop for recipe research, she found an email from Marta asking her to stop by the office ASAP.

Parker bit her lip, looking at that "ASAP." She wondered if Calli had lied about having permission to come on the hike. After the experience of the previous night, Parker should have checked directly with Seth and Marta. What if Calli had a tendency to make things up? Like, for instance, the existence of a note suggesting she break into Parker's room to leave flowers.

On her bed by the window, Mouse slept, long legs twitching. Parker hefted the canvas laundry sack out of the hamper in her bedroom, then remembered to grab the reusable grocery bags from the hook by the front door. The yellow slicker hanging on the next hook nudged a switch in her brain, and she grabbed that too. If Adam were still out fishing, she could leave it on his porch.

When Parker peered around Marta's office door, Marta was behind her desk, focused on her laptop. Parker knocked, awkwardly adjusting the stuffed laundry bag. "You wanted to see me?"

Marta looked up and closed her laptop, face arranged into a smile. This was the first time Parker had seen her without makeup, and she looked older, eyelashes invisible and her face wan. Blonde hair slipped from a loose ponytail instead of the usual chignon. "Parker! Yes, thank you for stopping by. I wanted to check with you about something. We're hosting a conference of rural police chiefs in February. It's the five-day retreat package, but they're providing a lot of their own programming. However, they do want mindfulness meditation training, an advanced course. Someone on their planning committee has been reading up on the value of mindfulness for law enforcement. Do you think you'll be up for it?"

Parker's heart pitter-pattered. Her fake expertise would be put to the test, but at least she had time to prepare. And she had come across the concept when she was prepping for her interview, so she knew there was information out there. "That's great! Wow, I mean, yes! I can do that. I'll put together a course. How much time will I have with them?"

"How much do you need?"

Parker calculated. Because of the short-term stays of the guests, her job was usually to give clients a taste of what meditation could do for them, hoping it would plant a seed of interest that might bloom back on their home ground. But for a group that had a stated intention to create a practice because of need, she would want to include a follow-up session on how to find support in their hometowns, how to make space in daily life to practice, and how to create habits that stick. At the same time, she didn't want to bore or overwhelm them, or it would all be counterproductive. "Can we do an hour a day? I'll blend lecture with different types of practice. And then I'll schedule an optional evening time, part discussion and part meditation." Parker was nearly breathless, the blurry picture of a future here coming back into focus.

Marta nodded and flipped her laptop open. "That sounds perfect, thank you. I'll mark it on the schedule. At some point, I'll need a description to put into their agenda, but it sounds like you practically have it written already."

"Can you email me the dates of their conference? And your deadline for the description?"

"I'll do that right now."

Marta bent again to her work, and Parker hefted the laundry sack. On the way out, she paused in the doorway. "No word on the murder?"

Marta met her eyes briefly, mouth twisting. "No.

I'm not sure there will be. They have no obligation to keep us updated."

"Right," Parker said. It felt like it should count for something that she'd found the body, but it could be the opposite; they'd be likely to keep her in the dark because she'd found the body.

"Have a good day off," Marta said, dismissing her, and Parker left.

Outside, she trudged toward the staff parking area with her load. Parking was at a premium in Nye Beach, and the little lot was a block and a half away on the other side of the street, behind a storefront. The laundromat was only five blocks away, so technically she could walk it, but it was up another steep hill. Plus, she'd have to lug the gallon jug of detergent.

The weather was still cool, with a brisk wind, but after the downpour the sky had cleared and was an even blue with scalloped silver clouds like decorative fish scales across the horizon. Parker smiled, still oddly happy at the challenge of the upcoming event. Despite the murder, despite Calli, she felt a surge of satisfaction. A year ago, this much stress would have had her running too many miles and/or trying to dull the pain with alcohol. Instead, she went hiking with Mouse and Calli, and had a positive interaction with her boss, who trusted her to put together something new and challenging.

"Wise, calm, compassionate, and responsible," Parker murmured to herself. And with that in mind, she tossed the laundry bag into the car and folded Adam's slicker over her arm.

The row of cottages where he lived was a couple of blocks further north. They were dilapidated but picturesque, with peeling paint on the windowsills, shingles weathered to silver, and front yards full of oyster shells, sea grass, and rusted anchors rather than lawn. His unit was a one-room cabin with a sleeping loft, shipshape and snug on the inside. When Parker had come for coffee, she'd felt like she was belowdecks in a boat, surrounded by cozy wooden planking and everything fitting just so as the rain streamed down outside.

Adam's old gray pickup was in the driveway, which meant he'd returned from fishing. Parker stepped up on the porch, thinking she might leave the slicker hanging over the back of an Adirondack chair so as not to bother him, but Pepper started yapping frantically from inside. Parker waited, but there was no gruff "Settle down," and no heavy step approaching the door. She hesitated, then knocked and called, "You around, Adam? It's Parker."

Pepper kept yapping. The door shook as he jumped against it from the inside.

Adam could be out back. There wasn't much of an out back, as the yard was barely big enough for his motorboat trailer, his project car, and a tiny shed, but she squeezed between the truck and the fence and peered around. A padlock secured the shed door. No sign of Adam.

He might have gone to visit a neighbor who didn't like dogs, or walked over to the little market to grab some milk or beer. She'd just leave the coat after all, folded over one of the Adirondack chairs.

Another bang and shudder of the door pulled Parker back as she was about to step off the porch. Pepper was always excitable, but this seemed excessive. Or was Parker still carrying around some extra paranoia?

She shaded her eyes to peer through the front window, but the slats in the blinds were too tightly closed to see much. Ignoring the hammering of her heart and the quick flash of Ryan's prone body in her mind's eye, she returned to the door, swallowed hard, and turned the knob. Nye Beach was not a place to leave doors unlocked, or tweakers would get your stuff, as Adam had been quick to tell her. He'd never leave his front door unlocked if he were out.

Adam knew how to take care of himself. He was probably right across the street.

The knob turned. The door opened. Adam was there.

****

The curved haft of a knife stuck incongruously out of Adam's black T-shirt like a Halloween prank. Parker froze in the doorway, fixated on his perfect stillness. There was no quiver of breath. In the dim light seeping through the closed blinds, a stain darker than the black cotton was perceptible. Her heart rat-tatted too quickly, and her face went hot then cold, but she couldn't move.

Then a growl came from the living room area. Parker jerked to see Pepper with his front legs on the top of the couch, facing her. His lips were drawn all the way back, the whites of his eyes showing. His whole body vibrated with stress. The musky reek of his fear mingled with the thick copper scent of blood.

She was going to puke, and she wrenched herself through the doorway and retched over the railing into the dry stalks of last spring's lilies. Behind her, Pepper landed with a thump on the floor, his growl increasing. Parker spat, wiped her mouth with the sleeve of her sweatshirt, and turned to him.

"Calm down, Pepper. Come on, boy. It's okay. It's just me."

He whimpered, trembling, and dropped to his belly.

She scooped him up, turning her head away from Adam's outstretched hand beyond him.

"I'm sorry," she murmured, not sure if she meant it for Adam or Pepper. "I'm so sorry."

Caught between the impulse to flee and the grim realization that she had to see how similar the rest of the scene was to Mrs. Gilford's murder, she nudged the front door so that it swung fully open. A scatter of books covered the floor in front of the built-in bookshelves, a kitchen chair lay overturned with a cracked leg, and peanuts and newspapers were strewn across the floor, soaking up a splash of coffee in front of the overturned coffee table.

Mrs. Gilford, a kind retiree with a fat brown cat named Cocoa and a fondness for cruises, died in her apartment when Parker was eleven. Stabbed to death. Unlike Adam, her babysitter was no minimalist, and Parker had picked her way through collections of seashells, church sale crafts, and knickknacks, lying broken and destroyed all over the living room as she searched for her, knowing something awful must have happened. Parker found Mrs. Gilford with a butcher knife sticking out of her chest, on the floor behind the kitchen island.

She closed Adam's front door softly and lowered herself onto the Adirondack chair with the rain slicker slung over the back. Pepper was a warm, trembling weight against her chest as she called 911 for the second time in two days.

****

This time, an Officer Mays showed up first. Parker watched him ease the patrol car to the curb and punch buttons on his dashboard before he climbed out and surveyed her, the row of cottages, and her again. He hitched his belt self-consciously and approached the porch. He was younger, skinnier, and shorter than Parker, and even though she knew it wasn't fair, she bristled with anger. Adam was her friend, and they sent a baby cop to his murder scene?

He said, "You're the one who contacted us? The injured man is inside?"

"He's dead," Parker said numbly.

She watched the cop turn the knob with one gloved hand and enter the cottage. After a few moments, he returned. "The detective is on her way, ma'am. In the meantime, can I get your name? Did you enter the residence?"

He looked down at her in the low chair, and she struggled to stand with Pepper still huddled in her arms. The dog eyed the newcomer with suspicion, hackles rising. "Is it Detective Balderas?" Parker said. "I can wait. There's something she needs to know."

"Sure, you should tell her everything," he said. "Could you confirm your name for me, ma'am?"

Okay, that was fair.

"It's Parker James. I was at the crime scene last night. Yesterday. Do you guys really have only one detective?" she added.

He cleared his throat. "We have two. But Elliott is on vacation. It doesn't matter, we'll call in the Major Crimes team."

Parker nodded. "Anyway, this is Adam's dog. The—the victim. When I got here, I opened the door and let him out, but my foot barely crossed the threshold. I could see Adam was—I could see the knife from the doorway."

"And then you got the dog?"

"No, he came to me. He knows me."

Pepper growled inaudibly and showed his teeth to the officer.

Mays swallowed and stepped back. He tore his eyes away from Pepper and back to Parker. "Okay. So you were friends with the deceased? With…Adam?"

"Yeah, somewhat. Fellow dog-walkers. We met a month or so ago, on the beach, but we kept running into each other because we both use the Nye Beach access."

The officer nodded. His radio spurted some static, which he apparently understood because he replaced the little notebook in his pocket and descended to the sidewalk, where he proceeded to have a conversation she couldn't make out.

One by one, other official vehicles joined Officer Mays', filling the street with patrol cars, black SUVs, and a fire truck. Neighbors pulled back their curtains and peered out.

Detective Balderas emerged from an SUV and climbed the porch steps. She raised her eyebrows at Parker and entered the cottage with another officer close behind. Pepper whimpered, and Parker mentioned to Officer Mays that it might be good to grab his leash and let him relieve himself in the grass. Mays retrieved the leash from a peg inside the door, and Parker let Pepper down to sniff in the strip of grass along the sidewalk.

When Detective Balderas came out, she looked at Pepper and said, "You have two dogs?"

"No. This is Adam's dog." Parker repeated the story of how they'd met, how briefly they'd known each other. Then she said, "There's something else I need to tell you."

Despite the sunshine, her teeth were chattering, and when the detective asked if they should talk at the station, Parker said, "Okay. I'm not sure what to do with Pepper, though."

"He'll have to go to the animal shelter if you can't care for him. At least until we find out if Mr. Reese had family or a friend that can take her."

With a start, Parker realized she hadn't even known Adam's last name. Adam Reese. He'd been older, seventy-something, but he could have living parents, siblings...even a separated spouse or children. Another family about to be gutted.

Parker looked down at Pepper. Marta would kill her. Mouse was quiet and rarely barked or even ran inside, as long as they got their miles in during the day. Pepper was a bundle of constant energy powered by frequent yapping. But Parker couldn't let him go to the shelter. She had to do this for Adam.

"I'll keep him with me for now," Parker said. "But I can't keep him permanently, not where I live."

"All right. I'll be talking to Adam's family later. I'll let you know."

Parker nodded.

"You don't know what family might live around here?"

"No, I guess—we were becoming friends, but I didn't really know much about him yet. I know he used to be a mechanic around here."

"That helps. I'll ask around, see who remembers him."

Balderas drove to TBI and stopped briefly for Parker to smuggle the dog up the fire escape. Mouse seemed astonished to see him, but greeted him happily enough.

Pepper was unenthusiastic about the bowl of kibble Parker put next to Mouse's. She hadn't noticed what brand he usually ate, or even if he had kibble, cans, or both at home. The two dogs sniffed each other, and Pepper jumped up onto Mouse's loveseat cushion. Mouse settled on her bed on the floor with a bemused look.

"I've got to go, guys," Parker told them. "Be good. Mouse, be a good host, okay? Don't let our guest get upset, he has to be quiet or we'll get in trouble. I owe you big time."

As she closed the door, Pepper yapped, and she gritted her teeth. She'd have to cross her fingers that he wouldn't claw at the door or chew anything that belonged to TBI.

At City Hall, the police department took up half of the second floor. Detective Balderas' office was crammed with an enormous desk and a collection of potted plants. Parker sat in an uncomfortable wooden chair. She had serious second thoughts. After all, there were a lot of differences between Mrs. Gilford's death and Adam's.

"I don't know where to start," Parker said. "And it probably doesn't mean anything."

"Ms. James," the detective said, glancing at her watch. "You know I have not one, but two suspicious deaths to investigate. I brought you back here because I trusted that you had something important to tell me."

"Okay." Deep breath. "These are not the first bodies I've found."

The other woman narrowed her eyes. "I'm waiting."

"My mom was strangled to death when I was five. Her face was covered with duct tape and she was shoved into a coat closet while my uncle distracted me with a game of hide and seek.

"My neighbor was murdered when I was eleven. It was a robbery. She was my sort-of babysitter. She was stabbed multiple times with one of her own kitchen knives, and bled out on her kitchen floor. I found her with the knife sticking out of her chest when I went over after school.

"So I'm feeling pretty weird about Ryan and Adam dying the way they did right about now."

Balderas nodded slowly and tilted her head. "I ran your name," she said. "Or rather, Officer Connelly did. We didn't see anything like that."

There was a note of challenge in her voice. Parker supposed that sometimes people made up elaborate lies to feel involved with an investigation. But that wasn't her.

"All that happened on the other side of the country," Parker said. "And I changed my name, because I was sick and tired of being—" She stopped. She hadn't planned to mention Britt, but if she was giving her real name, she had to, because it would come out, anyway.

Parker took a deep breath. "There was another murder, a third murder. When I was in high school. It was all over the papers and social media. Even though I was a minor, my name got out. I was a suspect for a little while."

"I see," Balderas said, sitting back in her chair. She tapped her pen thoughtfully against her cheek.

"I wanted you to know about Mrs. Gilford and my mother, because you're going to find out, anyway. I mean, you would, wouldn't you? You would have sent Officer Mays back to do more than a quick Google search, right? After Adam?"

"Yeah," she said. "We would have figured it out. It is better coming from you. Thank you."

"So, I'm kind of freaked out," Parker said. "I mean, am I crazy? Or is this too much coincidence?"

Balderas grimaced. "I'm sorry you've come across so many deaths. And we will check all leads. But I will say, this burglary; it wouldn't surprise me if it's an addict looking for something quick and easy to sell. Your friend was an old man. Maybe they thought he would be easy to intimidate."

Parker looked down at her hands twisting in her lap. She wanted to argue. Those cottages didn't look like they had anything worth stealing, but she knew sometimes that made no difference. But what about Pepper? Thieves hated dogs.

She kept her mouth shut. It was true, it could have been a random burglary gone wrong, just like Ryan's death could have happened for any number of reasons, the duct tape a coincidence. But Parker no longer believed it. Of course, she hadn't told Balderas about the lavender incident. But the lavender didn't count for anything, now that Calli had confessed.

Balderas seemed to read the trend of Parker's thoughts. She sighed. "Do you think someone is targeting you by killing people around you?"

"I'm trying not to be paranoid. But I don't know," Parker said.

Balderas nodded. "Generally, crime's a lot more straightforward. How could anyone have known that you'd be the one to find Adam Reese's body, or even Ryan Bennett's body last night? And those little cottages there, they get burglarized quite a bit, even though they look low end. They're close to a couple of bars, and the beach access, and a few of them are vacation rentals, so they're easy pickings for someone looking to grab a TV or some household goods. Generally no security."

"You really think it might have been a random break in?"

"I don't know yet, Parker. Or—what is your original name?"

"Corey. Coral Jantzen. Parker was my mum's maiden name, and I borrowed the last name from a boy I liked in second grade. But call me Parker. I've gotten used to it. Corey was a different person."

"Okay. Parker. I promise, we'll keep an open mind. Have you talked to anyone else about this? Have you told your boss or a friend?"

"No! I mean, no, of course not. All I did was call 911!"

"No, that's not what I mean. I mean, about your past. It's got to be really hard for you, finding a body, it's got to bring up terrible memories. Do you have someone to talk to?" She regarded Parker with tired kindness.

Parker's throat closed up, but she forced herself to answer. "It was all a long time ago. I've learned to cope." She could hear the defensiveness in her voice.

"I have no doubt you're good at coping. But my recommendation for you is to get some extra help. You just lost a friend." She stood.

Parker stood up too, nonplussed. She wasn't sure what she'd expected after sharing her past. More than mere acknowledgment, anyway. "What am I supposed to do?" she said.

"We'll need you to make an official statement. Officer Mays will sit down with you now. If I have any further questions, I'll let you know."

"I can just go do my laundry after?" Parker asked.

"Sure, honey, if that's what you want." Balderas ushered her out.

Chapter Eight

Parker left a witness statement with Officer Mays and refused a ride home. It was getting dark, but she needed air and motion and solitude. At the main road, she waited for the crosswalk, numbly watching cars full of people out for Saturday night fun whiz past.

Was Adam's mother or sister or daughter getting the bad news now? Did he have a brother, a cousin, a son? She knew none of that, only that if he had family, he hadn't mentioned them in their few conversations. She'd appreciated how he never pried into her life; she hadn't noticed how little he shared of himself.

And what about Pepper? Could she keep him out of the animal shelter? Mouse was gentle, quiet, and apartment-friendly by nature, which was fortunate because Parker's dog-training skills were nil, beyond knowing consistency and rewards were good. What that translated to when you were trying to calm a thirty-pound bundle of Pepper, she had no idea. Maybe Mouse could do the training.

If Marta learned Parker was harboring another dog, it would be a strike against her. Marta had turned on her so quickly when Calli lied, and just because she was currently happy with Parker's eagerness to please didn't mean she'd give her the benefit of the doubt moving forward.

As Parker neared Tyler Bettering, her steps slowed.

She couldn't think about laundry when Adam had just been killed. But her laundry still needed doing. It was going to sit there in her car, getting funkier with each passing hour, until she did it.

Adam had been a fixture of the beach. His death engendered a bone-deep angst in Parker that she could not define or settle with. Beyond that, memories of Mrs. Gilford were bubbling up, not just the horror of finding her body but the things Parker had loved about her: her exotic seashells, her homemade gingersnaps, her crotchety cat. Her kind and patient voice, gone from Parker's life and the world too soon.

Breathe, Parker told herself. Grief is normal.

She'd had the chance to know them both. It was something to be grateful for.

Bile rose, and she swallowed down acid. She stopped where she was on the sidewalk and tilted her head back to look at the overcast sky, pulling in a long breath until her lungs ached. Was her whole life going to be like this? Desperately clinging to rote positivity while lives crumbled around her?

She pushed that line of thought away. She wasn't going to veer off course again by sabotaging her own efforts to become happier. Leaning toward positivity was a mindset choice, not denial. And all this darkness was not her whole life. It was just a really crappy couple of days for her. For Ryan and Adam…it had been an ending.

Screw the laundry. Parker would take Pepper and Mouse for a long run on the beach—or at least a long walk. She wasn't sure what Pepper's capabilities were. On the way home, she'd pick up dinner, and they could all cuddle on the couch, and Parker would light candles for Adam and Ryan. And for her mother, and Mrs. Gilford, and Britt, too. All of the dead who had been on her mind.

Laundry could wait until tomorrow.

It seemed like an excellent plan until she noticed the guy leaning against a truck parked a few doors down from TBI's side entrance. Her heart jumped before she consciously recognized him.

It was Jess. Jesse Wyatt Harper, Parker's friend, and her late best friend's ex-boyfriend. The guy she'd fallen in love with and stayed in love with, despite everything, before, during, and after Britt's disappearance. In the warped mirror of the investigation, the relationship had looked suspicious to the cops, to the news media, eventually even to their friends. But neither had cared, because it was real and everything else stank of bullshit.

Neither cared, to a point.

"Jess," she said aloud, succeeding in a tone of perfect neutrality.

He straightened, slipping his phone in his pocket, and faced her. Uneven light from the windows of the Institute and the streetlight above picked out the angles of his face. He looked older, which was only fair, since it had been eight years. He'd settled into his looks, becoming more handsome. Parker stopped herself from running a hand through her wind-blown hair.

"Corey," he said, and held out his arms. His grandfather's wedding band still glittered on the ring finger of his right hand, in honor of the man who'd raised him.

"I don't go by that name anymore," she said, but gave him a quick, awkward hug anyway.

"Oh, right, you told me that," he said. "What is it,

again?"

"Parker. My mom's maiden name, as you so astutely remembered."

"Right." He smiled. "I'll try to adjust. It's great to see you."

She swallowed. "You got here fast. I didn't think you'd make it until tomorrow evening."

"Yeah, I didn't stop for much. I'm starving, actually. I didn't have lunch and now it's almost dinner time."

He paused, obviously waiting for her to take the hint. Instead, she said, "I need to take the dogs for a walk. Do you want to meet me after? There are plenty of places to grab a bite around here. You can just text me where you end up."

His face shuttered. "Um, no. I'll eat later. I'd rather come with you if that's okay. What I have to say is important."

She opened her mouth, trying to figure out a way to turn him down. She didn't need anything else on her plate right now. The wind was low, the tide was low, and starry purple sky showed through holes in the clouds. It was the balm her soul needed, that and watching the cavorting of the dogs.

But he was right. It was probably best just to get it over with. "Fine. Where are you staying?"

"I figured there'd be a hotel room around. There were plenty of vacancy signs." He shrugged. "Do you think I should figure that out now?"

"No, I just didn't want to break the bad news that I have no space later, when you're even more exhausted. I live at the resort where I work, but my apartment's pretty small, and I share it with a dog. Come on up, we've got to get them, anyway."

He followed her through the staff entrance, and they climbed the four flights of stairs. "How many dogs did you say?"

"I'm taking care of an extra dog for a friend who died. It's temporary," she said quietly, knowing how thin the doors were. Chances were her fellow staff members were out and about on this unexpectedly free Saturday night, but you never could tell.

Pepper heard them coming. His yips echoed down the stairwell, and Parker bit her lip. "Pepper, hush," she called in a semi-whisper, but he didn't stop. She took the stairs two at a time.

Pepper leaped from the back of the loveseat when Parker opened the door and scrambled toward her. Parker lifted him into her arms, where he switched from yipping to licking. She looked into his soft brown eyes, wondering what was going on in his doggie brain. Did he know his person was gone forever?

Mouse ambled over to investigate Jess, who stepped in and closed the door. Parker could feel him studying the small space, the lack of decoration beyond the hotel-like decor that had come with the place.

"What's your name?" he said, as he scratched Mouse's jaw.

"Mouse, Pepper, this is Jess," Parker said.

"Good to meet you both. I'm guessing the peppy one is Pepper? Even though the other one is more pepper-colored?"

"You got it. Mouse is named for her temperament, as in quiet-as-a."

Now that Pepper had calmed, Parker put him down, and he joined the new-person-greeting-party until Jess rose to his feet.

"You look the same," he said. "I mean, a little older. A little wiser. But pretty much the same."

Wiser, calmer, and more compassionate, Parker thought. She hoped. "We've both aged almost a decade," she said. "And I'm guessing it wasn't the easiest decade for either of us."

"No."

She sighed. "Okay. Give me a couple minutes to put on something a little warmer for the beach. Then we'll take these two for walkies, and you can tell me whatever's so important."

She immediately regretted saying walkies. Mouse disdained baby-talk, but Pepper was all about it and the yipping began again.

****

Ten minutes later, they left by the outside stairs. Jess took deep breaths of brisk salt air and looked out to the horizon, where the ocean was darker than the sky. Parker had grabbed a flashlight to navigate the stairs, but there was enough ambient light that they should be fine without it on the beach.

Just last night, Ryan had died at the bottom of this cliff, but the crime scene tape was already gone and most of the driftwood that had hidden the body had been scattered. No one, living or dead, lay in wait in the under-stair cave, and her shoulders relaxed as they reached the sand.

They turned south. There were no other beach walkers in sight, but Parker wasn't sure how well Pepper would listen in the presence of temptation, so she kept him leashed although Mouse ran free.

Jess remained quiet. Possible conversation starters ran through Parker's mind, but most of them sounded angry or bitter. Finally she said, "So, I'm really surprised to see you. I can't believe there's anything important left to say that couldn't have been better said years ago. What are you doing here, Jess?"

She'd tried to forgive him. She'd tried to forgive herself. When she thought of them as kids caught up in Britt's horrible death, she felt compassion for them both, but a layer of resentment remained under the surface. He hadn't stood by her when she needed him.

He raised his eyes from his feet with a pained look. "Corey. Parker. I know it's you."

****

Parker halted and stared at Jess. This was it. This was the betrayal she'd been reeling from for years, said face to face for the first time.

At the end of his leash, Pepper jerked to a stop with a squeal before sitting disconsolately at her feet. Parker ignored him.

"You really believe that?" she asked, voice surprisingly calm. For a while, she and Jess had been the number one suspects in Britt's death, at least according to the less scrupulous corners of the internet. It made a good story—Britt and Jess had a volatile on-again, off-again relationship. Britt refused to believe it was over—and suddenly she was gone and Jess and Corey were together every moment. It wasn't what actually happened, but it was believable, and apparently there were various social media photos that convinced people they knew the truth better than the police. Corey's 'triumphant' smile. Jess's 'hostile' eyes.

They hadn't kidnapped or killed her, of course, not together and not separately. They had both loved her. Until one last interview, Corey believed Jess knew that as well as she did.

Jess said, "Parker, just tell me. You've been sending the letters, the postcards. I already know."

It was so far from what she was expecting, she barely managed a single word. "What?"

His jaw tightened visibly, fighting down whatever retort was about to come out. Finally he said, "Please, don't play dumb. It has to be you. I don't know why you're doing it, but it's time to stop."

Parker shook her head. "I'm serious, Jess. Whatever you're talking about, it wasn't me. I have literally no idea what you mean."

He studied her face. "It has to be you," he repeated desperately. "I didn't think you would do something like that, and I resisted believing it for a long time. I guess you're punishing me, or working out your own issues. I don't know. But it's got to stop."

Parker grimaced. Yes, she had issues, and she'd done plenty of stupid things to work them out, but sending letters to Jess was not one of them.

Before she could respond, Pepper pulled on the leash with such abandon that his eyes bugged out. Parker took pity and started walking. The breeze blew lightly, cooling the heat in her cheeks.

Finally she said, "I really didn't send you anything. I haven't kept track of you since I left. I didn't want to know what you were up to. At first I wanted you to come after me, and beg me to come back. But I gave up on you a long time ago."

He was silent. When she looked over, his head was bowed, hands in his pockets.

Parker asked, "Were they postmarked from Oregon? Is that why you thought—?"

"No! They talked about our relationship. Personal stuff."

"What do you mean?"

"'Your kisses were sweet but your heart was black,' that kind of thing."

Parker snorted. "What the heck? That doesn't sound like anything I would ever say. It sounds like someone didn't want to believe you were innocent. We got used to that a long time ago, remember? Why would you think that was me?"

"'Your kisses were sweet?' It has to be someone I kissed. Someone who thinks I wronged them. And Britt is dead, so that leaves you. All this time, I've been sure it was you."

"You've got to be kidding. You haven't kissed anyone since I left? I find that a little hard to believe."

"I've had relationships, but nothing serious. You and Britt…I haven't had any other relationships nearly as intense. On purpose."

Parker met his eyes. "You know my handwriting," she reminded him. "And they can't be in my handwriting, because they're not from me."

"No, they're in block letters. Even the postcards. But, Parker, they mention where we used to meet. What we used to get up to."

What they used to get up to…wandering in the woods at night, looking for signs of Britt in the last place they'd seen her—and also delighting in their desire for each other. In the woods, in the shed behind the elementary school, in Jess's truck.

Parker circled back to solid ground. "Where are they postmarked from? I've only been here for a couple months, not even that."

He shook his head. "All over the country. I don't think it means anything. There are online services that do that. You can get your stuff mailed from anywhere for a fee. There's no rhyme or reason or pattern. One month it's New York City, the next St. George, Utah."

"Oh. Crap," she said.

"Parker," he said haltingly. "If it's really not you—I'm sorry. I'm sorry for thinking that all this time. I just—I just don't know who else would do that."

"It wasn't me," she said with finality, touching his arm. They paused and she looked into his dark brown eyes. "I promise, I would tell you if it was. I'm not saying I'm totally over what happened, but I've moved on. I'm not harboring the kind of demons that would make me torment you."

"I believe you," he said. A line remained between his brows. "But now I'm even more disturbed because I can't imagine who else it could be. And since I'm going to be away for a few months, all my mail is going to my mom's house. I really didn't want her to see that crap. I was going to ask you to stop, for her sake."

Parker shook her head. "Sorry. I can't even guess. Have you thought about hiring a private detective or something?"

"No. Because I was so sure it was you, I hadn't considered anything else." He shrugged and smiled weakly. "I'm glad, though. I didn't like to think of you still being angry after all this time."

The tide was coming in, and their steps meandered to avoid the line of surf. As they continued in silence, Parker wrestled with bringing up the interview he'd done before she ran away, the last straw where he cast doubt on her honesty. Rehashing that old pain didn't sound appealing, especially after finding their way to this small peace. Finally, she said, "So, you contacted my dad and came all the way here just because of the letters?"

He sighed. "I'm going to work on the fishing boats in Alaska to save up for another year of school. It's tough work, but it pays really well. This was sort of on my way, and like I said, I really hoped if you knew that you'd be stressing out my mom…"

"Yeah. I always liked your mom. If it were me, I'd totally stop. But like I said, the past is gone. I'm done with it."

"It wasn't all bad," he said, with a ghost of a grin and a sidelong glance.

They walked on. She thought of Ryan, disfigured by duct tape, Adam, stabbed in the back, and grimaced. If only Jess knew how close the worst parts of the past seemed tonight.

"Well, it's kind of nice to see you, anyway," she offered. Strangely, it was true. With the tension broken, they fell into a comfortable silence. They hadn't talked about their final fight…but it felt like they were even anyway. He'd publicly implied she knew something about Britt's death—and Parker had deserted him without giving him a chance to explain. He hadn't come after her, and it had felt like a betrayal of all they'd meant to each other.

Then. It felt like that, then. Now, it just seemed like one more fuckup in an enormous pile of fuckups, and it was time to let them all go.

Her stomach growled. They should eat dinner together, make peace, and wish each other well. Interview schminterview, she didn't care anymore.

"Are you still in touch with Keith?" Jess said, out of

nowhere.

"Keith Moore?" She barely remembered him, a redheaded kid who'd moved away after freshman year. The only reason she remembered him at all was because he sat next to her in algebra and tried to cheat off her paper.

"No. Krista's little brother. Keith Murphy."

"Oh. No." Keith Murphy hadn't even been in their grade. "I mean, Krista and I are still friends. She got me this job, actually. But I don't think she talks to her brother much." Parker tried to remember the last time Krista had mentioned him. "She said she saw him last Thanksgiving. Or it might have been the one before. Why? Are you thinking he would have sent the letters? That seems pretty unlikely." Keith suffered brain damage in a bicycle accident during high school—one of several things that led to Krista's Mom's breakdown. He'd been living in a group home for years. Parker remembered Krista joking a few years back that Keith still had a genius IQ, but used his 'so-called' brain damage as an excuse not to get a job. Sometimes Krista's humor was a little dark, even for Parker's taste.

Jess was silent for a few steps. "You're probably right. He was a weird kid, though. And he had a crush on Britt for a while. Well, what about Krista? Do you think Krista would have sent the letters?"

Parker snorted. "Okay, first, about Keith? There were probably seventeen guys who had a crush on Britt at any given time. Besides you and your best friend. And second, no. Absolutely not. Unlike most of the world, Krista remembers that you and Britt had broken up months before we started dating. She's not your biggest fan, but she has no reason to torment you. Whoever's doing it has to be someone who's angry with you. Krista couldn't care less what you and I got up to before or after Britt disappeared. Remember? She had her own shit going on."

Jess frowned. "I don't remember, actually. I wasn't as close to her as you and Britt were."

"Yeah. Well. She was having relationship issues." Parker remembered very well. She'd gone to Planned Parenthood with Krista for moral support and driven her home afterward. "Everything piled on," she said. "When people talk about how much they miss high school, I just look at them like, if only you knew. I mean, I guess things were okay into sophomore year. But we were all so stressed out, even before Britt got weird. Even before everything fell apart."

Jess nodded. After a moment, he said, "Wait, who were all these guys who had a crush on Britt? Because I don't remember you naming names to the police."

"I'm exaggerating, probably. But all the guys thought she was hot. I couldn't point a finger at someone obsessing about her, though."

"Did you say Eric?" Jess persisted. "You said me and my best friend. And he did not. He was a good guy. He wouldn't go after anyone I was dating."

Parker mimed shock. "Oh my god, Jess, he totally crushed on her. The whole time you were dating! I can't believe you didn't see it. He was always talking to her, trying to sit next to her."

Jess snorted. "Eric? Yeah, because he was avoiding talking to you and sitting next to you, that's why he was awkward! Britt was a safe space for him. He had a crush on you, Parker."

"He was a sarcastic jerk to me!"

"What I said."

She shook her head, laughing. Jess must have been blind not to see how Eric looked at Britt. Plus, Parker had been single through most of high school. If Eric wanted to ask her out, there had been plenty of opportunities. Not that she would have said yes. Eric was kind of awkward all around.

Now it was Jess's stomach that grumbled loud enough to hear over the surf. He made a face. "I think I need to get some dinner before I start digesting myself. Should we turn around?"

She checked their location. They'd come about a mile and a half, almost reaching the jetty, and fog was rolling in. It had that salty scent she loved, and she inhaled deeply and blinked away sudden tears.

"Hey, what is it?" Jess asked. He was always too observant for his own good.

"God, I don't know," she managed. "I actually—for a second there, I was feeling almost happy. Normal."

He quirked up his lips. "Yeah, and—?"

"You're just here as—I don't know. As an errand, right? I mean, you came because of the letters. It's not like you're here as a friend. For a minute, it just felt different, like I was living a different life. Like all the bad things didn't happen."

"Corey. Parker. What things? You mean Britt?"

She almost nodded, not wanting to get into it. Not wanting to pretend Jess cared.

He seemed to read her mind. "I want to know," he said. "You can tell me. I'm still a good listener."

He had been a good listener back then. Their friendship had become closer as their other friends were swept up in their own lives. They'd talked a lot about

Britt, even before she disappeared, but also about everything else. Life, the future, their parents.

Parker sniffled. "It's not a big deal. I mean, it is a big deal, but it's not about me." They were heading north again, and he shot her an encouraging look. She hesitated, wondering if this would be the last straw. He knew she'd been exposed to three murders in the past. Her body-count was now up to five. Would he run screaming? He should.

She took a deep breath. "I've found two bodies in the last, oh, twenty-four hours. One last night, one this afternoon. Dead bodies. Murdered people. That I knew."

"Oh my god, Parker, I'm so sorry. That's crazy!" He showed no signs of running away. His face in the dark was shadowed and solemn.

"Yeah, tell me about it. Like one wasn't enough."

"So, they weren't connected?"

She described finding Ryan, including the duct tape and the hat lying there as if intended to catch her attention. Jess knew the story of her mother, knew how much that one event had warped her life, and he shook his head.

When she talked about Adam, tears choked her up again. "It was like finding my neighbor, my babysitter, when I was eleven. She was stabbed, too, during a robbery. I told you about that, right?"

"I don't remember all the details, but I remember it happened. This is seriously messed up," Jess said.

"It really is."

"I don't know what to say. It's horrible, and it's unfair."

"You don't have to say anything. I mean, there's nothing to say. It just is."

They fell quiet as they climbed the steps back up the cliff. The dogs panted happily. Jess paused at the landing and turned to look over the ocean, and Parker broke the silence. "So, what kind of food do you want?"

He threw her a sideways glance. "Oh, you're going to eat with me now?"

"I guess so." She shot him a small smile.

"Well, is there anything good nearby?"

"Yeah, there's good Mexican, or good pizza, or decent Thai, but it's all the way across town. We could get it delivered, though."

"You know, I get it if you want to be alone. You don't have to—"

She raised her eyebrows. "I'm hungry too. And I was kind of being a bitch before. I'm sorry. Now that we got some of the weird shit out of the way, can we try the old friend thing a little more? Honestly, I don't even mind if you sleep on my couch. Although, full disclosure, it's actually a loveseat and kind of short."

He hesitated. "Really? I'd like to keep talking. But I don't want to put you out."

"You won't. And maybe we can talk about something besides murder and death."

"Here's hoping," he said.

Chapter Nine

They brought the dogs upstairs and settled for frozen burritos and snacks from the grocery store. Parker felt disturbingly comfortable with him, like years and bad feelings had just fallen away, but she kept reminding herself that this was a temporary thing. Tomorrow, he would continue to Alaska, and she'd be on her own, still dealing with two murders. Still trying to keep the momentum going in her new, fake life, even as she was drowning in death. Jess's appearance was a minor footnote in all this. She probably wouldn't see or hear from him again for years.

But it had been a long time since she'd been around anyone but Krista who knew her so well, and it astounded her how easily they fell into old patterns. She kept doing a double take, because he had days of stubble on his face, and his shoulders had filled out, his hands roughened. What changes had happened below the surface? He seemed more thoughtful, slower to react. Less likely to drop f-bombs every other sentence.

They ate at the kitchen table under the too-bright glow of the overhead light. Jess was down to the last of his four burritos. Parker had long ago finished hers, and they dipped veggies into salad dressing to balance out the grease and salt. "So, what have you been doing?" she asked. "A while ago, my dad said you went away to college."

Jess shrugged. "Yeah, after you left I dropped out too, but I took my GED that fall after our class graduated, and then applied to school. My idea was the farther away the better, but I ended up at the University of Maine for spring term. I was interested in marine biology. Anyway, that didn't stick. Even in a place where no one really knew me, I was still reeling from the fact that Britt was actually dead. I mean, we'd been so sure that she was living it up somewhere, laughing at all the fuss. It was like that imaginary Britt kept going inside my head even though I knew it wasn't true. On top of that, I kept thinking I saw you around campus. I thought you'd come back, and just, you know. Show up in my life. It was driving me nuts."

Parker had imagined that Jess would do the same. Each had been waiting for the other to come and find them.

"So you dropped out?" she said.

"I dropped out. I stayed with my mom for a while, but she kicked me out after a few months. I guess I was kind of hard to live with. I got a construction job, and then another one, and then, I don't know, months and years were going by and other people were graduating and getting real jobs and getting married and having kids, and I was spinning my wheels, working really hard but living in shitty apartments, partying it up on weekends.

"So, I decided to try school again. But I didn't want to take out loans, so I saved up, and did a couple years, and now I'm going to save up again."

"What are you going to school for?"

He grimaced. "It's going to sound stupid."

"Really? Now I definitely need to know."

"Architecture."

"What!" That was so far from anything she would have guessed. She remembered his doodles from high school. He'd been artistic in a cartoony way, but had never taken an art class. On the other hand, he'd always been in Honors level math classes.

"Yeah, crazy, right?"

"No, it doesn't seem crazy. It's unexpected, but it seems right somehow. I approve. You'll have to show me one of your designs."

"I will. Thank you." He grinned.

After they finished, she flipped off the kitchen light, and they moved out to the balcony, where they sat on plastic chairs watching the distant waves, close enough to each other that she could feel the warmth radiating from his body. She wondered if he still felt the old attraction, and if he also recognized it was probably a bad idea. But she was hungry for connection. Jess was the past, but he was one of the few good things about the past, even though he was all tangled up with the worst thing.

Mouse and Pepper relaxed at their feet. Jess asked what Parker wanted to be when she grew up, and she told him her own GED and spotty schooling story. "I couldn't figure out anything I could focus on. I couldn't believe I would succeed at anything. I was working at bars, drinking too much...dating guys I didn't even like. No health insurance, or long-term housing, or anything stable. Anyway, I was getting lower and lower, and I reached a point where I had to change or resign myself to the fact that my life was going to be all crap."

"So what happened?"

"Mouse."

"Mouse?"

"Yeah. This older lady that always came to my bar was a complete alcoholic. She would bring Mouse inside, and I'd let her smuggle Mouse under the table if it was pretty empty. She slept at her daughter's house sometimes, but sometimes she just lived on the streets. So, she finally collapsed and had to move into a nursing home, and she told her daughter to give me Mouse."

"Why?"

"I don't know. I think she knew how miserable I was, and that I was going downhill. Which is pathetic, that this random old lady who was half out of her mind could see that." Parker laughed uncomfortably, but internally apologized to Franny, whose kindness and insight had been much more important than her altered states.

"Jeez, Parker."

"Yeah. Well, she was right, though. I straightened out when I had Mouse to take care of. And when I realized I could end up where she was." *Thank you, Franny*, Parker added silently.

"So—Mouse and I started walking and then running, which ended up being really good for me. I realized I could choose not to hang out in sleazy bars for the rest of my life, which Krista and my dad had both been trying to tell me for a while, to be fair. I started a program at the community college…and eventually I got this job." Parker shrugged, feeling self-conscious about the massive hole in the middle of her story. False starts, money struggles, and more self-sabotage—not the stuff she wanted to share. The negative, cynical person she'd been for so many years hadn't believed she could really change.

She took a deep breath. Her existence as Parker still

felt like a miracle. "I think I'm doing the right thing. For me. For right now."

"This?" he said. Somehow, he was looking into her eyes, and his arm was around her, familiar and novel at the same time.

Parker's heart skipped a beat, and she kissed him.

****

Out of habit, Parker blinked blearily awake at six, although she and Jess had stayed up until almost two. With his warm back against hers, his even breathing tempting her back toward sleep, she marveled at how comfortable she felt. She should be panicking. But the tough times they'd gone through in the past were long over, and they were older and wiser now. No regrets, she thought, and almost believed it.

She slipped into the still-dark living-room, wondering if she could take the dogs out quickly and crawl back into bed. Her phone flashed on the coffee table. It was set to "Do Not Disturb," so there was no sound, no vibration, and she wouldn't have noticed the call if she weren't standing right there, but since she was, she had to look. There weren't too many casual reasons to call this early in the morning. What if it had something to do with the police investigations?

As soon as she picked it up, she recognized the area code on the incoming call. The same as her dad's, but not his number. She answered hesitantly, reminding herself that East Coast time was three hours ahead. It wasn't ridiculously early there, so her heart should chill out.

"Is this Coral?" a woman's voice asked.

"Who is this?"

"Coral Jantzen? Is this her?"

"Yes. Who's calling?"

"Ms. Jantzen, we haven't met, but I live on your father's street?" The voice was plump, officious, reminding Parker of the buttoned-up secretary from her high school whose face had wrinkled into an expression of permanent skepticism.

"Yes?"

"Honey," she said sympathetically, and cleared her throat. "Oh, I'm not doing this very well. I'm sorry."

Panic twisted in Parker's stomach. "What is it? Is he okay?"

"Honey, it's not too bad, we think, but your dad was in an accident. A car accident."

"It's not too bad?" Parker repeated.

"I mean, it's bad. I wouldn't have called if it were just, you know, a sprained ankle." Nervous laughter, quickly stifled. Parker imagined strangling the woman. "But he's going to be okay, it looks like. He is having surgery, though. I told the doctors I would call you, because I took care of his cat and his cactus before, you know, when he traveled? I still had your number from when he went to visit you."

"What hospital is he in?" Parker asked, and wrote down the answer, then hung up without listening further.

With trembling hands, she dialed the hospital and identified herself. A nurse said her father was in surgery for a compound fracture, he'd been in a car crash and had extensive contusions, but overall, he'd been lucky. After surgery, he would have a cast for a couple months, and physical therapy, but that would likely be the extent of it.

Parker didn't ask what the unlikely scenario was. She hung up and breathed with the phone in her hand. What should she do first? What should she do, period?

She pulled up Marta's number before remembering it was too early. Marta probably had her phone turned off, too. If Parker wanted to talk to the bosses, she'd have to bang on their door.

Should she? Yes. No. She noticed her hand was shaking and stopped to take some deep breaths again. It was a broken leg. People didn't die from that. Get it together, Parker.

But they did die from car accidents. How bad had it been? How dangerous was this surgery?

She should go. She should be there. What if something went wrong? Complications. A blood clot. Was he going to have to depend on the airhead neighbor who hadn't even given Parker her name?

Parker couldn't go, she didn't have vacation time yet and wouldn't for another four months while she was still on probation. Where was that TBI benefits binder?

She stood, rubbing her face hard as if that would clear her head, and glimpsed Jess hovering in the bedroom doorway in his boxers.

"Are you okay?" he asked.

She shook her head. "Not really."

He approached and folded her into a hug. She stiffened, needing to stay focused and not let the tears start, and he stepped back.

"What is it? Tell me," he insisted.

"My dad—" Parker began, and then the tears came despite her efforts. She collapsed into his chest. It was a brief storm, which gave way to self-conscious sniffling after a minute or two as she realized this was the second damn time he'd seen her cry in two days. She wasn't like this.

She pulled away to grab some tissues, not meeting

Jess's eyes until she'd blown her nose and mopped her face. Then she collapsed onto the loveseat, and he sat beside her.

Mouse nuzzled her in concern, and Parker said, "It's okay. I'm not sure why I'm finding this so upsetting. I mean, he's not dead or anything. He just—there was a car accident. I don't even know where or what happened, but he's in the hospital. And I was just realizing that I can't go see him. He's too far away, and I don't think he has anyone—"

Her throat twisted shut again.

"Hey, hey," Jess said. "He's a plane ride away. Talk to me."

"It's just—I mean, even if I could get plane tickets, I don't have vacation time yet. I started this job six weeks ago. I can't just zip over and visit him and see how he's doing. I would have to take days off, and fly across the country! And I can't learn much over the phone, they won't take the time to explain, they just—and his neighbor is such an airhead—"

"When's the last time you saw your dad?" Jess asked softly.

"A couple years ago. It wasn't—it wasn't a great visit. He was worried about me."

Parker and her father had argued about college and money and what her mom would have thought about being used as an excuse for Parker to throw her life away. They almost stopped speaking. Again. They'd managed to work through it and Dad had accepted her choices, even if he wished they were different. That was what she loved about him.

"I have to go," Parker said helplessly. Mouse's head was on her lap, and Pepper leaped up to get in on the comforting by fitting his body into the triangle between Parker and Jess. Parker scratched around his ears. "But— it's not just my job. I mean, I can ask for time off without pay," she realized. "Even though there's an event coming up this week, I can still ask. They would probably understand, right? But would the police let me go? What about the murders?"

"Parker, you can't seriously be a suspect," Jess said. "The police won't care."

"No, I know. I hope. They must think it's weird, but...I would have to tell the detective. I feel like I should."

"Okay. So you talk to your bosses and you call the detective on the case. Do you have money?"

"Yeah. I have an emergency fund and a credit card." She preferred not to touch Mom's trust fund and insurance payout, but in an emergency, she would do what she had to do.

The real issue was staring up at her from two pairs of concerned brown eyes. Mouse raised her eyebrows. "But two dogs! What am I going to do with the dogs? I guess, there must be a kennel around here. I haven't done that before, Mouse has never had to—"

"No," Jess said firmly. "Let me help. I'm not on a tight timeline. I'll take care of Mouse and Pepper, if you don't mind me staying here."

Parker bit her lip, staring at him. That would be better for the dogs, less scary for Parker, but—Oh, God. Marta and Seth would have to be told about Jess. Worse, they would have to know about Pepper! Her heart sank.

Jess said, "Parker, these things happen, okay? Your bosses know that. Don't worry, we'll make it work."

A little after seven, Parker called Marta's phone and

got through, then walked Jess down to their apartment to introduce him in person. He could be very charming, and in the light of the family emergency, he convinced them to allow him to stay, on the condition that he would keep Pepper and Mouse outside most of the time, and quiet when they were inside. For Parker's part, she promised she'd find a home for Pepper as soon as she got back.

By nine a.m., she'd switched out the dirty laundry bag in the hatchback for a carry-on bag, called Detective Balderas and left a message that she would be out of town due to a family emergency, texted Krista about Dad's accident—Krista had always liked him—and was on the road to the airport, where she hoped to pick up a last-minute standby seat on a flight scheduled to leave at one.

It felt surreal. Parker was like a stranger in her own body. Ibuprofen headed off the incipient pounding in her head, but she hadn't slept much or stretched or run or meditated—all the things she counted on to center herself in times of stress. She was on the road alone, without even Mouse to keep her company, unmoored, as if the murders had frayed her anchor, but her dad's accident had well and truly snapped it.

Jess had handed her a bag on her way out the door, saying, "Snacks," and when her stomach growled, she realized she hadn't eaten anything yet. The bag held energy bars, bananas, a peanut butter sandwich, and a water bottle. What was it that addicts had to remember? Don't get too hungry, angry, lonely, or tired—something like that. Well, that was her. Hungry, angry, lonely, tired, worried, scared. Sad. All the bad things. No wonder she felt hollow. Like she might get lost on the way to the airport and never come back. Not that she wanted that.

But she felt the dark magnetism of running away, of finding some unfamiliar life to take the place of this too-difficult one.

Parker bit into the peanut butter sandwich which Jess had sweetened with honey, then devoured the rest in five sticky bites.

Things were good too, she reminded herself. Don't lose perspective. Having Mouse in her life. Pepper was good; she was helping him. Seeing Jess, of all the crazy things, had turned out to be good, if potentially complicated. And laced with denial? Don't go there, not now.

Krista was good. Parker's job was good, except she didn't deserve it. She flinched away from that thought, too. She pictured Calli on yesterday's hike and smiled. Calli was good. Maybe the tiny bits of wisdom Parker had painstakingly started putting together from the train wreck of her life could be useful to Calli, if they continued to spend time together.

At the airport Parker dialed the hospital with trembling fingers, but her dad was still in surgery, which seemed like a bad sign. Such a long surgery for what she'd been told was a broken leg. She boarded the one o'clock flight.

During a layover in Chicago, she found a text from the nameless neighbor saying Dad was in the recovery room. Another text followed, with a smiley face.

—I'm so sorry I worried you! He's going to be fine. Don't tell him I called you!—

Parker ground her teeth and closed her eyes. Would she have sped across the country if the neighbor called post-surgery instead of mid-surgery? It didn't matter at this point. And Parker couldn't trust the woman's assessment, anyway. She'd talk to the doctors before completely relaxing. No, this was good. She was heading in the right direction.

****

Parker hadn't packed anything to distract her on the plane. On the second flight, she started reading a thriller from the airport bookstore, but stopped when the bad guys targeted the heroine's father. A nervous man crocheting a beanie in the next seat wanted to chat about the skyrocketing price of real estate in Seattle, but eventually he fell silent and Parker put her headphones on and pretended to nod off.

Eyes closed, she tried some slow, deep breath cycles to release tension, but pieces from the past couple of days derailed her. Ryan's cool bony hand gripping hers as he smiled hesitantly. Pepper's weight in her arms and the thick smell of blood and fear. Jess, leaning against his truck in the twilight, a harbinger of the past.

During the stopover, Parker texted Krista with the update about her dad. Krista asked about Mouse and when Parker replied that Jess was staying at her place to care for both dogs, she was incredulous.

—*Are you crazy?*—

Parker—*What do you mean?*—

Krista—*I mean, you know*—

Parker—*What?*—

Krista—*The things going on*—

Parker—*The murders?*—

Krista—*It's a huge coincidence.*—

Parker—*It's not Jess!*—She added an eye-rolling emoticon.

Krista didn't respond.

Parker—*Krista! Trust me. I just spent hours with*

126

him.—

Parker almost put "the night" but deleted it.

—It was never Jess.—

There was a delay. Parker bit her lip and watched the screen. Finally Krista responded.

—He hurt you!—

Parker hesitated. He had hurt her deeply, but only her feelings. Only her heart. And he had been hurt, too. It wasn't great, but it was a far cry from murder.

—We hurt each other. Kids in a bad situation.—

Krista—*Fine. Your call. So did you sleep with him?—*

Damn it. Trust Krista to sniff out the whole story.

—No!—

Krista—*That's good, at least. Save it for after he does the favor.—*

Parker—*Ha ha—*

When Parker stepped out of the deserted New Haven airport into the chilly night, frost sparkled on the sidewalk. She took a deep breath and snuggled into her light jacket, wishing she'd brought a hat. Had she really forgotten how cold autumn in Connecticut could be? When she was little on Halloween, Dad would roll the car from one block to the next, so that she could warm up between door-knocks. Year after year, she refused to "ruin" her costume with a coat, and Dad humored her, unlike most of the kids, whose mothers bundled them up in bulky layers. There had been many small things like that; Dad gave in where a two-parent family might have held firm. Parker's friends had been jealous and smug at the same time.

An Uber drove her straight to the hospital, where the wheels on her small suitcase echoed through nearly empty corridors. When she made it past reception and went to look in on her father, the lights throughout the corridor were dim, and the nurse tapping away on a keyboard at the desk suggested Parker just take a quick peek because he was sleeping.

Her heart pounded painfully, caught between fear and the strange banality of the moment: the smell of disinfectant, the squeaky wheels on an orderly's cart, a muffled news broadcast from someone's TV. Dad's door was ajar, and she peeked in to find a double room. Dad's bed was next to the window, and he lay on his back, a cast deforming the sheets over his legs. His mouth hung open, and his cheeks looked hollower than Parker remembered. She couldn't see much more than that, but his snore was steady and light, and some of her internal tension drained away. She settled on a chair next to the bed, legs as fatigued as if she'd run twenty miles, and watched him sleep.

Throughout the long trip, she'd assumed she'd spend the night sitting by her father's bed, or perhaps on a cot in his room. After about fifteen minutes, with the roommate snoring at intermittent intervals like a broken chainsaw, Parker realized that wouldn't work. Her dad was okay. She'd find a quiet place to sleep, come see him in the morning, and get the full scoop.

She debated going to Dad's duplex, but in the end, she used her phone to locate a nearby hotel and summoned a ride. After checking in, she texted Jess. He'd brought Mouse and Pepper on a hike around a local reservoir during the day, and then later taken another long beach walk. He reported both dogs seemed out of sorts, missing her and, in Pepper's case, Adam, but they had eaten, and were now curled up with him in the living room. Then he added an afterthought.

—*Your frnd Kelly stopped by*—

Parker—*Kelly? Calli? What did she want?*—

Jess—*I don't think anything. I said you had a family emergency. She offered to walk dogs. I said no need.*—

Parker—*Okay*—

Poor Calli. She needed friends her own age, or at least her own dog, although her mom would be a hard sell on that one.

Parker looked online for any updates on the two murders and saw nothing. Then, focusing on positivity, she did some gentle stretching, meditated, and tried to sleep. It was after two in the morning local time, but eleven o'clock back home. Past her bedtime any way she looked at it, and she was exhausted, but sleep didn't come for a long time.

Chapter Ten

The heater woke Parker at intervals all night with its unfamiliar noise, but by morning, being in a new place had done its usual magic. Space away from the murders, away from the sudden reversal of all things Jess, plus the pleasant anonymity of a hotel room conspired to energize her. She felt completely Parker, despite returning to where Corey should be strongest. This was a chance to reconnect with her dad and the places she'd loved as a teenager, but with more wisdom and perspective.

Before Jess's arrival, the murders had pushed her dangerously close to the kind of downward spiral that had eaten years of her life already—but not as close as she'd thought, she realized now. With a chance to process, to sleep, to breathe—and with the massive relief of seeing that her father was okay—her brain settled back to its new normal.

Not that all the anxiety had vanished. What would happen to her mental state if the police focused on her? What would happen when Jess left?

She swept the pointless worries away, dressed, and grabbed breakfast, then checked out of the hotel. Pulling her carry-on, she walked through the crisp air back to the hospital, enjoying the sight of bright autumn foliage on the maple trees along the sidewalks. Tonight, Dad should be home and she would sleep in her childhood room. Once she made sure he was fine, she'd fly back, maybe as soon as tomorrow night. And they would plan a longer visit for when her vacation time kicked in.

Dad was asleep when Parker poked her head into his room. His skin looked gray in the dim light seeping through the blinds, and snores rattled from his open mouth. The bed next to him was empty now, and she left her suitcase in a corner and walked back to the nurses' station.

"Can someone tell me how my dad is doing? Jantzen, Room 234."

The nurse, a skinny older man with bushy hair and reading glasses hanging from a cord around his neck, nodded and tapped at the computer. "Hmm, looks like he had a fever early this morning."

"Is that bad?"

He met her eyes and smiled reassuringly. "It wasn't too high. Surgery is hard on the body, and there's always the potential for infection. We'll see that he gets lots of rest, and he'll be fine."

"I was thinking he might be able to go home today."

"Mmm, it was a pretty nasty fracture. He's got several contusions too, and a mild concussion. I'm pretty sure Doctor was thinking of keeping him for another day at least, but we'll see."

"When will the doctor be around?"

He shrugged, glancing at his rainbow-patterned watch. "Within the hour."

Parker thanked him and returned to the room, settling into a chair but feeling uneasy. She didn't like the sound of that fever or how haggard he looked. The institutional atmosphere chipped away at the optimism she'd woken with. She watched Dad sleep and shifted in the uncomfortable plastic chair.

It wasn't just the hospital that was niggling at her. The last time she'd seen Dad, when he'd come out to California a couple years ago, they'd worked their way through the argument about money and her life plans and come out the other side, but at the time she'd been taking college classes. Since she quit, she'd kept their chats brief and infrequent to avoid having to explain. She wasn't looking forward to lying, but Dad had a knack for sniffing out the weak points in her stories.

Would he come out and ask how she'd qualified for a job with room, board, and health insurance—not to mention an ocean view, and gym and spa privileges—with no degree and a resume full of short-term waitress and bartender jobs? The short answer was, Krista had lied to get Parker the interview, and Parker went along with it because she deserved a break, goddammit.

But that answer wouldn't hold much water with her college professor father, who didn't seem to understand how much she struggled with mental health. Or, when she let something slip, he'd thought she should focus on fixing it. As if it were that easy.

She shifted again and watched him sleep, thinking about their last few interactions. She'd emailed him about the new job, and he'd sent flowers, but she hadn't updated him beyond a quick "All is well" here and there.

If she were ashamed about the way she'd gotten the job, she shouldn't have taken it. But the funny thing was, Krista had been right. Parker was good at getting other people to meditate. Clients kept telling her she had a soothing voice and a calm demeanor, even when she felt like a seething mess inside.

A short woman with buzzed gray hair and reading glasses on a beaded chain stepped into the room. "Ms.

Jantzen? I'm Dr. Swanwick."

Parker nodded, not wanting to get sidetracked by a discussion of her name change.

"Nice to meet you. Thanks for taking care of him. Do you think he should still be sleeping?"

"We'll wake him up soon. I believe the nurses are making their rounds right now," she said. "But sleep is good. He can go home tomorrow, if we're able to get him up and walking, and assuming there's no further sign of infection." She briskly tapped on her phone screen, then slid it back into the pocket of her lab coat.

"Tomorrow," Parker repeated.

"Yes, I'd like to keep him under observation for one more night. He was enormously lucky, but he's been through a lot. Let's make certain he's on the road to recovery." She patted the end of his bed lightly, smiled again, and left.

When the nurses came a few minutes later and gently shook him awake, he was groggy and out of sorts, but then he caught sight of Parker standing out of the way near the door.

"Parker?" he said, confused. She'd trained him well when he came to visit, and he seemed to have adjusted to the name change.

"I'm here, Dad," she said, throat thickened with emotion.

"Ready for a visit to the restroom?" one of the nurses asked, oblivious to the moment.

Dad blinked. "Umm, okay. Can I walk?" He looked dubiously down at the boot at the end of his right leg.

"Yessir," the nurse said brightly. "We're going to get you trained on crutches. Might as well start now."

Dad met Parker's eyes again as they helped him up.

He looked dazed, and she wondered how many painkillers he was on.

"I'll come back when you're all sorted out," she said. "Just going to get some coffee."

When she returned twenty minutes later, they were helping him back into bed. "Your father walked all the way to the end of the hall," one of them said. "He's a trooper!"

"Great," Parker said, knowing how much he hated being patronized, but when she tried to catch his eye, his face showed nothing but exhaustion. She sat back in the plastic chair, and the nurses settled him in and left.

"Parker," he said again. "What are you doing here?" He gave a weak smile. "Not that I'm not thrilled to see you."

"Your neighbor called me about the car accident."

"My neighbor? How would—*oh*. Mrs. Laine."

"Yeah. You didn't ask her to?"

"I wouldn't have bothered you. It was pretty minor. Well, the car is totaled," he admitted with a wry smile. "And so is my foot. But it happened in slow motion. This young guy went through a four-way stop, and if I wasn't such an old relic, I'd have been fine. Bones getting brittle."

Parker raised a brow. Dad was no fitness buff, but he'd always taken good care of himself, walking regularly, and playing tennis. It was just like him to downplay any injury. She said, "I needed to make sure you were okay."

He reached for her weakly, his hand barely lifting from the blanket. "The sedatives are too strong," he said. His eyelids fluttered. "Can you tell them not—"

She squeezed his cold fingers. "The doctor said you

can probably go home tomorrow. You should rest. You don't have to fight it."

"I want to talk," he mumbled.

"I want to talk to you, too, Dad. Don't worry. I'll come back."

He turned his head from side to side in apparent negation. "Don't go," he said.

Parker waited for his hand to relax, then rose and stopped at the nurses' station on her way out.

"If my father asks, can you tell him I'll be back in the afternoon?" she said to the unfamiliar gray-bunned nurse now staffing the desk.

"No problem. What room?" She scribbled a post-it note, and Parker left to find fresh air.

****

Out front, she sat on a wooden bench, mercifully free of smokers, to gather her thoughts. There was a bite in the air although last night's frost had melted, and she didn't fancy staying in the institutional dreariness of the hospital or dragging her suitcase around to coffee shops to while away the hours until afternoon. She knew where Dad hid the spare house key. She should just head home.

Within five minutes, an Uber picked her up, and in twenty minutes, she stood in front of the old Victorian duplex a half mile from the Yale campus where she'd lived for almost five years. Not long in the big scheme of things, but it still felt like home, because she hadn't lived anywhere else for half that long. The large maple on the lawn was aflame with yellow leaves, and yellow and orange chrysanthemums braced the front door. Dad kept the house up nicely, with gray and purple paintwork, and he'd added a ramp access to the shared front porch. Parker wondered if the current tenant on the other side of the duplex used a wheelchair. That could be the one who'd called.

The spare key lived under a rock along the side of the house near one of the recessed basement windows. Parker felt around in the long weeds growing in the narrow strip between fence and house and didn't find it. The dry stalks rustled against her hands as she combed through them. The key wasn't there, or on the windowsill or under any other rocks in the vicinity.

Dad must have moved it after she'd run away. Strangely, that hurt, even though she was twenty-six now and would have been long past moving out in almost any circumstance.

Abruptly self-conscious, Parker stood and brushed herself off. Midday on a Monday, there were a number of people walking and biking past, and there might be retirees and students and stay-at-home parents in the neighboring homes. Probably most of them wouldn't recognize her even if they had been here a decade ago. She could be anybody, some tweaker trying to break in.

As if paranoia had conjured her, a sturdy woman bustled up the sidewalk next to Dad's house with hands on hips and called out, "What do you think you're doing?"

She was a decade older than Parker, more or less, with bobbed brown hair, a denim dress over a turtleneck, and a round, sour face. Parker bristled, then took in a deep breath. Wise, calm, and compassionate, she reminded herself.

"Hello," Parker said, in a tone striving to be mild. "I was looking for something. Who are you?"

The woman narrowed her eyes. "I am Mrs. Laine, the head of the Neighborhood Watch committee, and you do not belong here, missy."

Ah, the infamous Mrs. Laine. Parker approached with a hand held out. "I do, but we haven't met. This is my father's house, the house where I grew up. Was it you who called me?"

The woman's eyes widened comically, and she stuck her hand out quickly and shook. "Oh my goodness, I'm so sorry! I just did not put it together! You're Coral!"

"Technically I—yes."

She folded Parker into a hug. The top of her head came up to Parker's nose and smelled like apple shampoo. When she backed away, a smile wreathed her face and she said, "I'm so glad you came! Dorreen, that's my sister-in-law, said I shouldn't call, but I knew you would want to know."

"Thank you, that was really thoughtful."

"Did you see your father yet? Is he okay? How is he?"

"Yes, he's okay. They're keeping him for another day, though, so I thought I would come by the house."

"Oh my goodness. Such a frightening thing to happen. So many careless drivers around here, mostly students, you know. Well, the students going too fast, and then the old ladies who can't see any more!" She tittered. "I drive as little as possible."

Parker smiled politely, although she would have sworn the woman was under forty, certainly not an old lady by any standard. "My father used to keep a spare key out here. Do you know if he still has one with any of the neighbors?"

Her face screwed up. "Well, I used to have one for when he went on trips, but not anymore."

"I suppose I could try one of the porch windows,"

Parker said, half-joking, "as long as you promise not to call the police." She realized even as she said it that it would be pointless. In her father's house, all the windows would be securely locked.

Mrs. Laine gave her a strange look. "Well, you could just knock," she said.

"Oh, you mean at the duplex? Is the tenant home? I wasn't sure if that was where you lived…" Parker trailed off.

Mrs. Laine shook her head adamantly. "No, no, honey. I meant you should knock at your father's door."

Now it was Parker's turn to be confused. There was a sly, almost victorious look on Mrs. Laine's face. Parker got a wilting feeling in her chest, suddenly realizing what the neighbor was implying. Dad was a grown man. Parker had been away for years, and only talked to him every few weeks. He might not mention a girlfriend, even if she had moved in.

Parker gave the neighbor a weak smile and approached the lefthand door. When she looked back, Mrs. Laine was still watching from the sidewalk. Parker shrugged and knocked, which felt pretty strange. She'd never knocked before unless she forgot her key and knew her dad was inside, and then she'd pounded, annoyed, as if this whole locking-up thing was something Dad dreamed up to torture her.

But now Parker tapped politely, and after a pause, rang the doorbell. As the chimes faded, she heard the deadbolt sliding and stepped back. The door swung inward, and a woman in a wheelchair looked up at her through the screen door.

Parker's heart skipped a beat in recognition, but the wheelchair threw her off and it took a few extra seconds to feel sure.

"Mrs. Ryden?"

After a flicker of surprise, the woman's face resumed the blankly pleasant expression that suggested that mentally, she was in a better place. It was the same distant look she'd worn through years of Britt's school plays, pool parties, and basketball games, and then, at the end, search parties and press conferences. Britt used to imitate the look with eerie exactitude, pursing her lips slightly to flatten the hint of a smile, raising the eyebrows the merest smidge, and then gazing beatifically into the distance.

Mrs. Ryden spoke in a cultured, overly enunciated way. Britt used to say her mom was trying to hide how many pills she'd taken. "Hello, Corey. I suppose you'd better come in. How is your father today? He hasn't called yet."

Numbly, Parker hefted her suitcase and reached for the handle.

****

Catherine Ryden had never been Parker's biggest fan. If Dad used Mom's money to move in society, it might have helped, although the unpleasantness in Parker's past would still have counted against her. But between the lack of conspicuous consumption and the unfortunate homicides everyone knew about, but no one mentioned in public, Parker was an 'unsuitable companion' for Britt. Parker's refusal to be cowed by Catherine's more-proper-than-thou act whenever they encountered each other had been the final nail in the coffin. Catherine's barely hidden dislike brought out all of Parker's snark, and that was before Catherine accused her and Jess of killing Britt.

Strangely, Catherine was more intimidating than she had been back in high school, even in a wheelchair. Probably because she was behind Parker's defenses, in her home. Was Britt's mother really living with Parker's dad?

Catherine led the way into the living room, where Parker spotted quite a few changes. The wood floors shone with a darker, more dramatic stain, the walls were no longer plain cream but alternated between soft shades of gray and mushroom, and a modular leather affair had ousted the old comfy couch, where Dad and Parker had spent a thousand hours cocooned with books or movies.

But more than these relatively superficial changes, what bothered her were the structural modifications. A pocket door wide enough for a wheelchair had replaced the narrow bathroom door in the hallway. And the kitchen, glimpsed through connecting archways, revealed not only new countertops but lowered counters.

Parker clenched her jaw. She tried to breathe her way through a surge of negative emotions, but she couldn't seem to slow the beat of her heart.

Mrs. Ryden maneuvered to face her from the other side of the glass-topped coffee table. Parker balanced on the edge of the couch, unwilling to sink in. A vanilla-scented candle guttering on a side table exuded a cloying scent, and she breathed shallowly.

"I should have asked if you wanted tea or coffee," Catherine said, but she didn't. She regarded Parker steadily, her hands folded over a forest green afghan that complemented her auburn hair. Confronted with her bony knees and stick thin wrists, Parker's anger should have faltered, but it only grew more entrenched.

"That's all right," Parker said, and grasped for

140

something else to say. Where to start? Yelling was probably a bad idea.

"So Brian's well," Catherine repeated. "I'll visit in the afternoon."

Parker managed a thin smile. "Yes. Me too."

Catherine nodded. "I was concerned when he didn't call this morning."

"He was sedated," Parker said. "He only woke up briefly."

"I thought it might be something like that."

Another awkward silence. Parker let it sit, although there was some part of her repeating "Kind, calm, compassionate." She'd been wondering lately if her mother would have forgiven Uncle Danny for killing her. It was possible. Mom had loved Danny, and Dad said she'd always been very empathic. But this woman, who'd been such a negative force in Britt's life and then in Parker's own—Parker didn't need to forgive her. She just had to cope with this situation. Somehow.

Catherine remained silent too, only her hands restless, massaging the swollen knuckles as if they were sore.

"So, you're living here," Parker said.

"Brian didn't mention me." A note of amusement.

"No."

"I'm sorry to surprise you."

Parker thought, "Yeah right, you are," but with some intracranial wrangling she said instead, "I'm sorry to barge in on you. I wouldn't have come if I'd known."

"Nonsense. It's your home." The word "too" remained silent, but Parker knew they both heard it.

After a pause, Catherine added, "Brian kept your room for you, of course. Not like a shrine. I believe he boxed up your things, but your bed is there, and you can bring your suitcase up." Her eyes darted away, and Parker wondered if they were both thinking of Britt's room in Catherine's old house. Did it still belong to Britt's dad, preserving memories of the past, or had it been cleaned out and sold off?

"Oh, I'm not staying here," Parker said hurriedly. "No, I have a hotel near the airport. It's fine. I just wanted to see the old house."

Catherine dropped her gaze to Parker's suitcase. "I'm sure your father would want you to stay here. Don't let me scare you away."

"No, I know, of course not. But I'm not staying long at all, just a quick trip to make sure he's all right. Then I have to head back for work."

"Very well," Catherine said.

They sat in silence. Finally Parker stood. "I'll go look at my old room and then get out of your hair."

Catherine nodded. "That's fine. You go up. If you need anything, I'll be in my studio." She saw Parker's blank look and added, "Brian retrofitted the guest room for me to work in. He extended it where the back porch used to be, so it gets a lot of natural light. The contractors did a beautiful job. Would you like to see?"

No more porch swing. No more barbecues, no more sunning on the back lawn? Of course not. Those days were long over. Why shouldn't Dad give their old places to this twisted, bitter woman?

Parker forced a smile. "No, thank you. I'll just go up. I don't want to bother you."

"Fine. Go ahead."

Parker left her suitcase at the bottom of the stairs, noticing there wasn't a wheelchair lift. Perhaps

Catherine didn't come upstairs? Either Dad had turned his old den into a ground floor master bedroom, or they didn't sleep together. Or he carried her upstairs? That sounded dangerous. And wouldn't work with a broken leg.

For a short time in high school, Parker had been her father's most diligent matchmaker, worried that when she went to college he'd be left alone, unable to take care of himself and going to seed like some absent-minded professor in an old movie. He'd dated the sister of one of Parker's teachers for quite a while, and she'd been happy with that. No, it was specifically the thought of him and Catherine Ryden together that made her stomach turn.

Parker's old bedroom had been repainted, the dated posters taken down, and the comforter replaced with a quilt. A colorful rag rug warmed the refinished wooden floor, and the scarred old bureau and vanity set had been polished to a shine, their surfaces cleared of clutter. Parker could stand in the middle of the room, shut her eyes, and see the way she'd left it, laundry and books strewn across every surface, closet doors hanging open. She could feel the echo of her last moments in here, shaking the detritus of high school from her backpack and filling it with hastily selected clothes, makeup, shoes, laptop. At the time, Parker didn't realize that was it. She expected to be caught and convinced to stay, or to cool down and return in a week or two and find a less devastating way to solve everything.

But neither of those things happened. And she'd never come back until now.

She imagined Dad sorting through the mess she'd left, trying to decide what to keep, what to throw away. Catherine had said her things were still here. Parker pulled open bureau drawers and slammed them shut one at a time: empty, empty, empty. Then she threw open the closet and found three good-sized cardboard boxes piled atop each other, with COREY in black marker on the sides. A few familiar jackets still hung on hangers, perfectly good fall and winter coats that her father probably couldn't bear to give away. Parker held one for a moment, thinking about bringing it back to Oregon, not out of sentimentality but because it was warm and waterproof and nicer than anything she'd been able to afford for herself. Then she let it go.

The top box wasn't heavy, and the contents didn't shift when she lifted it off the pile and set it on the bed, so she wasn't surprised to find it chock full of clothes.

The middle box was more interesting, with favorite childhood books and a few knick-knacks and souvenirs. She turned over a chipped brass rabbit she'd bought on a field trip in grade school, its smooth weight familiar and comforting.

The last box held a mélange of costume jewelry, as tangled as she'd left it, and a pile of notebooks which made her shake her head—old Algebra notes are not sentimental objects, Dad. Underneath was a layer of framed pictures, carefully wrapped, including her favorite of Mom and Dad and her infant self, and some unframed snapshots from middle school and high school that she used to have up on a bulletin board. Corey and Britt and Krista and Eric and Jess in different combinations. Since Jess had just asked about him, she noticed Krista's little brother Keith in a few. He'd been a cute kid, dark-haired and gangly, easily a foot taller than Krista even when he was a freshman and she a junior.

Parker laughed out loud when she found one of Eric leering in an exaggerated fashion at Britt's bikini and set it aside to show Jess. There were other friends, too, who'd spent a year or two as part of the crowd and then drifted away, and she studied their faces, reaching back through time for their names, wondering where they'd ended up.

With a half-smile, she shuffled through the whole stack. When she found a good one of Britt, she compared her lively, laughing features with her mother's cold and haughty visage. How could Parker have imagined they looked alike? And Jess. Parker had remembered his high school self well, but comparing the pictures with his adult face underlined the changes she'd noticed.

She wanted to keep all of these, she realized, and the framed picture of her young parents. She set them in a pile on the floor, then flipped through the notebooks, seeing that the class notes were interspersed with song lyrics and poetry and prose she'd written herself, her form of doodling in high school and probably why Dad had kept them. God, back then she would have been horrified to imagine him seeing these, but now she guessed they were probably no different from any other teenager's, as age-appropriate as the scribbles they'd all brought home from kindergarten, and heartwarming in their own way.

Reluctantly, Parker closed the three boxes and put them away. Someday, she'd bring everything out to Oregon, or winnow it down and ship what she really wanted. But for now, the photos were enough. They would fit in her carry-on without too much rearranging.

Downstairs, Catherine was nowhere to be seen, and instead of calling out a goodbye, Parker lifted her suitcase and let herself silently out the front door.

Chapter Eleven

Mrs. Laine was in the yard across the street, snipping at the smooth top of a low hedge with gardening shears. "Have a nice visit?" she called.

"Yes, thank you," Parker said. Unfortunately, even this cool response was enough to encourage Mrs. Laine, who barely glanced both ways before rushing across the street toward her.

Parker focused on her phone to order another Uber and pretended not to notice the neighbor's approach.

"Your father was so kind to take her in," the woman said, in a voice that intimated nasty secrets.

Hating herself for it, Parker fell for the bait. "Mrs. Ryden?" she said. "What do you mean?"

"Oh, my. That poor woman lost everything." Mrs. Laine shook her head regretfully.

Parker could tell where this was going. The neighbor's tone was rife with assumption and insinuation. Parker had developed an allergy to this kind of gossip while Britt was missing. Nevertheless, she said, "Well, she seemed okay. I mean, I hadn't known she was in a wheelchair now, but..."

"Oh yes, it's some kind of nerve disease. What's it called? It's truly awful, you can't imagine. She just went from walking around healthy as you please to being stuck in that chair in a matter of months."

"Multiple sclerosis?" Parker ventured.

Mrs. Laine nodded vigorously. "I think so. And of course, you know about her daughter being killed. And on top of that, her husband blamed her and her other kids aren't speaking to her!"

Parker's ears pricked up. "Blamed her for what?"

"For the middle one. Brittany? Was that her name, your little friend? Poor dear. Well, it turned out that Catherine had made her—you know—get rid of a baby! That would drive any girl away in this day and age!"

Parker looked at her blankly.

Mrs. Laine's voice dropped to a whisper. "She made her get an abortion!"

Parker blinked. There had been nothing about a baby or a pregnancy in the whole sordid saga of Britt's disappearance and murder, except possibly in the National Enquirer, right next to the piece on alien abductions. Her face must have betrayed shock, because Mrs. Laine nodded happily.

"Oh yes, I thought your friend would have told you, but then it would have come out in the questioning, wouldn't it, dear? No, it must have been a terrible family secret. When there are so many childless couples longing for a baby, imagine! There's no excuse, absolutely no excuse."

Parker lost her stomach for this conversation, probably due to the vile taste in her mouth. Her phone buzzed, and she looked up to see a dinged-up Toyota heading down the street toward her.

"That must be my ride," she said in relief. "Thank you again for calling me. I really appreciate it. Got to go!" She extended the handle of her case and hustled to meet the car, not looking back.

****

Parker's stomach reminded her that the hotel breakfast had been light, but she was too antsy to sit and eat. Thanks to Mrs. Ryden, she would need another hotel room. But what she needed first was some nature, and she knew where to find it.

When she moved to town at age twelve, the woods behind the grade school, bounded by a cemetery, a park, and the town reservoir, were a world in themselves with their own mysterious denizens, animal and otherwise. Sometimes there were tents pitched among the trees, and although Parker realized the people living there had probably been desperate, at the time they'd seemed mysterious, even romantic. People fished in the reservoir from dawn to dusk and sometimes kids on the path would startle deer foraging in the undergrowth or a heron hunting in the shallows.

The Uber driver dropped her at a playground near the start of the path. A bald and bearded guy supervised a couple of toddlers at a three-foot-tall climbing wall, but otherwise, all was quiet. Parker searched for a spot to leave her carry-on. In high school, everyone lugged backpacks everywhere unless someone had a car, but she really didn't want to drag her suitcase along for a hike. There was no perfect spot, so she detoured off the path to nudge it between the branches of a fallen tree, then headed down the main trail she and her friends used to meander along as teenagers.

With her quick stride, Parker passed a couple of dog walkers and found herself alone. Moving further into the woods, she shivered, but not from the cold. They had all been together here so long ago. The echoes of endless conversations between Britt and Krista and Corey still sounded in these woods. Silliness, intense discussions about the future, arguments, and angst. Romance. She often felt guilty that she'd run away and left so much behind; but now, in a bittersweet way, she remembered. She'd escaped more than the hotbed of rumor and gossip, the backstabbing of former friends and acquaintances. This place was saturated with her history and the pieces of her old self. When she'd left, it clung to her all the way across the country and up the California coast, the miasma off-gassing slowly as she traveled. And now here she was, soaking it up again despite her best intentions when she woke this morning.

Yet, it was a gorgeous fall day, the foliage in full yellow-orange splendor, the air crisp with promise. Parker wandered farther, following looping offshoots of the trail. They had loved it here, she and her friends. Most of their dramas had played out in this wood that felt like it belonged to them, separate from school and home, unsupervised by adults.

Eventually, she found herself back at the reservoir and settled on a boulder, comfortable despite the chill that seeped through her jeans. Her nose was cold, her fingers curled into the ends of her sleeves, but the stillness trumped all that.

Distant children's voices rose in laughter, some game at the school or the park, but she felt alone. Her eyes unfocused on the blur of light on water, and she let her mind go blank, fixing her awareness on the cool air entering her lungs, redolent of algae and the life-cycle of trees. Everything else faded into the background. Once in a while, she'd start thinking about Catherine or Britt or Adam or Ryan, but she let it go and relaxed into being here, breathing the same air and seeing the same sights that she had as Corey a decade ago.

Eventually, a dog barked nearby, and she roused herself to scope out the path. No one was visible, but she climbed down and stretched, once again feeling like she was getting the hang of meditation. Even here, in the heart of it all, she'd been able to center herself.

Moseying along, she finally allowed herself to consider what she'd been blocking out, what Dad's neighbor had said. She heard Mrs. Laine's voice in her head. *Catherine made her abort the baby.* Her tone held something suggestive and snide that made Parker cringe, but could it be true? Over the years, Parker had accepted that she'd probably never know exactly what happened to Britt, but she never stopped wondering. If Britt were alive, they might have grown apart by now, but that was part of growing up. Missing and murdered was different. It left a dangerous wound that spread pain and depression. Anything that shed light on what happened in Britt's life in the months before she disappeared might lead to understanding and healing.

So, Britt had been supposedly pregnant. Catherine supposedly forced her to terminate. Neither of those things was technically impossible. Britt had been sexually active. Her mother was massively controlling and viewed her children's lives as accessories that could flatter or detract from her lifestyle statement. A teen pregnancy in the family would have elicited gossip, judgment, and scorn in her social circles.

The part Parker couldn't swallow was Britt keeping it a secret.

Their small group had been through pregnancy scares together. The first, most frightening one, was early sophomore year, when Britt was barely fifteen. She and a guy named Travis Decker slept together for a couple of months, and she'd been on the pill since hitting puberty, but her period didn't come and didn't come. It was the first time any of the core group had that happen, and they whispered and searched the internet and debated urgently about whether to ask the health teacher how adoption worked if you couldn't tell your parents.

The only other scare Parker could remember was a year before Britt disappeared. Britt and Jess had been at the height of their relationship, not yet breaking up every other week. They spent all their lunches and hallway time in deep discussion and skipped classes to hold hands and stare moodily into the distance together.

Both times, Britt's period returned on its own. She would have told her friends if she'd had an abortion, because when Krista had one, they'd talked about nothing else for months. It wasn't in Britt's nature to keep something like that to herself. Sharing and venting were how she processed.

At the same time, Jess and Parker had never figured out what caused her to become distant and sometimes cruel before she left. So that was a check in the other column. Could it have been a secret pregnancy, a forced abortion? But why would she hide it from them, when they'd shared the details of everything else?

Walking through crunching leaves, Parker wondered if one or both of the earlier pregnancy scares could have ended by forced abortion. Britt would have had to lie in a way she didn't seem capable of, not just once, but over and over. And yes, her mother drove her crazy, and Britt was often angry with her—but not to the point of raging hatred, which would have been Britt's reaction to being controlled that way.

After her death, the police questioned every one of

Britt's friends up, down, and sideways, and they'd all been so young. Could they have lied or evaded questions so successfully that a secret abortion could stay hidden, even under that much pressure?

No. If it were true, Britt had kept it absolutely secret and Catherine had done an amazing job of hiding it from the media. So how would the annoying neighbor have learned about it?

Parker should let it go. It was too far-fetched, and Mrs. Laine had way too much schadenfreude showing. But there had always been unease in Parker's mind about the change in Britt before she disappeared. It had seemed like she was trying to manipulate her friends into begging for more information, but whenever Corey or Krista or Jess asked what was wrong, she denied it. They didn't know what to do but to give her more space.

In retrospect, whatever had changed her had probably been the end of Britt's world, and Parker was haunted by the fact that she hadn't tried harder to get answers.

She reached a fork in the path and had to decide whether to loop back toward the playground or keep going. She was close to the clearing where they all used to hang out, which wasn't far from where she and Jess discovered Britt's body.

Parker dreaded seeing either place because she was already knee-deep in memories. How much worse to be in the clearing. How much worse to look at the place where her stubborn optimism had collapsed under the weight of a devastating reality.

Parker's stomach growled, but she ignored it. She hadn't been here in more than eight years. She might not be here again for eight more. Like it or not, she would make herself look.

The trail had become narrow and overgrown, as if seldom used. Where did the high schoolers drink and smoke and hang out away from prying adult eyes nowadays? Parker's mind jumped to Calli, stuck at her parents' hotel, and despite the tragedy of her own group of friends, she felt a pang of sympathy. Even with everything that had gone wrong, they'd had each other. At least for a while.

Parker worried at Mrs. Laine's story as she eased past brambles. She wouldn't put it past Catherine to try to force Britt to terminate. But Britt would never let her mother bully her into anything. If there had been a secret pregnancy and a secret abortion, Britt must have cooperated for her own reasons. Unless Catherine had some way to blackmail her. Parker almost laughed. What could Catherine do, drug her and drag her to a clinic? How would she find a doctor who would go along with that? And how would she keep Britt quiet afterward, kill her? Not funny.

A flash through the trees startled her, and Parker halted. Something pale and swift, there and gone. A white-tailed deer, a startled bird? She paused, holding her breath, hoping for the deer. It would be a reward for coming out here and facing her past, a good omen.

Instead, her stillness revealed crunching footsteps through the dead leaves somewhere ahead. She couldn't see anything and stepped off the path toward the noise, then paused again. Silence. A thicket of bushes taller than her head, evergreen with shiny leaves, blocked her view.

Damn. She turned back to the path, and someone yelled "Ha!" and jumped out in front of her.

Screeching, she threw her arms in front of her face, ducking down as if that would protect from an attack. Britt's corpse flashed into her mind in a moment of terror and self-recrimination. Why had she come here alone, so close to where her friend had been murdered?

But instead of an onslaught of blows, a hand grabbed her upper arm, and a not-unfamiliar voice said, "Hey! Hey, Corey. Oh my god, I'm sorry! Calm down. It's me. It's Eric."

Parker blinked, and breathed, and blinked again, and her brain finally picked out a few familiar features in the man in front of her.

"Holy—holy shit! You idiot!" she cried, and smacked his arm like they were still in high school, but somehow she was smiling too, all that adrenaline washing out in a flood of relief. "What the hell are you doing out here? Oh my god." Her heart pounded like it would break her ribs, and her face was hot with embarrassment. There had been a moment—a brief moment, but still—when she had absolutely believed she was about to die.

"I couldn't believe it when I spotted you on the trail," he said. "Corey Jantzen, in the flesh. You grew up, girl! But I'd know you from a mile away."

Parker looked him up and down. He wore a white tech shirt, short running shorts that revealed muscular legs, and trail shoes without socks. In high school, he'd been a skinny tech-geek type, smart and intense and definitely not athletic, but he and Jess had been best friends and his dark sarcasm fit the group dynamic. Parker noticed a wedding band on his left hand, and abstract tattoos on both wiry biceps.

"You look great," she said, shaking her head. "I

honestly—seriously, what are the chances of us running into each other out here?"

"I live here! I mean, not here, in the woods, but I still live in town, and I run here on my lunch break almost every day. So the odds are good for you to find me, but what the heck are you doing here?"

"Yeah. Good point. I'm visiting my father. He was in a car accident, but he's fine, so I'm here for just a couple of days. I wanted to see where—you know. Where we grew up."

His face sobered. "Oh, yeah, man. You haven't been back in a while, huh?"

"Never."

She could see the memory of that last year flicker across his face. She hadn't said goodbye to anyone, she'd just left. Eric might still be upset with her. It must have hurt his feelings too, but she'd never given him a second thought. The big hurts were enough to carry. The two of them hadn't been that close, but thinking about it, Britt had disappeared and they'd all been wounded, no matter what degree of closeness they'd shared. And then Britt was dead, and Corey was gone too. It must have been hard. Parker had left a note for her dad, but hadn't been nearly as thoughtful to her friends, as if her anger at Jess slopped over onto them.

Eric didn't seem to hold a grudge, though. He slapped her on the shoulder again. "Huge coincidence," he said, grinning. "Awesome. Listen, I need to finish this run, okay, but do you want to get together later? Come over, have a beer, meet my wife and kid?"

Parker snorted. "What! Are you serious? You joined the legions of breeders. Wait, you're not really Eric, are you?" He'd been hugely cynical about the 'mindless rush to pair up and breed,' in high school, grumbling about over-population.

"It's pretty wild," he acknowledged. "Listen, I didn't bring my phone. I'll give you my number, you text me later, and we'll figure out a time."

"Yeah, okay. That sounds really nice, thanks."

He dictated the number. She keyed it into her contacts, and he raced off into the woods. Catching her breath, she stared after him.

****

Parker smiled to herself as she walked back toward the park. Like Krista, Eric had weathered their high school tragedy and segued into a normal life. Once she would have hated him for that and hated herself for being the weak one. Now she was happy for him. Mostly. Okay, there was still a tiny shred of resentment. How many murdered bodies had he stumbled upon?

Parker ignored that line of thought. It would be interesting to see Eric's home, meet his wife and kid. A break from her own family stuff. And no doubt good for her, to see up close that she was probably jumping to conclusions about his gloriously easy and fulfilling life. He must have his own challenges, his own hang-ups. Everyone did, or so she'd heard.

Krista had gone to the five-year class reunion a few years back, but Parker shut her down every time she tried to talk about it, so she wasn't sure if Eric had attended. You could have offered Parker a million dollars and she would have refused to attend. Dealing with everyone's morbid curiosity about where she'd disappeared to and what she'd been up to sounded awful. After Britt was found, nasty rumors about Corey and Jess spread like a virus, and Parker had been sure they'd smile to her face to glean information about her but continue speculating wildly and unkindly behind her back.

Possibly, she should give everyone more credit.

After talking to Eric, she felt like she could run into almost anybody from high school and be comfortable chatting with them for a few minutes. As long as they didn't want career details, she'd be fine. It probably wouldn't seem like a big deal to anyone else, but it was huge for her to let go of some of that anxiety, and she felt her shoulders drop.

At the playground, she retrieved her suitcase and called for a ride back to the hotel. Hospital visiting hours started at two, so she stopped at the Starbucks in the hotel lobby and picked up a bagel, then walked over to see Dad.

Her time in the woods had blunted the jagged edges of her encounter with Catherine, but she braced herself. This meeting with her father should be a happy one, but Parker deserved an explanation.

Outside his room, she paused, not liking the self-righteous tone of that thought. What had she done to deserve anything? She could argue it was her right as a daughter, but she certainly hadn't volunteered much about the ups and downs of her own life. They spoke every few weeks, but she avoided confiding in him. She wasn't planning to tell him about the recent murders when he should be focusing on his health, but he would surely prefer to know if he had a choice.

Was it the same for him? Maybe he'd felt the distance between them meant not talking about the relationship with Catherine, because she didn't need to know. And if she ever did visit—well, he could tell her then. He never would have predicted this emergency trip.

But it was Parker's childhood home, goddammit! And it was Catherine 'the bitch' Ryden!

She rode the surge of adrenaline through the door, striding in as if about to confront an adversary.

Instead, she found her father propped up in bed with an expectant smile, which warmed as he saw her. He looked thin and tired, but the gray color in his cheeks had warmed.

"I thought I imagined you this morning!" he said.

"No, it's really me!" Parker bent to kiss his cheek. They weren't a demonstrative pair, she and her dad. Too much time apart. But he looked so vulnerable, and her anger was undermined by a rush of concern.

"I still can't believe you came all the way across the country for this!" He patted the broken leg where it lay beneath a sheet, oversized with the boot-like cast at the end.

"Yeah, well. It's not a big deal." She sat next to the bed, noticed him trying to struggle upward to face her at a more natural angle, and leaped up. "Do you want me to raise the bed? Should I get a nurse?"

He laughed. "Parker, calm down. I'm fine. Look, there's a button here. I was just trying to find it." The bed whirred, and he attained a more upright position. "That's better. Sit down."

She sat and they looked at each other. There was a brief silence. Words about Catherine lined up on her tongue, but she still hadn't decided how to say them.

"So you got leave from work?" he asked after a moment. "That's good. Not all jobs would let you take off like that."

"It wasn't a problem," she said. "I told them it was a family emergency."

"And your dog? What's her name, Mousy?"

"Mouse. Je—A friend is watching her." Another topic to avoid, because she was still a little miffed Dad gave Jess her number, plus she didn't want him to assume anything.

"Good. How long can you stay?"

"Not very long, Dad. There's a lot going on back home. I just wanted to make sure you were all right."

He nodded, smiling. A silence, again. This time, she broke it. "Dad, I went over to the house this morning."

His face sobered. "Oh. Parker—"

"So I saw what you did, the bathroom and the counters and the ramp. And I talked to Catherine. Dad, how could you?" Her throat closed up and hot tears came to her eyes, and she realized it wasn't anger that she felt—it was betrayal.

He hesitated, looking lost. "She's not what you think." He reached for her hand. "Parker, you don't know her. It's hard, as a kid, to understand the adults around you. You just see one part of them, and you judge them harshly. It's natural."

"She hated me. She hated Jess! She publicly blamed us, both of us, for Britt's death! She is such a hypocrite!"

"I know. It was an awful time. Parker, try to understand. She was lashing out. She was so hurt, so heartbroken." His voice was soothing as he squeezed her hand. She yanked it away.

"No! We were kids, Dad. She was supposed to be an adult! And she permanently warped our lives because she was sad? She wasn't sad. She was an evil bitch to Britt, all the time. She probably killed her herself!"

Dad shook his head. "You know that's not true. Honey, I'm not sure we're going to see this the same way. I'm not trying to nominate her for 'Mother of the Year.' But there were pressures in that household you don't know about, and you got everything just from Britt's point of view. Yes, they had a poor relationship in the years before Britt died, but that made losing her worse, not easier. Parents always think that the next phase will come along, and they'll get along better with their kids then." His voice trailed off.

"She ruined our lives," Parker repeated stubbornly. He was her dad. He shouldn't forgive that, not ever.

"I'm sorry, honey. I'm so sorry you had to go through all that." His voice caught, and she looked up to see tears in his eyes.

Parker took a deep breath, and they sat for a minute. Then she said, "Okay. You're right. I don't think we're going to see this the same way. I'm just—I feel like I can't really go home anymore because *she's* there. I mean, is she your girlfriend? Are you sleeping with her?"

He flushed. "Parker! Don't—You can't—" He sighed deeply and started again. "I asked her to move in two years ago, when her MS flared up and she ended up in the wheelchair. We'd become friends, very close friends. It's complicated. Her illness, our history. Her grief. She's not a well woman, Parker."

"So she's not your girlfriend, but you basically rebuilt our house for her," Parker stated.

He narrowed his eyes, the way he did when she crossed the line as a kid. "I 'basically' did," he said. "If I'd imagined that you would at some point in your adulthood need to move back in, I may not have done that. But it seems extremely unlikely that will happen. Unless you get hit by a bus and need a place to recuperate."

"Or if you do," she said and nodded to the cast. "How is it going to work, her in the wheelchair, you in the cast? She can't help you, and you can't help her."

His face hardened. "I'm not her nurse, Parker, and I'm not going to need a nurse. Okay? Leave it."

She did. Her father seldom got angry, but the warning signs were there in his voice. Just like when she was in high school, she'd pull a strategic retreat and come in from another angle later.

Or not. He'd made his choices, and he was right. They didn't affect her day-to-day life at all. What she'd lost was the assumption that her old home was there, just in case, if she wanted it. Now she knew it wasn't.

"Okay." She tried a smile. "I get it. Well, I don't get it, but it's your choice and your house."

He relaxed. "Good. And Parker—I am sorry I never told you about Catherine. It was cowardly of me. I couldn't find the right time, and we don't talk enough as it is. But I should have."

Parker shrugged, done with the topic. "So, does it sound like they're letting you out tomorrow, for sure?"

He fell back into the pillows and groaned. "I'd be fine checking out today, but the doctor wants to keep an eye on me in case the fever comes back. I'm exhausted, and I know I'll rest better at home, in my own bed. But I guess I should stay. What do you think?"

Parker made a face. "I guess you're lucky they have room for you and aren't rushing you out the door. Or maybe you have fantastic insurance. I don't know, Dad."

He shook his head again. "I feel fine," he repeated, but he looked old and wan.

She stood up. "You should be resting." Belatedly, she noticed a couple of paperbacks and a stack of magazines by the bed, and a plant with a little "Get Well" balloon on the table under the TV. "You had some visitors."

"Yes, a delegation from the college. I don't know if you remember them, Chris and Patti? They brought a card from everyone in the department."

"I can't believe they're still there. Do you need anything else? Do you want anything from home?"

He smiled. "What, you'll brave Catherine again, for my sake?" Then he sobered. "No. She called and said she'd stop by and bring me some things. She didn't mention she'd seen you, though."

"It was brief," Parker said.

"Actually, you should go back over there. I have some boxes I packed with some of your old stuff you might want."

"I saw them. They're too big to bring on the plane. I'll ship them another time. But I grabbed the photos. Thank you for collecting them."

"I thought you might want the notes too," he said.

"The notebooks? No, those can be recycled. They were just doodles from old classes."

"No, the notes. I chuckled when I found them. You and your friends used to fold them up like origami, remember? Like that would keep anyone from reading them. But it worked, at least for me. I knew I could never fold them back up the right way and you'd figure out I'd been spying on you!"

"Huh, I didn't see any notes in there. It's okay. I'll get them next time. We'll plan another visit before too long, a real one." She moved toward the door.

He fought to keep his eyes open. "That pretty green box," he said. "Where did you get it?"

"I don't know, Dad." She wasn't sure what he was talking about, but it didn't seem important. "I'll come back later."

"Good night," he said muzzily.

"See you later."

Chapter Twelve

As she made her way out of the hospital, her phone dinged with an incoming text. She glanced down, expecting a notification from Jess or maybe Krista, who was probably salivating to hear about her visit home.

The text wasn't from either of them.

Calli—*Talked to ur friend. Hope ur dad is ok. Hugs—*

Parker—*Tx, don't worry. He's fine. Be back tomorrow or next day.—*

Calli—*Good—*

She was a sweet kid, obviously lonely, and Parker thought again about trying to get her involved with other kids her own age. Maybe she wouldn't let her parents interfere, but Parker was an outsider. She could be like the cool aunt.

While she had her phone out, she texted Krista.

—Ran into Eric. He's married?!—

She followed it up with a text to Jess.

—Ran into our biggest fan (C. Ryden) :(Hope the pups are good! Will tell all later.—

It was still early in the afternoon and there were hours before dinner at Eric's. She could hunt down a bottle of wine to bring—a walk to the liquor store and back didn't sound too bad. She could go for an actual run, as her stroll through the woods hadn't been all that strenuous. Or she could work out in the hotel gym.

The desk clerk informed her there was a nice wine shop two blocks away, and she walked over and picked out a mid-range bottle of red to bring with her, wondering if Eric would laugh. Doing something like this made her feel like they were just playing at being grownups. Although was it rude to bring wine when half of a couple might be breast-feeding?

Afterwards, she opted for the gym, knowing she'd sleep better if she got a workout. The three-hour time difference was weird, but she didn't want to adapt too much, since the trip would be so short.

It was while she was on the floor mat doing crunches that Dad's words clicked. "The pretty green box," he'd said. She'd noticed a shoe-box off to one side in the closet in her old room, but it had been orange.

One pretty green box from the past stood out, but it hadn't belonged to Parker. Britt had a carved wooden chest a little bigger than most shoeboxes, stained jade green, where she stashed her notes from middle school onward. The box had a hidden latch, so it was impossible to open unless you knew it was there. It was an illusory privacy, not hard to figure out, but good enough to deter casual spying.

Was Dad saying that Britt's box of notes was in Parker's stuff? How would it have gotten there? He must be mistaken, but he'd never been in Britt's room, so how would he know what the wooden chest looked like? Unless Catherine brought it when she moved in. That was possible, although it seemed weird that she would care enough about it to bring with her, and then lose it.

Parker was curious. Very curious. What if there was something in there that mentioned the supposed pregnancy and abortion? What if there was finally another name, someone who could account for Britt's missing months, between her disappearance and her murder?

But if Catherine had the box, wouldn't she have read all the contents already, not to mention passing them on to the police? There couldn't be any real bombshells in there.

Parker was hypothesizing without enough information. Fantasizing, more like. And there wasn't anything she could do about it, anyway.

She took her sweaty self back to the room and showered, and it was in the shower that she realized there was one thing she could do. She could go back to Dad's and say she wanted to look in her room again. What was Catherine going to do, bite her? Parker wasn't sixteen anymore, easy to intimidate or shame. She had a right to be there, and so, unhappily, did Catherine, and they would both have to deal with it.

"Kind, calm, compassionate," Parker reminded herself. Talk about fantasizing. She wasn't ready for compassion toward Catherine. Pulling a face in the mirror, she blow-dried her hair for the first time since the Tyler Bettering job interview.

She texted Eric to find out what time to show up and calculated a time allowance for a quick stop at Dad's. She'd have a good excuse to get out of there quickly, although she couldn't imagine needing one, because neither she nor Catherine would seek conversation. Knock on the door, be let in, run upstairs to her room, find the box, get out. And if the box wasn't in the bedroom, if it was in one of Catherine's spaces like her downstairs studio? Well, that meant it was off limits, right?

But now Parker really wanted to read those notes. She would have to play it by ear.

****

A few blocks from Dad's house, Parker said, "Just drop me here," and the Uber driver, a sixty-something woman with hoop earrings as big as bracelets, pulled up in front of a coffee shop. Parker hopped out. In high school, it had been a popular ice cream parlor, with lines extending down the block on hot summer days. She peered inside. Lights were off, and a woman with a broom was sweeping around an array of wooden tables, chairs overturned on top. The glass display cases held a smattering of baked goods. She could use a latte or chai tea as an excuse for minor procrastination, but when she tried the door, it was locked, and the sweeping woman shot her a dirty look.

Parker continued down the sidewalk. She hadn't wanted Catherine to see her being dropped off, so she could use the "I was in the neighborhood" defense. It was probably overkill, but Parker didn't want her to get curious about what might be in the old bedroom that was so intriguing she'd made a second trip.

The house remained quiet after she knocked on the door. She waited a full minute, then jabbed the doorbell twice in quick succession. When she was a kid, she'd hated it because it was loud and grating like an old-fashioned alarm clock, but it was definitely audible anywhere in the house.

Self-consciously, Parker glanced around. A curtain jerked in the window across the street. Was Mrs. Laine spying twenty-four seven? Maybe there was a Mr. Laine, and they worked in shifts. She had mentioned a sister-in-law, too. Could be a family undertaking.

When the door opened, Parker turned quickly with a polite smile. Catherine raised her eyebrows. A long skinny paintbrush was held carefully in one hand and there was a smudge of green on one cheek.

"I'm sorry," Parker said. "I didn't mean to disturb you."

"I was busy," Catherine said flatly. "I didn't think you'd come back." Then anxiety flashed across her face. "Is it Brian? Is he all right?"

"Yes, sorry. I didn't mean to scare you. No, he just, he mentioned some things in the boxes that I didn't take the time to look at, and since I'm probably going home tomorrow, I wanted to come back and look again."

"Oh. Okay." Catherine still sounded disgruntled, but she wheeled back from the door, and Parker stepped inside.

"Thanks. I really am sorry to disturb you."

Catherine continued down the hall and said over her shoulder, "Don't worry about it. You can let yourself out when you're done."

Well, that was easy. Parker trotted up the stairs and flung open the closet. Three large boxes with her old name. A couple of shoeboxes that, upon further inspection, held unused pairs of Dad's favorite sneakers. Miscellaneous outdoor gear shoved in next to Parker's old coats, and piles of extra blankets and pillows on the top shelf.

Frustrated, Parker pulled out the cardboard boxes again. The clothes box really was clothes, all the way down. She reopened the one with the notebooks and shuffled through it, but still didn't find Britt's green chest. A few folded notes had fallen down to the bottom. They were Parker's: a birthday note from Britt and a mushy love note from a guy Parker dated in eighth grade.

She put the boxes back and looked around for inspiration. The green box had to be here, unless Dad was really mixed up.

But where? And how would it have gotten here?

When Catherine moved in, or when the construction was happening downstairs, it could have been shifted from one of her piles to one of his piles. That seemed plausible.

Parker considered whether Catherine might be pretending to be confined to a wheelchair, à la far too many sitcom plots, and had retrieved the chest after Dad had seen it. That was hard to imagine. Even Catherine frigging Ryden wouldn't stoop so low as to fake needing a wheelchair. And why would she?

Parker pushed the sliding doors open as wide as possible to peer behind them. There was no light in the shallow interior, and the crammed rod made it hard to see well. In desperation, she pushed all the old coats and winter gear to one side and stood on tiptoe. Finally! It had been in plain sight all along, for anyone taller than five foot ten. The wooden chest was on the top shelf, way over to the right, partially obscured by a pile of blankets.

Narrowly avoiding pulling the blankets down on her head, she edged the chest off the shelf. Her heart pounded. It was a time capsule. It had been a feature of Britt's dresser for as long as Parker could remember, a treasure trove of secrets. She hesitated, anticipating the fresh pain that would come from reading their hopeful young voices, ignorant of all the shit that was coming down the road.

Nevertheless, Parker carried it to the bed and sat with it on her lap, fingers on the hidden latches that would release the lid. Dad must have opened it, since he'd seen the notes, but he'd always been good at puzzles. He would have turned it over in his long fingers, finally finding the pressure points. It had taken Parker more than a few sessions, hanging out in Britt's room and poking at the thing with increasing frustration as they chatted or watched TV, but once solved, it seemed obvious.

The lid sprang open. Notes were heaped inside, several inches deep in a velvet-lined interior, some of the paper still crisp and white, some soft and gray or yellowing. Some were folded into squares, but most were triangular, about an inch and a half long. The faint smell of pine cleaner wafted out, and in a flash of memory, Parker saw Britt sitting on her bed the day after Christmas one year, squirting a new bottle of floral perfume into the lining, then gagging in disgust and wiping it out with pine cleaner from under the bathroom sink.

Parker itched to open the notes, but she felt exposed sitting here with Catherine right downstairs. It didn't matter what sort of feelings Catherine had or claimed to have about Britt's death, what sort of narrative she'd created that allowed her to paint herself as a loving, grieving mother. It would be a betrayal of Britt's memory to accept that there was anything valid about Catherine's point of view. So Parker didn't want to talk about it. Catherine couldn't know Parker was taking the chest.

The suitcase was safely stashed back at the hotel, and she hadn't thought this far ahead. How could she hide what she was taking? She emptied some clothes out of one of the cardboard boxes, wrapped the chest in an old sweater and squished it into the leftover space.

Closing the flaps, she stuffed the extra clothes into the other two boxes and slid them back into the closet, rearranged the pile of blankets on the upper shelf until it didn't look like anything was missing, and closed the sliding doors. She gave the room a quick once over. Just the way she'd found it. At the last second, she grabbed the wine bag and looped the handles over her wrist, then clomped down the stairs, cradling the cardboard box awkwardly in her arms.

The foyer was clear, no sign of Catherine. Trying to be less rude this time, Parker called out, "Thank you! Goodbye!" as she grappled for the knob.

From much closer than expected, Catherine said, "Oh, you decided to take some of your stuff?" and Parker jerked around to see her sitting by the window in the front room.

Prickles of heat ran across Parker's face and chest in guilty embarrassment. "Uh, yes. I decided to ship it myself. Dad probably won't be getting around to extra errands anytime soon."

"Did they say, is he going to be able to drive?"

"I don't know, honestly. The boot is on his left leg, so probably."

She nodded.

Parker grasped the knob again.

"You know, Corey, it might not mean anything to you now, but Jesse Coburn really was an undesirable character. I know you were angry that I blamed him, but he was self-centered and short-sighted. Very spoiled. You have no idea what he put her through."

Parker stiffened. Had Dad told Catherine that Jess and Parker were in touch? Plus, had Catherine conveniently forgotten that she'd accused Parker too?

Catherine wasn't finished. She spoke with an urgency that implied she'd been waiting to say the words for a long time. "You were too young to see it back then. Maybe you still are. The quiet, charming ones are the worst. He was manipulative. He had a dark side."

Parker's hand squeezed the knob and then released it. She should just leave, but she turned to face Catherine instead. "You don't know what you're talking about. You barely knew him. You barely knew any of us."

"Teenagers always think that. But when you're older, you have more experience. I knew his type." She drew nearer, looked up into Parker's face with beseeching eyes.

"How?" Parker demanded. "Were you even in the same room with him, with any of us, for more than five minutes at a time? You were barely part of Britt's life until she died. She was an inconvenience, an embarrassment, and you jumped to conclusions about her and all the rest of us too." Parker's voice picked up speed, a triggered avalanche.

Catherine jerked back like she'd been slapped. "Don't tell me how I felt about my daughter. Britt lied to you, all of you. She twisted everything around."

"You're so full of shit." Parker grabbed the doorknob again, breathing hard and shaking with anger.

"Jess killed her for killing his baby," Catherine snapped.

A noise escaped Parker, somewhere between a gasp and a snort.

"Oh yes," Catherine continued. "Their filthy little sex games. They thought I didn't know, but I caught them. He wouldn't use protection, so guess what

173

happened? He ruined her life."

"That's ridiculous," Parker said. "Jess and Britt broke up six months before she disappeared. Whatever happened between them had nothing to do with it. Plus, Britt wasn't pregnant. I would have known."

"No. She took care of it early. She didn't want any of you to know. But he wouldn't stop tormenting her afterwards. He drove her crazy."

Catherine's words twinged uncomfortably in Parker's mind. Jess had just said something similar. Britt drove him crazy, to the point where he didn't recognize himself. Parker said, "Funny how all this happened without her closest friends knowing anything about it."

"You were fucking him. She knew you wouldn't believe her." Catherine's mouth twisted as if it hurt to curse.

"Oh, so she confided in you, her loving mother?" Parker pulled the door open at last, the wine bag biting painfully into her arm as the heavy bottle swung with her movement. "Keep your nasty fairy-tales to yourself. We loved Britt. You're the one who made her life a misery."

Catherine moved in close, so her chair hit Parker's legs. Her face was white, her eyes blazing. She'd seemed frail and small—but not anymore. Parker lifted the box up and away from her to avoid banging Catherine's head, but the older woman was doing her best to intimidate. And she was succeeding.

"I never laid a hand on that girl," Catherine spat. "I loved her. She was my daughter, and I did my best for her every—single—day."

With each of her last three words, she forced the chair into Parker, its normally quiet motor making an unhappy whine. Trapped against the door, Parker stumbled, dropping the cardboard box. The wine bag slipped off her wrist and she grabbed for it as the door hit the inside wall. Parker tripped over Catherine's feet and ended up on the floor as the glass bottle bounced on the wood with a thunk.

Catherine's ragged breath combined with Parker's in the new silence. Parker levered herself to a sitting position, reached for the plastic bag and checked the bottle. The heavy glass hadn't broken. Two feet away, though, the cardboard box had not landed well. It was on its side, contents spilling out, the corner of the jade green chest protruding from Parker's old sweater. She prayed Catherine wouldn't notice, but it was too late.

Catherine's face crumpled as she recognized the chest immediately. "Where did you get that?" she whispered. "I threw it away."

Parker climbed to her feet. Her right knee was going to have a hell of a bruise and her funny-bone throbbed from her elbow hitting the edge of the door. She backed away from Catherine and crouched to tuck everything back into the cardboard. "I guess my dad—" she started, but stopped at the look in Catherine's eyes.

"He wouldn't do that!" she screeched. "He wouldn't do that!"

"I'm sorry." Parker's anger had faded to a kind of hollowness. She stepped toward the doorway without turning her back on Catherine.

"That's not yours," Catherine said. "Leave it here. Give it to me."

"No," Parker said.

She backed through the storm door. Her eye caught movement in the street. Mrs. Laine had halted two feet short of the sidewalk with her mouth hanging open, oblivious to the possibility of traffic. This must be like Christmas for her, such a juicy fight with the door wide open.

Parker turned to close it behind her, to belatedly protect Catherine's privacy, but Catherine was right there and she met Parker's eyes again. "It's full of poison," she said, almost sadly. And let the door slam shut.

Chapter Thirteen

Mrs. Laine's mouth worked as she reached for something to say, but Parker hurried down the steps and onto the sidewalk, putting as much space as possible between herself and whatever had just happened. When she slowed two blocks later, readjusting the box and the wine bag to less painful positions, her heart was still pounding as if she'd run from a bear. Unless she got a handle on her mental state, she would not be good company.

The sidewalk was deserted. Parker set everything down and pulled out her phone, then hesitated. Did she still want to visit Eric and his wife? Not really. She wanted to run, fast and far, until she couldn't hear Catherine's furious accusations or feel the wheelchair hitting Parker's legs. If running didn't work, she had the whole bottle of wine. That would calm her down. And visiting Dad at the hospital, drunk or hungover, that would be lovely.

With some extended exhales, she slowed her pulse. Catherine Ryden had always been a bitch. She'd been testing Parker, trying to see which button would get the most reaction. Time after time, Catherine had tried the same strategy on Britt, offering different poisonous interpretations of events until she found leverage to drive a wedge between Britt and all of her friends. But Britt grew a thick skin and an excellent bullshit detector, and

Parker liked to think she had too.

Parker would be leaving tomorrow. There wouldn't be another chance to see Eric, and Catherine shouldn't be allowed to take that away.

Parker looked at the innocuous box on the sidewalk, which now felt like a time-bomb. Catherine's final words made Parker even more certain the chest held an important piece of the past. She'd have to bring it with her to Eric's house. What if Eric was curious and asked to look inside?

Parker snorted, realizing she'd entered the realm of ridiculous paranoia. Eric wouldn't know Britt's wooden chest was there unless she told him, and of all their friends, he'd probably care the least. No, Parker would say she'd picked up some stuff from her dad's house and leave it at that, despite the temptation to vent about Catherine. That little story could be saved for Krista. And Jess? Maybe an edited version. Or, however random and ridiculous it had been, should Parker ask him about Catherine's accusation?

She would think about that later.

Parker was about to let Eric know she was running late, but her phone buzzed and a notification popped up. Calli again.

—*Sorry 2 bug u. coming home soon?*—

Parker swiped the notification away. Calli must be bored, but Parker didn't have time to chat. She called Eric.

"Hey, I'm running late. Just leaving my dad's now. I'm gonna call an Uber."

"I'll come get you," he said.

"You don't have to do that."

"Not a problem. It's still your same house? That's

not far. Shoot, I could walk there in fifteen minutes."

"I've got a big box of stuff I picked up from my dad's. Don't worry about it. I can get a ride."

"No, seriously, that's silly. I'll drive over. Be there in a couple minutes."

Parker told him the street names at the intersection she'd reached, then paced restlessly. In a few minutes, an old Volvo pulled in front of her and Eric rolled down the passenger window as Parker hefted the box. He wore a button-down shirt and jeans, sleeves rolled up to reveal muscular forearms.

"Hey, little girl, want some candy?" he leered.

"I take it back. You haven't changed a bit."

"Want to put that in the back? Hang on, let me unlock the doors."

Parker set the box in the back seat and slid in the front beside him.

"Thanks for picking me up. You're bucking the trend," she said as he pulled out.

"Oh, yeah? What trend?"

"I was just noticing. Every single driveway in this neighborhood has an SUV."

He grinned. "Yeah. I'm my own man, though. Not bending to the forces of greater consumption for no real reason."

"What about snowstorms?"

He shrugged. "I've got four-wheel drive. Never had a problem."

"Nice." She wished she would see snow while she was here. That was one thing she missed from the East Coast. Out west, there hadn't been more than a couple inches at a time in years, in all the places she'd been, and even that much was rare.

The confrontation with Catherine was taking on a surreal cast in her mind. Terrifying but funny, and she could imagine Britt gasping, "Oh my effing shit, she didn't!" Horrified laughter and whispering in her bedroom while her mother stalked around downstairs like the Terminator with a stick up her butt.

"Hey, did you know my dad is living with Britt's mom?" Parker blurted. Eric was navigating through neighborhoods of one- and two- story homes on postage-stamp-sized lawns, mixed with student apartment buildings and duplexes.

He shot her a glance. "What! That's crazy. Wow, I didn't see that coming. How did that happen?"

"I have no clue. My dad didn't even warn me. I went over today thinking I'd stay in my old room tonight, and there she was. She's in a wheelchair now, M.S." Mentally, she added, *and I've got the bruises to prove it*.

"I wouldn't wish that on anybody, but it almost seems like karma. She was such a bitch to Britt," he said. "I mean, I don't think I ever met her, but I heard all the stories and I watched the news, you know—*after*."

Parker had forgotten. She'd moved to town in time for middle school, but Eric hadn't joined the group until freshman year, and by then Catherine had largely stopped showing up for school functions. Britt made the Division One girls' basketball team sophomore year, but even the championships didn't get Catherine to bleacher-sit in a noisy crowd. "Yeah, well, you really didn't miss out."

The car turned into a short, wide driveway in front of a modest brick ranch house. She said, "Hey, this is your place? It looks really nice." It was true. A few apples lay under a tree in the trim square of front lawn and a neat wooden fence hinted at the existence of a private yard out back.

"It's simple, but it's ours," he said proudly. She followed him to the front door, feeling a moment of shyness—now she would have to meet the wife and make small talk with nearly complete strangers all evening—but she quashed it quickly.

Eric reached for the knob, saying something about the house having been a fixer-upper, still in progress, and then frowned when it didn't turn. "That's funny. I thought Em would be home by now."

"Em is your wife?"

"Em is my wife and Katrina is my daughter. We call her Kat right now. Or KitKat." He dug in his pocket for keys.

"How old is the baby?"

"Eight weeks, as of tomorrow."

"Wow, you really are a new daddy! I hope your wife doesn't mind company."

Parker followed him into the house, which seemed dim and chilly, but he started flicking lights on and fiddled with the thermostat. Almost immediately, warm air started blowing, and a small but bright space took shape. Eric continued into a tiled kitchen separated from the living area by a breakfast bar.

"Em's maternity leave ends next month," he said as he stepped out of his shoes and set them by the door. "And I've been working from home, mostly, but today I ended up with a job downtown, so I thought she'd be starting dinner."

"Sorry," Parker said, feeling awkward.

He grinned. "Don't be silly. We're having spaghetti. I'll whip it up in no time. Let me text her real quick, see where she's at."

He fiddled with his phone. Parker set the box down near the door and hung up her coat, then settled on a barstool. When he put the phone back in his pocket, he said, "I forgot. KitKat had a checkup. Em will be home soon. She says to start without her."

"Is there anything I can do?"

He shrugged. "You want to look in the fridge, see if we've got salad stuff? All the veggies are in that separate drawer in the middle."

They chatted as he sautéed vegetables to go in the spaghetti sauce and Parker chopped carrots and cucumbers on a cutting board. She asked him more about Em and KitKat and his work, and he asked her about what had happened since high school, about moving so far away to exotic Oregon. She had to laugh at that as she described the sheer mundanity of the move, all the boring minimum wage jobs she'd worked, keeping it as light as possible. She couldn't help feeling like the truth under the story was coming through, the self-destruction and pessimism that had been her ball and chain for years. Something about his nice, normal life, his energy, his obvious happiness, made her feel ashamed of her crooked path. He'd been one of them. He'd lived through the tragedy. Why hadn't he gotten thrown off track, like her or Jess?

Of course, Krista hadn't either, but Parker knew she struggled internally. Eric seemed like he'd shaken the bad stuff off and grown into a normal guy. But then, he'd been more on the outside of their little circle.

Em and the baby got home just as dinner was ready, rushing through the door in a flurry of brisk air and cheeriness. Parker was surprised to recognize her as someone who'd been in the grade above them, a petite athletic redhead with braces and good grades, someone Parker had passed in the hallways for years but never gotten to know. Back then, Emily had been so far out of Eric's league that their romance now was like a fairy tale, and Parker wondered again what had transformed him from a sarcastic, self-conscious geek to a confident husband and father. What if Britt's death hadn't left him untouched, but just inspired him to live better?

Parker focused on making socially acceptable small talk for most of the evening. No murder or tragedy and as little as possible about herself or her work. She held little Kat after dinner, amazed at her tiny perfection and the powerful grip of her fist.

When the baby started fussing and Em took her upstairs, Parker sat in the living room with Eric, trying to motivate herself to leave. She'd drunk some wine and eaten a lot of pasta, and that, on top of jet lag and the warm house, was paying off in sleepiness. She wanted to check in with Jess about Mouse and Pepper and then go to bed. At the same time, Eric's little bubble of familial bliss was sweetly soporific, despite Em's wry comment that Kat had screamed for two hours straight the night before.

As the conversation lulled, Eric said into the silence, "Are you still in touch with anyone else from the old days? Have you talked to Jess?"

"Just a little. I hadn't talked to him for a long time, but he showed up just this week, on his way to Alaska. And Krista, of course. We've been in touch for ages."

"I had no idea." He sounded surprised, and maybe a little disturbed, but Parker wasn't sure about what.

"Yeah. I was surprised to see Jess, for sure. We

didn't part on the best of terms, but he came and found me, and it's been really good. He's taking care of my dog right now. Two dogs. It's a long story."

Eric laughed. "You have a new dog that you forgot about?"

Parker shrugged, not wanting to go there. "I was taking care of a dog for a friend when I got the call about my dad's accident."

"So Jess is helping you out?" he said.

"Yeah. It almost feels like none of those years had passed. I mean, we've both changed a lot, but we're still the same people, and we were close back then." She blushed at the understatement.

"Parker—" he said. He leaned forward, and then leaned back and laughed a little.

"What?"

"It's not my place to say, I just—I don't want you to get hurt again."

She hadn't expected that. "What do you mean? Hurt by what?"

"Jess. I mean, I like the guy, I always have, but—I'm not sure he's good news for the ladies."

Parker raised her eyebrows. "You are going to say more, right? You can't say that and just stop."

He took a deep breath. "Jess was my best friend in high school. And I stuck by him through everything."

"But…you're not going to tell me you think he killed Britt, are you?" Or that he tormented her? Raped her? Parker could hear the brittle edge in her voice.

"No," he said, "I never thought he killed her. But Parker, I knew about you two."

Her heart pounded. She felt automatically guilty, although she couldn't guess what he thought he knew.

He hesitated, seeming to pick his words carefully. "I know you guys were together a lot. When we all thought she had just run away."

Parker almost laughed. "Everyone knows that. It was literally in the papers. We started going out before Britt disappeared, and it might have seemed weird from the outside, but missing her brought us even closer."

"Fine. So. I'm just saying. You guys kept it pretty quiet, for most of that time, until everything hit the fan. But I knew before that. Because Jess told me. You guys were pretty hot and heavy."

Parker frowned. Jess had seemed so disturbed by the letters he was getting from someone who knew where and how and when they'd been together, which was weird if he'd gone around telling people. He may not consider Eric, who'd been his best friend, a possible suspect for the letters, but she did. She flashed to the photo stashed in her suitcase, of Eric leering at Britt. Was Eric telling the truth, or had he stalked Jess and Parker and now could not let it go? All this normalcy could be a façade.

"So what?" she said finally.

"So, I guess what I'm trying to say is—he wasn't exactly, I guess respectful is the word."

"He wasn't respectful," she echoed, not sure where he was going.

"He always wanted you, even when he was with Britt. And when he finally got with you, he talked about you like a trophy."

That didn't jibe with her recollection. She and Jess had been so tentative about getting together after he and Britt broke up, feeling guilty and defensive about their own happiness. It had been delicate, not planned, a strange relationship that might have fallen apart if Britt hadn't left, because they were both overshadowed by her. Britt and Jess had such a tempestuous relationship over the years that in the short time Jess and Parker had been together, she constantly felt like she'd wake up and find Britt had reclaimed him.

"I guess boys that age really are assholes, right?" she said uncomfortably.

Eric spread his hands. "Yeah, maybe. I'm only saying this because he's back in your life now. You should know what he was like when you weren't around. Britt messed with his head big time, and all that jerking around gave him really weird ideas about relationships. He hasn't had a single serious girlfriend since, well, since *you*."

Parker laid her hands flat on the cushions of the couch, trying to anchor herself. She said, "Today Britt's mother told me Jess was tormenting Britt before she disappeared, because he got her pregnant and she aborted the baby. Do you know anything about that?" The expression on Parker's face must have been a grimace. She was waiting—no, hoping—for him to tell her that wasn't what he'd meant at all.

Instead, he looked down. "I don't know exactly what went on between them at the end. I just know they got strange. You know how Britt was being such a cold bitch half the time—well, according to Jess, the other half the time, she was super hot for him, wanting to go at it constantly, wanting him to prove something by doing it all over the place. Like, risky places."

"Where?"

"Oh, one of the supply closets near the principal's office. In the woods, during the day, just off the path. The shed behind the elementary school."

Parker felt a stab in her heart. Those were *their* places—well, except for the supply closet. She would never have done that. "Catherine told me they were playing 'filthy sex games' and she caught them."

Eric shook his head. "I don't know. For a while, Jess had scratches and bruises all over his body, and he laughed it off and said that was the price of hot sex. Jess talked about you like you were some kind of angel compared to Britt, and it made me uncomfortable. Like he would screw with you the way she was screwing with him. Or like they were passing a disease back and forth and now he'd pass it to you, too."

Parker tried to contain an unexpected whirlwind of emotion without letting it show. Part of her wanted to lash out at Eric, for saying such things in his soft, kind voice, for regarding her with concern as he twisted the truth of Jess beyond all recognition. That hadn't been how it was with Jess and Britt, or with Jess and Parker. Parker would have known. But for a long moment, she couldn't think of anything to say that wasn't outright defensive and rude. Finally she said, "I don't remember it being like that at all."

He sat back and snorted lightly. "Yeah, well, Jess is a charmer. He dresses it up with the women, but you should hear him with the guys. That's the reality. The Jess behind the scenes. I wouldn't let him near my sister if I had a sister."

"You don't think that's normal? For most guys?" Parker made a half-hearted attempt to sound teasing.

Eric shook his head. "Not me, anyway. Not like that."

She wanted to leave, but had one more question. "So

Jess never said anything to you about a baby? About Britt being pregnant?"

He started shaking his head, then stopped and tilted it, looking up. "Umm, yeah. They had that scare, like sophomore year, right? And she wasn't pregnant. That was way before things started getting weird."

"No, I mean later on. Closer to the end."

"I don't think so. I mean, he might have joked about knocking her up, but I didn't take it seriously."

"What do you mean?"

"Like, harem stuff. Barefoot and pregnant stuff. You know."

Parker couldn't imagine Jess making light of Britt being pregnant. They'd been terrified both times Parker knew about. But she nodded and stood up. "It's been so great to see you and meet your family. I'm really glad you're doing well. You're going to be a great dad." Despite the distrust and defensiveness that had welled up in her heart when he was attacking Jess, she meant it. Eric had grown up and gotten his shit together. He'd been the smartest of the group all along, and they'd treated him like a tag-along geek, there on sufferance because of Jess.

He stood too. "It's been great to see you. I'm so glad we ran into each other! We should keep in touch. Are you on Facebook?"

"Um, as little as possible. But I'll keep your number, and hopefully I'll be back to visit my dad again sometime soon. I'll let you know when I do. And if you guys come out to Oregon…"

He laughed. "Sure. Listen, say hello to Jess and Krista for me, will ya? I mean, I'm not sure he's boyfriend material, but I miss the guy, you know?"

Chapter Fourteen

Parker maneuvered the keycard through the reader and pushed through the hotel room door. She dropped the box on the floor gratefully, rubbing the places where the corners had poked into her, and collapsed on the bed. Her phone had been vibrating on and off for the past twenty minutes, and when she pulled it out, there was a list of notifications from different people. She opened her texting app.

Dad—*When are you leaving? Would like to see you again.—*

Jess—*Mouse misses you. Pepper too. A little weird here, hope ur ok—*

Krista—*How's life in the East? Dad OK?—*

And even Calli:

—I miss you. When are you coming back?—

Parker hadn't arranged her return ticket yet, but she wanted a morning flight tomorrow. Checking online, she found a couple of options, and being so close to the airport, she could even visit Dad first if she took the 11:30 flight. She texted him back:

—Need to head back tomorrow but want to see you too. Are you getting released in the morning? What time?—

He replied that he was hoping to be out early and had arranged a ride with one of his friends from the college. Parker promised to be at the hospital by eight, so they could have breakfast or coffee together if he was up for it.

Then she stared down at Jess's text, biting her lip. Eric's supposedly well-meaning input on top of Catherine's crap—it didn't add up to anything, really. Catherine's accusation was meaningless. She'd always been venomous and manipulative, smiling coolly to their faces and pouring poison in Britt's ears behind their backs. Not to mention her baseless accusations of murder. It was a coincidence that Eric had some weird protective streak and went off on Jess's failings on the same day.

So why did Parker feel so uneasy?

Finally, she sent:

—Arriving PDX 1:30, home by 5ish—

It seemed curt, but she was too tired to untangle her feelings right now. He'd be leaving soon anyway, possibly as soon as she returned, and then she'd have space and time to figure it out.

Moving on, she tried to respond to Calli. She wasn't sure she wanted to encourage frequent texting or a real buddy-buddy relationship with the bosses' daughter, but she didn't want her to feel ignored either. Parker was shooting for positive adult mentor, but it might be hard for Calli to tell the difference without Parker spelling it out. Finally she texted:

—Coming home tomorrow. All ok?—

Sighing, Parker kicked her shoes off and padded over to solve the puzzle of the knock-off Keurig on the bureau. It eventually yielded a paper cup of chamomile tea, and she changed into pajamas and climbed under the covers before texting Krista.

—Time to talk?—

Krista answered almost immediately.

—*Sure. Yr dad ok?*—

Parker called her.

"Hey, what's up?" Krista answered warmly. "How's your dad?" Her voice was loud against a background of static.

"Is this a bad time?"

"I'm just heading inside," she explained, and the static dropped suddenly. "I was out for a walk in the wind. How's he doing?"

The sympathy in her voice made Parker's eyes tear up. She said, "He had to stay in the hospital an extra day, but he's going to be fine."

Parker didn't mean to get into all the details, but she ended up reviewing the whole day for Krista, from Catherine being Catherine to the nth power, to running into Eric, to finding the box of notes, to dinner at Eric's place.

Krista was quiet for most of the recounting, although she laughed in disbelief about Catherine and Parker's dad living together. The box of notes fascinated her. "Oh my god! I have to see those. I wonder if she saved our cartoons, do you remember? We used to pass them back and forth and add more and more details and we were such bitches!"

"Don't worry, I'll keep 'em until you visit. We can look together," Parker said, and impatiently went back to the part that was bugging her more than it should, Eric's warnings about Jess right on the heels of Catherine's accusation. Krista wasn't Jess's biggest fan, but she was Parker's best friend and she'd try to be fair. "So, what do you think of Catherine and Eric both going off on Jess?"

"We already knew Catherine considered him—and

you—major suspects. I always wondered why she didn't go after me, too," Krista said.

"Because you had all the parents fooled." Krista could fake sweet and responsible like nobody's business. "But it's not just that. The pregnancy story bugs me. Does it seem remotely possible to you that Britt had an abortion before Jess and I started going out, and then he was torturing her about it until she disappeared?"

Krista was silent for a moment. "I doubt it. Britt didn't keep things to herself. Christ, she practically took out a banner ad on the student website when she got a bladder infection, and it was a full-page ad when her period was late."

"Yeah. And I was dating Jess. How would I not have noticed if he was cyber-stalking her? Or any kind of stalking."

"Honestly? Guys can be weird. A guy on a mission can be very secretive."

"Krista, you don't really think this was for real?"

She paused long enough to make Parker uneasy. Finally, she said, "I doubt it. Catherine probably overheard something Britt said and completely misconstrued it. Remember that time we were making plans to meet at the Market Basket to get stuff for a birthday cake, and she accused Britt of drug-dealing? Like she thought we were speaking in code."

Parker laughed out loud. "I'd forgotten that. Jeez. That makes me feel better." She considered for a moment. "Well, that's Catherine. What about Eric?"

"Eric's just full of shit," Krista said.

"Right?" Parker said, relieved. "He was the geeky, less attractive sidekick all through high school. He may still have some unacknowledged resentment about that."

"No, I mean, Eric was just as nasty! High school guys are all misogynist pigs, Parker, you know that. If he's telling himself any different now, he's delusional."

"But you should see him," Parker said. "He's really happy. He's got a beautiful wife, a brand new baby he adores, a nice little house, a good job. He's even kind of hot. You wouldn't believe he's the same Eric we knew."

"Then that's the problem!" Krista said.

"What do you mean?"

She didn't answer. Parker could hear liquid pouring, and then a male voice in the background. Krista hadn't been dating anyone seriously since she moved to Washington, or at least hadn't mentioned anyone yet. Parker perked up her ears, but couldn't make out the words.

"Is that the sound of a man in your house?" Parker teased.

"Delivery guy," she said dismissively. "I'm starving. So, what if all that good stuff is too much for Eric? He's an awkward little geek inside, and he thinks he doesn't deserve what he's got. Imposter syndrome! In high school, he must have been mad with jealousy, and Jess was always cool, always good-looking, always well-liked…"

"And Eric had such a crush on Britt!"

Krista paused. "Did he say that? I always thought he was into you."

Parker snorted. "Jess said that too, but it's ridiculous. Everyone knew he liked Britt. There's no way he was into me. I don't think so, anyway."

"Well, you wouldn't, being you," Krista said. "He probably hated that Jess ended up with both Britt *and* you. Clearly not fair. So he rubs it in that he's now got it going on, and then he undermines your choices in the past. Textbook inferiority complex."

Parker laughed. Krista loved pop psychology and had a secret addiction to soap operas where everyone was motivated by petty ancient grudges, giant conspiracies, and blackmail schemes. "Okay, if you say so, Doctor Krista."

Parker's phone buzzed. It was Calli again. "Hang on a sec." She lowered the phone to look at the text.

—*Not really. Did something not-good. Talk tomorrow*—

Parker frowned and put the phone up to her ear. "Calli's being kind of weird. She keeps texting me. We barely even spoke until the day the wedding guest was murdered, and now she's texting me every few hours."

"She's a lonely kid," Krista said. "Don't encourage her. She needs to find friends her own age."

"Yeah, true." Did something not-good, though. That was a little scary. Should Parker call Marta? What if Calli had taken sleeping pills or something?

"I gotta go," she told Krista, who'd become distracted again. There were muffled voices on her end. "I need to take care of something. Call you tomorrow."

"Okay, good night," Krista said and hung up.

Parker bit her lip. She was being silly, right? Why would her mind jump to suicide? Calli said she'd talk to her tomorrow, so it couldn't be too bad. Right? But Parker couldn't calm herself down. She kept thinking, what if, what if—but she didn't want to terrify Calli's parents about what was admittedly a huge leap.

Parker texted Jess instead.

—*I have a big favor to ask you. Are you at my place?*—

Jess—*Just got in. Pepper sick, went to vet.*—

Her heart lurched.

—*Is he ok?*—

Jess—*Ate something bad. Ok now.*—

She wanted more details, but guessed Jess might have let him eat something rotten on the beach. She had to watch Mouse carefully to keep her away from dead fish, and she hadn't warned Jess.

Parker—*Good, thank you! Will pay you back. This is weird but could you check on Calli for me?*—

Jess—*Check on? Like, see where she is?*—

Parker—*Like, make sure she's acting normal. She sent strange text, said she did something not-good.*—

Jess—*Okay, hang on, I'll see if she's around downstairs.*—

Parker shook her head and smiled down at the phone. Eric's words had made her doubt her feelings for Jess and question what she thought about their shared history, but despite that, this was pretty awesome. Oh, there's a teenager that you think might be in trouble because of your traumatized tendency to jump to the worst possible conclusions? Sure, I'll check on that for you, no problem, be right back.

And her worry probably was born from her own trauma. What did "not-good" mean to a teenager? Did it actually mean bad, or did she just eat a whole pint of ice cream?

Parker texted Calli again:

—*Hey. Can talk if you need to tonight.*—

She got ready for bed while she waited for Jess to get back to her, and wished that Mouse were here. Speaking of feeling isolated. At least the cops hadn't attempted to contact her, so it was beginning to look as if the deaths had nothing to do with Parker, or they would have found some link by now. She had been self-centered to imagine there might be a connection, and a little ray of hope made itself known underneath the dread.

Jess still hadn't texted. Parker's phone sat face up on the rumpled bedspread, the screen dark. After stretching, she settled cross-legged on the second bed, and let her focus soften as she concentrated on the sense of her own breathing. Thoughts kept rising: the murders back home, Calli and her parents, Krista and Jess and Eric and Britt, Parker's teenage years which felt like a story that should have ended years ago but somehow hadn't.

She breathed slowly and evenly, and then more slowly and evenly, and time passed, and for an undefined moment, she let it all go—until the phone buzzed, and her eyes popped open, and she was back on the other bed with the phone in her hand before consciously deciding to pick it up.

Jess—*Don't see her anywhere, but her mom is on the front desk and seems fine not worried*—

And almost simultaneously, a text from Calli:

—*I'm ok, c u tomorrow, tell u then*—(followed by a horrified emoji)

Parker texted back to Jess:

—*Tx. Overreacted. C u tomorrow.*—

He sent back a little yellow heart. Parker wondered what yellow meant. She almost looked it up, and then castigated herself for being so foolish. He was a guy she used to know, doing her a favor, on his way to earn a shitload of money in Alaska to pay for college. He was not going to be her boyfriend. He was not going to stay in Newport and walk her dogs with her and go out to breakfast with her and lift what suddenly seemed like a stifling burden of loneliness from her heart. He was not.

Her emotions had been all over the place in the last hour, not to mention the whole day. She was hollow and weary, and went to bed, thinking, "Calli, I'd love to tell you it gets easier, but…"

****

Several times during the night Parker surfaced from an ongoing nightmare, helpless to resist falling back into it, but when morning came, nothing remained but a sense of dread. This was familiar from her morbidly depressed days, so she attempted to smack the sticky cobwebs from her mind with a sweaty round of speed work on the treadmill and a steaming hot shower. After that, she felt more like herself, although the shadows of the night were packed under her eyes.

No bad news awaited on her phone, which was something. She decided to focus on gratitude for the rest of the day; her dad was okay, and it had been good to run into Eric and meet his family. There was even a silver lining in the little spat with Catherine, whose nastiness made Parker feel closer to Britt and more sympathetic to how erratic she'd been in the months before she disappeared.

Parker was not thankful for all the aspersions cast on Jess's character, since she'd just forgiven and jumped into bed with the guy, but she would have to deal with that later.

Otherwise ready to leave, Parker stared thoughtfully at the large cardboard box next to the door. She hadn't forgotten about it, but she'd mentally glossed over what she would do with it. Did she have time to go to the post office or a shipping store? Would the airline let her check it as baggage?

She had a brief fantasy of carrying the wooden chest onto the plane and reading the contents during the two flights, but then she pictured the few square inches of the meal tray she'd have for personal space. Instead, she emptied a bazillion folded notes into her oversized purse. The chest fit back into the cardboard box, wrapped in the same wool sweater to protect it from dings.

Not only did the hotel's front desk have packing tape, but they would also ship the box for her if she addressed it. She checked out, leaving the box behind, and walked to the hospital, pulling her carry-on. It was colder than the previous day, with a heavy, overcast sky and a strong wind, and she shivered, wishing she could go back and retrieve the sweater.

Dad was dressed and waiting in the hospital cafeteria, duffel bag on the floor at his side. A plastic brace engulfed his lower leg and a pair of crutches leaned against his table, but the doctor had pronounced him good to go and his ride was coming at 9:30. They both selected fruit salad, toast, and eggs from the buffet line and surprisingly excellent coffee from the carafes by the wall, and tucked in.

"So now that I know what it takes to get you to visit, I'll have to drive less cautiously," Dad said after decimating his eggs.

"Nope. This was your one hospital visit, ever. From this point onward, you're required to remain in perfect health," Parker said lightly.

He leaned forward. "Seriously, Parker, I'm so sorry. I should have visited you this past year. There's always some excuse. Finishing up a project, someone retiring at

work. These last couple months I told myself I was giving you space to get used to your new town, your new job, without being in the way. I should know better. We never know how much time we have."

He trailed off. For as long as she could remember, Dad had radiated a sense of controlled optimism, as if spending more than two seconds acknowledging a negative sentiment would make him a terrible role model. Come to think of it, that might be why Parker had gone so far the other way, staking out her right to show rage and grief. But she didn't blame him for the way he was or the way he'd raised her. He never pretended not to be sad, he just processed it differently.

She wondered, in passing, if he'd perceived her downward spiral as a rebellion somehow targeted at him.

"It's okay, Dad," was all she said. "I could have visited sooner, too. But I was afraid to come here. It was silly."

"It wasn't silly," he said. "This town has to be full of memories for you, memories you might not be ready to face yet."

Her throat thickened. She nodded. "I don't want to wallow in the past. But I am glad I came." She squeezed his hand. They smiled at each other.

After a moment, he said, "I heard you and Catherine argued. I hope you don't hold it against her. It's still hard for her. It's always going to be hard."

Parker wondered what Catherine had told him. Had she shared her theory that Jess had been stalking Britt, tormenting her about a terminated pregnancy? "She seems to remember things the way she wants to remember them, not the way they were."

He nodded, but distractedly. "Listen, Parker. I really

thought that wooden box was yours, or I wouldn't have put it in your room. Catherine was downsizing as she moved in, and things just got mixed up. She wanted it to go to her storage locker, and I thought it was something of yours that had ended up in the garage."

"Oh? She told me it was supposed to go in the trash."

"I don't think it matters, Parker. What matters is that it belonged to Britt."

"Yeah, well, Britt would have wanted me to have it, not Catherine." Parker heard herself sounding as mature as a seventh grader and tried to regroup. "It's too late, anyway, Dad. I had the hotel ship it out to Oregon." The notes filling her purse seemed to rustle, and she wondered if he'd noticed how unusually full her purse was.

"Oh." He seemed perplexed. "Well. Catherine would like it back. Could you send it when you get home? I can pay for shipping…I'm sure Catherine wouldn't even mind if you read them first. You could photocopy them."

He was such a peacemaker. Parker was positive that Catherine would mind, and mind a lot. And Catherine wouldn't have her panties in such a twist if she didn't already know exactly what the notes said. At the very least, there would be lots of notes detailing some of the harsh interactions between Catherine and Britt, if Parker recalled correctly.

She shrugged. "Sure, I can ship them back. Don't worry about it."

Dad looked hugely relieved. "Thanks, Parker. I knew you wouldn't hold a grudge."

Her phone buzzed for the third time during this conversation, and she used it as an excuse to look away.

There were eight new texts showing. She was certain there hadn't been eight buzzes—they must have been coming in right on top of each other. Her heart beat a little faster. Was Pepper okay? What if he'd been sicker than the vet thought?

Her mind jumped naturally to the dogs, but when she pulled up the message screen, the top two were from Calli. The first one said:

—*call me when you get in tomorrow*—

Parker scrolled down to see who else was burning up her in-box. Eric had texted

—*good to see you yesterday*—

And several were from Jess.

She tapped his name. Early this morning, six-thirty in Oregon but nine-thirty here, he'd sent three in a row, around five minutes apart.

—*Calli in touch with you?*—

—*Calli not around, did she text u today?*—

—*Marta crazy worried, please call.*—

Parker scrolled down and saw that Marta had texted, too.

—*Calli missing. Where would she go? Call me NOW.*—

Parker's hands shook. She looked at Dad, whose expression had tightened into concern. "Are you all right, honey? Bad news?"

"Um, yeah. I suppose. I mean, it's probably nothing. My boss's daughter has been acting a little weird, and now they can't find her."

"How old is she?"

"Seventeen. She's not a little kid, she should know better. But she's smart. I'm sure she can take care of herself…" Parker was babbling, and she heard her own words with a terrible sense of inevitability. That was the kind of thing people had said when Britt disappeared, thanks to her habit of punishing her parents by not telling them where she was.

"I'm sorry, Parker." He laid his hand on hers. "I'm sure this is more upsetting because of what happened to Britt, and I don't know all the background here, but it really is probably fine. A lot of people who 'disappear' just need a little time alone. And teenagers are more volatile than most."

"Yeah, I'm sure you're right," Parker said, but weakly. She hadn't told him what had been going on in Oregon when his accident occurred. The two murders, similar to deaths in their shared past, were thrown into sharp relief again. The story of her life: murder by suffocation, murder by knife. Disappearance—followed by murder.

She called Calli's number, then texted when it went straight to voicemail. Her fingers felt like alien tools handled from a great distance.

—You okay? where are you? text me right away pleez—

Dad laid his hand on the table in front of her. "Parker, I hate to say it, but it's already nine-thirty. My ride's here. What time is your flight?"

She looked up. "Shoot," she said. "Um, eleven-thirty. I'll head over to the airport. I'm sorry we didn't get more time, Dad."

"Don't be sorry. I'm so grateful you came. Will you update me when you get home?"

"Yeah, sure."

They rose, him awkwardly balancing with the aid of the table until he got the crutches in place. She hugged him. "No more accidents," she said firmly.

"If it's the only way to get you to visit…" he said.

A tall, bearded man stopped in the cafeteria doorway, looking lost, and her father waved. Parker slung her stuffed purse over her shoulder and grabbed her rolling case. "I'll call you." She kissed him quickly on the cheek and walked away.

****

At the gate, Parker found a seat and checked the time stamps on Calli's texts. About six and six-thirty a.m. East Coast time, which would have been three and three-thirty a.m. for her. She texted Marta.

—*Calli txted me at 330am your time, just said to call her. any news?*—

No reply.

She tried texting Jess.

—*sorry, was with my dad. what's going on?*—

The airline staff were already calling the boarding groups, and she had to join the queue. In moments, she was down the ramp and in her seat, carry-on tucked away up above and purse by her feet. She focused on her phone.

Jess—*It's crazy here. Seth is gone too.*—

Parker—*What? Calli is with her dad?*—

Jess—*No, Marta is sure not. Has called police.*—

Parker—*Where did Seth go?*—

Jess—*Not sure. Talked to ur friend Ellen at front desk. Rumor is fight with Marta, stormed out.*—

Parker—*They never fight*—

Jess—*Until now? Maybe fight made Calli run.*—

Parker—*Maybe. Keep me posted?*—

Jess—*Will do. Have a good flight.*—

She took a minute to figure out how to set up in-flight texting, then sat and stared out the window. Then checked messages again. No one had contacted her. Her thumb rested on Calli's name, but she decided not to bombard her. Calli must know by now that everyone was worried. If she wasn't answering, it was because A: her phone was dead or had no service, B: she didn't want to, or C: she couldn't.

Parker sat back and took a deep breath, not sure what to think. Calli being missing must have something to do with Ryan and Adam's deaths. Two things could be a horrible coincidence, but three?

At the same time, if Seth and Marta had a major fight for the first time ever, Calli could be punishing her parents. Kids who were used to their folks fighting thought it was no big deal, but Seth and Marta were always in sync, always modeled communication and affection and appropriate modes of disagreement. If they were so angry that they'd resorted to a good old-fashioned yelling match, Calli could be terrified that her world was ending.

Thinking about it that way made Parker feel like she'd overreacted. The tone of Jess's texts and Marta's text had been panicky, and she'd bought into that, but with the forced downtime of sitting on the plane, she had the gift of perspective. This would probably be okay, like Dad had said.

Nevertheless. A triple coincidence was disturbing. Parker fished around in the zipper pocket of her purse and found Detective Balderas' number.

—*Are you handling Calli Tyler disappearance?*—

No response after five minutes.

Parker followed up anyway.

—*Just FYI. My high school friend who was killed*

went missing first for months. I am flying back to OR now. Please txt if questions.—

She stared at her screen for the rest of the flight. Jess texted once, saying no news, that he wasn't in the loop. Nothing from Marta, nothing from the detective.

During the layover in Chicago, she bought an overpriced sandwich and picked at it with little interest, compulsively checking her phone and tuning out the rush of humanity around her.

Detective Balderas got back to her while she stood in line at the gate for her second flight.

—I would like to speak with you, when will you arrive?—

Parker—*ETA 430-5pm—*

A pause.

Balderas—*Tomorrow morning, 9 am, my office.—*

Parker's stomach shriveled. If the detective was scheduling meetings for tomorrow morning, it must mean she wasn't expecting Calli to be found by then. Or Parker's info wasn't urgent. She turned it over in her mind and couldn't figure out how to interpret the delay. She should be optimistic and assume it had nothing to do with Calli. Probably the detective wanted to touch base about Ryan and Adam.

It was hard to believe that yesterday she'd felt she had perspective on the murders. On the plane, she leaned back and closed her eyes, progressively releasing the tension in her scalp, forehead, and neck, but no matter how deep the breath, the clamp around her chest would not let go.

Chapter Fifteen

The night air was cool and misty, with a salty tang, when Parker finally hefted her carry-on case out of the hatchback. She was nearly three hours later than expected, thanks to delays at the airport and on the highway. Her legs released some of their travel stiffness as she climbed the hill toward Tyler Bettering. Near the main doors, she hesitated, wondering if she should check in with Marta, but that could wait. Parker would talk to her after she was forewarned about Marta's mental state and whether there had been any news.

She rounded the building to climb the fire escape, pausing to enjoy a glimpse of the ocean. Or just procrastinating her homecoming. She'd made peace with Jess, slept with him, and then depended on him in an emergency. Her renewed faith in him shouldn't be so easily undermined by Catherine and Eric, but despite her best intentions, this reunion was going to feel weird. She pasted a smile on her face and tapped on the door before walking in.

Pepper bounced like a rubber ball and Mouse put her front legs on Parker's rib cage, going for a full-face lick. Jess entered from the living room and lifted Pepper so the small dog could join in the sloppy greeting. Parker had a second to wonder if Jess was standing so close because he was going to hug her, and if she should move away, but then it was too late. She was encased in a one-armed, dog-filled squeeze, Jess's forehead against hers.

"Welcome back," he said softly, so close she could smell cinnamon on his breath. "You okay?"

At the sound of his voice, something in her relaxed. She squeezed her eyes shut, enjoying the feeling, but it only took a moment for her brain to start yammering again. Everything was way too complicated. She pulled back without answering and Jess set Pepper on the floor, smile fading.

Parker crouched to pet both dogs, hiding her face and buying time to think. Gladness and relief warred with confusion and exhaustion. Jess was a temporary anomaly in her life. And she should be worried about Calli, not stuck on herself and Jess.

She finally said, "Sorry, I'm starving and kind of strung out, I guess, but I'm pretty okay. How about you?"

"I'm pretty okay too." He tilted his head, studying her. "But once you've settled in I'll update you on what's been going on."

She stood up quickly. "Calli?"

"No. I mean, yes, she's still not home. But there's more."

She looked at Mouse, who looked back, panting happily. Pepper seemed no worse for wear. "Okay, I give up. Just tell me."

"I wanted to wait until you got a chance to eat and unpack—"

"Jess!"

"Okay, okay. I should have realized that wasn't the way to go about it. How about this? Sit down, and I'll make you an omelet while I talk. You like eggs, right?"

Parker slung her purse on the table and parked the

carry-on next to the door, then sat in one of the wooden kitchen chairs. "Sure. Talk."

He started setting ingredients on the counter. "Well, I told you Pepper got sick, and I took him to the vet. What I didn't tell you was the vet thought it was chocolate poisoning. I told her there was no chocolate in the house and she said, well, maybe he found some when you were out for a walk. But Pepper was leashed for all of our walks. I would have seen if he was munching on garbage. And then I remembered; there was a delivery guy who asked if he could give the dogs a biscuit. He said they were organic. Pepper gobbled his right up, but Mouse sniffed hers and left it."

"A delivery guy from where?" Parker said.

Jess shrugged. "He must have been bringing something into the lobby. He was parked in a van out front when we left the building."

"But you think his biscuits were chocolate? There would be complaints everywhere he went."

"I don't know. I guess it could have been an accident. I mean, they looked like regular, bone-shaped dog biscuits, just like the ones you have. I can't explain it. But I'm positive there's no other way Pepper could have eaten chocolate without me noticing. He was never more than a few feet away from me when we were outside."

Parker nodded, although she wasn't convinced. Dogs could snarf things up pretty quickly. It took almost a week for symptoms to appear for salmon poisoning, so it couldn't have been that, but dead sea birds, seals, and jellyfish could all be found on the beach—carrion that would smell fascinating to Pepper and could conceivably cause diarrhea and vomiting. Would the vet have been able to tell the difference between that and chocolate poisoning, after the fact?

"I'm so thankful you brought him to the vet," she said. "I'll pay you back. Pepper seems okay now?"

"Yeah, he's been fine since then. And Dr. P. said she would send you the bill. She recognized Pepper. I had to break the news about Adam. She was really upset. But Mouse was with me, so she was willing to trust that you were the responsible party. She looked at Mouse too, just in case, because I told her they'd been together constantly."

"I'm sorry you had to deal with all that."

"It's not your fault. It's my fault. I should never have accepted biscuits from a stranger. I wanted to report him, but I don't even know what company he was with. His van was plain white, and he had a baseball cap and a button-down short-sleeved shirt, but…I mean, I barely looked at the guy. He had sunglasses, clean-shaven. Dark hair."

"No name tag? No logo?"

Jess shook his head slowly. "I don't remember. I'm sorry, Parker. At the time, he was just some guy. I was thinking about other things. We could probably ask at the front desk, see if there's a record of what deliveries came in around that time."

"We could ask, but I doubt it. There's a loading dock for all the kitchen and housekeeping deliveries way on the other side of the building. A delivery van out front would have to be something small and quick, probably for a guest, and I'm not sure how long we'd keep a record. Once the guest receives a delivery, there's no point."

Jess nodded reluctantly. "Okay. We'll let it go for

now. But I'm looking out for that guy. It had to be that biscuit, I'm positive." The dark look on his face said he didn't believe it had been an accident.

By now, the eggs were releasing a rich odor of mushrooms and basil from their pan on the stovetop. The toaster popped, and Jess grabbed butter from the fridge. "You want jam?"

"Yes, please." Her stomach rumbled. "Now I'm afraid to ask, but was there more?"

"So, the other thing was minor, and totally unrelated."

"Okay, what?"

He set the plate in front of her. "Breakfast for dinner! Do you want some coffee? Or water, or something?"

She grabbed her fork. "Thank you! If you put water on, I'll take a cup of tea."

He put the kettle on and sat across from her. "My tires got slashed."

Parker swallowed quickly. "What! That's not minor. Like, with a knife?"

"Pretty much." He shrugged. "A random act of minor vandalism. Someone didn't like my out-of-state plates."

"Half the license plates around here are out-of-state," she protested. "I've never had any problem, and mine are from California." Someone had stabbed Jess's truck. That was pretty violent. Her face heated.

He reached for her hand. "It's okay. It's just tires," he said.

She dredged up a smile. "Wow, I'm really exhausted. And sick of people. Do they know who did it?"

"They who?"

"The police?"

"Parker, seriously, they wouldn't care. I mean, they have better things to worry about. I needed new tires anyway."

She stared at him. "Jess, isn't that going to be like, a thousand dollars? Someone did a thousand dollars of damage to your truck, and you didn't report it."

"I was going to have to spend the money soon anyway," he said. "There will be snow where I'm going. Little did they know, whoever did it probably saved me from skidding off the road."

"You're scared of the police," she said.

"I don't want to bother—"

"No, you're *scared* of them. You're worried— what? You call attention to yourself, and they'll suddenly figure out they have a onetime murder suspect in town in the middle of two murders?"

"That would be ridiculous, Parker. Just as ridiculous as you being a suspect. Which you're not."

She shook her head and reached for a forkful of eggs, only to realize they were gone. Her plate was empty. Regretfully, she slid it away and sighed.

Did it make her a bad person to be glad that she and Jess still had matching police paranoia, all these years after Britt's murder?

She said, "Well, I think you should reconsider. Maybe your insurance would pay if you reported it."

"I don't think I'm covered for vandalism. But it might be worth asking. Okay." He nodded at her. "Thank you. Do you want another omelet?"

"Yes, but not now. I should let Seth and Marta know I'm home. So, nothing on Calli?"

"Not that anyone mentioned to me. The only reason I heard anything at all was because Marta knew I was staying here and thought Calli might come looking for you. Plus, I picked up some gossip when I went down to the lobby for coffee, but I don't know how much is true."

"You told me there was a marital spat. That would have been just last night, right?"

"I think so. When you asked me to check on Calli after dinner, I went to the lobby and Marta was sitting at the front desk, working on the computer. So whatever happened hadn't been too catastrophic up to that point."

"Marta's very controlled," Parker said. "I'm not sure how much you can tell from her face most of the time. But they never fight. They're the poster children for how to have a perfect marriage. Professional in front of the staff and clients, but there're always little hand squeezes or smiles or jokes. You know how some married couples are always sniping, even when they're smiling? Marta and Seth are the opposite."

Jess shrugged. "There's a first time for everything, I guess. Around ten-thirty, Marta came up and knocked on the door. She said she and Seth had an argument, Calli left the apartment in a snit, and did I know where she was? Your friend in the lobby—Ellen, I think?—told me later that Marta and Seth were so loud she heard it through the wall, and she swears they were fighting about an affair."

"That's impossible."

"Ellen said the same thing. But she swore that's what the yelling was about. They had a huge fight, he stormed out, and Calli was apparently so disturbed she left too and didn't come back."

"Did she leave a note? Did she and Marta have a

fight, or did she just…walk away?"

He shot Parker a sharp look. Much had been made of the fact that Britt had 'walked away' from her life without any initiating factor. She'd gone to school in the morning as usual, attended the homecoming game, and left without a word, unless someone was lying about a dramatic final interaction. At least Calli had a reason to be upset, so there was some motivation.

Jess said, "No one mentioned any kind of note or text, except for what she sent you. Not that they told me, anyway."

"So, I got that weird text last night, you go to check on her and think that Marta seems fine, so it must mean that Calli is fine. Hours later, Marta comes and tells you Calli's gone. I found more texts this morning, which Calli sent in the middle of the night. But they're not anything dramatic. They're just like, talk to you soon." Parker showed Jess the screen with the three texts and her responses. Had she missed something important between the lines? If she'd said the right thing, could she have prevented Calli from running away?

But they didn't even know that she had run away. Calli may have left on her own, or she may have been forced to leave.

"You have to wonder what the 'not-good thing' was," Jess said.

"Yeah. That freaks me out. I have an appointment with Detective Balderas tomorrow morning. I was going to show her the texts, too. But do you think I should tell her tonight?"

"You look exhausted," he said. "I think the morning would be fine."

"I am exhausted. I'll text Marta, though, let her

know I'm here if she needs anything." Parker messaged her as she spoke, and got an okay sign in response. Nothing else came through, and after a moment, she set her phone down and rested her head in her hands.

"I did almost nothing but sit around on airplanes all day," she mumbled, "but I've been wishing for my bed the whole time."

"That's an easy one," Jess said. She felt his hand warm on her shoulder. "Let me grab my stuff. I'll sleep on the couch tonight."

Parker lifted her head and crinkled her nose at him. She'd been anxious about this moment, considering they'd been a bit, well, premature, right before she left. Not to mention the input from people who didn't know any better. Now it seemed obvious. "Don't you dare. I mean, unless you really prefer it. Just sleep with me. I want you there." She was too tired to blush.

He grinned. "I can do that. Watch this," he said, and pointed to the living room where Mouse's dog bed lay. "Dogs to bed!" he said, and they both obeyed immediately, Pepper fitting himself easily against Mouse's long skinny side.

"Wow, how did you teach them to do that in two nights?"

"Necessity is the mother of dog-training," he said, as he flipped off the light switch. "With you gone, Mouse wanted to sleep with me, and Pepper was lonely too, in a strange place without his person. Until I figured out that they could comfort each other, I had both dogs whining and trying to jump on the bed for an hour. Mouse tried to convince me she always slept with you, but I didn't believe her, because there wasn't any dog hair on the pillow."

"You checked my pillow for dog hair?" It hadn't been that long since Parker washed the sheets, but that didn't mean she wanted someone to inspect them.

"And didn't find even one. She's a terrible liar."

She felt the tug of dirty dishes in the sink, the still-packed suitcase, the satchel full of unread notes which she hadn't yet mentioned to Jess…but she took his hand and turned her back on it all, following him to bed, and to sleep.

****

Parker's watch woke her at six. Jess was snoring lightly, the muscles in his back shadowed by gray light seeping through the blinds. She snuggled close, enjoying his warmth and the familiarity of her own bed. The dogs were still quiet. It would be a good morning to drowse back to sleep, but her easy contentment unnerved her. There had been other boyfriends since Jess, of course. The good ones had been convenient distractions, the bad ones her special way of punishing herself. The one really good one that had gotten more serious had an especially painful ending. Caused by Parker.

Back in high school, spending the whole night together with Jess and waking up in the same bed had been a fantasy that never happened. Despite that, she was enveloped in an emotional déjà vu, overtaken by a past self who still clung to a belief in happy endings. Before Britt was found. Before the world recast Jess and Parker as evil and made them doubt themselves and each other.

She slid out of bed, her mood plummeting from sleepy happiness to familiar heartache. In the living room, Mouse and Pepper greeted her excitedly, bringing a reluctant smile to her lips. She hugged them both before working through some yoga poses on the living room floor. Time to face the day. Calli could be home by now, leaving Parker with only the pile of problems she'd had before Dad's accident. But there were no new texts on her phone, and the dogs needed to go out.

Jess was stirring in the bedroom. Wanting solitude, Parker crept out the kitchen door to the fire escape with the dogs. In the cool morning air, she paused to look down at the ribbon of beach narrowed by high tide. The sky was pearl gray, the ocean darker steel. Only a couple of other walkers and dogs were visible far below. Adam should be out there with Pepper this morning, breathing the salty air, enjoying his little dog's gamboling. She let the grief wash over her again, took a deep breath, and clipped on Pepper's leash as Mouse led the way down the steep metal steps.

On the beach, loose sand shifted underfoot, and her eyes watered as a chill breeze picked up. The wind came from the south, and she pushed against it for a mile, squinting to keep sand out of her eyes, then turned and let the wind chivvy her toward home. She felt more awake and calmer, the stone in her chest less heavy.

On the way back, she diverted into town for fresh bagels. How long would Jess stay now that she'd returned? How long did she want him to stay?

The Alaska job, earning money for school, was his road to a better future. No matter how either of them felt, that was important. But Parker couldn't deny that the doubts sown by her trip had eased immediately in his presence. There were still rifts in the trust between them, but if time was allowed to heal them, what would their relationship become?

Would Parker feel the same desire for him if it weren't for the murders, the past rearing up like a tidal wave? Maybe she was clinging to him in desperation and didn't want to admit it.

The garlicky scent of the bagels made her even hungrier, and she picked up her pace, jogging up the fire escape so that when she threw open the door, she and the dogs were all panting. Jess sat at the kitchen table, phone in hand, and looked up with a smile.

"Good morning!"

"Morning," Parker said. She plopped the bagel bag down on the counter and dug for butter in the fridge. There was a nearly a full pot of coffee, and she poured herself a cup after putting the bagels in the toaster oven. "Fresh bagels," she informed him. And then, not to pussyfoot around, she said, "Are you leaving today?"

He didn't answer immediately. Mouse and Pepper lapped at their water bowls, then settled together in front of the sliding glass doors to watch the ocean and the beach below.

"I guess I should, but I don't really want to," Jess said finally.

"Isn't your employer expecting you?"

"No, I have until next week to check in. As long as I'm there and do all my paperwork, and get a physical by the time the boat leaves, I'm good." He looked down and then up to meet her eyes. "I'd like to stay longer. I'd like to spend more time with you."

She felt a thrill of pleasure. "Yeah," she said. "I mean, stay as long as you can. As long as you want. But things are weird now."

"Feels like old times," he said, and took her hand. Then, somehow, they were kissing, a long deep kiss that felt exactly like old times, and her heart skipped a beat.

When they pulled back from each other, she

whispered, "Is this messed up? Are we repeating the past?"

His brown eyes were steady on hers. "No! Everything is different. We've grown up, Parker. I've got to leave in a few days, but everything is going to be okay. The past is the past. We still have now."

"The past is the past," she repeated. "I know. We couldn't go back if we tried." She cleared her throat. "I've got to get ready to see the detective, and I want to see if Marta's around before I go. I'm not sure how long I'll be."

"Do you have to work today?"

"I don't know yet. No one contacted me about it. But with Calli missing, and Seth possibly away, I don't know if we're canceling things or what. I'll ask Marta." Just in case she'd missed an announcement, she checked her phone again. Nothing appeared in text or email, or showed up in the schedule app.

She felt an urge to dress up to meet with the detective but curtailed it defiantly and trotted downstairs twenty minutes later, freshly showered but wearing jeans and a sweater. Anxiety about Calli came in waves: one moment, she'd feel resentful about being sucked into teenage drama, and certain that Calli was already home or at some inappropriate friend's house, possibly without a phone charger, possibly being a jerk on purpose. Then Parker would remember the first days without Britt, the same rollercoaster of exasperation, anxiety, and terror, and it would all be too familiar. She knew how that story ended, and Calli's could not end the same way.

Calli wasn't anything like Britt, though. Britt had been popular, charismatic, sophisticated, manipulative. Calli was lonely, awkward, immature. Secretive.

Well, they had that last one in common, anyway.

She left her purse, with its stash of folded notes, in its customary spot on the sideboard despite a brief impulse to hide it in a drawer. She didn't want Jess to see the notes before she did, but she'd trusted him to stay in her home all weekend without a second thought. On the other hand, she hadn't had anything very personal in the apartment. It was the notes making her paranoid. Arguably, by virtue of being Britt's most serious and long-lasting boyfriend, Jess had as much right to read them as Parker did. She just wanted to read them first. What if there was something about her?

What if there was something about him? Catherine's words came to mind.

She rejected the thought immediately. She chose to trust Jess, but if he unfolded and read the notes, she'd be able to tell, and then she would kick him out of her home and her life for going through her bag without permission. There. Issue settled.

The lobby was empty, the front door still locked to walk-in traffic and only a couple of cleaning staff visible in the hall. Parker went through to the back, where a group in the staff room drank coffee and ate breakfast. Marta wasn't there, but Ellen was sitting with a few people at one of the larger tables. They looked serious, and Ellen was speaking softly while they listened, so Parker didn't interrupt.

She recognized an older woman with a semi-shaven head at the coffee maker and joined her. Petra led team-building and communication workshops for corporate clients. She could be abrupt and sarcastic, and Parker wasn't sure they would ever be friends, but Petra would tell her what was going on.

"Good morning," Petra said. Her blue eyes had dark shadows under them, and Parker detected the faint scent of cigarettes.

"I just got back from a family emergency. I heard Calli was missing yesterday. Is there any news?" Parker asked.

Petra shrugged. "Marta's in her office. You should ask her."

"Is there a staff meeting today?"

"She hasn't said yet. We've got a group scheduled starting tomorrow midday, so we can probably push our meeting until tomorrow morning. That's what I told her."

"What about Seth?"

Petra shrugged. "He's gone."

"What do you mean, gone?" Seth was the backbone of Tyler Bettering. Marta handled the business end, sure, but Seth was the voice that carried the message.

"Don't ask me. Go talk to Marta. I'm sure she'd love to see you, since you're such great friends with her daughter."

Yeah, there was the sarcasm. Parker opened her mouth, shut it, and backtracked through the hallway to the closed door of Marta's office, where she listened, heard nothing, and knocked.

"Who is it?" Marta demanded.

"Parker."

"Come in. And close the door behind you."

Marta looked almost normal, blonde hair sleek and make-up fresh, but her eyes were bloodshot and her hands shook as she slid some papers into a folder and tucked it in a drawer.

Feeling a jolt of sympathy, Parker took one of the visitor chairs. "Have you heard anything from Calli yet?"

"Not a word. You would have said if you did?"

"Of course. We're not usually in touch, either. She just started texting me last week, mostly after the—" Parker found she didn't want to say the word murder. "Last week," she repeated.

"I see," Marta said.

"I'm going to talk to the detective this morning. I'll show her my phone. Can they track the texts, do you know?"

Marta shrugged helplessly. "I don't think so. If they could track her phone, they would have already."

"I don't know if I can be any help, then."

Marta sighed. "Did you know Seth was having an affair?" Her eyes jumped to Parker's face.

"Are you serious?" Parker said. "I mean, you guys are—No. Are you sure?"

"Calli knew. Calli said everyone knew."

"I don't think that's true," Parker protested. She wasn't on gossiping terms with the rest of the staff, although she was probably a subject of gossip, but surely she would have picked up on it if people thought something like that was going on. Instead, everyone talked about Marta and Seth like they were larger than life, like they embodied the success and self-actualization and vitality they sold. Krista had never mentioned anything about an affair, and she'd given Parker the scoop on everything from the housekeeper with a fetish for men's used socks to the chef who'd had his kids taken away last year.

Marta said, "Well, it's true. At least, the affair occurred. I don't know who knew about it."

Parker wondered how Calli found out, and she wanted to ask who the woman had been, but didn't want to pry. "So, where is Seth now?"

"I don't know. I don't care."

"But…does he know Calli's gone?" she pressed. "Do you think she might be with him?"

Marta shook her head emphatically. "He wouldn't do that to me." But she choked on the words, and then she was crying helplessly, shoulders shaking and manicured hands covering her face.

Parker hesitated, not sure if Marta would want to be comforted, but she couldn't watch her cry and do nothing. She walked around the desk and patted her back awkwardly. Marta pulled her down and sobbed into her shoulder, enveloping Parker in a cloud of citrus perfume. "Hey," Parker said helplessly. "It's okay. It's going to be okay."

Marta's sobs eventually slowed to hitching breaths, and she pulled away, leaving a damp spot on Parker's shoulder. She grabbed a tissue from a drawer and noisily blew her nose. Parker retreated to the other side of the desk.

"God, I'm sorry," Marta said. "I don't know what's wrong with me. Calli's punishing us. That girl. She has no sense of perspective. The world is full of cheating bastards, but her father betrays us, and it's the end of everything." She tried to smile. Her mascara had stayed perfect, but her nose and cheeks were red and shiny.

"You're pretty sure that's what this is about?" Parker asked.

"I don't know what else it could be." Marta's gaze dropped to the top of her desk.

"You're probably right. Teenagers never do have perspective," Parker said.

"How about you? Is your father okay? I wasn't

really expecting you back this soon," Marta said.

"Yes. He's out of the hospital already. His leg was pretty badly broken, and he'll be in a cast for a while, but he's going to be fine. Thanks for letting me go see him."

Marta shrugged. "Family. Just because you're still new here doesn't mean shit doesn't happen."

"Thanks," Parker repeated. There was silence. Marta looked down at her desk. "Well, I should go," Parker said. "I'm supposed to be at the police station at nine."

Marta looked up, her eyes tearing again. "Call me if you hear anything. Right away."

Chapter Sixteen

Parker had planned to walk to the police station, but now there was no time. She hurried up the hill toward her car, tension humming through her gut. Marta's anxiety for Calli was contagious, and it exacerbated Parker's hollow grief, which felt like it had been there all along, beneath her reconstructed positivity, beneath her spark of reconnection with Jess. A river of sadness running through her soul for all the lonely, all the grieving, all the dead.

She sank down into the driver's seat, face hot and chest tight, and realized she couldn't go see Balderas until she got herself under control.

When she reached inside for strength, all she found were tears, and she had to let them come. She cried not just for Marta but for Ryan's parents, steeping in the same loss that Marta dreaded. For Adam, who'd weathered many storms only to die from someone's act of violence. For Calli and her loneliness.

And of course, behind, under and through—Mom. Mrs. Gilford. Britt. Parker's own dead, whom she would always carry with her. If they weren't a part of her, who would she be?

And then she cried for the person she could have been without all this sadness.

At last she tipped from needing to cry to feeling like she was wallowing in it, and her sobs slowed to heavy breaths. She blew her nose on a napkin. She was late for the appointment now, of course. That would look good to the police. She texted Balderas quickly that she was on her way and peered into the tiny mirror on her sun visor. Her face was blotchy, her eyes red and watery, her lashes stuck together with tears. Her hair looked fine, though, so that was something.

****

"Can I see the texts?" Detective Balderas said.

"Sure." Parker passed the phone across her desk and looked around at the few personal items in the room as the detective studied Calli's words. Oversized plants in front of the windows, a photo of a dark-haired woman and a little boy on the deck of a boat, and several glass floats on top of a file cabinet. Pieces of preschool-art were taped to the drawers, and Parker tried to decipher what they represented. Dinosaurs, she thought. Or cows? Or dogs. Something with long legs and toothy smiles, standing next to giant flowers.

"So, you don't know what the 'not-good thing' she did was supposed to be? She hadn't talked about it with you before you left?" Detective Balderas said.

"No. I hadn't talked with her much at all. Like I told you, I've only worked at TBI for a couple months, and she's my employers' daughter. She's home-schooled, so she's around a lot, but I hadn't really gotten to know her."

"So you're not close. But she sent this to you," Balderas stated.

"I think she's lonely. She doesn't have friends her own age, and I'm probably the youngest person there. And she likes my dog. She's always asking if she can walk her."

"Have you let her?"

Parker shook her head. "I'm a single woman with no social life. Pretty much all I do is work and go on hikes and runs with my dog. I don't really need help." She flushed, thinking she sounded both petty and lame. "I should be nicer to her, but I don't want to encourage her to spend time with me instead of finding friends her own age. Anyway, the day Ryan was killed was the first time we had more than a two-minute conversation."

The detective pursed her lips but didn't respond.

"Do you think there's a connection between what's going on with Calli and what happened to Ryan and Adam?" Parker asked, afraid to hear the answer.

Balderas' phone buzzed, and she glanced at it, then set her hands on her desk as if about to stand. "It's extremely unlikely," she said. "Kids this age take off, often for reasons that make no sense to anyone over the age of twenty-five. I'm told it's a brain development issue. But as you know better than most, we have to take it seriously, just in case."

Parker had hoped for a more definitive answer, but followed the detective's cue and stood.

"How's your father?" Balderas asked.

"He's okay. Broken leg."

"Good. So you won't be leaving town again for a while?"

"Not unless there's another family emergency."

"All right." The detective nodded. "It goes without saying, but I'll say it anyway. If Calli gets in touch with you, tell us immediately. And be careful yourself."

Parker met her eyes. The detective's face was expressionless. Parker couldn't tell if she was implying something accusatory or being solicitous, so she just nodded back.

****

Stepping into the bright light of a cool October morning with a hint of salt in the air, she inhaled deeply. The ocean wasn't visible, but the wide blue-gray sky seemed to reflect it. In the time since she'd gone into the station, the brisk wind had calmed into an amiable breeze.

Her feet carried her past the parking lot. She wasn't ready to go back to Jess and TBI just yet. It felt wrong to be contemplating a walk without the dogs, but still she turned toward the bayfront, where she seldom took Mouse because the sea lions agitated her. Either their insistent barks taunted her or she wanted to go for a swim and make friends, Parker wasn't sure which.

Midday on a Wednesday, the shops were open, but only a few older couples and a family with four kids wandered by. Parker strolled the boardwalk to admire the fishing boats, and wondered what would happen to Adam's little boat. She should have asked the detective whether she'd found his family, and if she'd remembered to ask about Pepper.

Parker's thoughts moved to Calli. One hike together, and Calli thought Parker was her best friend. Instead of being happy about it, Parker had blown her off for her own good.

She should have listened better, asked more questions. Was something going on beyond Seth's supposed affair? It must be tough to be the daughter of a charismatic self-made success story. Everyone who met Calli would feel like they knew her father intimately, because his self-help books were soul-baring, and he wrote frankly about his early struggles with marriage and parenthood.

If she loved her father, if she believed in him, it may have rocked her foundations to learn he was having an affair. He was a liar, a cheat—only human after all. Where would she have gone, though? Had she gone after him? He must know that she was missing. Even if he and Marta weren't speaking, the cops would have checked in with him when they learned about the fight.

But since Calli's face wasn't shining from every news website already, Seth must not be as worried as Marta. He would never hold back on notifying the media. Sure, now he'd retired and was living a quiet life away from Hollywood and the public eye, but he must still have friends and favors he could call in.

Parker turned that thought over in her head, leaning on the fence as the water frisked against the shore. The smell of the bay was thick and fishy, the boats with their complicated rigging and glossy wood picturesque in the sun.

Marta was devastated, but based on his actions, Seth was less so. Marta was letting the police do their thing the way they wanted to do it, and Seth was uncharacteristically staying out of the way. It could be shame, Parker supposed, but that seemed unlike him. Even if he'd done wrong, was he capable of owning up to it? Well, she thought he probably was, in the sense of making a public apology and allowing himself to be interviewed about whatever led him to cheat on his wife. He'd probably try to talk Marta and Calli into being part of the interview, and his sorrowful gaze would seem so sincere to the viewer that they would root for him to be forgiven.

If Seth wasn't worried about Calli, should Parker be

worried?

Some deep-seated restlessness had claimed her, and she still couldn't bring herself to turn back toward home. She'd had a half-formed idea that if Jess didn't leave today, she could take him north, hike Cascade Head with the dogs. They could even bring a picnic. But she kept walking, turning the pieces over in her mind.

Even if Seth had no shame and walked out without a second thought about Calli, Parker was carrying some guilt. She had the uncomfortable suspicion that she was to blame for something, if not everything. There was nothing she could do for Ryan, besides hope that his killer was found. Nothing she could do for Adam, besides taking care of Pepper as he would have wished. It was only Calli that she might be able to help. It was only Calli that she might be able to find, if she'd run away and was hiding. Calli trusted Parker, she'd wanted to talk to her. But if she wasn't responding to her phone anymore, how could Parker let her know she was ready to listen?

Her thoughts coalesced. She would speak with Seth, pin down what he knew, what he suspected. That might help her figure out how to reach Calli.

She stopped on the sidewalk next to a T-shirt shop and texted him. Both he and Marta were "The bosses" to the staff, but Marta was much more in charge of day-to-day operations. However, Seth made a point of saying any of the staff could talk to him anytime. Parker doubted he had this particular time in mind, but she didn't let that stop her.

—I want to help find Calli. Can I speak with you?—

There was no immediate answer. She stared at her phone impatiently for a minute, then slid it in her back pocket and headed toward TBI to update Jess on her plans.

****

Seth still hadn't replied by the time Parker reached home. Her backup plan was searching for Calli around town, even if that meant checking random coffee-shops and calling her phone at various intervals. Then Parker could drive down to Cape Perpetua, near the natural area where they'd gone before. Calli couldn't have gotten there on foot, but she could have hitchhiked, or contacted a friend no one knew about, who'd driven her.

When Parker opened the door, Jess was in the kitchen, pulling on his jacket. "I was just about to take the dogs out," he said. "I wasn't sure how long you would be."

"Sorry, I should have texted." She looked at the dogs, who were waiting eagerly. Mouse's tail thumped against the floor. Parker scratched her head fondly.

"How was your meeting with the detective?" Jess asked. "Is there any news?"

She shook her head. "It was pointless, and there's nothing. But I was thinking. Calli's dad is a media magnet. If he were worried about Calli the way Marta is, he'd have her face all over the news, and that hasn't happened."

"So, you think she's with him?"

"No, she can't be. There's no way the cops wouldn't have checked that. But he may know something that leads him to believe she's fine."

Jess nodded. "Well, I don't want to freak you out, and I could be jumping the gun, but what if he's received a ransom demand? Would he tell the cops, or would he be the type to keep it secret and follow the kidnapper's instructions?"

"I don't know," Parker said. She hadn't considered ransom. She'd gone straight from runaway to killer and back, with nothing in between. A kidnap for ransom seemed unlikely, didn't it? Seth was, or had been, some species of celebrity, but although he was a household name in some circles, there were a lot bigger targets. On the other hand, although Seth and Marta lived modestly enough here, they also had a vacation house in Italy. Perhaps they could afford a decent ransom.

Mouse and Pepper sat upright and poised next to the fire escape door. Parker looked at them, feeling guilty for delaying their expected outing.

"I texted Seth and I'm hoping he'll agree to talk to me," she said. "I mean, why wouldn't he? I'm not his wife, I'm not the police, I'm just a staff member his daughter likes. I'll ask about a ransom, see what he says."

"Okay," Jess said. "What do you want me to do?"

She shrugged. "Um, you can still take the dogs out if you want?"

He looked at their panting grins. "Yeah, I kind of have to at this point. But do you want me to come with you if Seth gets in touch? He could be involved somehow. I don't know him, but a lot of times it's family who screws you over." He rotated the ring on his finger, an unconscious habit.

Parker shook her head. "No, that's okay. It's not that kind of thing, I'm pretty sure. Calli discovered her father was having an affair, got upset, and confronted him and Marta. So he might be angry with her, but he'd never lay a finger on her. Both of her parents dote on her."

"You never know," Jess said.

"Sadly true. But I'm pretty sure. You take the dogs. I'll text you if I leave before you get back."

He pulled her close and kissed her on the way to the door.

In his arms, she asked, "So, what are you going to do later? I mean, did you decide? Are you staying?" Her heart wrenched a little. How had she come to depend on him so quickly?

"A couple more days, if that's okay?" he said. She nodded.

When the door shut behind him, she checked her phone and grabbed a snack. Seth hadn't replied by the time she was done, and she debated texting him again, but decided to wait. She would check some of the possible hangouts in town for Calli, drive down to Cape Perpetua, and then, if he still hadn't responded, she could call. Being too insistent might put him off.

On her way out, she reached for her purse and realized it was still stuffed with Britt's notes. It would only take a few minutes to get a sense of whether Britt had kept only special notes or whether these were all the mundane bullshit that they'd spent years sending back and forth. "Did you see Katie's skirt? OMG it's about an inch long!" kind of thing. At the very least, it would be a roller coaster of nostalgia.

Parker forced herself to leave it. Time to focus on the present. She grabbed her keys and wallet and strode out, only to feel her phone buzz as she trotted down the stairs. It was Seth.

—*Having coffee at Nye Beach. Meet me?*—
Parker—*I'll be right there*—

****

Seth was visible through the window, bald head bent

232

over his laptop, an oversized mug of cappuccino beside him. He looked intent but not particularly stressed.

Parker watched for a moment, then pushed through the glass door and bought a green tea at the counter. The shop was warm, folk music playing softly in the background, the air redolent of coffee and cinnamon. When she turned after ordering, Seth looked up and smiled, flipping his laptop shut. Parker's shoulders tightened.

She paid three bucks for her twenty-five-cent tea bag and one minute of labor, then gritted her teeth and sat down across from him.

Before she met Seth, she'd been only vaguely aware of his existence. She'd heard his name and glimpsed him on television talk shows as she flipped through the channels, but she didn't know what he was famous for. When Krista started working for TBI and every other word became "Seth said," Parker looked him up online. His self-published memoir, featured on a morning talk show, had propelled him to bestseller-dom, but when it was discovered to be almost entirely fictional, his popularity plummeted. When he admitted on national TV that he'd lied because he couldn't face discussing his real childhood of abuse and what he'd had to do to survive as a teenager on the street, public opinion turned in his favor once again. With soulful eyes and an oversized, expressive mouth, he became a charismatic figurehead for public discussion of the effects of chronic child abuse on individuals and society.

To Parker, despite all she had in common with Seth—they were both runaways who'd gone off course and then embraced different aspects of the wellness community, not to mention both bald-faced liars—his charisma felt too slick. It was a kind of armor, and she sensed a gap between the deep sincerity with which he spoke, and the mind behind his eyes, which measured everyone he met and, she suspected, found them wanting. Despite that, she wasn't immune to his charms. He made her feel like they had a secret understanding. He probably made everyone feel that way.

Krista had laughed when Parker tried to explain why he made her uncomfortable. "Parker, he's a shrimp and about as intimidating as a koala bear!" But being five inches taller than him made it worse, not better, because some shorter men felt like they had something to prove around her, so she became pre-emptively defensive. And so far, familiarity hadn't helped either.

He studied her across the table. She studied him back. He didn't look nearly as careworn as Marta, and Parker felt resentful on her behalf. Why should Marta bear the whole burden of worry? Not to mention, shouldn't he be looking shamefaced about his affair?

"How are you, Parker?" he said in a concerned tone. He must be reading the past days of stress and travel on her face even as she was seeing the lack on his.

"I'm hanging in there," she said.

"This must be an awful time for you. I'm so sorry about your friend. Adam, was it? And then your father?"

"My father's okay," she assured him. "The accident was frightening, but he's going to be fine, and it was good to see him. Good to go back home."

"You hadn't been back in a long time," he observed.

There was an element of careful non-judgment in his voice, and she bristled. How did he manage this when she came here to talk to him about his missing daughter? As she'd headed over, she'd been composing ways to ask about Calli that wouldn't imply blame. And yet here she was, on the defensive herself.

"I hadn't," she confirmed. "Listen, Seth, thank you for asking, but I came here to talk to you about Calli. I got a few texts from her while I was away, and then I came back to find her missing. Marta's really worried. I know it's none of my business, but I can't help but worry, too."

His face sobered. "I know," he said. "I think Calli would be sorry to know she's drawn you into this."

"What do you mean?"

"Calli's furious at her mother and me right now. And she learned as a little girl that emotional storms won't move us. Now, to make us understand how hurt and angry she is, she has to take major action." He shrugged, as if it were obvious. "But it was meant for us, not for you. I'm truly sorry."

"You're positive that she's run away?"

"Entirely." His voice was one hundred percent sincere, as if the shadow of a doubt had never crossed his interior landscape.

"Are you so certain because you've heard from her?" Hope twitched inside her, although she knew it couldn't be that simple.

He paused, just for a microsecond. "I haven't heard from her, no. But I know my daughter. I know how she thinks. She needs some time to calm down, and then she'll come back to us. I told Marta this too, but she's all worked up, conflating the recent killings somehow with our family troubles."

Yes, how silly of Marta, Parker thought. "You're not worried about the murders?"

"They can't have anything to do with us. That poor

young man who was your client. It was terrible, but none of us had ever seen him before the wedding party. And your friend—horrible." He shook his head. "Violence is a terrible thing, but it is part of the human condition. It persists even, or especially, in small towns that seem safe and insulated from the worst of the outside world."

She noticed it was *her* client, *her* friend. Her stomach clenched. "You think the murders have something to do with me?"

"No! Of course not. That's as ludicrous as thinking they have anything to do with Calli."

He laid his hand on top of hers, and she suddenly remembered this man was an adulterer. She pulled away.

"So you don't think we should try to find her?" Parker asked.

"I'd love to find her," he said. "But I have no idea where to start. Calli has her own friends. She's an independent young woman, and we give her space."

That was not Calli's take on it. But Parker supposed what felt like space to a parent might still feel constricting to a teenager. She tried one last thing. "You don't know any friends or boyfriends she would have gone to stay with?"

"If I did, I would have told the police."

"Okay," she said, scooting her chair back. "Thanks for meeting with me. Are you coming back to TBI soon?"

He made a face. "Our little institute is very like a family, isn't it? No secrets. I suppose Marta has told everyone of my fall from grace, the better to punish me. No, no, that's not fair. She has the right not to hide her pain."

He paused, composed himself. "I will make it right,

somehow," he said. "Don't worry, your job is safe."

Her eyes widened with horror and he laughed.

"Don't worry! No, I'm joking. I'm sure you're genuinely concerned, just as you are genuinely concerned for Calli. It's okay. Listen, Parker."

He grabbed her hand again, squeezing it. "You have enough on your plate. Seriously. I'm a dog and a cad, and my daughter is a dear but self-centered teen, and neither of us deserve the affection of a woman like Marta, but we'll both make it up to her, and we'll all be fine and live happily ever after. You take care of you."

Parker stood, leaving her tea untouched on the table. "Thanks again for meeting me," she said, and turned away, pushing through the door and out into the fresh air. Somehow, she felt worse than ever. As she turned up the street, she glimpsed him again through the window. He'd already opened his laptop and was leaning toward the screen intently, reading glasses on.

Chapter Seventeen

Instead of heading home, Parker walked around Nye Beach and up to the skate park, looking for Calli. Seth had offered nothing useful and made her suspect he lived in a different universe than she did. He'd interpreted his daughter's actions, knew there was no chance he was mistaken, and neatly switched focus to other things. He talked a good game, and Parker didn't think he was lying, but she couldn't help drawing a comparison to Britt's disappearance. Not even Catherine had been totally nonchalant about Britt "running away." But it was different. To Catherine, Britt had seemed unpredictable because Britt and Catherine spoke two different languages. But Calli seemed transparent to Seth. He trusted his understanding of her so thoroughly he felt no fear.

He was crazy, Parker decided. For someone who had once been abused to assume that the best possible scenario was true—how could he be such an optimist? She certainly couldn't. Her scars differed from his, of course, but they had made her pessimistic, to say the least. Obsessed with death, tuned into despair.

She caught herself. That was the old Corey thinking. Wasn't Parker more like Seth? She couldn't let herself fall prey to her old, self-defeating habits. Realistically, Seth knew his daughter better than Parker did.

She wandered downtown and through the library.

Free Wi-Fi might draw Calli in. If she didn't have her phone, she might want access to public computers. Inside, there was no sign of her, but Parker realized quickly that Calli could be standing fifty feet away and still unseen. Even this tiny town was too big for one person to search on foot. It would take a coincidence of large proportions to run into her, even if she was in a public place and not at the private home of an unknown friend, like her father assumed.

Was it a fair assumption? It could be. Seth thought she was online making friends that her parents didn't know about, but Calli had seemed awfully lonely. She'd told Parker she didn't have friends her own age. What if she meant she had older friends?

That was a chilling thought. Parker's mind jumped from older friends to older men to inappropriate, manipulative relationships. To abuse and drugs and, yes, murder.

Okay. That was definitely the old Corey. Get a grip, Parker. Flow from a place of grace, or, to put it another way, get your mind out of the frigging gutter.

She was running out of places to check within walking distance when her phone buzzed with a call. She fumbled it out, hoping it was Calli, but it was Krista.

"What?" Parker said grumpily.

"Well, hello to you, too. I'm good, thanks. How are you?"

"Not great." Parker turned her feet toward TBI, passing a dog-walker and, oddly, a stout old woman striding along in a bathrobe and slippers with a cigar in her hand. Despite the beautiful weather, the sidewalk was otherwise empty.

"What's wrong?" Krista said.

"Same stuff. I'm wandering around looking for Calli. What did you want?" She knew she sounded peevish, but she'd been deep in her private headspace, slogging her way through guilt and fear.

"So she's still missing?"

"Yep."

Krista waited for elaboration, and then asked, sarcastically, "I don't suppose you care to share any more news? I mean, considering I've known Calli longer than you have."

Parker rolled her eyes. Krista had told her she and Calli hadn't hit it off. She'd described Calli as an over-privileged baby hipster, from her green hair to her angsty scribbling, and Calli had called Krista—what was it?—Smooth.

On the other hand, you could make fun of a kid and still be fond of them. Plus, the situation was doubtlessly pressing Britt-buttons for Krista too, bringing up bad old memories. Parker softened. "I've talked to Marta and Seth separately," she offered. She told her about the supposed affair, which Seth hadn't confirmed or denied, exactly, and about their vastly different responses to Calli's disappearance. "Marta is certain that Calli's in danger. She's fixated on the murders, and Calli being young and stupid. Seth is positive that Calli is either punishing them or taking some time alone, and he's not worried at all. Marta reported it to the police anyway."

"So Marta and Seth are not even talking?" Krista sounded scandalized.

"Yeah, hard to believe, right?"

"I thought they'd be together forever, hand in hand," Krista said. Her voice had an unpleasant edge. Parker decided to get off the phone. Krista probably wasn't happy about their troubles, but she enjoyed gossip and could easily spend the rest of the afternoon hashing it over.

Parker said, "I'll text you later, okay? I'm going to grab some lunch and see if I can figure out where else to look."

"Oh, hey, wait," Krista said quickly. "I was thinking I should come down and help too."

"What? Really?"

"Yeah. I mean, I should, right? We can look for Calli together, and look through Britt's old notes too. It'll be perfect."

Parker wasn't sure. It wasn't like the cops were organizing a search party at this point—they didn't have enough to go on. Plus, Calli could turn up at any minute. "Not yet," she equivocated. "I'm not sure what you could do that isn't already being done. Plus, it's a five-hour drive. Chances are, she'll turn up before you even get here." Also, Krista would expect to stay with Parker, and three people in the tiny apartment would be weird. Especially if two of them were Krista and Jess. Parker tried to picture going through Britt's notes with Krista and Jess together and shuddered. They used to hang out, sure, and they were both more mature than they had been back then, but they'd always tended to dig at each other unless there were other people around.

Krista said, "Okay, we'll talk about it tomorrow if she's not back. I just hate to think of her out there somewhere alone. Is anyone searching the beach? Doesn't Calli love the beach? And there're miles and miles to search."

Parker knew Calli walked on the beach sometimes. Did she love it? Would she sleep rough on the beach if she were angry? There were little semi-protected places in the dunes and scrubby forests where people sometimes camped, but Parker doubted Calli owned a tent or a sleeping bag. That seemed kind of outdoorsy for her, based on their one hike, and her mom would have mentioned if camping gear were missing. On the other hand, Calli had to be somewhere, and no one had found her yet.

"That's an idea," Parker admitted. "I'll do that. And I'll mention it to the cops. I hadn't thought of it that way."

"You can't search miles of beach by yourself," Krista said.

"Jess is with me. We'll go south from Agate Beach, and when we hit the jetty, we'll check south of the bridge. Thanks, Krista."

"Jess is still with you? I thought he was just staying with the dogs while you were back east." Her voice had curdled slightly.

"He might stay for another day or two. Listen, thanks again. I'm back at the hotel. Talk later!" Parker hung up.

Krista's suggestion had lit a fire in her. There were miles of coastline where Calli could have found a camping spot within hiking distance. There were three stretches of beach that Parker visited regularly on her runs, separated by two headlands and comprising almost seventeen miles.

She burst into the apartment. Jess was at the table with a giant sub sandwich in front of him, Mouse and Pepper sitting attentively on either side.

Parker chuckled. Mouse gave her a quick, shame-faced glance, but then turned back to the sandwich. "Tell me you're not giving them pieces of your sub," Parker said.

"There's way too much meat," he said. "It was clogging my arteries. They're helping me out of the kindness of their hearts." He grinned, and she gave him a quick squeeze and dropped into a chair.

"So it looks like, aside from undermining years of dog-training, you're all doing well without me?"

"We're doing fine. I got you a sandwich too. Figure I should stop eating up all your food supplies."

"You don't have to worry about that. The cupboards were bare when you got here. What did you get me?"

"I wasn't sure if you ate meat, so I got you a veggie. Is that okay? You can have some of my meat if the dogs don't finish it off."

"It's perfect, thanks."

He got up and grabbed the second sub out of the fridge, and she unwrapped it. It smelled deliciously of vinegar and pickles. "No begging," she told Mouse and Pepper, who looked at her mournfully and slunk over to the patio window to watch seagulls, knowing the rain of treats had ended.

"Did you meet up with Seth?" Jess asked.

"Yeah, he texted me back, and we met at a coffee shop. He believes he knows his daughter so well that he understands what she's doing perfectly and therefore he's not worried about any other possibilities. She's staying with some unknown friend, and she'll be back in her own time, period."

"Do you believe him? I mean, do you think he's right?"

"Not…entirely? I've still got a bad feeling about the murders, and then Calli missing—it feels weirdly personal to me. I know that's crazy, that everything is different and I'm stretching the interpretation to fit my situation—"

Jess shook his head. "I'm freaked out, too. I'm glad you told the cops about your mom and your neighbor and Britt. It could be just weird bad luck, but it's freaky. I don't like it."

Parker wasn't sure if his validation helped. He hadn't seen the bodies, so he was depending on her impression to draw his conclusion, and her impression was biased by her past. Plus, she didn't want to be validated in her fear. She wanted to be un-validated. She wanted it to be all coincidence, and Calli was with some gorgeous boyfriend or girlfriend, oblivious to her parents' worries or deliberately punishing them, and poor Adam and Ryan had been killed for random reasons by random people.

She gave Jess a wry smile because at least he was trying to help. "Thanks. Well, Krista called and gave me a good idea, though."

"Oh yeah?"

"She suggested Calli might hide near the beach. There are lots of little nooks and crannies out of the wind along the dunes where people camp sometimes."

He looked dubious. "I don't know Calli at all, but would she be comfortable roughing it? Her whole green hair and false eyelash thing seems pretty high maintenance."

Parker shrugged. "Huh, I haven't seen the eyelashes yet. But from what I know, she does like the beach. And when I took her hiking, she enjoyed it. Who knows, maybe she was prepared, maybe she bought a little tent and sleeping bag, or borrowed one from a friend."

"Can't hurt to try."

Parker gulped her water. "You don't have to come with me. I mean, I realize, even if she's there, it's probably pointless. We could walk right by her and not see her, if we're looking in the dunes and she's out on the beach or vice versa."

"I'm coming," Jess said, grabbing a napkin. "I'm definitely coming. Mouse and Pepper and I will help you cover all the ground. Plus, Calli's green hair will help. Not many people with a bright green head around here, right?"

"It's windy and cold. Almost everyone has hats or hoodies."

"Dang. You're right."

"Are you up for running at least part of it? I was thinking we could go south, across the bridge and as far as we can get before dark."

Jess gestured to the empty butcher paper in front of him, scattered with pepperoncini and black olives. "Sure. All fueled up. I don't see why not."

Parker texted Marta:

—No news from cops, have looked around town, now going to check beach—

Marta didn't answer, but Parker felt better knowing she'd tried. She wished she could give her some of Seth's serene confidence. Marta was suffering, he was sailing along, and most likely neither attitude was having any effect on Calli's current state of mind, wherever she was.

Parker changed into running gear and added a hat and a windbreaker. Jess changed into track pants. Because of the likelihood that they'd be trekking around all afternoon, Parker packed a small backpack with water bottles, a collapsible dog bowl, and some energy bars.

There were about six hours before dark, and from her weekend long runs, she knew it was about ten miles down to Ona Beach. Calli probably wouldn't have gone that far, but she was capable of it, and there were trees to camp among and a public restroom and fresh water source there.

A knock sounded on Parker's door as she finished packing. Pepper yapped excitedly, and Mouse pricked up her ears. Parker answered and Ellen stood at the top of the stairs, holding an enormous bouquet.

"Hi, Parker, sorry to bother you." She aimed a grin over Parker's shoulder. "Hi, Jess!"

"Hi, Ellen, what's up?" Parker said.

She held out the bouquet. "Well, flowers!"

Parker looked back at Jess, who'd crouched down to keep Pepper from investigating the visitor. Jess shook his head, frowning slightly.

"Who are they from?" Parker asked.

Ellen thrust them toward her again. "I didn't open your card, but the delivery lady left them at the front desk, so I figured I'd bring them up."

"Wow. Thanks." Parker accepted the arrangement. It was exotic, with tiger lilies, stalks of pussywillow, and sprays of red berries. Definitely not something she would have picked, and the powerful smell made her point it away from her face. There was no lavender in it, but she thought immediately of the 'prank' Calli had pulled just last week.

Jess rose with Pepper in his arms to stand beside her. Mouse nosed between them to get her own view of what was going on. "No word on Calli, huh?" Jess asked.

"Oh my god." Ellen brushed back her caramel curls. "That girl is driving her poor mother crazy. I think Marta is going to explode. But I told her—Calli is a piece of cake compared to me at the same age."

"You're not worried?" Parker said.

"Well, I am, because Calli's probably better at hiding things than I was. But I'm not saying that part, for Marta's sake. I wish Seth would come back," she added wistfully. "Without him, she's just lost, especially with the, you know—" she lowered her voice, "murders."

"Thanks again, Ellen," Parker said, not wanting to get into it. "We were just about to head out."

Ellen took the hint and gave a quick smile. "No problem. I'll tell you if I hear anything. See you later!" She trotted down the stairs, her steps echoing in the narrow stairwell.

Parker closed the door. Jess set Pepper down on the floor and peered at the flowers.

"Should I be jealous?" he said lightly.

"I can't imagine who these are from. Unless…either my dad, or someone trying to cheer me up about my dad?" She carried the bouquet to the kitchen to look for a receptacle. There were no vases, but she was pretty sure she'd saved a giant pickle jar that would do the trick. She rifled under the sink, leaving the bouquet lying on the counter, but came up empty.

"Someone trying to cheer you up about the murders?" Jess suggested.

"That's not typically a flowers occasion. Let's find out the easy way." Momentarily distracted from finding a vase, Parker plucked the small envelope from a plastic spike among the flowers. A burr of anxiety vibrated in her belly, but she squashed it and tore open the card. Part of her, ridiculously, expected it to be from Uncle Danny. But Danny didn't know her changed name, and Dad would never have shared her address or anything else with him.

The card read "With Sympathy" in gold script across a photo of a field of lavender. She opened it with shaking fingers. In tiny, precise block letters, someone had written, "I'm here for you."

Danny's letters had always been on torn-off sheets from a legal pad with scrawled blue ink and messy, urgent printing, sometimes illegible. So that ludicrous theory went straight down the drain. She wished she had another one.

"Well, what does it say?" Jess asked.

Wordlessly, she held it out. Jess took it gingerly, touching only the edges, and examined it inside and out.

"No signature." Parker stated the obvious just to break the silence.

He stared down at the card.

"Jess?"

"Yeah," he said, as if agreeing to something she hadn't said. Then he met her eyes. "But, Parker?"

"What?"

"This handwriting? I swear. It's the same as in the letters."

"What letters?"

"My letters. The ones I thought you might be sending."

"Are you sure?"

"Mostly. It's block letters, like someone's trying to print in an unrecognizable way. But it's also a little spiky, do you see? Especially the first letter of each word."

"Did you bring—"

He shook his head. "No. I had no end game beyond

trying to get you to stop. I tossed them."

"Damn," she said.

Mouse nudged her leg. Pepper had given up and returned to the sliding door to watch the beach, but Mouse had faith that they were still going out. Parker rubbed the short fur on top of her head.

"What are you going to do?" Jess asked.

"What can I do?"

"Tell the police?"

She snickered. "Oh, Detective Balderas? By the way, someone sent me flowers. Can I get round-the-clock protection, please?"

Jess shrugged, his face troubled. "Someone is messing with us. And people have died."

"This is Mr. I-needed-new-tires-anyway speaking?"

"Yeah. Not the first time I was ever wrong."

She squeezed his hand, and followed his somber gaze back to the ugly bouquet, shockingly bright and mundane within its crinkly plastic and tissue-paper sheath. A bubble of anger rose within her, and she yanked off the wrapping and stuck the flowers, head down, into the compost receptacle under the sink.

Jess set the card on the counter. "Keep that," he said. "Just in case."

"I will." Parker didn't want to look at it. "It doesn't make a lot of sense. If it really is the same person, they've been threatening you all along, and suddenly they want to threaten me too? Why?"

"Because I'm with you? Or maybe you're supposed to find it comforting. Supportive."

She snorted. "An anonymous sympathy card saying, 'I'm here for you?' I feel like I'm on a hit list. Nobody could think that was comforting." Then she thought back to the lavender. Her stomach flipped.

Jess shook his head. "I know. I don't like it. It's one more thing that's too much of a coincidence."

Angrily, she grabbed the plastic wrapping off the counter. It crinkled loudly as she shoved it into the trash. She said, "This is stupid. It's only flowers, and you know what? It's probably not the same as your letters. We're just spooked. I have a socially awkward secret admirer among the staff here. It's a distraction from what's important. Calli is still gone, and Mouse and Pepper are still waiting for us."

Jess looked from her to the little square of cardstock on the counter. "You still want to go?"

"Yes. Let's go look for Calli. Burning off a little adrenaline should clarify things."

He rolled his eyes. "I'm starting to think that's your answer to everything."

"That and meditation," Parker assured him. "And dogs."

Pepper scrambled to join them at the door. Backpack, snacks, water, leashes. A hat against the October breeze. They were set.

Jess lingered at the table after lacing his shoes, looking troubled. Parker grabbed his hand. "Don't let it get to you. Come on. We're going to the beach."

Chapter Eighteen

They exited by the inside stairway so Parker could check the lobby on the way out while Jess waited out front with Mouse and Pepper. No one was behind the reception desk, so she lifted the barrier and went through to the staff room. Ellen and Marta and some others were at one of the round tables. Marta tapped on her phone. She didn't look too bad.

"Who's on the desk?" Parker asked.

Everyone looked up and Ellen hurried over. "Is someone waiting?"

"No, it's okay," Parker said. "I was just wondering, were you the one that signed for the flowers?"

"Yes, I thought I told you. It was the Jose's Flowers van. Is there a problem?"

"No. Just checking." She wondered if florists had a confidentiality policy. If she told them someone forgot to sign the card, would they look up the name of the person who paid for it? They would probably refuse. Secret admirers weren't against the law, but Parker could try.

She lowered her voice and gestured toward Marta. "She okay?"

"Yeah," Ellen replied with a sideways glance at Marta. "She sent an appeal to the local news blog and they posted it."

"What kind of appeal?"

"Asking Calli to come home. It has her picture and says if you see her, call the police."

"So, everyone still believes she's a runaway?"

Ellen blinked at Parker. "Wait, oh my god, no one told you about the note, did they? Sorry, I thought you knew."

"What?"

"Marta found a note in Calli's room, in the trash, like she changed her mind about leaving it. It was a goodbye note."

"What did it say?"

"The usual stuff. You guys suck. I need some time to think. Don't worry, don't come after me. I'll be home soon."

That was good, right? It pointed to Calli leaving under her own power. Although runaways could quickly become victims, as Parker knew well.

She shivered. "Jess and I are going to look for her on the beach," she told Ellen.

Ellen nodded. "Marta mentioned that. Good luck! I bet she's at a friend's house, though."

If she has a friend, Parker thought. But she said, "Yeah. You're probably right. But it's something to try."

Ellen shuddered. "I know how you feel. It sucks just sitting around. Oh, hey—Marta canceled everyone except the Holistic Dentists Association. Marta and Petra have been calling the other reservations and offering free upgrades for a later date."

Parker vaguely remembered the dentists being on the master schedule. "What time are they coming? Never mind, I'll check the app."

"Tomorrow lunch, but they're mostly providing their own activities. I don't think you have any appointments scheduled until Friday, but you should double-check."

"Thanks, Ellen."

Ellen looked back at Marta and lowered her voice. "She's refusing to think about next week. We'll have a full load again Monday. If Seth's not back, or if Cal—" She looked sickened.

"I know," Parker said. "But I don't blame her for not wanting to think about it. Worst comes to worst, we'll all do what we need to do."

Ellen nodded. "It's an impossible situation."

Parker squeezed her arm. "Keep me posted, okay? We're heading out."

She told Jess about the note as they descended to the beach. A thick cloud cover had blown in, and the wind was a steady breeze from the south that stung Parker's eyes. The beach looked so deserted, she began to doubt the plan. There was no one out but a few dog walkers. She and Jess jogged to the jetty, then clambered up and down some of the steep trails that led through the dunes near the lighthouse, hoping for some sign of Calli. Among the line of twisted trees that grew hunched over from the constant wind up along the cliffs, they spotted a couple of tents, but one seemed abandoned, sagging and mildewed, while the other was home to two weathered middle-aged guys who were smoking out front.

Parker called "Calli," a couple of times, feeling foolish. Her voice was thin and weak in the wind. Even if Calli somehow heard her, if she didn't want to be found, she'd duck into the next gully or disappear over the crest of a hill, and Parker would never know. The dogs at least seemed hopeful, sniffing excitedly as if about to discover Calli's trail.

"Should we keep going?" Jess asked, catching his breath.

"There's a campground with restrooms and showers on the other side of the bridge," Parker said. "Not far. More dunes and forested trails where it would be easy to evade attention. I don't know how much money she has. She might be staying at a legit campsite."

They backtracked up to the road and crossed the bridge over the bay. Cars, trucks, and RVs rushed by, forcing them to hug the rail of the narrow sidewalk. Jess stopped at the apex to gaze out to sea, while far below, a pair of fishing boats made their way toward safe harbor in the marina. "It's beautiful," he said.

"Yeah, it is." Parker looked toward the horizon, away from the merry-go-round of anxious thoughts circling in her head. Jess squeezed her hand, and she squeezed back, grateful that he was with her.

They made their way down the south slope of the bridge and a set of curving concrete stairs. For a moment, South Bay stretched before them; a maze of tiny neighborhoods and curving streets with a myriad of paths where a teenage girl might easily evade notice indefinitely, if she had food, drink, and a blanket.

But checking it out was something no one else was doing, and it felt better than doing nothing. Plus, the dogs were loving it.

Jess and Parker jogged down a paved bike path and diverted into wood-chipped trails through the trees, then wound their way around a sprawling campground populated largely with RVs. There were dogs everywhere, and they stopped frequently for doggie greetings as they traveled the loops. The few tents they saw were on campsites that also had an RV, and they spotted no one between the ages of twelve and thirty-five.

Off the paved paths, they startled mushroom hunters poking around in the scrub, but discovered no secret campsites. A few hardy souls clustered close to the main beach access despite the weather, but as they topped the rise, the long stretch of beach to the south looked barren and deserted.

"I don't know what to do," Parker said. "I was thinking we'd go to the headland, but now I'm doubting Calli would have come even this far. It would have seemed daunting unless she came here regularly. She might have been more comfortable on the north side, but here? I'm doubting it."

He nodded. "Okay. We've covered a lot of ground. Let's head back for today and see if anyone else has news. If there's nothing by tomorrow, we can always try again."

"If she's still gone tomorrow, and it's voluntary, she's got to be inside someone's house or apartment. Two nights outside already, for someone not used to camping, in windy, damp weather? Of course, if it's not voluntary, all bets are off."

On the way back, they diverted into town to buy ingredients for dinner. After a chilly day, fish stew, a loaf of bread, and a dark beer sounded perfect. Parker tried to switch gears from thinking about Calli sleeping rough or being held against her will to thinking about spending the evening with Jess. It felt just like the ambivalence of old times, wandering through the woods half-looking for Britt, half enjoying each other's company.

She was so over her head.

Cara Johns

They walked the last few blocks back to the hotel with hands linked, but in silence. After years of living close to the edge, Parker valued stability more than anything. She'd been content and optimistic about slowly growing her client base, beefing up her credentials and experience into something legitimate, and someday, in the distant future, owning her own business.

There was nothing in the plan about romance. There was no room for it, beyond a very hypothetical, shadowy impression of love and marriage and kids in the unimaginable future. Most of the people she grew up with were already there, but Parker's life had been skewed by murder, and she'd come to terms with having a different path. She'd had to climb out of a pit of morbidity to get where she was, and she was proud of it.

Right?

She snuck a glance at Jess. His cheeks glowed from exertion and the cool, damp air, and his hair held a nimbus of silver droplets. He looked intent and serious, as if he, too, were thinking about big life choices.

"What are you thinking about?" Parker asked.

"I don't know. Calli, I guess." He met her eyes. "And us. Back when we were that young and stupid."

"Is that what we were?"

"Yup, pretty much. Me, anyway. I should have done everything differently."

What was he regretting? Being with Britt? Being with Parker? Or something worse?

Could she really be falling in love with someone and then feel sudden suspicion at a simple turn of phrase?

Parker released his hand, and they climbed the stairs.

256

After feeding the dogs, Parker texted Krista while Jess was in the shower.

Parker—*Your beach idea struck out*—

Krista—*No sign of Calli yet?*—

Parker—*Not on beach, haven't heard from Marta or cops. Calli left goodbye note in garbage too.*—

Krista—*In garbage?*—

Parker—*Maybe she couldn't get the words right*—

Krista—*Maybe. Damn*—

Parker—*Yeah*—

Krista—*You should check the beach again later tho, or downtown. She's got to be somewhere*—

Parker—*Could be anywhere.*—

Krista—*Where'd you look?*—

Parker—*All the way down to south bay thru campground*—

Krista—*Not north?*—

Parker—*No*—

Krista—*Try north. Tonight*—

Parker—*You're crazy. would be her 3rd night sleeping on beach. she's got to be at a friend's. or enemy's*—

Krista—*I would try. I should come down*—

Parker—*You shouldn't. you have no vacation time yet.*—

Jess came out of the shower and started putting the stew together in the kitchen. Parker took her turn under the pounding spray. She tried to rebalance her mind after the unsatisfying exchange with Krista. Hot water ran down her body, relaxing her, and when a layer of disgruntlement had washed off, she thought about Krista again.

She probably wanted Parker to keep checking the

beach because that's where she would have gone at that age. Krista had more empathy for Calli than Parker had given her credit for. Or, Parker thought sourly, Krista just liked to be in the middle of things. It must be hard for her to feel left out. If she were instrumental in helping to find Calli, it would put the spotlight back on her.

Parker rolled her eyes. She'd long ago accepted Krista for who she was. No point getting irritated about it.

The fish stew came out rich, salty, and delicious, with fresh sourdough bread and butter on the side. They ate ravenously, and drank the beer. She told Jess what Krista had suggested.

He shrugged. "We could try. It wouldn't hurt anything. But I don't have high hopes."

Parker thought about the night she'd discovered Ryan's corpse, when Calli had walked up to her and Mouse at the base of the stairs. She'd come from the north that evening. What if she had a favorite place or a friend up there?

"We should go," Parker decided. "After I clean up. Just in the name of being thorough."

At the sink, Jess pulled her close and kissed her, and she had second thoughts. They could stay in tonight, get a fresh start tomorrow. But Mouse looked up at her with enormous eyes, and Parker knew that no matter how much exercise they'd had today, Mouse and Pepper would need a final bathroom break, anyway. They might as well make it a full walk up the beach. The bed wasn't going anywhere, after all. Even though Jess was. Tomorrow or the next day or the day after.

She refused to think about that right now, and they bundled back up a little more warmly. Some of the overcast had cleared, but Parker brought a flashlight, just in case. They descended the fire escape, then made their way carefully down the cliff stairs.

Parker had received a text that there would be a staff meeting to prepare for the dentists Ellen had mentioned, but she wondered if any of it would happen. Without Seth and with Calli still gone, what would Marta do? What should she do? She had to pay the bills, but it would be impossible to act as if it were business as usual.

What if Calli never came home, but ran off to Los Angeles or Mexico or joined a cult, and Marta and Seth just had to move on? They wouldn't, Parker was certain. They would hire a private detective or a deprogrammer or whatever was necessary to get their girl back. Which was why disappearance was so poisonous. They would be unable to rest until they had an answer other than a crumpled note.

Parker bumped Jess's hip with hers. "Nice out here, huh?"

"Gorgeous," he agreed, but he was looking into her face.

She blushed. Too mushy for her taste. She yelled, "Come on!" and they scrambled down the slope of the sand toward the water, the dogs leaping in joy. Unlike Jess and Parker, they continued straight into the ocean until Parker yelled, "Mouse! Get back here!" They'd both need a good toweling and brushing tonight, but the panting grins on their faces were worth it.

Jess said, "So, north?"

"Yeah. Let's get away from the water, walk closer to the cliff. There are more places to camp up there. I've noticed a bunch of little driftwood shelters, too, though I wouldn't want to sleep in one."

They walked briskly to fight the chill, watching for beached logs and rocks in the gathering gloom. Above, the first stars appeared between cloud formations and Parker was trying to find the Big Dipper when Jess suddenly said, "Is that a bonfire?"

The glow was nearly hidden by a fold in the sandstone cliff near a creek that threaded across the beach to empty into the ocean. "Looks like it. A campfire, anyway. It's pretty small."

They slowed to a stroll. The dogs explored the scents along the edge of the beach more thoroughly. Parker clipped on Mouse's leash in case there was food or another dog near the fire. As they approached, faces turned toward them. Eight or ten teens, in hoodies and warm jackets, sat on logs that had been dragged into a rough triangle with cans and bottles upright in the sand at their feet. A couple were making out on a plaid blanket off to one side. Parker got a whiff of pot, but it blew away on the salty breeze. No one looked familiar in the flickering light.

"Hey," Parker called out.

The kids quieted and someone said, "Hey."

"We're looking for a friend. You guys know Calli?"

They shrugged.

"She's got green hair and she's about as tall as me. She wears a lot of black," Parker said.

"Oh yeah, I seen her at Starbucks a lot. She's with that blonde girl," a kid in a yellow beanie said indifferently.

Parker's heart sped up. "What blonde girl? What did she look like?"

"Like, blonde hair, longish. Kind of normal looking. I don't know, I wasn't, like, staring at them."

"When did you see them? Today?"

"Nah. It was a while ago."

Frustrated, Parker bit her lip and looked at Jess.

He said, "She ever hang out with you guys?"

A couple of the kids shook their heads. The two on the blanket sat up and pulled away from each other. Neither of them had green hair, either.

Parker said, "You see her anytime recently?"

Yellow Hat shrugged.

"If you see her again, could you tell her please contact Parker?"

"Sure, whatever."

As they turned away, the kids' voices picked up again, a couple of them rising into laughter.

Discouraged, Parker said, "There might be a dozen girls with green hair in this town."

"It's a pretty small town. And most of them wouldn't be so tall," Jess said. "You never know, it might be her."

"Yeah, and now we can expand our hunt to include a normal-looking girl with long blonde hair," Parker said wryly. "Useful."

He squeezed her hand. They continued in silence to the cliff that marked the headland between this stretch of beach and the next. A lighthouse cut a shining beam over the ocean.

"Damn," Parker said.

"It was a good walk," Jess offered.

"I got my hopes up for a minute there. I'll have to tell Krista we almost got a lead, thanks to her."

On the way back, the kids were gone, the fire covered with sand. In front of TBI, Parker and Jess stopped and looked up. A few bare windows provided a clear view into the gold-lit rooms beyond. Parker located her balcony, the room beyond the wide sliding door lit dimly by a nightlight. A dark figure was silhouetted against the glass.

Parker caught her breath. The break-in Calli had confessed to had receded in importance in Parker's mind. But if someone was there now, could it be Calli again? It was impossible to discern details this far away. As she squinted upwards, the silhouette narrowed and disappeared into the gloom beyond the glass.

"What is it?" Jess asked.

"Someone's up there. In my apartment," Parker said.

He followed her gaze. "Are you sure?"

"Positive. What if it's Calli?" She was frozen, wondering why Calli would be there, how she could have gotten in again, whether to call Marta or Detective Balderas or just rush upstairs.

Pepper yipped impatiently. Jess stuffed Pepper's leash into Parker's hand. "Only one way to find out," he said, and took the first four steps in a single leap before racing upward.

"But—" Parker protested, too slow. Jess was halfway up already. She looked around for Mouse, who was sniffing a tangle of seaweed twenty yards back. "Mouse!" she called, and lifted Pepper into her arms.

Something caught her eye, in a place her eyes tried to skip over but were magnetically drawn to. Something green, and knitted, and shaped like a frog, tossed like refuse in the scrub next to the turn of the wooden stairwell.

"Jess!" Parker cried, but her voice was small and strangled. Mouse arrived, panting, and stood at her side.

Parker stepped forward, then again, to bring the cave under the stairs into view, where Ryan's body had been hidden only days before.

Thumping footsteps alerted her that Jess had returned. "What's wrong?" he demanded.

No body, only a hat. Only Calli's hat.

Parker took a breath, heart pounding so hard her chest quaked, and pointed. "That's Calli's hat. I'm sorry, it's okay, there's nothing else here. Go, go up, I'm coming too. We have to catch her."

Jess looked torn. He glanced up at the windows high above. "We should call the cops," he said. "They'll want to see this."

"We will," Parker said. "But go! Hurry! I'll be right behind you."

With a last uncertain look, he turned and raced up again, his footfalls shaking the stairs.

"Stay back. Stay!" she commanded Pepper. She wasn't sure if he could be trusted, but when she placed him next to Mouse, he sat and looked at her alertly.

Parker kicked through the sand in the low-ceilinged nook under the stairs, finding nothing, not even cigarette butts, thanks to the cops' recent evidentiary cleanup. She edged back out, skirting the hat, and peered into the scrubby brush along the cliff side. Not spotting anything manmade except for a crumpled pop can so old she couldn't tell what kind it was. She picked the hat up gingerly, by one of its froggy eyes, and looked underneath. Nothing but sand. She shook it gently to see if anything fell out, but nothing did.

Parker dropped the hat and stood. Jess was more than halfway up the fire escape already, eating up the metal stairs with his long legs. Parker scooped up

Pepper. "Come on," she told Mouse, and they started up as fast as they could. Parker should have asked Jess to wait. What if it wasn't Calli, and she'd sent him into danger?

"Jess!" she yelled breathlessly from the parking lot. She couldn't see him anymore because the fire escape looming above blocked her view. "Jess, wait!"

A couple on the sidewalk glanced at her curiously as she swung up onto the metal stairs, still cradling Pepper. Mouse barked and trotted ahead.

Jess had disappeared inside the apartment. Parker's steps slowed. As she climbed from the third landing to the final set of stairs, Jess popped his head out just as Mouse reached the door.

"There's no one here," he said. "But someone did break in. The fire escape door was open. They broke the glass."

Parker's heart pounded. "They're gone? You sure?"

"Yeah, I looked everywhere. Plus, the inside door was hanging open, and I saw you deadbolt it before we left. Careful, watch the glass."

Pepper wiggled in her arms. Parker stepped carefully past the mess and set him down in the living room where Mouse was already sniffing around. Parker turned back to the kitchen to see the damage. Pepper followed her to lap at the water bowl and she swooped to pour it out and refill it, conscious that stray shards of glass might have landed inside.

Deep breath. "You looked everywhere?" Parker asked again, voice constricted.

"Yeah, it's okay, Parker. There's no one here. It's not too bad. The windowpane in the door is the only thing broken; they didn't trash the place. You'll have to look closer to see if they took anything. Hey, do you want to sit down?"

Her face was cold and clammy. Adam's place flashed through her mind: coffee table overturned, peanuts and paper scattered across the carpet, Adam lying there past all caring. Parker swallowed and shook her head. "I need to see."

Jess joined her as she followed the dogs into the living room. It was a small space she could scan in an instant, with the loveseat and coffee table facing the sliding doors, a couple of armchairs in front of the TV, and a bookcase on the opposite wall. The narrow sideboard near the entry held her keys and purse, as well as a couple of candles and a small jade tree.

At least, it normally held her purse. The oversized satchel that doubled as a bookbag and/or lunch bag, that also happened to be holding the notes she'd taken from Britt's wooden chest, was gone.

She rushed to the bedroom door, eyes darting to the dresser where she'd found the lavender. Nothing there, and nothing looked disturbed, but she opened and closed drawers and threw back the covers. The closet had two sliding panels, and she checked both sides.

In the living room, she scanned the bookcase, then hurried back to the kitchen to throw open all the cupboards and drawers. Mouse followed her from room to room, sniffing, and Pepper followed Mouse.

Jess followed too, hanging back and watching with concern on his face.

Parker slammed the last kitchen drawer and turned to Jess.

"You okay?" he said.

She shook her head, wandered into the living room,

and collapsed onto the loveseat as if her strings had been cut. "I don't know. I can't believe they took my purse. I had hardly any cash in there, nothing anyone would want."

He sat beside her, his leg warm next to hers.

"You ready to call the cops now?"

"I should call Marta and tell her first." But Parker didn't move. This time, no one had used a key card to get in. They'd broken the windowpane, then turned the doorknob from the inside. She would never feel safe in here again. She would never feel like her stuff was private.

She had a mini-billfold with her license, one credit card, and a little cash inside, small enough to carry while running, that had been with her on their travels today. But her actual wallet, with her debit card, her checkbook, her library card, membership cards…all that was gone. Her mom's sterling silver compact mirror, one of the few mementos Parker had, was gone, and that, along with the notes, was irreplaceable.

Jess squeezed her shoulders sympathetically, then stood. "Where's your broom and dustpan?"

"Um, next to the fridge. If they weren't stolen."

"Okay. I'll get the glass, give you some space to make your calls."

"Let's leave the mess for the cops to see, for now. Can you bring me the detective's business card from the fridge?"

She stared out toward the ocean. Mouse's head nudged onto her knee and Parker rubbed her velvety ears until Jess handed her Balderas' number. Then she sighed, set it aside, and called Marta.

Chapter Nineteen

When Detective Balderas and her partner arrived as Jess and Parker were sipping tea in the kitchen with Officer Mays. Mays had insisted that Parker shut the dogs in the bedroom, and Pepper gave the occasional soulful yap to remind everyone it was torture.

Balderas dismissed Mays, and Parker introduced Balderas to Jess. The detective's eyes flicked between them with interest, and Parker guessed that she'd done her homework and recognized his name. Parker had told her earlier she was single and lived alone, both of which were true, but now looked false. She stifled the impulse to explain his presence.

Balderas sat at the table while her partner leaned against the counter, making the kitchen feel crowded.

Parker offered refreshments. Balderas shook her head with a perfunctory smile. "Just topped up, thanks." She gave them a measuring look and said, "Listen, I don't know what's going on, but there are a few things I don't like. I don't like that Calli is still not home and hasn't contacted anyone."

"Yeah, of course, us too," Parker said.

"I don't like that her hat was where our victim was found."

Parker and Jess nodded.

Balderas leaned forward, meeting their eyes in turn. "And I really don't like that Calli's new best friend and her best friend's boyfriend were previously involved with another runaway, which ended badly. Newport is a peaceful town, and now we've had two murders and a missing girl within a week, and all within half a mile of Little Miss Hidden Past. I hope to God that you have nothing to do with any of it, but if you do, I will find out. You best just tell me now."

"That's not fair," Parker protested. "We had nothing to do with what happened to Britt, and have no idea what's going on with Calli!"

"Do we need a lawyer?" Jess asked.

"I don't know, do you?" Balderas said, raising one eyebrow.

"We don't need a lawyer. We haven't done anything but try to help," Parker insisted, shooting Jess a quelling look. She had a sinking feeling. This kind of suspicion and antagonism were what she'd feared from the start.

"Oh? Explain this again. Start with why you were hanging out on the beach at the site of your client's murder."

Balderas had believed in her innocence before, Parker was certain. She'd seemed to understand that Parker was a decent person with extraordinary bad luck. On the other hand, Balderas was a cop. She moved through the polluted backwaters of human nature, and it was her job to question everything. Calli's disappearance was a coincidence too far, and she could no longer indulge in small kindnesses. Parker understood that.

Still, the detective should be fair and open-minded, even if she had to be skeptical.

Parker gave Jess an apologetic look before asking Balderas, "Seriously, do we need a lawyer?"

She shook her head and sat back in her chair. "You

certainly may consult a lawyer at any time," she said. "It would be a shame to slow things down, though, considering we have a missing child."

Ouch. She pretty much had to say that, and it wasn't untrue. The most important thing was for Calli to be found, but Jess and Parker had to tread carefully. Once Catherine Ryden had plastered her unfounded suspicions about them all over social media, the press had eaten them alive. What if the police got distracted by their history? How would that help Calli or find justice for Ryan and Adam?

"What do you think?" Parker asked Jess.

He shrugged, his mouth in a grim line.

"We reserve the right to change our minds and get a lawyer later," Parker said to Balderas.

"You don't have to reserve that right. You have that right," her partner pointed out wearily.

"I know. I'm just trying to tell you, your suspicion is pointless. Please don't waste time thinking that we did anything to Calli."

"How were you trying to help?" Balderas asked.

Jess answered. "No one was looking for her. Parker said Calli liked the beach. We thought she might be hanging out there, even sleeping there."

"There, at the bottom of the stairs?" Balderas said.

He said, "No, there on the beach. Earlier today, we went south across the bridge, looked along the little trails in the dunes and cliffs. Tonight we walked north, toward the lighthouse. It was on the way back that we found the hat."

"It wasn't there when you left?"

Parker thought back. They'd been joking around, and at the bottom of the stairs, they'd run toward the surf with the dogs, who'd been as rambunctious as if they'd been cooped up all day instead of outside all afternoon. Would they have noticed the hat when they were focused on each other and the dogs' craziness? But it hadn't been so dark then, and Parker had been wary of that spot. She must have at least glanced at it.

"I don't think it was," she said. "I'm pretty sure we would have noticed."

"What time was that?"

"Umm, six forty-five? Seven? We'd eaten dinner, spent some time relaxing before we came out one last time."

"So it was dark."

"It was getting dark. Ish. The sky was clear, and the moon reflects off the ocean, so sometimes you can still see okay on the beach. Plus, we had a flashlight, although we weren't using it at that point."

"You really think you would have noticed a hat in the sand?"

"Not positive," Parker said. "But I think so. I would've glanced down automatically. It wasn't bright and reflective like Ryan's hat, though. And it was more in the grass. I'm not totally sure."

"One of us would have noticed it," Jess argued. "That's what happened on the way back, after all."

"But at that time, you were facing the other direction, and you were at ground level," the second detective pointed out.

Parker nodded.

"Okay. So you went down to the beach thinking you might find Calli conveniently sitting in the sand in the dark. What next?"

"It was more that we were thinking if she had no

place to go, she might think it was safe to sleep on the beach. People camp in the dunes all the time," Parker said.

"Were you thinking you'd go knock on the door if you saw a tent? Or, even better, unzip it and look around inside if no one answered? Because if Calli didn't want to be found, why would she answer even if she was there?" Balderas said.

Okay, it sounded dumb when she put it like that.

"Sometimes kids are just looking for proof that someone cares," Jess said. "For all we know, she wants to be found. Plus, we did come across a group of kids that said they'd seen her."

"Tell me about that," Balderas said.

Jess told her about the bonfire and the supposed Starbucks sightings with a blonde girl, and then the rest of the walk up to the headland and back.

"And then Parker spotted someone up in her window, so I started running up to see if I could catch them. But she yelled when she saw the hat and I came back," he concluded.

"Did you see anyone in the window?" Balderas asked.

"No, I wasn't looking. I had Pepper's leash, and he was going nuts sniffing around the sand and not listening. I was about to pick him up and carry him."

"There's no question someone was up here," Parker said irritably, gesturing to the broken glass. "They came in that way, and the inside door was open too. Someone came through."

"We'll get back to that," Balderas said. "Bear with me. So, you two are down at the bottom of the stairs, Parker sees the hat and calls Jess. Parker, you recognized

271

it?"

"Yeah. I took Calli hiking the day after Ryan died. She was upset, I was upset. It seemed like a good thing to do. She wore that hat then."

"Okay, so you thought an intruder was in your apartment and you'd found something belonging to a missing girl. At that point, you called the police?" Balderas' voice sounded neutral, but the sarcasm came across loud and clear.

Jess answered. "Parker thought it might be Calli up there. She wanted to rush up and check."

"So you left the hat, and you both go up as fast as you can, but Parker carried the dog, yes? During that time, did you see anyone else in the windows, or in the parking lot, or around the beach access?"

"No, it was deserted," Jess said.

"I saw a couple, a man and a woman, pass on the sidewalk," Parker said. "But they just looked like they were out for a walk."

"And then what?"

"Well, Jess got there first, and he ran up ahead of me."

"Toward an unknown intruder." Balderas' voice was flat, but Parker prickled defensively.

"Yeah. I realized too late that it might be dangerous, and I tried to call him back, but I was almost certain it was Calli and that she might run away if we didn't catch her."

"Okay, so you get to the door, Jess first—"

He nodded. "And I saw the window was broken, and the door was ajar, so—"

"So you went in."

He shook his head, but not in denial. "At the time, it

made sense. I'd pounded up the stairs, they're metal, they made a huge amount of noise. And the dogs were barking behind me. If someone was in there, they'd had plenty of time to get away."

Balderas said, "And what if they waited because they wanted to harm you?"

Jess looked down, embarrassed. "Yeah. I didn't think it through."

"So, you burst in, and there was no one here, and you checked to see what was missing. And then, eventually, you called the police."

"Yes," Parker said. "And then they came and implied that we were kidnappers, or killers, or both." She knew it sounded childish and her face warmed, but she stared at the detective defiantly.

Balderas ignored her.

Jess said, "We called when we knew what to report. It made sense to see what was missing, and when we were pretty sure Parker's purse was the extent of it, we called."

"After you called your boss."

Despite Parker's effort to give Marta a heads-up this time, she'd had to leave a message, and the cops had arrived first. Marta rushed up the stairs soon after Officer Mays arrived and had been sent back to wait in the lobby.

"She's been going crazy with worry. I wanted her to know about Calli's hat," Parker said stubbornly.

Balderas looked from one to the other and shook her head. She pushed back her chair and stood, shrugging into her coat. "Okay. Well, Officer Mays will come back in for a report about the break-in and the missing purse. If I were you, I'd get that glass fixed as soon as possible and consider a more secure outer door. I'll mention it to your boss when I speak with her."

"That's it?" Parker said in disbelief.

"That's it," the detective said. "Unless there's something else you want to tell me."

"No, it's just—we have questions! What about Calli? And do you think it was Calli in here? Are you going to get fingerprints? And will I get my purse back?"

"I don't have any answers for you right now. Contact us immediately if you have any further issues."

Jess and Parker walked Balderas and her partner to the inside door, eliciting a fresh volley of yips from Pepper in the bedroom. "You still have my card," Balderas confirmed.

"Yes." Parker glanced at the coffee table where she'd left it.

"Good. We'll keep in touch."

Parker returned to the kitchen and Officer Mays had her go over the information about the missing purse. She left after a reminder to report the stolen credit cards to the credit card companies, and suggested that Parker freeze her credit score. She also repeated Balderas' advice about the kitchen window.

"That's so helpful," Jess said sarcastically as the door closed behind her.

Parker tried to remember which cards had been in the wallet and realized that the phone numbers to report them stolen had been printed on the back of the cards. She rubbed her temples. An irritating headache had formed behind her eyes, and the thought of wading through multiple online banking sites made it multiply. Dumping her lukewarm tea into the sink, she said, "We need a break."

They went into the living room. Jess freed the

canines. Pepper tumbled out as if he'd been pressed up against the door and Mouse stalked out moments later, as if she hadn't noticed the door was closed. Then Parker flipped off the living room lights for better ocean viewing. They gazed out at the waves from the loveseat for several minutes until the kettle whistled and she made another round of tea.

But instead of relaxing, she felt worse. Her mind paced like a tiger in a cage, coming up against the bars no matter which way she turned. She couldn't fix anything, couldn't help anyone, didn't know what to do, and the thought of someone rifling through her bag and maybe tossing it in a dumpster, maybe keeping Mom's silver mirror, made her nauseous.

"You should head out tomorrow," Parker said, finally.

"What? No!" Jess said. "There's no way I'm leaving you in the middle of this."

"This is nothing," Parker said unconvincingly. "This is a bunch of nasty coincidences, and you being here isn't helping. It's just making the police look at you, too."

"You don't believe that, do you? Someone left that hat for us to find, Parker. Someone broke into your apartment. Those flowers! You should have told Balderas about that."

"That would have made it worse, not better."

"Well, you didn't send them to yourself. I didn't send them to you. It would have shown that it's not us, that someone else is involved."

"Involved with what, though? With Calli's disappearance? With poisoning Pepper? With Ryan's death? Plus, the hat—there was no reason for anyone to think we'd find it there. We could have gone the long way around, I often do."

"But they could have watched us come down those stairs and bet we'd go up the same way."

She shook her head. "I'm sorry, Jess. I have the worst headache. I don't want to think about it anymore, but I know I need to."

"Parker, someone is toying with you," Jess said. "With us. The letters I was getting, my tires, the chocolate dog biscuit, the flowers, the hat…"

His list was incomplete. Hesitantly, she said, "There's one other thing I didn't tell you about. Calli broke into my room the night of Ryan's murder and left flowers on my bureau. Lavender. She said she got an anonymous note telling her to do it, but I didn't believe her. I thought she was bored and pulling a stupid prank." Parker's eyes felt hot.

He blinked. "Parker, that's messed up. She broke into your apartment? And you didn't tell the cops?"

"I talked to her about it. She was already in trouble with her parents for other stuff, and she was crying when she admitted what she'd done. I thought she realized how stupid it was, so there was no point in making it worse. I took her hiking."

"But what if it has something to do with what's going on?"

Parker raised her shoulders and dropped them. "I don't know. My brain is like a stress tornado. I'm going to meditate."

"Really? Now?"

Despite the vise around her temples, she chuckled at his expression. "I meditate a lot. I mean, *a lot*. It's sort of an addiction. I'm surprised you haven't noticed yet."

"I know you teach meditation, right?"

"Yeah. But it's not just a job, it's a part of how I cope. Where other people take a few deep breaths in a stressful moment? I try to do some kind of full-on practice a couple times a day, even if only for a few minutes. And all this craziness has thrown me off."

"If that's what you need to do now, I can get out of the way."

She closed her eyes. This felt strange. Jess's Corey hadn't been a runner, hadn't been a dog person. Why did it feel like bringing meditation into the mix was one difference too many, like he might suddenly realize she wasn't the same girl he'd loved in high school?

That could be a good thing. If he left, it would be one less complication, and he could disentangle from whatever was happening around her. She couldn't figure it out right now, or anything else, either. "Yeah, I think I do. I'll go out on the balcony, you can stay here. Don't worry. I'll try not to feel like you're staring at my back."

"Why don't I find some cardboard and cover the kitchen window? That's really bugging me."

"Look in the recycling bin under the sink, and there's tape in that junk drawer under the cutting board. Thank you." She stood and squeezed his shoulder. "I won't be long."

****

The chilly breeze from the ocean cut through Parker's fleece jacket, but she stayed on the balcony, hypnotized by the roiling ocean. Meditation had centered her somewhat, in that she'd been able to notice all the intrusive worries were about things she couldn't control. That was freeing. Now she felt calmly fatalistic. Would someone else get murdered? Would her car get stolen? Or someone could burn down the Tyler Bettering

Institute, or she would turn out to have a brain tumor. Who could say? It wasn't up to her.

All she could do was take the best care she could of herself and Mouse and Pepper, at least until he found another home. Jess was outside of the bubble, because he could take care of himself, and also—he would leave. And chances were, his life would keep him from coming back. He'd save up his money, head back to school, earn his degree, and live happily ever after, far, far away.

So what? She wasn't going to change the course of her life just because she'd spent a few days reigniting a teenage crush.

When she heard a noise behind her, she turned to see Mouse pawing at the door. Mouse was accustomed to Parker sitting on the balcony, but not leaning on the balcony railing. The dog's brown eyes tracked Parker with concern and Parker gave in. With one last glance at the powerful waves, she slipped through the door and scratched Mouse under the chin.

"You're not going anywhere, are you, Mouse?" she murmured.

With a relieved sigh, Mouse settled next to Pepper, who appeared to be watching the ocean with one eye shut.

In the kitchen, Jess laid a final strip of duct tape over a cracker box to cover the broken windowpane.

"Thanks for doing that," Parker said. "Sorry if I was abrupt before."

He turned and smiled wryly. "You were fine. Anyone would be stressed out. I'm stressed out. This is all nuts."

She plopped down into a kitchen chair, put her head down in her folded arms, and closed her eyes.

"You don't look like you're feeling much better," he observed.

She heard the chair pull out next to her and raised her head. "I am. Kind of. I realized it's a waiting game. It's not my preference, but there's nothing I can do right now. Nothing in my control. So…just ride it out, and hope that Calli comes home, and hope that there are no more murders or break-ins or vandalism or dog attacks. And let the police do their thing."

Jess laid his arm on the table next to her, palm up. She looked at his grandfather's silver ring shining against his calloused skin, and the way the hairs of his tanned forearm left a smooth swath along the inside of his wrists. Her heart tugged with regret, but she squashed it down. It was time to appreciate the present. His hand felt warm and strong, and he squeezed hers gently.

After a moment he said, "You know, I'm down with pretending to be normal and letting the police do their thing—at least for tonight—but do you want to stop your credit cards first? When my wallet got stolen a couple years back, someone ran up four thousand dollars at Best Buy before I realized it was missing."

"Right. Yes. I'll do that. And do you have any other brilliant advice for someone who feels like they got run over by a steamroller?"

"Netflix? That's about all I feel up to."

She hesitated, wondering if she should pull back to the old-friend zone. What would she be doing if Jess weren't here? Probably having a marathon conversation with Krista, chewing over everything that had happened since they last spoke. Parker hadn't updated her on the break-in or Calli's hat, but relaxing with Jess sounded better than rehashing everything again. Trying to be honest with herself, she amended; relaxing mindlessly with Jess sounded better than almost anything. She'd talk to Krista tomorrow.

Jess cleared his throat. "So, does that sound okay, or do you need to meditate on it?"

"Ha, that's funny. Yeah. Let's just chill for a while."

Chapter Twenty

After Parker wrestled with the credit card issues, they settled on a creepy thriller that neither had yet seen. Jess pronounced her furniture arrangement unacceptable, and they pushed the uncomfortable and seldom-used armchairs out of the way and moved the loveseat around to face the TV. With her legs curled under a blanket, she leaned against his chest, watching actors move around on screen without registering the plot. Jess's warmth seeped into her muscles, and she began to feel sleepy, until the vein of unease she'd tapped into on the balcony gradually took hold of her thoughts.

"Jess?" she said, laying her hand on his chest. "Can we stop the movie for a minute?"

He clicked the pause button. "What is it?"

She sat upright and faced him. "What are we doing? And don't say 'watching a movie'."

He blinked. "I don't know, Parker. Enjoying each other's company? Providing companionship and support during a tough time? Do we have to pin it down, exactly?"

Her heart sank. "No. Not exactly. But you wander in, you help me out, you let me lean on you, and then what? Then you're gone again. You know what? There's nothing you can say that changes this, so I'm sorry I brought it up. I appreciate everything you've done." Hot tears sprang to her eyes, but she blinked them back. She sat upright, shook the blanket out, and folded it on her lap.

He gently took her hand. "Parker. I get it. It's weird being here with you. I mean, I'm glad to be here, I'm glad I can help, but it brings back a lot of memories. Things I haven't thought about for years and years. I didn't think I was still that guy. Now, I kind of feel—"

He stopped. His face flushed.

Her heart lurched. "What?"

He looked down, avoiding her eyes. "I loved Britt," he said. "I was so crazy about her. She drove me frigging nuts, too. Sometimes I didn't recognize myself. At the time, that seemed like a good thing. Intense." He laughed a little.

"Yeah, I remember."

He met her eyes. "But after all the ups and downs, me and Britt broke up for real. And then there was you. And it was different, totally different in a really good way, like things with us didn't have to feel edgy to be legit. But when she disappeared, everything got so strange. We were confused, and lost, and hurting, but still in love. I've thought about it a lot. I'd lost myself with her, and with you, I was more myself."

Parker tensed against the rush of emotion. That was it. That's how it had felt to her, too, like they were better together. The world made more sense once they were figuring it out together. Until it just got too complicated.

For eight years, she'd danced around the pain of his loss, hating him, trying to understand him and forgive him, trying to avoid the whole tangled mess in her mind. Time had provided perspective, but the wound was still there. "That's not entirely true," she said. "That

282

interview you gave. The things you said. How is that love?" His interview with a friend-of-a-friend who had a big YouTube following went viral. The guy eventually took it down after getting legal pressure from Britt's family, but soundbites and quotes turned up here and there for years afterward. It had been too late, anyway. Everyone Parker knew had already watched it.

On a loop, over and over—Jess, staring down at his lap, a wing of his hair sweeping his cheek as he looked into the camera: "Maybe Corey killed Britt."

That was the out-of-context clip, permanently etched in Parker's memory. The entire video hadn't been a whole lot better, but at least you could see Jess tripping over his tongue and backpedaling. "Maybe our relationship freaked Britt out more than I knew. Maybe Corey said something that made her run, got her killed. I don't mean she actually killed Britt. I mean, maybe the two of us—it could have been harder on Britt than I knew. Corey can be a little too honest sometimes. Maybe something she said put Britt over the edge."

Jess looked away from Parker with his jaw clenched. "I know, that was messed up. But you hurt me too. You didn't give me a chance to explain or apologize. I was an idiot. I never should have done that interview with Donny. I should have known he'd mess with me, that he'd do anything to get more followers. But you just left. You had my back, you anchored me, and all of a sudden you were gone, and I was washed out to sea."

She shut her eyes and breathed through the pain, a deep breath in, a slow breath out. She'd been protecting herself. He'd betrayed her, made it seem like there was something shameful about their love. Made it seem like Britt could have been so wounded by something she said that she'd gone and gotten killed. Parker had *had* to leave. He had been her last bastion against a world that hated her, and then he'd piled on.

She breathed deep again and opened her eyes. His were fixed on her face, brown irises with flecks of green and gold.

She'd been in so much pain, so confused, and no one understood that there hadn't been any path but away.

What would have happened if she'd stayed? If she'd tried to talk to Jess again before she left? She'd been drowning in death, the flashes of finding Britt's body, the emotional echoes of the long uncertainty and hope, then the final plummeting knowledge of loss. And the aftershocks that radiated out, suspicion and rage and fear magnified by the press.

Would she and Jess have learned to weather that poisonous environment together?

"But why did you do it?" Parker whispered. "Why did you say I chased her away?"

He looked pained. "I never really thought you did, Corey. Parker. It just came out wrong."

"You said—"

He talked over her. "I said in the interview I thought you might have known where she was. Who she was with. You and I were disgusted with her when she left—remember? She'd been distant and bitchy when she communicated at all, and we'd had it up to there. And then it started sinking in that something was wrong. She would never leave like that. And we both wanted to go back in time, to find out what was wrong and fix it instead of getting pissed at her. I was ashamed that I'd let her push me away without trying harder, and so were you."

Parker nodded. A tear dripped down her nose and she wiped it impatiently away.

"And we talked, and we searched, and we tried to imagine where she could have gone and why, and we spent hours and hours in the woods. And then—it was almost like a switch flipped. I mean, it was both of us, I see that now, but we sort of realized—hey, we had each other, Britt wasn't coming back, and even if we never learned what happened to her, we had each other, and that was really good."

It *had* been good. And Parker had felt guilty about it, too, in the spaces between being with Jess and worrying about Britt.

It took weeks for everyone else, including Britt's parents, to realize something bad must have happened, because she would never leave for so long without any contact. Or without using her bank account or a credit card. Later, it came out that her parents thought she'd gone to stay with Catherine's estranged sister, who wouldn't return her calls. Their reluctance to admit they didn't know where Britt was meant the police didn't start searching until November.

But when people started thinking something was wrong, they started looking at Parker and Jess funny. The best friend and the ex-boyfriend. Rumors flew in the halls of the high school, but worse, on social media, where it wasn't restricted to classmates but could be seen by anyone, and Catherine had fed into that.

"And then we found her body." He swallowed hard. Parker knew he was seeing that hollow in the earth, Britt laid out on fallen leaves with hair mercifully veiling her sunken face.

Jess went on. "I couldn't believe it had come to that.

That we hadn't saved her. The guilt got about a thousand times worse."

Parker nodded wordlessly.

"And I started thinking. I started doubting my feelings. Eric asked me how long you and me were getting it on before Britt and I broke up—he was messing with me, just being a dick for the sake of it. He knew all those rumors were bullshit. But it stuck in my head like a thorn. Had I not loved Britt enough? Was it my fault that she'd run to the guy who killed her? And did I really love you? How could I have switched gears so quickly?

"I doubted myself and doubted you. I thought, what if it was just sex between us, a rebound thing?"

Parker sniffled. The heartbreak of finding the body cast doubt on everything for her, too. Had they tried hard enough to find her? Had Britt left because Parker wasn't a good enough friend, happy to take her sloppy seconds and back off when she got bitchy? But Parker had also believed she and Jess transcended all the bullshit. They were transparent to each other, and despite everything, their love was golden.

Jess continued, "So I started thinking, what about Corey? What's really going on there? Because I'd gone to this paranoid, suspicious place. And I thought, maybe she knew where Britt was all along, maybe that's why everything's easier for her. And when I looked at you, most of the time you seemed okay, deep down, in a way that I was not. Like because you'd been through death and grief before, you had some special knowledge that made it easier for you." He shook his head. "I wondered if you were glad Britt was dead. So that we could move on."

Parker opened her mouth to protest, and he shook

his head. "Don't. I know it sounds terrible when I say it out loud. I didn't put it into words back then. It took me years to realize what a crazy rationalization process that was, putting all the weight of us being together on you. I guess it was some kind of survivor's guilt."

"I was never glad. It wasn't like that." Her eyes filled with hot tears and her throat thickened. She clenched her jaw to force the sobs back.

He gave a humorless smile. "I know. But I was so overwhelmed with everything. Horror, grief, guilt, shame. God, we were kids. I couldn't begin to fathom how Britt could be gone forever."

"So you turned against me," Parker said in a small voice.

"No. I needed some space to sort my head out. I was trying to make sense of everything, and when you were around, it made me even more confused." He reached and wiped tears from her cheek.

"When I tried to talk to you after the interview, you yelled at me. You said I killed Britt," she reminded him.

"No, I said *we* killed Britt," he said. "By saying the wrong things. By letting her go. By finding each other. I was in such a dark place that I wanted you to hurt the way I was hurting. I didn't mean—"

She nodded. "You wanted me to leave you alone. And so I did." Why hadn't they at least tried to talk after calming down? They'd meant so much to each other, and it had all gone away. She had gone away.

"But that's the funny thing. I really didn't want you to leave. I wanted you to argue, to prove I was wrong. And I *was* wrong, Parker. Whatever happened to Britt, there's no use playing what-if. We didn't kill her. And we deserve to have a life."

Parker stared at the rug. A life, yes. But it could never be the same life it would have been.

He said, "The weirdest thing is, when I came out here, I thought we would be strangers. I didn't think I had that old Jess still inside me. I thought he was gone. But it turns out I'm still him in a lot of ways. And you're still the girl I fell in love with. I still love you."

She looked up to find a question in his eyes. A giddy relief washed away some of the darkness in her heart, like a sunrise revealing that the blue of the sky remained after a night of storm and thunder.

Parker shook her head. "God. I must be a little crazy too. You're going to leave in how many days, and my heart is already breaking."

He leaned in and kissed her, and she kissed him back.

When they pulled apart, they looked at each other self-consciously. His eyes shone. She laughed a little. Feeling this much after striving for mere contentment for so long was terrifying. Almost as terrifying as thinking there was a killer in her safe haven, almost as terrifying as thinking someone was toying with her. With both of them. But in a completely different way.

****

Parker woke sweating under covers that had become too heavy, heart pounding. Her ears strained for a half-remembered noise, but all was still and quiet. The light arrowing through the blinds struck the blankets in bright, hard-edged lines.

Her phone said 9:42 a.m. She hadn't slept this late in years. Had she forgotten to do something, be somewhere? No text notifications, no news. No noise outside the closed bedroom door.

Disgruntled, she padded to the kitchen in stockinged feet, and found a scrap of paper on the table. "Thought you could use some rest. Dogs to beach, back soon.—J"

Parker yawned. Maybe she had needed some extra sleep. The cross-country trip had been brief but intense. And the holistic dentists' conference started today, but she'd checked, and she had no sessions until tomorrow morning. She should go over her notes for the group presentation, but that could happen anytime.

The fridge was nearly empty except for a couple of unidentifiable takeout containers that Jess must have gotten while she was away, and in the freezer, the bag of ground coffee held a scant teaspoon. All this murder and travel had really thrown off her housekeeping.

After getting dressed, she went to grab breakfast in the staffroom, but Ellen waylaid her in the lobby. "That man of yours is so handsome," she said, looking hopefully past Parker.

"Sorry, Ellen, he's out with the dogs. Just me, getting some coffee," Parker said.

"Oh, wait a sec. Mail came already. You want it now or later?"

"It's okay. I'll take it," Parker said, and paused while Ellen rifled under the counter. Parker expected a bill or two, but Ellen hefted up a familiar cardboard box. When Parker had taped and addressed it at the hotel in Connecticut, she hadn't realized it still said, "COREY'S CLOTHES" on one side in Dad's messy scrawl.

If Ellen thought that was strange, she didn't comment. She said, "You want to leave it under the counter here and grab it later? It's not heavy, but it's kind of big."

"Sounds good. I'll get it on my way back up.

Thanks, Ellen."

Parker moved to walk past her, but Ellen said, "Oh, wait, Parker, one more thing. Petra wants to talk to you."

"Do you know why?"

"Marta's not working today. I don't blame her. It's hard for any of us to focus with Calli still gone. I can't even imagine what Marta's going through. But yeah, talk to Petra. She may have penciled you in to cover something."

"Thanks, I will."

Petra wasn't in the staff room, but Parker found her in her small office near the gym. Petra pulled out a clipboard as soon as she saw her. "Oh, good, Parker. I know it's not on the schedule, but could you lend a hand with the conference today?"

Parker looked at her askance. "What do you need?"

"It's the spouses. We were providing a van to the outlet mall to keep them busy while their significant others were schmoozing, and Marta was going to drive. She said you wouldn't mind."

"I've never driven one of the vans," Parker said. "Honestly, I haven't even been to the outlet mall yet."

"Perfect. It'll be a good opportunity for you then." Petra smiled. "There are twelve people signed up. It'll be a tight squeeze, but there are fourteen seatbelts aside from the driver."

"Is the van an automatic?" Parker asked, hoping there was a graceful way out of this.

"I think so. The group will meet in the lobby by two. Why don't you get the van at one-thirty and take it around the block, get comfortable with it? The keys are at the front desk. Just ask whoever's at reception, and there's a gas card there, too."

"Great," Parker said unenthusiastically, accepting the clipboard. It had a list of names and cell phone numbers, the initial pickup time and place, and the ending meetup time and place. At least Parker wouldn't be expected to walk around the mall with them. Leave here at two, get back at six. It wouldn't be so bad.

"Give them each your business card so they have your cell number, too," Petra said. "Just in case. Good luck!"

She waved Parker out of her office, and Parker headed back toward the lobby, reminding herself to grab the box after she got her breakfast.

Despite all the mushy stuff last night, she had yet to pin down when Jess was leaving. He had to be in Anchorage on Monday, was all he'd told her. Soon, possibly even today, he'd have to head out, and Parker hated to miss spending the afternoon with him. How unprofessional would it be to meet him at the mall? Would anyone care? Actually, if Petra was right about the numbers, there would be an extra seatbelt in the van and he could come along.

At that thought, her spirits lifted slightly, and she hefted the awkward box up the four flights to her suite, realizing she should have left a note. She'd only meant to be gone for a few minutes, and it had turned into a good half hour. But Jess would have texted if he were worried.

She burst in, ready to greet dogs and man, and stopped short when she encountered silence. Nothing had changed since she left. The kitchen light was off, the dog bed near the balcony door untenanted. Dropping the box on an armchair, she hurried to check the bedroom, bathroom, and kitchen, although she already knew. No one was here.

Her phone had no notifications, and it was almost eleven thirty. On a normal day she and Mouse often went out around six a.m., but considering how late they'd stayed up last night, Jess and the dogs probably left shortly before Parker woke up. It wasn't too weird that they were still out.

On the balcony, she squinted until her eyes adjusted to the glare of the October sun. A brisk wind lifted dry sand in streams across the beach, visible from here as snaky patterns against the darker sand beneath, that would sting against her bare skin if she were running. Maybe Jess was taking his time enjoying the invigorating weather.

Deciding to take advantage of the solitude and silence, Parker lowered herself onto her mat, and gazed with soft focus toward the distant horizon. Tension had tightened her neck and shoulders, even her eyes and forehead. She focused on each body part separately, consciously loosening the strain, but she couldn't forget the empty apartment looming behind her. Last night's intruder, Jess's absence. A panicky irritation rose with a bloom of adrenaline. Her skin prickled with a sudden chill, and unease washed through her, though she wasn't sure why.

She tried to breathe through it and let the emotion pass, but it was too strong. Frustrated with herself, she rose and returned to the somnolent apartment, where dust motes danced in rays of sunshine. Seeking distraction, she grabbed the cardboard box and brought it to the bedroom.

The room remained austere except for Jess's oversized duffel bag unzipped and spilling underwear and T-shirts along his side of the bed. She flipped on the overhead light and set the box on top of the plain white duvet cover, then ripped off the shipping tape quickly, like tearing off a bandage. Upending the box, she let the contents slide out. The green wooden chest landed on its side in the midst of crumpled clothing.

Lifting it from the mess, Parker marveled at the intricate carvings of flowers and vines, the way the green stain on the wood deepened in the centers of shapes and lightened around their edges. Automatically, she pushed the pressure points to pop open the lid. Emptiness gaped at her, the flat rectangle of the felt-lined bottom draining her good intentions to sort through the clothes and get things done. The sting of the missing purse hit her again, and the uneasy feeling she got knowing a stranger had been in the apartment with bad intentions.

She plopped down with the chest in her lap, feeling her weight jounce gently on the mattress.

Britt had been gone a long time. Parker hadn't even known the notes existed until a few days ago. But out of nowhere, they had promised a lifeline to the past, to the real Britt. To the real Corey, too, and all of her friends, the people they were back then. Their struggles, their preoccupations, what they thought was funny or maddening or important.

The notes might have held a reference to someone or something that would shed light on why Britt died and where she had been all those months, but they might not have. Mostly, Parker wanted to hold proof that Britt had been real, that they had all been real and worthwhile, and that period of their lives had been special and more than a prelude to tragedy.

No use dwelling on something she no longer had.

She thrust the chest off her lap, stood and regarded the mess of old clothes once more. Reaching for a crumpled piece of blue jersey, she wondered if it was that scoop-necked dress she used to like, when her brain caught up to her ears.

When she'd set the chest aside so roughly, something had thudded inside. The apartment was quiet except for the humming of the fridge and the occasional distant seagull or police siren filtered through glass. The out-of-place noise still echoed in her mind. A light kerchunk.

She could have left the cover unlatched, and when it fell, it jarred itself shut. But there had been layers to the sound. Had there been? She lifted the chest in both hands.

A gentle shake shifted something back and forth. When she held it to her ear, she heard not only the light kerchunk but also a whispery friction.

She popped the box top open again and poked and prodded at the felt glued to the bottom. In the corners, the fabric was thick and fuzzy, coming away from the wood. She picked at an edge until she could grasp it and pulled upward, holding her breath. Was there a false bottom?

The felt tore in her hand. She set it aside, remembering she'd promised Dad to ship the chest back to Catherine. That wasn't a priority, but for his sake, she should probably keep it in one piece.

Something was hidden inside. It had to be in the bottom; the lid was carved from a single piece of wood. Because the lid's release was a pair of hidden pressure points, maybe there was another one for the inside floor? She ran her hands over every surface, pushing and prodding, and remembered how Britt had giggled when Parker tried to open it the first time she visited Britt's house. Parker, who'd considered herself good with puzzles, had tried everything. No false bottom had opened then.

She scrutinized each side of the chest and rolled her eyes when she reached the rear panel. The "secret" compartment wasn't secret, just well-camouflaged. A gap a hairsbreadth thick outlined an area about eight inches wide and an inch and a half tall, just above the chest's stubby back feet. A pair of discolored toothpick-slim hinges marked the bottom of the panel.

Parker pried at the gap with a fingernail before noticing a bit of flower in just the right position to get some leverage.

The hinged panel opened downward. She cleared a space on the duvet and dumped the contents.

Chapter Twenty-One

Various items avalanched from the narrow opening and fell in a pile below: folded papers, triangulated notes, ticket stubs. The envelope from a greeting card, over-stuffed and held shut with a rubber band. A thin gold chain tangled with a dull silver chain. A set of keys on a metal key ring that read "BRITTANY" in red block letters. A couple of tiny plastic bags, crumpled and worn.

Parker peered into the back of the compartment and shook free two papers that had gotten stuck. Then she set the chest to one side, feeling as if she were in a dream. She had wished for a piece of Britt and their childhood, and what did she find? Something better. Britt's most precious treasures. The ones she kept secret from even her best friends.

Catherine had said the chest was full of poison, but Parker doubted she'd discovered the hidden compartment. If she had, she wouldn't have had the patience to return the tightly packed contents when she was done.

Parker hesitated, but not out of fear that she'd discover something hurtful. It was that Britt, who'd shared so much, kept these few things back. What would Britt say if she knew Parker was about to look at the things most private to her?

An image of Britt's face veiled by a curtain of blonde hair arose in response. Britt would say nothing.

Or she would wish she had shared more before she died.

Parker ran her hand through the pile, spreading items across the bed to see everything better. She picked up the "Brittany" key ring, the metal cool and heavy in her hand.

For her sweet sixteen, Britt's parents had surprised her with a red Lexus, complete with a high end stereo system, sunroof, and white leather seats. The key ring she ended up using was a later gift from Jess, an oversized silver heart, and when she disappeared, that was the one lying in the center console of her car, where she wasn't supposed to leave it but always did.

This must be her spare set of keys, with the keyring her parents had given her on her birthday morning. Parker set it to one side and reached for the baggies.

The first one held two perfectly rolled joints, probably the work of Britt's older brother Thomas, who usually hooked them up. The second held half a dozen Xanax, which had been freely available in the Ryden master bathroom. Parker set those aside, too.

As she lifted the tangle of gold and silver necklaces, her phone vibrated. Hoping it was finally Jess, she swiped with one thumb to check.

Krista—*What are you up to? Time for a call?*—

Parker considered her response, but if they spoke she'd spill the beans about the chest. Selfishly, she wasn't ready to share. Plus, she'd end up talking about Jess, and Krista would give her a hard time. Parker sent a quick*, later,* then scrolled to Jess's contact info. She hit "Call" and listened to it ring until his voicemail picked up. Heart sinking, she hung up without leaving a message and turned back to the necklaces.

They were so knotted together they would have

taken hours to untangle, but it wasn't necessary because the pendants were visible. The thicker silver chain held two half-heart charms, the kind that said, "BE FRI" and "ST ENDS." Krista and Parker each had a necklace just like it, from Christmas of freshman year when they'd each exchanged them with each other. She'd never seen the pendant on the fine gold chain, though. A dolphin with a tiny sapphire eye. Maybe a gift to Britt from her parents when she was younger?

Parker set the tangled chains back on the bed. All that was left was the papers and the envelope, but she was still fighting her own reluctance. She wished Jess were here, so she could stop worrying about him and Mouse and Pepper, and they could look at this together. She should wait.

In case she'd somehow missed a call, she checked her phone again. Then, with a sudden certainty that he'd driven somewhere, she stood. His note said he was going to the beach, but it didn't say which beach.

Parker reminded herself she was being silly. If he left right before she woke up, he'd only been gone three hours. It wasn't that hard to take a three-hour walk on the beach. Heck, he could have headed south across the bridge like they'd done yesterday and gotten turned around on the trails at the park. He might have dropped his phone or forgotten to plug it in last night.

But if he'd taken his truck, he could have gone farther. He could have driven to a northern or southern beach access. He was a tourist. Maybe he wanted to see Devil's Churn or Cascade Head before he left for good. Nothing to worry about, and if she added drive time, three hours for a beach trip with the dogs made sense.

She trotted down the interior stairs and peered out

the window in the staff door. Her heart sank. Jess's dusty black truck was still parked up the street near the real estate office, so wherever he'd gone, he'd gone on foot.

More slowly, she made her way back upstairs, fighting involuntary negative thoughts she knew were ridiculous. Jess wasn't lying at the bottom of the cliff stairs with his mouth and eyes taped shut. And Jess hadn't kidnapped the dogs. Even if he'd decided he and Parker had gotten too deep, too fast, he wouldn't have taken her dogs and left his truck and duffel bag.

No, he'd gotten carried away on a long walk, and his phone died, and he was trudging along with Mouse running circles around him. Poor Jess, he probably had to carry Pepper by now. He'd be cursing himself, too, knowing how worried Parker would be.

She returned to the bedroom and her discovery. This time, she roughed the loose pile of papers into a stack, then sorted through them. Britt's birth certificate, the title to the Lexus, her social security card. A couple of birthday cards: a really sweet one from her grandma and a hand-drawn one from her younger sister. And then notes—four little triangles, and a few notebook sheets folded in quarters and crumpled from being squished in the compartment with all the other stuff.

Parker's hand hovered over the pile of notes then landed on the over-stuffed envelope, because the distended shape hinted at its contents. When she eased off the rubber band and unfolded the flap, she found a stack of Polaroids.

She hadn't seen a Polaroid camera in years, not since Britt's, and wasn't sure they were still around. Back then, they were retro-cool. The Polaroid camera took non-digital, self-developing photos, which printed instantly on special film. The pictures developed in a couple of minutes, popping out of the plastic box nearly white and the image magically taking shape, first ghostly, then sharp and vivid.

The top two pictures showed Krista, Britt, and Corey hamming it up the day Britt got the camera for her thirteenth birthday. Parker's nostalgic smile dropped as soon as she flipped to the next one, and she shuffled through the rest. Naked and semi-naked teenage boys, horrifyingly including Jess, and then, at the bottom, a couple of Britt wearing lingerie.

Parker squared the stack back together, wishing she could un-see them, but before she wrapped it back up, she snorted a laugh as a memory came to mind. The very first thing Britt had said when she tore the gift wrap off the camera had been, "Thanks Mom and Dad, now I can take my own dirty pictures!" Sarcastically, to be sure. No adults were in earshot, her parents having gone out and left them in the care of the housekeeper, who was in her room watching soap operas. Britt had received her big gift from them, a new laptop, that morning at breakfast, and they'd left the rest for her to open with her friends.

In school, the students had been lectured repeatedly about not sending anything online that you didn't want all over the internet for the rest of your life. Experimenting with the Polaroid camera could have seemed safer to Britt. But like anything else, these prints could be photographed with a smartphone and uploaded to the cloud in less than a second. Parker wondered if Britt had ever let any of these out of her hands. Were there digital copies somewhere, or had she truly kept them locked away?

Parker shuffled through again. Jess was at the top of

the pile, leaning back against the headboard of Britt's old bed with a grin and nothing else. He looked terribly innocent, in a horny teenager kind of way.

She flipped through the rest. Dave Sheehan, onetime captain of the lacrosse team, naked on the same bamboo-patterned sheets. Mitchell Younger, who'd graduated two years ahead of them, shirtless in the backseat of the Lexus, ignoring the camera in favor of masturbating intently with eyes squeezed shut.

Okay, Britt had gotten kinkier than she'd shared with Corey and Krista. Parker blushed, thinking of herself and Jess making out in the shed. Parker wouldn't have told Britt all the details, either, even without the ex-boyfriend piece. But it was hard to believe Britt hadn't ever mentioned dating these guys.

Had they even dated? When?

Parker set Mitchell's picture aside, planning to ask Jess if he'd known Britt had an intimate relationship with him, and went on to the next.

Another one of Jess, in Britt's bed again. This one was dimly lit, with deep shadows obscuring a lot of detail. Jess was cross-legged against the headboard, one hand cuffed to the wooden bedpost. His head tilted back as if he were faking relaxation, but his jaw was clenched, his eyes narrowed. A pillow held over his lap hid his level of arousal, but he looked seriously pissed off.

He'd said more than once that Britt drove him crazy, but Parker hadn't realized she actually handcuffed him to the bed. Were those real handcuffs? They looked real.

The next one was someone else, and at first, Parker was just relieved it wasn't Jess or Eric or anyone else she knew. A skinny boy with dark hair, whose face was bisected by the edge of the shot. He must have jerked away at the last minute, blurring the picture. He was shyer than the others, with tanned arms and legs dotted with mosquito bites, wrapped around to cover as much of his chest and genitals as possible.

Recognition and denial arrived simultaneously. It looked like Keith, but it couldn't be Keith. Krista's little brother had followed them around intermittently like a nerdy, humorless puppy. He fetched upon request and got teased unmercifully, and whenever he ceased to be useful or amusing, Krista would order him to get lost. He watched Britt with puppy-dog eyes and she barely registered his existence. At least, that's what Parker had believed. Until now.

She flipped to the next photo. Keith—and although she couldn't see his face from this angle, she recognized the distinctive dark hair—lay diagonally across Britt's purple batik bedspread on his stomach with hands cuffed behind him. There were red stripes on his butt and thighs, as if he'd been whipped.

This time, Parker shoved the pile back into the envelope without second thoughts. Rising, she paced and worried at her lip, trying to think. Why would Britt have Keith in her bed? Was there any way he could have been in her room, with her camera, with someone else? Then why would she keep this picture?

Parker hadn't had doubts about the other guys, even though she'd never known Britt slept with Mitch or Dave. Why did she have doubts about Keith?

Because Keith was Krista's brother. Because Keith was two grades behind the group, and that was a huge difference in high school. Because Keith was humorless, awkward, geeky, and Britt was gorgeous, older, popular, rebellious. It didn't fit.

On the other hand, Keith had been on the swim team and looked it, with well-muscled shoulders and slim hips. Yes, he was skinny, but he was already taller than Britt, and not un-cute. Just young. And Krista's brother. And…

Parker huffed angrily and popped off the bed to pace into the living room. Had Krista known about this? It must have been before the accident, before Keith disappeared into months of rehabilitation and then a special school. How long had the relationship gone on? When had it happened? Was it after Jess and Britt broke up, during the months Parker and Jess were dating, and Britt was becoming more and more bitchy? Parker pictured the marks on Keith's legs and shuddered. They weren't just pink. They'd looked bloody.

Then she slowed herself down. It was probably consensual. In Jess's picture, he'd looked pretty fed up with the cuffs, but he'd probably agreed, at least initially. He and Parker had tied each other up with a pair of nylon stockings once, which wasn't all that different. Except the stockings would have come loose with a tug, and the handcuffs weren't coming off without help.

In Keith's case, it felt worse. Consent wouldn't mean much, because he was so much more of a kid. Britt had too much power over him.

Parker guzzled a tall glass of water at the sink. With no one else around, the silence loomed. The sound of her own swallowing was magnified, and the old building rattled in the wind off the ocean. She set the glass down, nauseous.

Britt's pile of papers still awaited her, but when she returned to the bedroom, she couldn't bring herself to go through them. Suddenly decisive, she beelined to the dresser instead and grabbed her running gear. Screw waiting around. She would run down the beach. Jess was a tall guy, traveling with two distinctive dogs and not trying to be subtle about it. He'd be easy to see. And if Parker happened to glance under the bottom of the cliff stairs to reassure herself it was all clear, so much the better.

She was about to leave by the fire escape when she glanced at her watch and swore. Unless she came across Jess almost immediately, she would be late for the trip to the outlet mall. And even if that happened, could she leave knowing that they had to talk about and look at Britt's stuff together? She swore again. Sure, Marta shouldn't have to work when she was falling apart with worry for her daughter, but Parker wasn't much better off right now. She couldn't imagine climbing into a van and driving out of town. Her entire body would rebel.

Her fingers hesitated over the phone, then she texted Seth and Petra.

—I'm sorry, something has come up. Cannot drive party to outlet mall as planned. Please find cover or cancel. Apologies, will explain later—

It was cowardly to send a text, but she couldn't handle questions right now.

She stared at the phone for another few seconds, chewing the inside of her cheek, then shot a text to Balderas.

—Haven't been able to reach Jess who is out with both dogs for 3+ hrs now, much too long, not responding—

Parker couldn't think of a good way to explain how worried she was, and decided to let it lie. She hit send.

Tucking the phone into a side pocket, she went

down the stairs two at a time, then started west through the parking lot. The salty air carried the scent of sugar from the taffy shop's open door. The bright sunshine should have lifted her spirits, but the glare against the green waters of the ocean seemed like a personal attack. She picked up her pace, deciding to skip her usual stretches and go straight to the beach.

"Hey!"

The word was windblown and indistinct, but Parker glanced back, hoping it was Jess, or even Calli. There were a few people hurrying by on the sidewalk, and as she watched, a woman in a trench coat turned toward her, waving one arm broadly. She had large round sunglasses and a scarf tied around her head à la nineteen-forties movie star, and Parker didn't recognize her until she took them off. Parker rolled her eyes and started back across the parking lot.

****

"What did you do to your hair?" Parker couldn't help laughing. Between Krista's trench coat, sunglasses, and newly brunette locks, Parker wouldn't have recognized her if Krista hadn't called her over. "Is this all the rage up in Seattle?"

Krista hugged her, then stepped back, patting her hair self-consciously. "Does it look ridiculous? I just didn't want to be recognized."

Parker snorted. "By who? If you were coming down to—" She stopped, humor waning. "Wait, are you here to help look for Calli? I told you, there aren't any search parties or anything. Did you talk to Marta?"

Krista clasped Parker's arm. "I came for you. I was worried."

Reflexively, Parker glanced down at the beach,

where her own worries were currently focused. No sign of Jess. She shook her head. "I'm fine, really," she said. "A lot has been happening, but nothing I can't handle. I can't believe you came down, though! That's so nice. Did you get time off?"

Krista waved away Parker's concern and looked her up and down, from T-shirt to capri tights to running shoes. She shivered melodramatically. "Aren't you freezing? I thought we could get lunch and talk, but you'd probably turn into a popsicle."

"I was about to go for a run," Parker said. "But, um, okay. I'll go later. How long are you going to be here?" *And where are you staying,* she wondered. Parker meant to buy an air mattress so guests could sleep in the living room, because the loveseat was so short, but she hadn't gotten around to it. Also, was she ready to deal with the shit Krista would give her about Jess? Not to mention, even if Krista got a hotel room, Parker would still have to let her into the apartment to hang out at some point. Parker pictured the mess on her bed. The photos of Krista's brother.

"I'm not sure," Krista said, glancing absently up and down the street. "Maybe a night or two. So what do you think? Do you want to change clothes and grab some lunch?"

"Lunch sounds good. I'm fine, though, as long as we're going somewhere casual. I've got my credit card on me. Did you have somewhere in mind?" Parker pulled her phone out as if to demonstrate the credit card pocket, and checked for notifications. Petra had responded to her text according to the locked screen snippet:

—*I can cover this*—

Moderately relieved, Parker slipped the phone back

into her pocket.

"Sushi," Krista said, predictably enough since it was her all time-favorite.

"Does that mean we're driving?" Parker said. There was a hole-in-the-wall sushi place a mile away, but it was up a steep hill. They could walk, but it would add a chunk of time and effort.

"Do you mind?"

Parker shrugged. "Your car or mine?"

"I'm parked right here. I'll drive," Krista said, pointing across the street to a sleek white van with tinted windows.

"New wheels?" Parker asked. Krista had been driving a forest green SUV for years and loved it.

Krista shrugged and clicked the key ring she'd pulled from her bag. The van flashed its lights in response. "The RAV-4 was acting up. I got a rental."

Parker climbed into the passenger side and glanced into the spacious rear compartment. Two rows of seats and a cargo area, like an airport shuttle. "Not sure about your taste," Parker teased. "Unless you're planning on providing taxi rides while you're here. Uber anybody?"

"Yeah, well, you take what you can get."

Krista turned south, and Parker relaxed. Krista's timing was perfect. Parker had been over-reacting to a grown man spending an extra hour on the beach. Big deal! It would be great to step away from the fraught atmosphere of TBI and eat sushi. Between the blood sugar boost and Krista being her snarky self, it was just what Parker needed.

"I really appreciate that you came," Parker said again. "You surprised the shit out of me, though! It's really okay with your work?"

Krista waved a dismissive hand. "It's fine. What are friends for, anyway? I may have slightly exaggerated the emergency nature of the situation, but oh my god, I needed a road trip. And I miss it down here! The resort is great, but it's total immersion, much more than TBI. It's practically a cult."

Parker nodded. Krista's new workplace was very corporate and slick, part of an international chain. Parker could imagine a sort of Stepford feeling to being surrounded by all the super-groomed, super-fit, super-positive staff all toeing the party line. And where TBI had thirty-two guest suites on four floors, The Waverly was a gated resort which included rental houses and cottages, a luxury hotel with over four hundred rooms, and even a small shopping center.

She asked, "Are you really avoiding Marta and Seth? I thought you guys were still close."

Krista grinned. "Nah. I was joking. The hair is just an experiment. But if this is the response I get…"

"Show me again," Parker said.

Krista popped both hands off the wheel to frame her face and hairdo, then resumed control as they arrived at a stop sign. The rich chocolate bob overpowered her pale skin and light eyes and narrowed her naturally round face. It was a completely different look for her.

"You're always gorgeous and you know it," Parker said. "But some highlights might give it some depth. What do you think?"

Krista squeezed her knee. "Yes! I thought that too. You're so good, Parker. So diplomatic. And who else can I count on to tell me the truth?"

As they passed a stretch of beach, Parker suddenly realized they hadn't turned east toward the Momiji. "Oh, did you change your mind about sushi?"

"No, no. I wanted to go to that other place. Down the highway."

"Okay." Parker's heart sank a little. She was grateful for the break, but driving to Seal Rock and back would add an hour to the trip. Good thing she'd made arrangements with Petra. But it would be more of a delay than she'd counted on in looking for Jess and the pups. They would doubtlessly be home by the time she got back, anyway. Parker sighed.

"Is something wrong?" Krista said, shooting a concerned look over the tops of her sunglasses.

"No." Parker squeezed her eyes shut, frustrated with herself. "Maybe. Yes."

"Oh, honey, I knew it. Tell me."

Parker opened her mouth to say how the murder craziness and Calli being missing had gotten her anxious about Jess being gone for so long this morning with the dogs, but then she stopped. Mouse. Krista hadn't asked about how Mouse was doing, or even where she was or why Parker hadn't taken her out for the run she'd planned to do. And Krista was practically Mouse's godmother.

Parker stole another look at Krista in her disguised movie-star getup. An uneasy feeling tightened her gut. With as casual a tone as she could muster, she said, "Did you know Britt and your brother dated?"

Krista raised one finely threaded eyebrow. "Dated? Keith didn't date."

"Okay. Well, what would you call it?"

Krista paused, and Parker thought she would deny any kind of relationship between them. But Krista said, "Fucking."

The hostile tone stole Parker's breath. Krista kept her eyes on the highway. After a long moment, Parker forced a tiny laugh to break the tension. "Wow, I had no idea. That's…shocking. Why didn't you tell me?"

"I would have gotten around to it. How did you find out?"

Parker mentally kicked herself. She'd planned to tell Krista about the chest eventually, but had hoped to talk to Jess first. No choice, now.

"I found some pictures that Britt had hidden," Parker said. "When I visited back east this week. There were a couple with Keith."

Ahead, a slow-rolling RV lumbered onto the highway from the state park, forcing Krista to slam the brakes. Parker clenched the armrest, and the tires skidded, then caught. Krista continued at half-speed as the heavy vehicle in front of them attempted to accelerate up the hill.

"Britt screwed my brother over, big-time. She full-on ruined his life," Krista said finally. "It doesn't need to be a secret. Not anymore."

Parker's brain fought for purchase. Krista had worn a disguise to visit Parker. Krista hadn't asked about Mouse. Krista was pissed off—still—because Britt had treated Keith badly.

"Britt was seeing him after she broke up with Jess, while me and Jess were going out?" Parker said, floundering.

Krista smirked. "Before, during, after…she was seeing him whenever she wanted. And he wasn't the only one. I'm not defending his taste, that's for sure."

Britt had always been a flirt, but it hadn't meant anything. Certainly not what Krista was implying, which made it sound like Britt was making booty calls all over town. No one else's name had come up during the murder investigation, which meant Britt and anyone she dated must have been crazy discreet for high school students. Or maybe the police had discovered other relationships and dismissed them. It was hard to believe that kind of thing wouldn't have leaked all over the media, but impossible to know for sure.

A passing lane opened up, and Krista jammed down the gas to swerve past the RV. Parker gripped the van's dashboard. "Watch out!"

Krista ignored her. "For a long time, I tried to protect you from the fallout," she said. "But then I realized you may not have known exactly what she was doing. But you knew what she was."

"What she was? You mean, sleeping around? Because I didn't know that." Parker flashed to the boys' pictures. What had Britt been? Sexually adventurous? Possibly sadistic? Parker definitely hadn't known that, and still wasn't sure. Six or seven photos didn't pigeonhole a person, not without context.

But Britt had kept them. Even the one of Keith with belt marks on his thighs. That meant something.

"She was a cruel, manipulative bitch," Krista said.

"She was our best friend!" It sounded weak in her own ears.

Krista shook her head, as if disgusted. "How many times did she taunt you about your clueless dad and his stupid rules? How many times did she rub her money in both of our faces? How many times did she play us off against each other? And then she passed Jess on to you like sloppy seconds, when even she got disgusted by how much shit he put up with from her! I still can't believe you fell for it."

"She had nothing to do with it. They'd broken up!"

"Yeah, for the seventieth time. She was like, 'oh, it's so hard to see Jess and Corey together but I'm glad they're happy,' like some kind of martyr, and you guys ate it up with a spoon. Checking in with her all the time about her feelings. All the while, she's screwing my brother! Who was barely fourteen!"

That was not how Parker remembered things. Britt had been clear that she was fine with Jess and Corey being together, even though she herself hadn't moved on to dating anyone else. She'd become distant and moody, and yes, Parker had felt a little manipulated, but no one had pandered to her. They'd just been trying to figure out if Britt was okay, like any friend would do.

But, as it turned out, Britt had been seeing someone else. Keith, at least. The other boys? Impossible to know exactly when any of those pictures had been taken.

Yuzen, the Seal Rock sushi restaurant, disappeared in the rear window. Parker's stomach sank. "You missed the turn," she said, but her voice was small.

"I changed my mind about lunch," Krista said casually. "Surprise! We have other plans."

Chapter Twenty-Two

"Aren't you going to tell me how worried you are, Parker?" Krista asked. She turned to Parker briefly, her face arranged into a concerned smile. "Aren't you going to share how, just like always, people around you are dropping like flies and you're afraid that there's something about you that attracts violence? Your poor mother. And your poor uncle, because he was a victim too, wasn't he? Mental illness is such a bitch. And then your babysitter. And then your best friend. And now, well, fuck, it's everyone, isn't it? Clients, friends, lovers, dogs…"

Parker swallowed hard. "Krista, do you know where Jess is?"

Krista smiled as if in congratulations for a job well done. "Yes, I do. You know, I rushed all the way down here last week to protect you from him. And look at you now, practically fainting with worry because he won't answer his phone. How quickly we forget."

Parker blinked. Last week. Jess hadn't arrived until Saturday. But Parker had texted Krista looking for sympathy the same day he called, the same day Ryan died.

"Where is he?" Parker demanded, voice high with panic.

"He's come for a visit. And your little dog, too! Well, both dogs, but it sounded better, don't you think?"

"What are you saying?"

"I hadn't wanted to tell you so soon. I was hoping to play things out for another few days, but look at you! Even though I took away all your clues, you still sniffed me out. Good on you."

"Krista, where are they?"

"Don't you worry, we're going to see them right now."

"And Calli?" Parker asked. "Is Calli 'visiting' you too?"

Eyes wide, Krista zipped her lips, repressing a grin. Parker's phone pressed against her left thigh, clearly outlined through the fabric of her running tights. Her fingers itched to pull it out and dial 911, but she was afraid to call attention to it.

"I don't get it," Parker tried. "You've been one of my best friends since we were kids."

A smile played around Krista's mouth.

"Are you pissed at me?" Parker asked. "Or Jess? Both of us?" Krista used to have a wicked temper, snapping in sudden anger, but she'd never been one to hide when she was upset. She'd mellowed a lot in recent years, too. But now Parker sensed a deep vein of rage which must have been there all along, below the surface. Like Uncle Danny's. Her fear solidified like ice in her veins.

"Why ever would I be pissed at you?" Krista said. "I came to help you, remember?" She veered suddenly into a gravel driveway on the ocean side of the highway. Parker tipped toward her, then rebounded hard into the passenger door. The van bounced, bottomed out, and descended steeply through a thick stand of scrubby beach pines. The highway disappeared behind them and moments later, under the rough-hewn portico of a stone beach cottage, Krista parked and turned off the engine.

Hands shaking, Parker yanked off her seatbelt, threw open the door, and stumbled down from the high footwell. Her ankle twisted, and she landed on her knees on the gravel. Thinking she'd dial 911 and run toward the highway, she struggled to her feet. Krista did yoga, lots of yoga, but Parker would win a footrace any day. All she needed was a few seconds to call for help.

Krista's footsteps crunched closer while Parker fumbled with the lock screen. "Stop," Krista said coolly. Surprised by the quiet tone, Parker glanced up mid-swipe. Krista stood unperturbed, aiming a gun at Parker's face.

Gun. Parker's thoughts evaporated in an explosion of terror. Instinctively, her hands went up, the phone with them.

Krista came closer, smiling her half-smile. "You don't want to leave now, do you?" she said. "This is where your honey is. And your dog."

Parker swallowed and nodded. "Okay." The gears in her mind ground slowly, unwillingly. Would Krista really pull the trigger?

Had she killed Ryan and Adam just to taunt Parker?

And Calli. Krista's anger at Britt made it sound like all this was wrapped up with the past. Was Calli a convenient teenage stand-in for Britt?

Krista directed Parker back around the van and gestured at a narrow white door next to the garage. The yard was private, surrounded by scrubby trees, a chimney to the north betraying a neighboring house.

"Don't bother screaming," Krista said. "It's just another vacant vacation rental. Now open the door."

Static blurred the edges of Parker's vision and she thought she might faint. A hysterical thought bubbled up. Having a gun held on you didn't look this incapacitating in the movies. Did everyone go weak in the knees and want to vomit?

Parker didn't have time to faint. She breathed in deeply, twice, as she fumbled with the knob, then let all the air seep out as the door swung open.

Krista shoved her hard, and Parker stumbled into a narrow mudroom with a tiled floor. As she tried to catch herself, the phone dropped from her hand and bounced to a stop on a colorful rag rug. Parker caught her balance and whirled to face Krista.

Muffled but nearby, Mouse's familiar bark rang out, and then Pepper joined in with some yips. Tears of relief filled her eyes. They sounded so close they must be in the adjacent garage.

"Shut up!" Krista yelled, and there was silence, except for a whimper from Pepper. Krista turned to slide the deadbolt into place, her back toward Parker, the gun pointing vaguely to one side. Parker was five inches taller and twenty pounds heavier. She calculated her chances of tackling Krista before she fired, but hesitated too long. Krista turned even as Parker tensed to move. "Now, now, don't get any big ideas. You'll ruin the party." Krista's glance fell on the fallen phone. "That's a good place for that."

"Krista, please, what are we doing here?"

Krista shook her head. "You'll find out if you do what I say. I will shoot you if I have to. Don't think I won't. Turn around and go up those steps and through the door. You'll be in the living room, and trust me, there's nowhere to go from there. I'll be right behind you."

Stymied, Parker faced the three wooden steps rising to another white door. The knob turned in her hand, and she stepped through, feeling the crawling sensation of the target on her back.

The space she stepped into was a large open-plan rectangle, with ocean-facing floor-to-ceiling windows making up most of the far wall. A kitchen and eating nook took up one corner and a partial loft above also faced the sea. Parker's adrenaline-fed alertness cataloged the basic layout even as she zeroed in on the people. A fit-looking man with gauze covering one eye regarded her with unsettling intensity as he trotted down the spiral stairway from the loft area. Calli was closer, sitting upright and pale on a sectional leather sofa. She met Parker's gaze briefly, looking forlorn, but then her eyes slipped away and down to the floor. Lacking her usual dramatic makeup, she looked years younger, her green hair lank around her face.

Parker discovered Jess last, bound to a kitchen chair in the far corner, facing away from her. Silver duct tape wound around his torso and arms, and he was motionless, his head bowed.

"Jess?" Parker called. He didn't react, but the dogs started barking again and out of the corner of her eye, she saw Calli flinch.

"Shut the hell up!" Krista snapped. She'd come up next to Parker from behind and Parker felt what she assumed was the gun prod into her back.

The barking continued.

"Shut up!" Krista screamed.

Calli whispered, "They heard Parker. Can't we just let them in? They'll calm down if they're with her."

Pepper's yapping reached a crescendo Parker hadn't heard since finding Adam's body, and Mouse let loose with throat-tearing volume.

Krista narrowed her eyes. "You would like that, wouldn't you?" she asked Parker.

"I can make them quiet down," Parker promised.

"Fine. Do it," Krista said. Calli made her way to a door next to the one they'd just entered through, and Mouse and Pepper flew past her and were on Parker immediately, panting and jumping and still barking, now with joy.

"Quiet down, guys," Parker said, crouching to hug them both and check for injury. "Quiet down. It's okay. I'm here." She patted them all over, finding no wounds, but smelling the musty reek of fear. Both dogs pressed up against her legs as she stood.

When silence reigned again, save for the panting of the dogs, Krista said, "Make them lie down out of the way. I would hate to have to shoot innocent animals, but I will if they cause problems."

"Oh, you can't shoot the dogs. Shoot Jesse James here before you shoot the dogs," Keith protested with a wince. Parker recognized him now, matching the blandly handsome features and the one dark eye she could see to what she remembered of the teen in Britt's photos. He remained standing as Parker settled the dogs, then sat on the tweed couch facing the sectional where Calli perched. His voice was deep, with a sincere note of concern.

Krista narrowed her eyes at him, then fake-smiled at Parker. "Parker, you sit next to my brother. And no funny business. You know I love Mouse, but I cannot take any more canine hysterics."

Parker lowered herself onto the couch next to Keith and patted the cushion on her other side. Mouse jumped up and settled herself as if they were on the loveseat at home, followed by Pepper. "Good dogs," Parker said. She asked Krista, "What's wrong with Jess? Is he okay?"

"We didn't do anything to Jess that he didn't ask for. Look at this!" Keith pointed at his bandaged eye. "Just because I invited him into the van for a little chat."

Krista ignored both of them. "Slide over more, Parker, behind the table. Keith, scooch closer to her."

Parker moved to the center cushion, noticing with a start that the thigh pocket in her tights, where her phone had been, was still distended. She had her pepper spray. Her heart kicked up a notch. It wouldn't do much against a gun, but it was something.

Krista had positioned her so she was trapped behind the coffee table, a substantial wood and glass affair topped by fresh flowers and magazines. *Men's Health* was open to a photo spread of pushup positions. Keith sat in the corner of the couch, angled to look directly at Parker with his unbandaged eye. His hair was combed forward with long bangs in a style that had been popular in the early 2000s. Extending from the hairline, a raised line of scar tissue twisted around his left eye socket, giving him a permanent rakish squint.

Krista tossed her coat on the back of the sectional, revealing a flowered blouse and a short lavender skirt. She clicked something on the gun and shoved it into a holster under the skirt's flirty ruffle. Parker knew nothing about guns apart from what she'd seen in movies, but she hoped that sound had been the safety.

Krista settled close to Calli, who inched away from her as if to focus better on the open notebook.

Keith leaned across Parker to speak to his sister and Parker could smell cinnamon on his breath, like he'd been sucking fireball candies. "So, sis, could we go talk in the mudroom?"

Krista rearranged the ruffle of her skirt over the gun, then caressed Calli's hip possessively. Her eyes were on Parker, watching for a reaction, as she said, "You want to leave our guest all alone? There's really nothing to discuss. I told you Parker might come over today."

Parker tried to keep any reaction from her face. Calli hadn't responded to Krista's touch, but neither had she shown surprise or annoyance.

"You told me that was Plan C," Keith corrected.

Calli clapped her notebook shut. Parker glanced at her, but Calli's hair veiled her expression as she fumbled to clip her pen onto the notebook's cover.

Krista said, "Well, remember how you fetched all the notes for me, so there was no reason for Miss Parker here to become suspicious?"

"Yeah?" he said. "Sorry," he added parenthetically to Parker.

Krista sneered. "You didn't get them all."

"I did so. Didn't I, Corey?" he appealed.

Parker looked back and forth between them. "That was you? You stole my purse. You broke into my apartment. What the hell?"

"I had to," Keith said. "To protect you."

Parker opened her mouth to ask, "From what?" but realized she knew. To protect her from learning something. To protect her from ending up here. She looked at Calli again. The girl was now leaning into Krista, with Krista's hand kneading solicitously at her shoulder. Calli must have been doing Krista's bidding when she broke in and left the lavender, but that wasn't to "protect" Parker, not back then. Krista had been toying with them both, messing with Parker's head and getting Calli to do her bidding.

"What do you guys want?" Parker pleaded. "I don't get it. Who cares if Keith was sleeping with Britt when we were kids? Nobody! Just let us go. I'll give you the photos!"

Mouse whined, and Parker patted her neck.

"What photos?" Keith demanded, face pale.

Krista said, "That's what I'm saying. You missed something."

"There were some things Britt had in a different hiding spot. I found them later," Parker hedged, trying to figure out if she could use this to her advantage. "Photos. Papers."

Krista said, "And where are they now?"

"In the office at TBI, in the safe," Parker lied. "The police might want to see them. And since my place had been broken into, it didn't seem smart to keep them there. But I can get them for you, if you let us go. Honestly, I couldn't care less about them."

Krista tilted her head. "So exactly what do you have? How did you know Britt and Keith were together?"

Boy, did Parker wish she had read through everything before leaving to find Jess. Maybe something in there would have helped her now. "Oh, you know. Title to the Lexus. Birth certificate. Cards with sentimental value. Polaroids. That kind of thing."

"What Polaroids?" Keith demanded shrilly.

"Something with you, or she wouldn't know about you and Britt, obviously. Don't worry," Krista said.

"We'll get them back."

"Why does it matter?" Parker said. Krista ignored her. Parker turned to Keith and repeated, "Why does it matter?"

He shook his head, but his forefinger rubbed absently at his left temple.

"Your scar?" Parker hazarded. "From your accident, right? But what does that have to do with—" She shuffled the bicycle accident together with Britt and Keith's kinky relationship, but couldn't make it mean anything. "What does Britt have to do with the accident?"

Krista smiled mirthlessly.

Keith stared at the floor, avoiding Parker's eyes. Parker addressed Krista. "He wiped out on his bike. You told me that. Everyone said that. He wasn't wearing a helmet. Every single kid in town got a new helmet after that."

"I didn't wipe out!" Keith blurted. His voice cracked with emotion. He sounded like he had back then, like the kid she had known. "*She* chased me."

"Who?" Parker said, but she knew. The girl who loved to drive boys crazy so much she sometimes left welts.

It still didn't make sense, though. "Britt was chasing you when you fell in that ditch? She didn't even have a bike, did she?"

Krista laughed derisively. "Nope. Bikes were for peons. She had a car."

Calli was watching Parker, measuring her reaction.

Parker couldn't hide it. She looked at Keith with dawning horror. "She ran you down with her…*car*?"

He nodded, then shrugged. "I only remember a little.

She was parked at the pullout when I rode by. Sometimes we would meet there. I stopped to see if she wanted to hang out. She called me a retard, said she didn't want a retard baby. And she screamed at me to get the fuck away from her. I'd never seen her like that before. I took off. All I wanted to do was get home. Then I heard the engine revving. I don't remember anything after that until the hospital." He rubbed his cheekbone, worrying at the scarred skin.

"Stop that," Krista hissed. Keith's hand fell to his lap.

"Holy shit," Parker said. "God, Keith, I'm sorry."

A snort escaped from Krista, and Parker turned to her. "What?"

"Well, that's the point, isn't it? You should be sorry. You should be a hell of a lot sorrier than you are. And so should that *bastard*."

She had the gun in her hand again, and she gestured toward Jess, who was still and silent, head hanging forward.

"I don't understand," Parker said. "How could we be sorry? We didn't know what happened. Why didn't you tell the police? It was a hit and run!"

"She didn't hit him," Krista said. "She scared the shit out of him, and he crashed into a ditch and hit his head on a rock. There was no proof that she had anything to do with it."

"My mother said I was confused," Keith whispered. "About the car. About the baby. About Britt. She said if we talked to the police, I'd get in trouble for following her. For bothering her."

"Bothering her?" Parker repeated.

"The little idiot was stalking her," Krista said. "For

like, a year. Because every once in a while, she would take pity and fuck him." It was impossible to tell if she was more disgusted with Britt or Keith.

Parker shook her head, but she kept her eyes on the gun, not liking the way Krista gestured with it as she spoke. She hadn't heard the click she thought was the safety, so that was good. Unless she'd missed it. Or she was wrong, and it wasn't the safety. She managed, "Okay. But why Jess? Why me? We knew nothing about that, I swear."

In one move, Krista stood and aimed the gun straight at Parker with both hands. Parker froze, unable to breathe. Krista stared into her eyes. "You make me sick," Krista said. "You always have." Then she turned, aimed at Jess, and pulled the trigger.

The sound of the shot rang through the room like an obscenity even as Parker screamed. Jess's body jerked and a raw cry tore from his throat. The chair pitched sideways and fell to the floor. Mouse howled and Pepper disappeared behind the couch.

Parker had no conscious thought but found herself on her feet, attempting to scramble across the coffee table and get to Jess. It was useless. Arms like iron bands closed around her, pulling her down so she landed heavily on Keith's lap, his breath quick and moist on the back of her ear. Mouse growled as Parker attempted to twist her way out of his grip, but Keith only laughed. She surrendered into furious stasis, but Mouse was on her feet, hackles raised and a disturbing low growl emitting from her throat.

"Mouse, hush," Parker said tremulously, afraid the dog would be Krista's next target. "Calm, girl."

"Calm, girl," Keith echoed with a giggle. He eased

the pressure around her torso slightly, and Parker sucked in a breath.

Jess groaned. He was alive. Parker glanced at Krista, who stood with a half-smile on her face, the gun at her side.

Calli said, "I'll check on him?" Krista nodded, and the girl scampered across the room. "He's bleeding from his shoulder," she called a moment later, "And I think— he might have hit his head again when he went down. He won't wake up."

"Help him," Parker managed, but Keith had squeezed her tight again and it came out strangled by her inability to draw a full breath.

"What do you want me to do?" Calli said, voice trembling.

"Leave him. He'll be fine on the floor. Come back over here," Krista said. "And Keith, you can stop man-handling Parker now. She's not going anywhere."

Calli looked uncertain, but she turned her back on Jess and walked slowly towards Krista. Parker jerked against Keith, who hadn't loosened his hold. Krista pointed the gun toward Mouse, and Parker froze.

Krista smiled. "Britt deserved to die for what she did to my brother. And you? Little Miss Strong-in-the-face-of-adversity? Little Miss I-get-the-man-even-though-I'm-a-beefy-cow? Little Miss I-don't-need-Mommy's-fortune? You deserve to die for being such a clueless asshole and Britt's best friend. And Jess? He should have been the one she was screwing, not my baby brother."

The hatred on Krista's face washed away years of making excuses every time Parker felt worse instead of better after talking to her. Years of assuming she didn't mean her praise to be backhanded, her encouragement to be condescending. Years of gratitude that she had a friend who stuck by her despite everything.

Keith's grip finally loosened. Parker pulled upright, sickened. "The two of you killed her? You killed Britt?" Again she saw the corpse, stiff, emaciated, ruined.

"We were just going to scare her for a while," Keith said in her ear. "It was therapy. But then we couldn't let her go home."

Krista said, "It was justice. She almost killed my brother. She ruined his life."

"She killed my baby," Keith added.

Parker shook her head. "I don't understand. Where was she all that time?"

"We found an old root cellar back in the woods," Keith said proudly, oblivious to her reaction. "Me and Krista fixed it up."

Parker swallowed. There were ruins throughout the woods, old pieces of stone walls and hand-built cottages dating as far back as Puritan times. A root cellar might be anything from a stone structure to a dirt hole in the ground, but either way, no windows, no light. Like a tomb. "You imprisoned her," she said dully. "You practically buried her alive." She twisted to look at Keith behind her. "Did that really make you feel better?"

"It was just going to be temporary," Keith said. He turned his face away.

Parker could've sworn he was ashamed, but like a naughty kid who'd stolen a pie from the kitchen, not like someone who'd captured and locked up and starved his girlfriend in a hole in the woods. She looked at Krista, who wore an aloof expression. When she met Parker's eyes, she shrugged and smiled. "I don't know what to tell you. It was very therapeutic," she said.

Abruptly, Calli, who'd been fiddling with her notebook, knocked the pen out of place and it rolled under the couch. All eyes watched her bend and fish her hand into the narrow space to retrieve it. She returned to her seat next to Krista, blushing, and set the notebook and pen aside.

Parker swallowed down bile and gathered herself. Not really wanting the answer, she said, "What about Ryan? What did he do to you?"

"Funny story, Ryan was a suicide," Krista said, almost as casually as if they were chatting over coffee, but Parker heard a zing of mean glee in her voice. "Poor guy. He was all doped up, planning to walk into the ocean that night. I just redirected him. Less ocean, more alcohol. Improvisation, right, Calli?"

Parker looked at Calli, who was staring at her own knees. "I only brought the tape," the girl said.

"And Adam?" Parker demanded. Someone should know the truth about his death, however briefly, but she had a sinking feeling there was no way out of this for her and Jess, and possibly for Calli, either. If this were a TV show, Parker would play for time, but there was no rescue on the way. No one expecting her, no way for anyone to know where she was.

Calli paled even further, looking at Krista beseechingly. "Who's Adam?"

Krista shrugged and waved her off. "Just an old guy Parker liked. It was an accident, I swear. Keith got jealous. He has a bit of a thing for you, Parker, as you may have noticed. It worked out nicely, though. Another piece of the pattern."

I am so sorry, Adam, Parker thought. *And Jess. And Dad.* She blinked away tears.

Cara Johns

"I do not have a thing!" Keith protested.

"I think he's still hoping not to have to kill you," Krista said in a conspiratorial tone. "But I keep telling him no one has root cellars on the Oregon coast. Too much rain. I'm just not sure what we would do with you."

Calli cradled her hands in her lap.

"Where does Calli fit into this?" Parker said.

Krista threw her arm around Calli's shoulders and squeezed. "Calli is a beautiful young woman, full of potential, who understands the importance of justice," Krista said. "She loves me, so she's helping me. Right, darling?"

Calli met Parker's eyes briefly with an unreadable expression. Her face flushed, and she looked down again. "I do love you," she said. "But I didn't know it would be like this."

"I told you what they did," Krista said. "They deserve to die, both of them. You agreed."

"I did, in theory," Calli said, voice low but mulish. "But I didn't think we would *kill* them. Keith's really okay now, isn't he? He's basically okay. No one else has to die because of what happened."

"My brain is scrambled!" Keith roared next to Parker's ear. She felt flecks of spittle settle on her neck. "What do you mean, I'm okay? I lost everything. I can't work. I can't live on my own. I lost my baby. I lost Britt. I will never, ever be okay."

Parker could feel his chest quaking, knew he was suppressing sobs.

"Stop that," Krista snapped. "You're fine, and better every day. And Calli, I get it. It's natural to have second thoughts. This is a serious undertaking. Of course, it's not as important to you, you weren't there. And you're a kid. You still think when someone is hurt, it erases all the shit they did. You're wrong, but that's okay. Why don't you go outside, and Keith and I will finish this?" She sounded so sensible, so adult. If Parker didn't know she was seducing a teenager into being part of a murder.

"Don't listen to her!" Parker said. "This—" Keith snaked one hand up around her mouth. She wriggled and thrashed her head, hoping to slam him in the face, but he shifted so she only hit his shoulder. Parker wrenched forward and gnashed her teeth, but he yanked his hand away and delivered a short sharp punch to the side of her head.

Her vision exploded in a scattering of light. She heard Mouse's bark transmute into a pained yelp, then blinked back to blurry awareness a moment later to find Keith was rocking and crooning in her ear, "It's okay, it's okay, don't worry, all over soon…" He cradled her in his arms. She blinked again, and some of the blurriness cleared. She sought Mouse, who crouched to the right of the coffee table, growling softly. On the dog's lower jaw, a scrape and some swelling showed where Keith had gotten in a lucky kick. Parker telepathically beseeched her to stay back, out of harm's way.

Calli stood in front of the other couch with her hand outstretched toward Krista.

"You're all over the place," Krista said. "I thought we just agreed you weren't ready to be part of this."

Calli set her jaw. "Give it to me. You're right. I'm not going to wimp out. I told you I'd do anything for you. I want to prove it."

Krista studied the gun, seeming to consider.

Calli pleaded. "You said if we did this together,

we'd be soulmates. You know I'm not a kid. I just had a weak moment. Let me."

Finally Krista nodded. "We'll compromise. If you do Parker, I'll put Jess out of his misery. And Keith gets cleanup."

"I thought we were going to keep Parker," Keith protested.

"What about the dogs?" Calli said. Her eyes flicked to Mouse, who had somehow moved about six inches closer to Parker and Keith.

Mentally, Parker implored her, *stay back!*

Krista slashed the air with one hand, her mouth tight. "No Parker, no dogs. No loose ends. Okay, do it." She handed Calli the gun, and Parker crumpled inside as the girl accepted. Feverish spots of color brightened Calli's pale cheeks, and her eyes were hectic and darting. Parker's gaze dropped to the gun, obscene in those plump white hands.

Across the room, Jess slumped on the floor, no longer groaning. She couldn't see him clearly beyond the shape of the chair.

In Calli's white throat, the pulse fluttered visibly like butterfly wings, and her jaw clenched. It seemed as if she moved in slow motion as she glanced again at Krista, who gave her an encouraging nod. Shakily, the gun rose in Calli's arms.

Surreptitiously, Parker edged her left hand into her thigh pocket. With everything she had, as suddenly as she could, she yelled, "Mouse, down!" and pulled out the tiny canister of pepper spray. Squeezing her eyes shut, she aimed backwards over her shoulder at Keith's face. She depressed the trigger even as a shot rang out. The concussive noise and a flash of brilliant light had to be death, and Parker's muscles seized in anticipation of agony.

Then Keith was screaming hoarsely and shoving her off of him. She landed on the corner of the coffee table, which knocked the air from her lungs. Gasping, she choked on pepper spray, and half-fell, half-rolled onto the floor, eyes streaming. Pepper growled from under the couch, and Mouse barked hysterically, but Parker couldn't make her eyes stay open to check on them. Her whole mid-section throbbed, and she waited to pass out and die, waited for an arterial rush of blood or a growing feeling of cold. But none of that happened. Chaos continued around her. She struggled to one elbow, eyes tearing, unable to comprehend. Had Calli's shot hit Keith instead?

But it was Krista who lay on the floor, Krista with her cute, flowered shirt already soaked with blood, Krista splayed gracelessly across the tile. Keith was a maddened animal by her side, his sobs interspersed with great snorts to clear his streaming nose. He rocked back and forth, rubbing his pulled-up T-shirt over his face with one hand and grappling to put pressure on her wound with the other.

Calli watched without expression, standing above them, the gun hanging loosely from her hand. Parker pushed to her feet. Her eyes burned, her nose dripped, and her abdomen felt like one enormous bruise, but she gently tugged the gun from Calli's fingers and fumbled with it, trying to figure out if there really was a safety thingy.

As she turned it over, her brain fixated on Calli. Seduced by Krista, manipulated into becoming a killer, but really just another victim. Would she, like Parker, have to pay the price of years lost, and a promising future gone off the tracks?

Krista had warped so many lives, and Calli's action had saved Jess and Parker from certain death. Parker couldn't protect Calli from all the fallout, but she might be able to protect her from some. She pointed the gun toward where Krista had been standing and fired into the wall.

Keith barely seemed to notice. He had collapsed further over Krista now. Pepper poked his snout out and then hid again, while Mouse whined anxiously. "It's okay," Parker said. "It's over. It's going to be okay." Her hands shook hard. She couldn't figure out what to do with the gun, so she hung on to it.

Calli blinked at her in shock. "What—?"

"Go wash your hands," Parker tried to say. She coughed, cleared her throat, and tried again. "Wash with lots of soap and water, all the way up your arms. Scrub. Okay? I shot her, not you. You had nothing to do with it. You were kidnapped."

"I love her," Calli protested. Her eyes fell to the siblings on the floor but skimmed quickly away. "I loved her, but I had to—I shot her."

"You were so brave," Parker said. "You saved us. Let me help you. You were kidnapped by a disgruntled ex-employee you barely knew, and I got the gun and shot her. Is there anything on your phone, texts from her or Keith?"

Eyes glassy with shock, Calli shook her head. "We had burner phones. She got rid of them already. But—"

"Do it. Wash. If you can, change those clothes, start the washing machine."

"What about Jess?"

"I'll take care of Jess."

With a last entreating look, Calli disappeared through a door.

Keith was still rocking back and forth, cradling Krista's head. Parker struggled to her feet.

"Gotta call 911," she called across the room to Jess's back. He'd flinched at the sound of the shot. He was alive, he had to be still alive. In the mudroom, her phone lay on the rug where Krista had left it. Parker's fingers unclenched from the gun to dial the phone, then she hurried to reach Jess with the dispatcher still on the line.

Chapter Twenty-Three

Jess's hand felt chill and bony as Parker grasped it gently on top of the pale blue hospital blanket. His face was swollen and discolored, long lashes nearly invisible against the dark bruises above his bandaged nose. He'd been sleeping a lot for days, and she'd been sitting a lot, quietly, being with him. Not meditating. Just thinking and listening to her own thoughts, allowing them free range into areas of the past she'd avoided for too long. Feeling melancholy, but in an okay way. And waiting for him to wake up.

A hand landed on her shoulder and she jumped and opened her eyes, realizing she'd dozed off despite the hard plastic chair.

"How is he?" Marta said.

Parker blinked at her, trying to parse what she was doing at the hospital, if there might be some emergency with Calli. But no, Marta was her polished self, calm and collected in a cashmere sweater and leather jacket with her hair up in a chignon and her lipstick just so. And anyway, Calli had been texting back and forth with Parker extensively. Physically, she was fine, and she'd been sent home the same day everything happened.

Parker stood, not liking the sense of being loomed over, and faced Marta. "He's getting better. He was lucky Krista only had a twenty-two. He'll be recuperating for a while, though." She caught herself babbling and stopped, realizing Marta had only asked out of politeness.

"Shall we get some coffee?" Marta said.

"Sure, okay." Parker's stomach tightened as she led the way toward the cafeteria, checking her back pocket for her wallet. Her stolen purse had been found in the vacation rental where it all went down, but she didn't have it back yet and wouldn't until the case was resolved.

Once they were seated at a circular table with steaming mugs in front of them, Marta said, "I don't know if you've talked to Calli. You may have already heard this. But I wanted to tell you in person." She paused. "We're letting you go."

Parker almost laughed in relief. "Yeah, I know. I mean, Calli told me. But I'd resign, anyway. You probably figured it out by now, but I don't deserve this job. I didn't study meditation in India or anywhere else. I did the first four weeks of a massage course once, in California, and I've got about a year of credits toward a bachelor's degree in English."

Marta gazed into her cup. "I guess Krista—she was just awfully convincing. She was good at getting people to do what she wanted." Her face crumpled, but she rearranged it quickly, biting her lip. Parker knew Seth had moved back into the TBI apartment when Calli's trauma had been revealed, but she had no idea how things actually stood between Seth and Marta. Krista's seduction and manipulation of Seth, which had led to Parker's hire as well as the destruction of trust in the relationship, had to be a bitter pill to swallow.

So far as the relationship between Krista and Calli, the girl had poured out most of the story to Parker, but Parker wasn't sure how much she'd told her parents or the police.

Parker pretended not to see the depth of Marta's pain. "Krista was a force of nature," she said. "I won't pretend she didn't have something to do with me ending up on your doorstep. But she only offered the opportunity. I'm the one who accepted it, I'm the one who confirmed that crazy resume was legit. I took the job, because I was afraid if I didn't, I'd end up in a downward spiral and there wouldn't be another chance. That's all on me."

Marta met Parker's eyes. "I keep hearing that from Calli too, you know. That Krista didn't make her do anything. That they loved each other. That she was attracted to her right off, and she couldn't believe her luck when Krista returned her feelings."

Parker nodded. "It's going to take some time before she can put everything into perspective. But she saw through Krista at the end, when it mattered most."

Marta looked at her sharply, and Parker wondered whether she knew it was Calli who'd shot Krista after all. Parker had encouraged Calli to confide in her therapist, at least. Thankfully, the police accepted Parker's version of the story, in which she'd claimed to have grabbed the gun while Krista was distracted by the dogs, then panicked and fired recklessly when Keith and Krista came at her.

Parker's story wouldn't save Calli from guilt and confusion over falling for a killer and then shooting her, but she'd protected Calli from being labelled for the rest of her life as the girl who shot that psycho-chick. Parker made it a point to remind Calli she was a badass hero every day, but she doubted the world at large would be so understanding.

Meanwhile, Parker's psychological scar tissue was standing up pretty well to the headlines. *Murder-victim finder becomes murderer! Young woman, tragedy magnet, averts final tragedy*. Jess had escaped more than glancing coverage since he'd conveniently been in intensive care, but Parker's past had quickly become fair game.

Marta stood. "I've been trying to convince Calli not to contact you anymore," she said. "But her therapist tells me to let it be, that it could be good for her to have a relationship with you. Please." She met Parker's eyes and took a deep breath, searching for words. Then she sighed. "Just be responsible. If she does keep in touch."

"I will," Parker said, also rising.

"And thank you for Pepper. She's crazy about that dog. I think he's been the only thing to make her smile these past few days."

"He's lucky to have her," Parker said, throat thickening. "Oh, and Marta? She really wants to audition for a play again. It would be so good for her, if you'd let her. I told her I'd help her, but—"

"I'll help her," Marta said firmly. "Can you be out by the end of the week? I've got job listings out already. I need to slot someone into the position as soon as possible."

Parker hesitated. Even before Calli had called yesterday in tears with a warning about Marta's decision, Parker had accepted she'd have to leave Tyler Bettering. Krista's manipulations and Parker's own lies had put her somewhere she didn't deserve to be, and even if no one cared, she couldn't stay. But she'd pictured leaving in the abstract future, when Jess was out of the hospital and Parker wasn't limping anymore. Having to pack and clean and find a place to store her stuff in the next couple of days, when so far it was all she could do to sit by Jess's bed and occasionally nap and eat, was a little hard to swallow.

She gritted her teeth. "I can be out by Friday afternoon. Will that work?"

Marta nodded. "Good luck, Parker. I hope things work out for you."

"Thanks." Parker sank down and watched her disappear through the door. She could get a hotel room and look for another job, another place. She could break into the emergency fund if she needed to. But her heart was leaning elsewhere, though not without reservation. She pulled out her phone and called Dad.

"Remember how you figured I'd never need to stay at home again unless I got hit by a bus?" Parker said. "Is it still okay if I do, just for a few weeks? I'll be nice to Catherine, I promise." Catherine must also be processing the knowledge that Britt had been alive and suffering, so close to home, for those months she'd been held prisoner by Krista and Keith. It wouldn't be hard to sympathize with Catherine, for once.

****

Jess was awake when Parker returned to the room.

"Parker?" His voice was raspy.

"I'm still here. Just popped down to the cafeteria to get fired." She sat and wrapped his chilly fingers with her warm ones.

"Fired? Really?"

"Yeah. It's okay, I deserved it, don't worry. I'll tell you the whole story when you're better."

"Okay. Was my mom here?" he asked, his eyes shifting to see if she might be behind Parker.

"Yeah. She'll be back later. She's gonna fly home with you in a couple of days, feed you up and get you to your doctors' appointments. You talked to her yesterday. Remember?"

"I thought that was a dream. Did I agree to that?" he said.

"You did. And guess what? You're not the only one returning to the nest."

He stared at her blankly, waiting for a punchline.

"Seriously. There's nothing keeping me here anymore. I'm going back, just for a little bit. A couple of weeks or so. Talk to Catherine about what Keith and Krista said, so she can hear it from me. See how it feels to be there, now that we know the truth about what happened to Britt. And also…figure out if I want to go back to school or do something else."

He smiled cautiously. "So…you'll be on the East Coast."

"For a while."

"At the same time I'm on the East Coast."

"Maybe."

"Maybe we can get together."

Parker bit her bottom lip, suppressing a grin. It was a terrible idea. Their lives had been derailed by Krista again, and here they were, spinning off in a crazy rebound relationship. Or could you call it "re-railed," now that Krista's evil had finally come to light?

Parker wasn't sure she liked the sound of that, either. They weren't on a train track. Whatever shape they made their lives now, together or separately, was going to be intentional and guided by honesty and love, not by fear and betrayal and running away.

"We'll definitely spend some time together," Parker said, squeezing his hand. "Whatever comes next."

A word about the author…

Cara Johns lives and writes in Oregon's Willamette Valley.

Thank you for purchasing
this publication of The Wild Rose Press, Inc.

For questions or more information
contact us at
info@thewildrosepress.com.

The Wild Rose Press, Inc.
www.thewildrosepress.com

A word about the author…

Cara Johns lives and writes in Oregon's Willamette Valley.